Momma's
Got the Blues

Essential Prose Series 196

Canada Council **Conseil des Arts**
for the Arts **du Canada**

ONTARIO ARTS COUNCIL
CONSEIL DES ARTS DE L'ONTARIO

an Ontario government agency
un organisme du gouvernement de l'Ontario

Canadä

Guernica Editions Inc. acknowledges the support of the Canada Council
for the Arts and the Ontario Arts Council. The Ontario Arts Council
is an agency of the Government of Ontario.

We acknowledge the financial support of the Government of Canada.

Momma's Got the Blues

David Sherman

GUERNICA
EDITIONS
TORONTO · CHICAGO · BUFFALO · LANCASTER (U.K.)
2022

Guernica Founder: Antonio D'Alfonso

Michael Mirolla, general editor
Gary Clairman, editor
David Moratto, cover and interior design
Guernica Editions Inc.
287 Templemead Drive, Hamilton, ON L8W 2W4
2250 Military Road, Tonawanda, N.Y. 14150-6000 U.S.A.
www.guernicaeditions.com

Distributors:
Independent Publishers Group (IPG)
600 North Pulaski Road, Chicago IL 60624
University of Toronto Press Distribution (UTP)
5201 Dufferin Street, Toronto (ON), Canada M3H 5T8
Gazelle Book Services, White Cross Mills
High Town, Lancaster LA1 4XS U.K.

First edition.
Printed in Canada.

Legal Deposit—First Quarter
Library of Congress Catalog Card Number: 2021949347
Library and Archives Canada Cataloguing in Publication
Title: Momma's got the blues / David Sherman.
Names: Sherman, David, 1951- author.
Series: Essential prose series ; 196.
Description: Series statement: Essential prose series ; 196
Identifiers: Canadiana (print) 20210358823 | Canadiana (ebook) 20210358971 |
ISBN 9781771837149 (softcover) | ISBN 9781771837156 (EPUB)
Classification: LCC PS8637.H485 M66 2022 | DDC C813/.6—dc23

For Reisa.
She always hits the right notes.

Sometimes MaryAnne thought it was madness: words and words, widows and orphans and wandering phrases; sometimes a verse or two, scribbled on legal pads, scraps of paper, backs of envelopes, restaurant napkins, a bloody cliché, that. Words that meant nothing, words that meant everything, idle thoughts waiting in line to be turned into songs—one day. Though her thoughts were rarely idle, especially when she sat at her table, her guitar on her lap, computer at her fingertips, cell recording to catch bits and pieces of chord progressions melded with a lyric or two. And the ubiquitous working tool, her ashtray and hand-carved walnut box of kush to jump start her brain. Get lost in that space. Until the phone rang.

"Maryanne, you sitting down?"

"I'm standing, scribbling words," she said, putting her phone on speaker, pressing the red dot that killed the recording.

"You're stoned? Of course, you're stoned, you're working."

"What's up, Joey? I got a sweet melody. I'm mining for lyrics."

"Phoning to see how you're doing."

"Give me a break," she said. Her kid never called to see how she was doing. "What's up? I need a couplet."

"You need a grandkid?"

"I need a couplet."

"Sorry, no couplet. Maybe a grandkid."

MaryAnne put the pencil neatly on the table, perfectly parallel to the lined page of the latest sheet of lyrics and scratches and dark Xs. Too many verses, too many ideas, too much of nothing. She felt her heart rate accelerate.

"You're pregnant." She needed time, chew on this new reality a little. But her brain was cumulus, a bit of cirrus, with a jet stream blowing them around inside her skull.

She was going to be a grandmother?

"How are you?" she asked her daughter. "When? Was this your idea?"

"No, but I think someone's trying to tell me something. You know, tick tock, tick tock ... I'm great. Over-the-moon."

"You're enjoying life too much, might as well drop anchor, jump overboard and tread water for a coupla of decades?"

She stashed her stash and started packing her long-stemmed glass pipe. Easy on the throat.

"That what I did to you?" Joey said. "Threw you overboard? I love talking to you when you're stoned and the panties come off and you get all macho aggressive."

"I'm not stoned. But I will be any second and my panties are on and I knew how to swim, Joey. And, I had my shit together. There a guy in the picture?"

"Wasn't immaculate conception, mother. Believe me. Though it was rather heavenly. I did see stars a few times."

"I'm happy for you. What're you going to do?"

"Give me a break, Mother. I have no idea. I'm not yet down with the reality of diapers, nannies, jammies and crib shopping. I think I'm maybe six or seven weeks. I'm going to see a doctor. Don't know when. Maybe I can go viral. Take a belly bump picture every day and post it on Instagram and do something with it when I pop the zygote."

"You know the guy?"

"Course," Joey said. "Met him in the washroom at the Meat Market."

"Joey?!" MaryAnne figured this called for sternness, staunch motherhood.

"I know the guy, I know the guy," Joey said. "I stopped doing guys in bathrooms in January. It was a New Year's resolution."

"I'm happy you're maintaining your sense of humour. Joey, I know this isn't about me, and I'm happy for you, if you're happy for you, I think, but this is what you want? Now? The world is a fucking mess, you have no job, you drink too much, and what're you going to do with a kid?"

"Bounce it on my knee?" Joey said, not really enjoying this exchange, contemplating the bottle of red beckoning. She looked at her watch. It was almost noon. Close enough. "What does anyone do with a kid? Screw it up, I guess."

MaryAnne took a deep puff, held it in. Exhaled.

"I'm too young for the grandmother shit, Jo."

"MaryAnne, believe it or not, when … uh … Felix and I were having a drug and wine-drenched evening of multiple orgasms, I didn't have a single thought of you. Not even a trace of one of your melodies floated through my mind as I screamed, 'Do me again, Big Boy.' I was in another dimension."

"Exactly."

"And I don't have a clue what to do. That a lyric for you, Mother? 'I got screwed and I don't have a clue what I should do.' It sings, doesn't it?"

"I don't need images of you rolling around a bed with some guy who probably wears a baseball cap and his pants around his knees when he's out buying groceries, if he knows how to buy groceries."

"You think the only guy that would sleep with me is a loser?"

"No, I think you pick losers to sleep with. It's a self-esteem thing fueled by your appetite for alcohol and drugs."

"Thanks, MaryAnne, you've always been so supportive."

"Jesus. Daughter, if you're happy, I'm happy for you. Stop the scotch and the rum and Coke and the coke and the dope and the wine and get more exercise. And keep the quantity and quality of your happy endings to yourself. It's good you're remembering them so vividly 'cause as the belly expands the sex life contracts. Actually most of life contracts until you're nothing more than an incubator. You want to do this? Abortion's legal here, you know?"

"I'm not sure about anything. But, MaryAnne, thanks

for the feel good, mommy dearest moment. I'm going to go get drunk." And she was gone.

MaryAnne took the latest sheet of scribbles and ripped it into a few thousand pieces and threw it over her shoulder.

"Mama said there'll be days like this, there'll be days like this, Mama said," MaryAnne sang, kind of downbeat, not even close to the Shirelles.

Joey, phone in one hand, extra-large lime-green plastic cup in the other, sat on the stoop and watched the world go by. The stoop was a refuge from the home she called My Little Dump. The sofa and arm chair she had been so proud to find at a Friperie for $25 now revealed itself as junk, just like the carpet worn of its pattern, and the coffee table she had fashioned from abandoned wood crates discovered in the back alley. The walls were faded or yellowed, depending on what substance she was abusing at the time and the whole place needed an injection of energy and cash, neither of which she had in sufficient quantity. Her Little Dump was a shithole, she knew, and refuge was found on the front stoop, at least in warmer weather.

Things moved out there. She didn't know where everyone was going or why but they were going. Zoom, zoom, zoom.

Guys and women on bikes, couples holding hands, a tall kid on a skateboard, and cars, always cars, making the turn off Van Horne and accelerating. She took a 12-second video of a guy on a board rolling by.

My life, she thought. *Watching the world go by.*

It was either give up the booze or give up the pregnancy, she thought, sipping hungrily at the cold, thin wine, enjoying the way it immediately coddled her brain. She had read the warnings on the bottles, seen the warnings on TV, even read the research on the Internet one night when she was a half a bottle over the line, suddenly curious what she was doing to herself.

"The choice, Ma, is stay drunk or stay pregnant," she said to no one. "Or, stay drunk and pregnant and have a very fucked up baby. Whatya think, MaryAnne? What would you do? Course, you're a doper. You probably smoked when I was in the womb. Think that's why I seem to have an unquenchable thirst? No shit, Sherlock."

People rushing by were no help. Maybe she should go somewhere, too, but it was easier to sit here and watch other people blowing by, sometimes film them, transfer it to her computer. My life in video. Trying to edit it was a mind bender. Especially since she didn't understand the software.

"Why was everything so complicated?" she'd mumble, usually *EUI*, editing under the influence, or trying to.

The glass was filled with eight square, glossy ice cubes and the cheapest red the dep had, a litre of Chilean at about $14 with tax. The ice killed the bitterness and one thing she had a lot of was ice. Bought 12 trays at the dollar store, filled and froze one as soon as she emptied it. It was compulsive. A freezer well stocked with ice calmed her. The fact that it was void of edibles didn't bother her at all.

So, she sipped from the big, tall plastic cup and contemplated where everyone was in a hurry to get to. Sometimes she figured she should get off her ass, get off the stoop and get going. But where? And why? Especially now. She was fucking pregnant. Again. Jesus!

Thing that nagged at her, even after half a litre, was maybe she should be doing something. Maybe paint. Or write. Lap dance. Work a bar. Work in a supermarket. No. Bookstore. Did they still exist? Café? There were a million right here in the 'hood. Travel? But where? Pretty fucking moot now.

"Yeah, I'd love to work here but I'm taking mat leave in seven months, that okay?" she said aloud. Had to watch that. She was talking to herself.

A woman in running shoes and a short, flared skirt, Spandex top, all in white, good haircut, just long enough, walked by holding hands with a guy in jeans and a T-shirt a few sizes too small. Showing off his pecs. They were laughing and enjoying each other too much for Joey's liking. She emptied the glass, filled her mouth with the vestiges of sweet ice and decided to kidnap the bottle waiting for her on a shelf on the fridge door.

She climbed up but the hallway started spinning too fast. Now, that was funny. She had had too much wine to go and get more wine. If you want to drink more, she said to herself, you're going to have to learn to drink less. She tried not to, but she couldn't help but giggle.

She lay down in the narrow corridor, spilling the red-stained ice onto the plastic Persian carpet, its shades of burgundy perfect to hide wine accidents. And, glass in hand, was out cold.

Michael was chopping onions, MaryAnne was smoking and changing strings absent-mindedly. The kitchen was steamy, scented with garlic and hot oil and marijuana, but only Michael could smell the grass. She was immersed in it.

"Ya know, I wasn't a bad mother. There for her. After school. 'Tell me the best thing that happened today' at dinner, every damn night when I was home. 'Nothing happened, Ma.'

"Jo didn't even need me. She learned living online. She won't do Lamaze, she'll use a birthing app. Hope she remembers to charge the phone before she goes into labour."

Michael had moved to chopping ginger. He was doing Chinese tonight. MaryAnne liked to watch him cook; he seemed so sure of himself, pirouetting between fridge, pantry, counter and stove with razor-sharp German carving knives in hand. Get a good buzz going and talk at him. He only half-listened—he was building the meal—but half-listened well. Didn't mind her rambling, foggy monologues. She was like background music. The guy was a catch. A tad self-contained, a little remote, but a catch. He let her live and breathe.

"So, like, I'm not sure if I have to be thrilled by this, or maybe I'm a real bitch," she said. "I want Joey to be happy, she wants to have a kid, great, but leave me out if it. I don't have to watch her screw up her life."

"Sure, you do," Michael said, grinding salted black beans in the pestle with garlic, ginger and soya sauce. "You'll be drooling over the little turkey like all grandmothers. It's the nurturing gene, comes with breasts and the womb. You'll see your factory-fresh grandkid, you'll melt."

"I musta got a Walmart special," she said. "The nurturing gene was left out of the box of reproductive goodies. I want to finish the CD. I know it'll disappear without a trace but I have to. And I'm doing that little tour around Northern Ontario."

"Put the grandkid on a video, go cute, go viral, like YouTube kittens," Michael said. He fired up the gas under the wok. "If she has the baby."

"Michael, I sing about teenage hookers, rusty factories and homeless kids—can't think of a better way to illustrate all that than with a cootchie cootchie coo baby video," she said. "Have they recruited you to reprogram me? I'm not going back to mothering, no matter how bloody grand it's supposed to be."

She took a deep puff, continued tuning.

"Kids are antidotes to cynicism and despair," Michael said.

"How would you know?"

He paused, a cloud passed in front of his eyes and then he went back to work.

"Musta read it somewhere," he said.

"Besides, she won't have the kid. Who are we kidding? Her head's a mess."

"Darling, your kid might have a kid," Michael said, using a metal spatula to make his dinner do backflips in the wok. MaryAnne was mesmerized by the spinning meat and broccoli.

"Life's a bagel," he said. "Mrs. Gross told me. It's the way it's supposed to be."

"Bagels are about cream cheese and smoked salmon," she said. "I've done my Earth Mother thing."

MaryAnne eyed what was left of the joint, took a last puff and carefully killed it, saving the rest for dessert.

"She has no business getting knocked up. She has some philosophical disagreement with the pill, patch, IUD, so she opts for condoms and guess what?"

"I thought you didn't talk to your daughter about birth control."

"I found them when I was snooping through her shit before she moved out. That and a couple of grams of coke. Which she's probably still doing. And drinking. And who the fuck knows what else."

"What'd you do with the coke?" Michael said, emptying the wok onto a hot serving platter he pulled from the oven.

"Didn't sleep for three nights," she said, pouring a glass of wine. "Don't know how I used to do that. You know, she's too young to be doing all that shit. And she's too young to be pregnant and too fucked up to be pregnant and who the hell knows who the father is?"

MaryAnne removed the ashtray from the table, grabbed dishes from the cupboard, cutlery from the drawer and laid them out in perfect symmetry.

"When you had her what kind of shape were you in?"

"That was different, times were different," she said.

Michael started serving, pushing beef in black bean sauce and broccoli onto her plate, then a scoop of rice. He was careful. He knew she didn't like the sauce commingling with the pristine white rice. She loved him for that.

He'd been pushing her to switch to brown rice but he couldn't argue with her when she said, "Show me a single Chinese restaurant that serves brown rice."

"What's different, darling, is you don't wanna be a grandmother," he said, filling his own plate, spooning the beef on the rice. Commingling didn't bother him. Not much did, she thought.

"Being a granny reminds you of your age, you can hear the grave calling and you're worried you might have to be on call 'cause Joey'll probably need help navigating this."

"Michael, I had a kid, good kid and I did when I could and didn't do when I couldn't. Marriage was a nightmare then the asshole … died. I didn't mourn. No long black veil for me. Marijohn Wilkin, rest her soul. Great tune. Maybe I should cover it.

"Anyway, I did the mother and the father part. I'm almost 60, I'm not doing mother redux for the rest of my life. I'll look after you, darling, not that you need lookin' after. But if this bundle of soiled joy, should it hatch, wants to get to know his or her grandmother, he or she best wait until he or she can zip over in his or her Miata, roll a joint and tell me what's up."

"Sure, baby," Michael said.

"I'm pissed this colossal intrusion into my game plan, my future, was perpetrated without even consulting me."

Michael could sense her temperature rising, confirmed when she went back and retrieved her ashtray and her box of herb, papers and mechanical grinder.

"And you know what, sometimes you're too fucking logical and together. This is a major fuckup, and you're standing there worried about your dried black bean sauce.

You ever get upset by anything? It's not that your feathers don't get ruffled, I'm not sure you even have feathers. Can you please support me on this not-anxious-to-be-a-grand-mother thing? I did not sign on for this upheaval. So please go fuck yourself."

"If I must," he said to himself. "But after dinner, okay?"

But she left the kitchen at high speed, smoke billowing behind her and he sat down to savour his cooking.

The guy who interviewed Felix was about his age and didn't give a shit. About anything. He was dressed in jeans and a worn, faded dress shirt. Felt like he had gone through this process a few thousand times. To keep his job, he needed warm meat to do the job. The pay was a dollar above minimum wage plus bonuses. Beat the quota, make another dollar an hour. Really beat the quota, you could earn as much as 15 bucks an hour. Doing the math, Felix figured he could gross 600 a week, decent coin. Bring it on. He signed a bunch of forms he didn't read—pledges to secrecy, pledges not to steal, pledges to give a minimum of notice when he quit—and everybody quit, sooner rather than later—and not to work for a competitor when he did quit.

Then he was handed off to a woman, also about his age, in jeans and a black spandex top, to tutor him in the fine art of fulfillment.

The corridor was narrow. Her name was Jeanine.

"First thing," she said as they walked down the long hall with closed doors on both sides, "is this place is full of shit. Best advice I can give you, get out now. The work sucks. It kills you, mind and body. After 5, if they let you go home, all you can do is crawl into a bath and smoke a shitload of dope, get drunk or both. Anything stronger really fucks you up the next day and they'll be on your case like ticks on a dog."

"What's the downside?" Felix said.

"That there's always a tomorrow," she said and pushed open a set of double doors revealing an insanely bright room big enough for several Dreamliners with row after row after row of tall shelves stretching beyond the horizon. There were self-driving carts on thin tracks moving silently between the shelves, forklifts with pallets of boxes going in all directions and people just like him frantically plucking stuff off shelves and dropping them into baskets balanced on a blinking, rolling, motorized device the size of a coffee table. No one was walking, everyone was doing a slow trot behind the electric footstools, made for anything other than resting your feet on. The light made him squint.

"Yeah, you'll have headaches almost every day," she said. "Bring Advil. And drink a lot of water—give you an excuse to go to the can. They probably have hidden cameras in the can so they'll know if you're pissing or not … This is a good place compared to others I've worked. Let you piss when you need to."

He was staring into the chaos, kind of mesmerized.

"Why do you stay if you hate it so much?" he said.

"I like to eat, pay the rent," Jeanine said. "C'mon, I'll walk you around, show you how it works."

The amount of stuff was overwhelming. Anything anyone could possibly want was on a shelf somewhere.

"We don't have perishables, here. No refrigeration. That's at another centre. We have everything else."

"Who, like, owns all this stuff?" he said. "Who's actually selling it?"

"They don't tell us. We just run around filling orders, putting them on those little robots we chase that are sent by computer and then they're forwarded by the computers to the proper station or to shipping. You're assigned to, let me see your papers, Station 12Q. That's mostly pharmacy stuff, OTC drugs, toilet paper, makeup, you know, shit you'd find at a big pharmacy, which is almost everything these days, but here it's mostly stuff for the bathroom: shampoo, shaving cream, toilet paper, diapers for kids and oldsters, whatever. Follow the robot. When it's done with you, it tells you and moves on and another robot will beep at you, tells you it needs filling."

"I'm working for a robot? Really?"

"Really," she said. "They're cute, aren't they? If you try and fuck them up, they know it and they report you. You get fired immediately. You can take a dump in aisle six, maybe get reprimanded, but fucking with the little mechanical bastards is a firing offence. But, don't worry, the robots, unlike us, are indestructible. You can play basketball with them and they keep on rolling."

"What company's web site are we working for?"

"Doesn't matter. They don't tell us. Everyone sells everything so who knows. They don't want you to know. It could be Amazon, Walmart, Costco, Shopper's, could be all of them. Doesn't matter. You fill the order as quick as you can so you can get the next order and fill that as quick as you can. Welcome to your new life. When you've had enough, razor blades in row 112B3."

He had no idea what that meant.

She led the way, pointing out sections, helping him get his bearings. There was nothing in the world that could fit on a shelf that wasn't here. From corn flakes and canned soup to car parts and stuffed toys for humans and dogs. Everything wrapped in shiny plastic, everything packed with the promise of a better life. If Santa, or Satan, had a warehouse, this would be it.

She stopped him near the entrance to the employee locker room. There was a traffic light shining green attached to the wall over the door.

"That tells you if you can go home," Jeanine said. "Green means, when your shift ends, you can get felt up or security cleared, as they put it. Usually takes about 20 minutes and they don't pay you for it. Same at lunch if you wanna leave. Yellow means you might be able to go home, OT is optional, if they get enough volunteers. Red means you're trapped like a rat, you can't go home, OT is obligatory. Light rules your life. You burn the red, don't come back. Green means it's slow, you might not get your eight hours, they might send you home after two or four, whatever they feel like."

"That legal?"

"If you read what you signed, you agreed to be treated like a robot yourself. As I said, razor blades are at 112B3."

Yes, Michael was chill. Almost frosty. He had done a stint with anger and rancour in a previous relationship and had spent 30 years or so with rock 'n' roll crazies, rigging sound and lights for shows that often sounded as musical as jet engines. Front of stage, back stage, it has always been out of control, miraculous and simply nuts. He had served his time in the land of This Makes No Sense at All and now preferred to reside in No Drama Today, Please, which was what life was usually like with MaryAnne.

Michael had always loved screaming guitars, honky tonk piano, horn sections, swing bands, girl backup singers, Motown and the Wall of Sound. But he knew there was no money in it, not for 99 per cent of the people who were like him: kids who could spend their days and nights smoking hash between two large speakers or camped out in a field for a few days listening to act after act and watching the girls go by. What could be better than sex, drugs and rock 'n' roll?

He never picked up a guitar or a horn. He didn't have what it took to be a player. He figured you had to be born with it.

So he picked up books: the physics of sound, tensile strength, light, speakers, staging, rigging, scaffolding, everything he could find at the McGill libraries, everything he could pick from his professors' brains and from crews at shows, trading info for hash and beer when he had to.

By the time he was 20, Michael knew as much as there was to know about building a stage, stacking giant speakers, monitors, hanging lights, building fog machines, turning wide-open football fields into decent concert halls.

Michael became the man in Montreal and soon, Canada. He made the music pop. And more than a few acts passing through paid him big money to come on tour with them; Europe, Australia, the Orient. Soon it was operas and ballet and symphonies. He saw the world from back stage and up in the air.

By the time he was 45, he had banked some serious coin, owned a few duplexes and triplexes in Montreal, bought for a song every time the Parti Québécois's independence platform threatened. When he hit 50, he called it a day. His ears and nerves were shot, as were his shoulders and knees, as was his fascination with the whole business. Kids and venues were using computers or subcontractors and cheap labour to replace him. Yeah, a few stages collapsed, lighting towers toppled, but there was insurance to take care of the fallout.

Most of the music sucked today, nothing he could tap a toe to, and he had begun to loathe climbing on planes, commercial or private. He had had his share of women. He was, to quote Dylan, who he sang incessantly, "Keeping away from the women ... giving them lots of room." Until he met and heard MaryAnne.

Michael had popped into the café she was playing. He knew Phil, the owner, and he had seen MaryAnne a couple of times before, having coffee and shooting the shit, usually between sets. One night he stayed to listen to her. MaryAnne was trying out a trio of new tunes and as she sang, she watched him looking back, intent and intense.

He was touched by the songs but more, the simplicity, the tenderness, the no-bullshit performance. He had seen them all and so few stayed who they were. But MaryAnne struck him as who you see is who you get. She was counting the cash when he asked her out.

"Did you write those songs?" he asked, looking out the picture window. Her tunes had touched him, the poignancy cut through his decades-old cynicism.

His shyness attracted her. He couldn't seem to look her in the eye.

"I did," she said. Three hundred, forty dollars. She used to make $3,500 a night minimum. Before that, there were years of $5,000 nights. Paid the band $1,500, hotels, meals, she still came out with a couple of thousand and a good feeling about life. Three hundred and forty dollars. Who was this guy?

"Good tunes," he said. "Something about them. Evocative. No broken hearts and tears-on-my-pillow soap operas. Smart stuff."

"Thank you," she said, folding the cash and putting it in the breast pocket of her performance-only embroidered denim shirt. She'd been hit on thousands of times and she'd succumbed to more than a few. Attraction, loneliness, anger, fatigue or boredom. What else was there to do playing three nights in Hayfield, Manitoba? Or New York, New York, for that matter. All that was waiting for her was a bar and a room, maybe one more elegant than the other, but still a barstool and an empty bed.

But this guy … calm, confident, in shape, lots of hair, deep eyes—when she could see them—seemed worth spending time with.

"I'm rigging the Stones at the Big O next week when I get back to town," he said. "You can hang out backstage if you like that kind of thing and we can go out to dinner when I'm done or listen to the show, whatever you like."

Turned out he wasn't rigging. The Stones travelled with their own crew. Michael, never Mike, supervised. He knew the idiosyncrasies of the venue, how the sound bounced, he told her later over Thai.

She watched him work from the side of the gigantic stage, bigger than any club she worked, even if you threw in the parking lot. The Stones toured with an armada of 18-wheelers. She toured in an old, rebuilt Saturn wagon. The crew was scrambling, they were running late, but Michael was in control, his hair delightfully rumpled, looking as if he could fly a 747 through a hurricane and not break a sweat.

Then Jagger walked by in tight jeans and an oversized silk blouse, short and thin, stood next to Michael, who ignored him.

"We're running a tad late, ain't we, mate?"

"Yeah, we are," Michael said.

"We going to be ready for curtain?" Jagger said.

"We will," Michael said.

"I hate being late," Jagger said.

"Me too," Michael said. "But I hate having a guy in the crew kill himself rushing. And I hate when the artists can't get their extravagant gear together on time. If you need to perform with a portable Carnegie Hall, gotta get it here on time."

"I guess that's true," Jagger said, laughing. "What's your name, man? Whatya do?"

"Michael. I make sure the lights and sound go up and

don't fall down and kill a few hundred ticket-paying customers or the guys in the band. What's your name and
what do you?"

She remembered Michael never looked at Jagger, kept
his eyes on what the crew was doing.

"I'm Mick. Like in Mick Jagger and the Rolling
Stones. Maybe you've heard of us." He laughed.

"Pleased to meet you, Mick. Why don't you let me
concentrate on what we're doing so this shit doesn't fall on
your head when you're singing?" And Michael walked
away, leaving Jagger alone, stage centre. The curtain was
closed but the noise from the 50,000 or so on the other side
was building, the beast growing restless. Jagger turned,
smiling, and walked past her, nodding hello. Seemed a
decent sort.

After, she followed Michael to his choice of dinner
spots. Pretty great meal. The guy knew the restaurant, the
owner and his way around the menu. She felt looked after.

"You gave Mick Jagger shit," she told him over a table
weighed down with platters.

"Well," he said, grabbing a sliver of curried duck from
the plate they were sharing. "Into everyone's life a little shit
must fall. He'll be a better man for it."

She wanted to take him home. But thought, no. This
might be worth savouring. Let it simmer, then with luck,
bring it to a boil. He drove her home, walked her to her
door, kissed her on the cheek, said, "I'll call you, okay?"
And did.

The girl behind the glass was in ripped leggings, tats and piercings, tiny torn top and exposed rainbow-coloured bra straps strung over bony shoulders. She was singing about her broken heart and the billion tears she had cried for Ricky. With her phone in her hand. MaryAnne figured it was her security blanket, a lifeline to the world beyond the soundproofing, wondered if she had turned it off. The tale of badass Ricky was backed up by a drum and synth loop. Everything was electronic but the girl, MaryAnne thought, though she wasn't completely sure. But her future was un-doubtedly rosier than MaryAnne's. The girl had the pipes and the body and the hottest commodity in the universe of streaming and YouTube—youth.

MaryAnne wasn't sure what she was doing here. In a basement. Wires slithering everywhere. A 20-year-old skel-etal nerd behind a desktop wall of screens, pulling faders and pushing keys and talking to himself as he tapped his feet and nodded his head in time to the boom of the elec-tro beat.

She remembered when studios were studios: fine fur-niture, carpets, space, good drugs, lots of booze, a thousand or more a day, pills and powder extra. This was 25 bucks an hour.

The tale of Ricky continued. It was monotonous shit to MaryAnne but she had to admire the work that had gone into the countless layers of electronic sound. That's what it was, she realized. Not music, but layers of repeti-tive, digital sound. Beats.

"Boop a doop, boop a doop, boop a doop, Rickeeeee, my beautiful boy. Boop a doop, boop a doop, boop a doop, Rickeeeee, my beautiful boy."

MaryAnne thought about going home, doing a joint in the car, hiding under the bed, forgetting the whole thing. Or maybe just strangle the chick in the studio, save her the tears for ol' Rick.

Everyone in the place was young enough to be her grandchildren, had she started the whole conception thing in her 20s. But she had been too busy playing, touring, partying. Nothing she regretted.

She was no Bonnie Raitt, she knew that, and today it was a game for viral children, but it's what she did. Or would do if this woman in her underwear would take her sound machine and skinny body and get the hell out.

She began to feel her age, remembered when it had been easier. For a dozen good years in another lifetime, she hadn't felt like she was carrying a Marshall amp on her back 24/7. It had been all icing and chocolate mousse.

Despite what her mother had said.

"Kids are a full-time job," the woman had said when MaryAnne was making her plans to leave the nest, packing her bags, lining up her guitar cases by the door, Victor— where was Victor now?—waiting outside in his father's car to drive her to their new place, a huge, filthy, warped-floored, paint-chipped upper on Pierce St., heart of downtown.

Six rooms that hadn't been cleaned in eight decades, it seemed. Kitchen and bathrooms old enough to be classified antique. Two hundred dollars a month, a fortune. But the future was full moon. He was working at a photo shop, selling cameras, framing black and white pictures of her he had shot and developed in his own darkroom. Her band was booked solid. She was making $100–$200 a week, easy. A label was talking record deal. International tour. And there was Mom, standing by the door, glass in hand, scorn on her face.

"You get pregnant, you'll be putting a pin in that balloon."

MaryAnne had heard the tale. Mom had been a torch singer, played the best hotels, her and a piano man, from one end of the country to the other. Dropping down to Florida, crooning for the snowbirds in Miami Beach, Catskills in the summer. Usually two-month gigs, room and board included. Luxury all the way. Marriage and kids derailed it all, her mother had told her whenever she drank, and the drinking accelerated as the kids grew and needed her less. She and her two brothers carved two decades and a career from her mother's life, haunting MaryAnne forever.

Yeah, the old lady lost 20 years, gained 47 pounds, waiting for the kids to grow up and out. She drank quite a bit then but turned it into a job once MaryAnne drove away to play at being an adult on Pierce St.

"Don't worry, Ma, everything's going to be fine."

It was, as long as the old lady drank enough.

Ma missed the stage lights, applause, autographs, encores, train rides, bus rides, plane rides, money. And never let her kids forget it.

"MaryAnne, you can't have it all, especially not if your husband is an asshole. Men can ignore their kids, do what they want. They got no conscience. Be careful what you wish for."

When the kids no longer needed their mother, the music business didn't either. It had changed. Hotels were not eager to book middle-aged women, less of them booked anyone at all, and her mother disappeared into a bottle with her brother Danny, the good-looking one, everyone said, the one MaryAnne's friends all wanted.

Booze, drugs, white nights got to the good-looking one. His heart stopped at 50. Her mother died of a booze-related cancer a few years later. Last she heard, her other brother, James, was trolling for adolescent sex workers in Thailand and Vietnam, teaching English as a second language to pay for it. MaryAnne had a family torch to carry, a point to prove. She could have a kid. She could have a career.

Maybe there was a song in there somewhere, she thought, and started scribbling as she waited for her studio time.

From touring solo in her 20s, she put a three-man band together, bass, drums, electric guitar, signed a great deal with A&M, hit the road. The guys were good men, neither addicts nor sexists, students of the blues. Robert Johnson, Elmore James, Muddy Waters, Howlin' Wolf, Willie Dixon were their grandfathers. Cultural appropriation not in the lingo yet. Soft spoken, mean players, happy for the work and didn't mind playing for a woman. They liked to get liquored up and play, as they said, but they never missed a beat or destroyed a hotel room.

In summers, when Joey was older, the band acted like uncles as they cruised the festivals. Good years. Some nights 300, some 3,000, some 30,000. Some festivals the crowds were bigger than her dreams, stretching to the horizon, or so it seemed from in front of those monstrous white lights, lost in fake fog. She banked a little, spent a lot. Loved to strap Joey in and roar down the highway in whatever set of wheels she had, wisps of carbon monoxide and marijuana in the rearview. The world was not simply her oyster, it was a tray of scallops.

Then Sid called. He was in town. Wanted to take her to Moishe's. That could mean really good news. Or really bad. He rarely came to Montreal and the few times he did he liked to flirt with her at the Ritz bar. A couple of vodka martinis, lots of compliments, assuring her her future was platinum, his suite was spectacular, wouldn't she like to see it, have some Champagne?

This time it was steak, and the scent of cigars and unlimited heaps of good dill pickles and cole slaw. He gave her the bad news as he attacked the seared rib, chewed happily as he buttered a dinner roll.

"Sweetheart, you're a great artist but, you know, hey, you've hit 40, the biz is changing," he said, slicing through the charred meat. "God knows where it's going. Your last CD sold 28,000 copies, got radio play on only 71 stations in the U.S., about the same in Canada, but let's face it, a lot of that is Cancon."

Might as well've been slicing her throat.

"We're contracting, letting a lot of our contracts lapse, only producing sponsored tours, doing a few with Budweiser, a couple with Coors, Pepsi, no risk, and we shoot it, saves on video production. They … uh … their demos are skewed younger. Not much, 18-35, you know. And that's the breweries. Pepsi, Coke, they're going after kids, six to 18, teenieboppers. Big market. Huge, beautiful teen market, God bless 'em."

He was still chewing, between bites of bloody meat, he was ripping at his buttered roll, shoving it in his busy mouth, pausing only for a sliver of pickle and a spoon of slaw.

"It's all about tits and ass now, MaryAnne," he said. "And it's not that you don't have 'em, but you're not in the demographic. And the tweed thing is ... uh ... old. We have guys, make a lot of money, all they do is study this shit. They know. Using computers.

"And Sweetheart, your songs, they're esoteric, you know? They're great songs, don't get me wrong, you're a great writer, but listeners, you gotta grab 'em in the groin, the feet, the heart, make 'em want to screw. Your songs, for the brain, tough sell. You remind me of that other guy from Montreal, Cohen. Did great in Norway, but ..."

Sid shrugged, grabbed a pickle with his hand and bit off half, smiled, and went back to work on his steak. She wanted to shove the pickle up his ass.

"So, you're not renewing my contract?" MaryAnne said. She put her cutlery down, afraid she might ram the steak knife through his eye. "That's it? We have three years left on it."

"There's a termination clause," he said. The asshole didn't stop chewing. Like he hadn't eaten for a month. "But, last tour, you lost $37,358. We're going to forgive it. I went to bat for you, Mary ..."

"MaryAnne," she said.

"Sure, sure, and I got them to write it off, so whatever royalties accrue from record sales and songwriting, you'll still get your share."

"So," she said. "The new CD won't happen? I have half the songs for it."

"Not by us, but," he said, grabbing the bowl of cole slaw and emptying it onto the section of his dinner plate made vacant by the steak he had ravaged. He reminded her of a wolf ripping at the entrails of a deer. "We're trying to sell your contract. Maybe someone else will pick you up and you'll be back in business. Or maybe you want to hang it up. I mean you got a kid at home, right? Frankie?"

"Joey, my daughter's name is Joey and what the fuck does she have to do with anything? You have three kids at home, don't you? You're working."

"Maybe you want to spend more time with her," he said, grabbing another roll. She realized she might as well be talking to herself. He was here for an expense-account dinner and she was just another piece of meat to destroy without conscience.

Cancelling contracts made the bastard hungry, she thought.

"I worked with you, what? Ten years, 12? Gave me a good break, I made a few bucks, you probably made more than a few ..."

"MaryAnne, we made you a star, we were always straight up with you, we made you ..."

"I made me, Sid. No one made me but me," she said, raising her voice. The suits at tables around her were glancing at her, an older woman in jeans and worn tweed jacket, patches on the elbows, no plunging neckline, no bling. She was disturbing their power lunches.

"You didn't play guitar hours every day, twist yourself into knots trying to find organic rhymes that hadn't been done a thousand times. You didn't fucking make me."

"MaryAnne ... Sweetheart ..."

"Don't Sweetheart me, you old bastard. You made 10 times what I made from me than I did and don't start telling me what kinda mother I should be. You were the son-of-a-bitch convinced me to tour the Orient for a month and paid for the nanny 'cause, you said, as I remember, 'Chinks and Japs love white ass, we'll make a killing' and I listened to you. And now you're kissing me off."

She stabbed her fork into her untouched steak, picked it up, stood up, and dumped it, fork and all, in his lap.

"Go fork yourself," she said, and walked out, head high, dying inside.

That was the beginning of this, MaryAnne remembered, waiting for the chick to finish another take about Ricky so she could get on with her life. Beginning of that temper, too. Shouldn't have told Michael to screw himself. Shouldn't let the shit get to her. But there was so much of it.

Yeah, the biz had changed but so had everything else, and she wasn't waving a white flag yet, wasn't going to lay down and die, even if it killed her. This is what she did, who she was. To hell with the Sids of the world. She last heard Sid had died in the saddle in a beautiful suite with a 16-year-old boy singer he had promised to make a star, full of surprises right to the end.

The kid finally stopped wailing about Ricky and was rabidly texting as a techie in jeans and T-shirt went into the studio and started taking apart mics and cables and the spit shield. The girl stared into her phone, waiting for a reply.

Exasperated, MaryAnne looked for an exit and found a steel door covered in Styrofoam behind sound baffles sealing off a set of drums. She wondered if anyone used them anymore with all the electronic beats they had in their computers. She put her hip into the door's panic bar and stepped into an alley. A black cat tore off through a busted, tall wood fence of grey, weathered one by sixes, red streaks of rust running from the nail heads.

There were a few garbage cans and a lot of garbage that hadn't made it to the cans, booze and beer bottles and aluminum cans and McDonald's wrappers, a few used needles, a condom, a stained, bent mattress, cigarette butts and cigarette packs and plastic supermarket bags tied off at the top, their bottoms swollen with lumps of dog shit and two young guys from the studio, laughing, having a good time at least until they saw her. They were sharing a joint.

MaryAnne pulled a long, expertly-crafted three-paper blunt from her shirt pocket and fired it up, promising herself to take only a couple of puffs. Raw was not the sound she was aiming for, not for this track, a mother's lament for a child lost to addiction. Talk about irony. She hadn't found the right groove yet. She wasn't looking for maudlin. She wanted a slightly detached air. If she could make the voice somewhat commonplace, matter-of-fact, day-in-the-life, she figured it would make the tune chilling, get 'em in the guts.

She had a good bottom of bass and drums and a great, clean rhythm guitar track to work from. She had rounded up the guys and they made a slightly drunken marathon of it, laid down a foundation for three tunes and had a good time doing it. Lots of good comps to plant her voice on. They insisted on taking only union rates, not a penny more but never looked at a clock. She loved those guys.

She took a short puff, wanting the buzz but not the burn.

"Whoa, that's a spliff, Mama," said one of the kids, the

studio engineer. He was maybe 22, in baseball cap, face punctured with acne scars, his jeans filthy and hanging down below the waistband of his cheap Jockeys. Skin pale, looked like he needed to get out more. She thought that style had seen its day. The other kid looked pretty much the same except he was sprouting a beard that seemed made of alfalfa sprouts. The studio gofer.

"If I was your Mama, I'd've taught you how to dress properly."

"Yow, lady, that's a dis," Acne Face said. "That shit's supposed to mellow you out."

"I'm as mellow as I get," she said. She handed the kid the joint. He was the engineer and she needed him on her side. But why were white Canadian kids trying so hard to sound African-American?

"Good shit," he said, holding his breath, letting the vapours saturate his brain cells. "You sure ain't like my Mom."

"Obviously," MaryAnne said.

"Yeah," Alfalfa Sprout said. "You're a real MILF, lady, the real deal."

MaryAnne took the joint back and slapped him across the face. The kid rocked back a few steps, his eyes crossed with pain and shock, filled with tears.

"Show some respect, you little prick," she said as the kid stared at her. "The only thing you'll ever fuck is your hand or maybe your friend here. So, shut up and let's go lay down these tracks. And don't ever talk about someone's mother that way. Understand?"

She killed the joint carefully, rubbing the burning tip along the brick, dropping it in her breast pocket, and walked in, closing the door in the kids' faces. There was that temper again.

It was three in the afternoon. Time was she used to get up at three, God bless her nanny. Now she felt ready for bed.

The sanctioned and silenced techies were setting up her mics, one in front of her face, one over her head. They weren't smiling anymore but MaryAnne didn't care. She was running through lyrics and exercising her voice, stopping only to stretch her face, loosen her shoulders, babble with her lips. Three in the afternoon wasn't optimal but it beat nine in the morning.

The lyric brought her daughter into focus. Pregnant daughter. Better not to go there, the guilt nibbling at her edges instead of concentrating on where the song should go. Or maybe it would ease her into the song?

No, she wasn't the mother perhaps she should be and the studio and the techies weren't what they should be. Maybe it didn't matter. It had always been about the song, the audience, the warmth, the adrenalin of the stage. Her little girl couldn't replace that, no man could match it, no drug topped it and the studio was a cold, unforgiving place.

She was a mother and a lover but she had always been a performer. The little girl grew up, men walked or were thrown out, but the voice hung in, the songs needed to be written. Who the hell knew why.

She had asked Michael why she still did it. They were two years in and she was climbing out of a warm bed and his hard, long arms to grab a cab and catch a plane for 15 shows in Nova Scotia and New Brunswick. She didn't want to go, but she did.

"Why am I doing this?" she asked him, pulling on underwear and jeans and a black wool sweater. "Why can't I be a normal person, binge Netflix, make pizza, do crosswords or Sudoku, sit and talk with friends for a few hours? Maybe 'cause I don't have friends. Maybe that's why I don't have friends."

"'Cause birds sing," he said, watching her, his beautiful, long body on its side smiling at her. "They don't have a choice."

She didn't seem to have a choice, he was right, even being here in this rat-hole studio. But nowadays, you could record anywhere, you didn't need a label, you didn't need an agent, you didn't need a distributor, you didn't need a producer. She'd even mix it herself and put it online and she'd sell 20,000 here and there, get a few hundred thousand YouTube hits and move onto the next.

It's what she did. Her brain bouncing around like the blue ball in a racquetball court. Give her a guitar, a legal pad for writing lyrics, an iPad for recording tunes and Michael to cook for her and to love and all was right with the world. As right as it could ever be.

Gaetan was a fulfillment pro. Had the moves, the kinetic energy, the wardrobe of sweatshirts cut off at the shoulders, neck and belly; blue jeans washed and worn to white with stylish tears at the knees and thighs, the hems shredded to threads that dragged along the floor like a rag mop. He knew every inch of the place, absorbent cotton to shock absorbers. He also knew dead spots where cameras couldn't find them.

He caught Felix pounding on the Tylenol dispenser in a washroom. Felix's shoulders were aching, as were his back and knees, and yesterday the machine spit out handfuls. Five hundred milligrams. If he took enough, the sugar-coated drugs did little for the pain but wrapped his brain in a not unpleasant fog. Made the day almost tolerable. But, the company's painkiller gift seemed to have dried up.

"That stuff bad for your body, man," Gaetan said. "That's why the company gives them to you. They don't give a shit what happens when your liver dies."

"They don't seem to give a shit about how my body feels right now, 'cause there's none left," Felix said.

"'Cause they're fucking cheap," Gaetan said. He was looking over his shoulder and checking the ceiling for cameras, on his knees in the toilet stalls, inspecting the toilets for listening devices.

"Gotta check every few days," Gaetan said. "Can't trust the bastards."

Stood up and reached into his pocket and handed Felix a little blue pill.

"Take that. You'll feel no pain, brother, no pain at all," he said. "Life will be good. Five dollars."

"Five dollars? Nah, c'mon man, I'm not paying five dollars for … what is this?"

"It's magic, my man, magic. Five dollars is nothin' and it'll last you all day. How you think I do this? Been doing it eight years, all because of these little things."

"What are they?"

"Tell you what. I give it to you, you don't like it, don't pay. You like it, come see me tomorrow. It's harmless. Half the place is eating them."

"Uppers or downers? Meth?"

"I don't sell illegal drugs, man. I'm cool. That's legal shit for people in chronic pain. It's legit. Call me Doctor G. You need something, anything, come see me. Long as it's legal. I also got smart pills, man. Modis and Ritz ..."

"What you talking about?"

"Modafinil and Ritalin and ... let me see ..." He reached into his breast pocket and pulled out a blister pack. "Adds. Adderall. Make you focus like a son of a bitch. Day goes by like fries and gravy. But doesn't kill pain. Take one of each, you fly like a bird, work like a dog and nothing hurts. It's beautiful. ... We gotta look after each other before Big Brother and the machines eat us up and shit us out, yeah? Know what I mean?"

"I'll take the blue tab. For pain."

"In ten minutes you'll feel real. Gotta go. Gladys is waiting," Gaetan said, and pushed his way out of the washroom.

Felix let the pill dissolve on his tongue and followed Gaetan into fluorescent-lit hell where Gladys, the blinking, impatient robot, waited silently.

"C'mon Gladys, let's roll," Gaetan said and he began a quick walk, the machine following, lights flashing, a faithful dog on wheels.

Every day, aching, tired and reticent, Felix found him, hiding from the cameras in the lavatory, slipped him five and received a tablet that melted in his mouth. He'd chase it with a cup of coffee and within a few minutes he was on the floor chasing latex panties and silicone lubricants, winter tires and toaster ovens, on autopilot, dreaming of beaches and women and cars and better dope and a perfect life.

Unfortunately the pill wore off in about six or seven hours and the aches slowly permeated every limb and joint and his thoughts turned to the job at hand and the hell he was enduring for a paycheque that never lasted the week. At least his mother had sympathy for him and made his meals and washed his clothes and tidied his room and his father finally stopped bitching at him. Just looked at him as if he was alien seed.

"This what you're going to do with the rest of your life?"

Who the fuck knew? So, he added smart pills to his working breakfast and the absurdity of his routine under the white lights vanished. Life was perfect.

When Joey finished throwing up, her face on the cold ceramics of the bathroom floor, she started to run through ways to off herself. But without pills or pistol, her options were limited. She thought of her father and that accelerated the rock 'n' roll in her stomach. Did he really jump in front of a metro? No wonder she was a drunk. Craziness was in her gene pool.

Morning sickness mixed with killer hangover. Maybe she was already dead and didn't know it. She lay, a wet cloth on her face like a mask, wondering if she had killed her kid or just given him or her fetal alcohol syndrome.

Maybe she just destroyed her own liver. Hangovers weren't strangers but this was the mother of them all.

How the hell could she be a mother? Maybe it was too late. Maybe she already screwed up.

"Yeah, kid, I'm sorry. You're mother's a drunk and you're already a mess. I apologize, pass that bottle. I'll hold yours and you hold mine."

She rolled over, holding onto the tub, lifted herself off the floor, first onto her knees, then onto her feet, shifting her hands to the sink, legs wobbly, her head feeling like it was under the wheel of a subway car. How could she do this to a kid? To herself?

"Character was what you were when there was no one watching," she had read on a bathroom wall in a bar as she chopped lines on a toilet tank with her maxed-out Visa card. Bloody embarrassing.

Maybe a baby could help give her a life of substance without substance abuse. She *must* be sick, was the after thought.

She kind of bounced off the walls, the house a moving train, making her way to the kitchen and coffee.

Yeah, but … her belly was going to go blimp-like. There were countless indignities that would be visited upon her pretty buff bod, a bod that would probably never be the same after all the stretching and tearing and sagging and screaming. And what about a Josh or Paul or even Felix, wherever the hell, whoever the hell he was? Men were like storms. They screamed in like a tornado, you rode out the awesome lightning and the big booms of thunder, shock and awe, and then hung on during the bad, or maybe not, then they blew out and you tried to repair the damage. Sometimes all you could do was patch the holes—booze, pills and powders were reliable patches, though not cheap.

How long was anyone going to hang in when she started to look like a school bus, when her perfect small breasts became sore and her belly blew up, her moods darkened by roller coaster hormones, exhaustion and complete shut down of her sexual self?

Wasn't hard to get an abortion.

Not something men dealt with. Except to try and make it illegal. She shoulda been a man. They could drink, go through two-fours in front of a TV and no one gave them shit. They could wear white without checking the calendar. And they didn't fucking get pregnant.

Then again, she thought through the foil that wrapped her scarred brain, almost everyone had kids. How bad could it be? So, you can't sleep, you waddle rather than walk, pee all the time, any guy that looks at you and thinks of sex needs therapy or incarceration.

But, as she chewed the first drops of espresso, road-testing her digestive system, it was done in a year, she thought, testing the colours of the grass on the other side. Nine months of discomfort and inconvenience and oozing, three months rehab, she'd be back to herself, except for a mini-person to look after. Really ridiculously mini. Plump, screaming parasites for, well, could be 20–25 years. They grew up but she knew there was a good chance her progeny would burrow in her basement or their room, coming out to use the can, the fridge, smoke her dope and drink her booze.

No wonder she was feeling nauseous.

What would the kid do for a father? What would she do for a man? Did she even need a man? Sure, she needed a guy watching football while she changed diapers and made baby food.

Even if it was Josh's and he came along for the ride, that would make him as permanently planted in her life as the kid. A package deal. Forever. Josh was a good guy, but the rest of her life? She had stopped believing in forever a few mad, obsessive love affairs ago, several "this is the guy" guys.

The baby wasn't just a baby. It was blowing a tire on her life at high speed and she was spinning out of control. Why would she want to do that?

"Because everything else is bullshit," Manon said. "Having a baby, it's not about consuming, it's about creating. It's a trip."

Easy for her to say. They were in a café on Monkland. Manon liked NDG. Joey found it too white bread, liked Mile End, which was turning white bread too quickly for her taste, but Manon had driven to the rescue, scooped her up, stuffed her into her glittering Lexus, chauffeured her across town to a bagel café and ordered her a plate of greasy eggs and sausage and soggy potatoes and, of course, a sesame-seed bagel. Just looking at the plate had Joey's stomach tossing on rough seas.

She didn't see Manon often but when Joey needed a shoulder Manon seemed to appear. Manon had a two-year-old that was in day care or under the scrutiny of a babysitter while mom sold over-priced homes. She loved her daughter, just didn't have a lot of time for her.

"Do you know who the father is?" Manon whispered, leaning over the table, her breasts just an inch above her eggs. Cleavage helped close many a deal and she made the most of hers.

"I think I know who he is, I just don't know him, you know?" She poked at her eggs, wondering how far the washrooms were.

"Doesn't matter," Manon said, chopping her fried eggs and spooning them onto a slab of bagel. Joey watched as diners, willing to pay $14 for two-dollars' worth of fried food and a bagel, coffee extra, sliced, diced, chopped, crushed and tortured their eggs before sliding them into their mouths between bites of bagel and slurps of coffee.

She sipped water, trying to keep her stomach from revolting. She imagined heaving over Manon's plate of luxurious grease.

"Have a kid, sure, there's no real time for lazy espressos and $100 dinners and making sure you see the whole season of your favourite theatre," Manon said. "But, best thing I ever did. Her father gives me five thousand a month and I never have to see the asshole. If you're going to marry the wrong guy, might as well be a lawyer. And my parents insist on giving me another thousand for the kid, pay the nanny. They have the money and it makes them happy. And I make pretty good cash selling houses. Prices are crazy. I mean, you wouldn't believe what people are paying for shitboxes that used to sell for $35,000. So how many do you have to sell to live well?

"I like spending time with my girl. If I wasn't working, I'd spend all my days just with her. You know, the park, the library, the Botanical Gardens. I bullshit all the time selling homes. At least with Cara, I'm real.

"And you know what? I'm tired of running around, looking for guys, trying to find the 'one,' trying to get laid, worrying about my hair, my shoes, my boobs. Be surprised at how many husbands call me for a private showing without the wives. Just what I need. Get a rep as the real-estate home wrecker. Having a kid was freedom to be home and not feel guilty about it. Really."

She loaded some more egg-topped bagel into her mouth.

"'Go forth and multiply,' said I don't know who," Manon said between chews. "I concur."

"It was be 'fruitful and multiply,'" Joey said. "I read the bible at night when I was a kid. I thought I'd have to become a nun to cleanse the evil thoughts I was enjoying so much. Maybe I shoulda listened to myself."

"Right," Manon said, laughing. "Sister Joey, making the priests happy."

The clouds were clearing from Joey's poisoned synapses and she was seeing Manon as wanting someone to share her foxhole. She was painting single motherhood as akin to peace in the Middle East, with mom and pop and the ex footing the bill, but Joey had no cash flow to ease the burden of multiplying. Maybe she could find a lawyer to bed, wed and shed.

There were only a dozen tables in the place, half of them taken by women in ones, twos or threes. The rest of the restaurant was buzzing and clicking with kids on laptops and iPads and phones. Where were the men?

"When you seeing the doctor?" Manon said.

"Today, supposedly. In about an hour. Remember? You said you'd drop me off. Really sweet of you. You sure you can do it?"

"Sure," she said. "I'll even hold your hand when he's got you in the stirrups." She scrolled through her phone with her thumb as she chewed. "Yeah, my only appointment today is not until ... Oh, shit. ... Now. Now! I'm late. I'm supposed to be there already. Jesus. I'm so fucked. It's a great house. They'll let it go for eight fifty, a steal, and I think the buyer's hooked and I get a full commission, make a good part of my year. I gotta run, Jo. Can you get to the doctor on your own? I'm sorry, I'm sorry, but this is like landing a blue tuna. Sorry, sorry, sorry. Next time, if I hook this one, I'll buy you dinner, best in town."

She gathered her phone, her little bag, her keys, her jacket, kissed Joey on the cheeks and half jogged out of the restaurant and down Monkland. One thing she didn't grab was the cheque. Joey's plate was untouched, Manon's was wiped clean. Two plates of eggs and sides, four espressos, three of them to fuel Manon's go-go life, tax and tip, almost fifty bucks. Joey dug into her back pocket for her credit card. She didn't have it. Didn't have her debit card, either. In her front pocket she had two tens, a five and two toonies. She was screwed. Maybe if she let herself puke all her bacon and eggs, they'd tell her to forget the bill. Hmm.

MaryAnne ran through the song five times, listening to the rhythm tracks in one ear. It didn't feel right. And the kids on the other side of the glass had their mad on and said nothing. She probably shouldn't've slapped the little shit but someone had to.

She pulled off the headphones and joined the guys behind the board.

"Can I hear it through the speakers?" she said.

Alfalfa pushed a couple of buttons and a couple of faders.

"How loud?" he said.

"Loud."

The bass came first, she loved that. Stephen had a great attack. A few long notes, then he broke it down to half and quarter notes, then the drums and electric guitar, then her voice, not bad for daylight, but not great. She listened to all five versions, all decent, all wanting.

"Give me a few minutes," she said, then left them and made her way to the alley. Not to smoke. To think. It was rush hour and traffic sounds were ricocheting off the brick walls behind the fences. She checked her phone, hoping Michael had called with a word or two of encouragement. But, he never did. He was always afraid he'd bother her. Instead she found a message from her daughter.

"Uh, yeah, uh ... nevermind, you're probably busy," and the line went dead.

MaryAnne called her.

"What's up, Joey?"

"Ma?"

"No, it's Lady GaGa. What's up?"

"Nothing. I called 20, 30 minutes ago."

"I'm at the studio. What's a matter?"

"I'm in NDG. Manon was going to take me to the

clinic, you know, get checked out, but she forgot she had an appointment and I'm stuck here with the bill, not even money for a cab. Killer hangover and the bill's fifty bucks and I don't have my cards or enough cash and ... nevermind. What they going to do to me? Make me wash dishes?"

"Joey, you're almost 30. I'm in a session here, booked for five hours and I can't run across town to pay your bar bill and you shouldn't be drinking. Shit. What're you doing?"

"Don't get all sanctimonious on me, Mother, please. And I'm in a café, not a bar and I'll work it out. I'm sorry I bothered you. I should've known better."

"I can't stop working to run to your rescue, Jo. Fucking studio costs money, techie, engineer, lose an afternoon. It's your womb, Joey. Look after it."

"MaryAnne, why are you such an asshole?"

"I am not the one who ran across town with a huge hangover and no money."

The line went dead.

MaryAnne thumbed a key on the phone to call her daughter back, blanketed by remorse and failure but thumbed another key to kill it.

"I am an asshole," she told a squirrel who stopped, looked at her and ran up the Hydro pole.

MaryAnne dug into her pocket for the charred half a joint but changed her mind. She was angry, but not sure why. Then she was. She was working, Goddamnit, and she wasn't going to drop it all to bail out her hungover daughter. Again. Joey was 28. She had to learn to swim. Now. MaryAnne had songs to finish before she drowned.

She pulled open the door to the studio. The guys were

watching a music video, a girl with little clothes and less talent dancing and lip-syncing.

"C'mon guys, beam me up and let's do it."

She pulled the headphones on, nodded to the boys, heard the baseline and then the drums and found the groove she was looking for. It was anger. She just wasn't sure at whom. And that confused her. But the groove felt great. Did it in one take. Then another for good luck. Then the last, 'cause, well, three times lucky.

Felix was working aisle 48—lawn chairs, black and white lawn jockeys, pink flamingoes, pale blue flamingoes, yellow flamingoes, beach umbrellas, inflatable beach toys, insecticides, pesticides, electric bug zappers, foam snakes, life jackets, life boats, boat motors. Some days it felt the aisle stretched to Ottawa. Felix prayed for roller blades, new knees, new back and new shoulders. Today, there was a new pain in his hips and a new cramp in his neck.

But his saviour arrived. Gaetan seemed to be a kind of rover, working here and there, keeping the flow flowing, keeping the blue pills coming. The sight of him soothed Felix's pain.

Gladys was behind him as Gaetan palmed him a pill for the five folded in Felix's hand, just two working buddies shaking in comradeship beginning their shifts.

"How's it going?" Gaetan said, looking around for the eyes in the sky as he dropped flamingoes into a basket clamped to Gladys.

"I wake up every day and say, 'Thank you Jesus,' and

I'm fine, except every part of my body is aching. How you do this? Eight years, man? Eight years?"

"I could be doing heart surgery but I don't like the sight of blood," Gaetan said. "Wherever you work, you're working for the man, man. I just work the angles, do my job, stay in shape, sleep my eight, don't drink, eat a good breakfast, whole grain cereal, no sugar, just lots of berries and nuts and yogurt, man, keep you going and gotta watch the caffeine, makes your blood sugar drop. And bacon, four strips, fat and protein, need that protein, man. I do some stretching to warmup, like before a game, you know."

"Sounds great, Gate. Wear my aching body down before ya even start working. What're you looking at all the time?"

"Cameras," he said. "Never know where the bastards put them. See them up there, in that little bubble, see the little red light too? I know they're watching us. They're always watching us. Can't fool me."

They worked with their back to each other, their robots between them and the rows and rows of suburban necessities.

"What colour's the light?"

"Motherfucker's red," Gaetan said. "Might be a two-pill day."

"How can they do this?" Felix whispered. "Force us to work. I feel like a fucking slave."

"See, that's your real lack of education showing," he said. "Compare your little points of pain to what enslaved lived. Man, that's ignorant. That's also why you're here rather than making real money at a real job."

"What's your excuse?" Felix said, keeping his aggression

on hold. Can't piss off the medicine man. "If you're so brilliant what're you doing here?"

"I never said I was brilliant. I'm just aware of my ignorance, which is a step toward enlightenment. Learn your history, man, or die. They can get away with this shit 'cause there's no union."

Gaetan still had his back to him but his voice dropped lower.

"Without a union, man, they'll use you up and then have Gladys here drop you in the recycling bins out back."

"Union? Someone …"

"Shut up," Gaetan said. "Keep it to yourself. I'm working on it. If you're interested, just nod, don't say anything, just nod."

"You're getting all James Bond on me, man. I'm nodding. See, I'm nodding."

"Think I'm being paranoid?" Gaetan said. "Guys who talk unions get green-lighted permanently so don't talk to anyone about it. I'll keep you posted. C'mon Gladys."

"Wait, wait. Tell me about Jeanine. She single or what? You know?"

"Jeanine not in that club."

"What club? Oh. She gay? Really?"

"Really. Tough broad. Butch. Thought you had a girlfriend."

"Just asking," Felix said.

"Happy wife makes for happy life," Gaetan said. "That's what I hear. I believe in the healing powers of porn. Don't have to buy anyone dinner. And I can keep the toilet seat anyway I want. And don't mention the U word. See ya."

"The 'you' word?" Felix said.

"Union, asshole, union. Shut the fuck up."

And he did his fast walk, Gladys, his mechanical blinking buddy, following close behind.

The good thing about the job was you didn't have to think. The bad thing about the job was you didn't have to think. Joey's mind wandered. And mostly it wandered to wine. Glasses, bottles, ice, the softening of life's sharp corners, the sweet balm for all her troubles, the assurance that, despite the evidence, she was witty, wanted, successful, fulfilled. Wine perpetrated the lies, assuaged the guilt, and, especially useful at this moment, stopped her hands from shaking.

Joey had to give change. The register told her how much, no brain cells prodded, but she did have to remove paper and coins from the cash, hand over a receipt and her damn hands had started to dance.

She was trying to hold on till lunch, another hour. It was her first day on the job, first day sober. How people did this every day, she had no idea.

She had to wait until the rush subsided. She started at 8 for the office crowd desperate for buckets of swill to kick-start their day at the desk. At 10 they came to reload during their 15-minute break. They were even more anxious mid-morning than their breakfast visits; their somnolent, ambushed air had given way to desperation, fear and a pervasive "What the hell am I doing here, six hours and five decades to go?"

She figured some would be back at dinnertime to keep the engine revving for the homefront.

Joey had briefly worked an office job and didn't have to imagine the horrors that whipped cubicle denizens into a buggy-eyed, caffeine-craving frenzy.

In her fresh Starbucks green apron, she took the order, punched the appropriate button on the cash, asked for money, waited while the ditzes on the other side of the counter dug into pocket or purse as people behind them danced nervously from one foot to the other as if they needed to pee.

Joey wondered didn't they know they'd have to pay for whatever over-the-top concoction they ordered? Why did her world come to a stop as the ditz searched for the three, four or five dollars or a card or even a cell phone app Joey was waiting for so she could take money from the next one in line and the next one and the next one and the next one. There was no end to it.

"Can I have a bagel with cream cheese? No, I'll have a carrot muffin. No, wait, sorry. I'll have a gluten-free marsh-mallow dream bar. Are they good? Are they fresh?"

"No, they're shit," Joey wanted to say.

"Awesome," she said. It was an all-purpose word for all occasions. Samantha used it with every customer, a cue for the big smile.

"Cappucino?"

"Awesome!" Blazing smile.

"I'll take a brownie and a large dark roast."

"Awesome!" Blazing smile.

Guy in front of her was still counting change. Didn't they get it? Couldn't they grasp her desire to drown herself in red wine was all encompassing? The need to drink screamed at her from every cell. Even her toes demanded alcohol. It was insane doing this sober.

Not so damn awesome.

"Make up your mind, give me your money and go away," she was about to say.

The moron facing her had asked for a frappocaffa something or other and Joey was amazed she punched the right button on the cash and pulled the change out but missed the guy's hand and rained coins all over the counter.

Great, she thought. *I'll get canned my first shift.*

She started picking at the change, silver lint from a stainless steel blanket of a counter, but the moron wasn't a moron at all.

"No worries," he said. "I've had mornings like that." She would've kissed him if she didn't feel like throwing up. She smiled. He was a good-looking guy with long dreads and a smooth, dark face, big eyes, big hands.

How'd you like to hook up with a bottle of wine and a preggers alkie? she thought. He gave her another big smile and all was right with the world until he moved on to the barista station and a 50–50 pulled up, 50-plus years and 50 lbs overweight. Of course, she wanted something with whipped cream and chocolate sauce and sprinkles over a half-litre of milk drowning a shot of coffee.

The drink disgusted her, but she didn't have to make it. That was the nauseatingly happy barista's job. She saw herself in the tired woman waiting for her change, 25 years down the road, waddling under the load of life, too many disappointments and too much wine. She checked the clock on the cash. Fifteen minutes to break and a drink.

She tried to give the 50–50 her change but the woman said, "Keep it, dear," and waddled toward the barista, balancing her load from one foot to the other.

Samantha was arranging muffins in plastic in the display case that had been shipped in from Joey knew not where. She came over to where Joey was wrestling with the cash.

"We can go to my car," Samantha whispered in her ear. "I have a thermos there. Iron out the wrinkles. And mints."

Joey looked at her, surprised. Was she wearing a neon sign?

"I can tell, Sister," Samantha said. "Just a little something to get you home. Coffee doesn't do it." Joey wanted to hug her.

She had said, "Hello, pleased to meet you," this morning at 7. Samantha was tall and heavy and racially indefinable. She wasn't Caucasian, African, Oriental, Aboriginal; just a big, beautiful mix Joey now wanted to marry.

Sam had a little Corolla, dusty inside and out, cardboard coffee cups and McDonald's wrappers on the floor, the stench of hard smoking imbedded in the roof and seats and carpets. Sam slid the windows down and pulled a thermos from under the seat as she lit a cigarette.

Making her way slowly through the parking lot was the overweight, overwrought woman, face etched with a lifetime of weariness, a plastic supermarket bag making her list to one side. Where were all the promises?

Sam poured a little clear vodka, looking as fresh and cool as lake water, into the thermos cup and handed it to Joey, keeping it below the windshield. Their little secret.

Joey took it, her face still on the woman struggling to get across the parking lot. She looked at the liquid relief, could almost see her reflection, looked out the windshield, pushed the cup back at Samantha.

"No, thanks," Joey said. "I'm okay. I'm good. Maybe at lunch."

God, she could taste it. Even the scent made her want to eat the cup.

She was good until her shift ended and she started to shiver. Was this what DTs were about? She signed out, wrapped her sweater around herself and headed for home. She counted the blocks. One to Jeanne Mance, ignore the dep that was on the corner of Parc, head straight north, Saint Viateur, Bernard, at least three deps to slip by, then a right on Van Horne, a dep-free zone, then a right to her house, lock the door, soak in a hot tub. Stay there.

Felt more like fall than early summer. Least in her bones. The sun offered no warmth. Joey walked fast. She needed to get home. She ached for the sanctuary of the tub—the succor of the tub as familiar and necessary as the succor of the bottle.

There was a dirty red-brick schoolhouse, circa 1930s, its chain link fence bent and rusted. Behind it the colony of daycare kids screamed and ran and skipped and kicked balls, most lucky enough to have no idea what the world had in store for them, Jo thought. She kept walking, kicking it into high gear. But in the corner of the yard, sitting on the asphalt, a little boy in a faded blue T-shirt stared through the fence, looking at nothing, shivering, blowing on his hands, oblivious to the bedlam behind him. Joey tried to keep walking but couldn't.

"Are you all right?" she said.

The boy looked through her. She knelt down, talked to him through the fence.

"Are you cold? Do you miss your mummy?"

The boy stayed silent, blowing into his tight little fists.

"Not warm, eh?" Joey said. "Is your mummy coming soon?"

The boy glanced at her then continued his focus on nothing she could see. Joey shrugged off her sweater, clumped it into a ball and tossed it over the fence. It landed on the boy's head. He giggled and pulled it off and held it in his lap as if it was a plush toy.

"Put it on, you know, put it on. You'll be warm."

The kid wrapped it around himself but said nothing, just stared through her.

Joey waved to the boy and walked faster, chilled to the cells of her soul, the bath calling louder. She didn't look back.

MaryAnne was listening through the takes a third time, making mental notes for the mix. A lot more bass just about everywhere; she wanted it melancholy. They had recorded the drums with eight mics and she wanted the snare and the brushes up a bit, the cymbals way down, and she'd have to play with the tom and kick drum. She wasn't sure which way to go.

Then Jeremy blew in, always like a man on too much caffeine. Maybe it was meth but it wasn't her business. He kissed her on the cheeks three times, dug a hard drive from his back sack and slid it across the board to Alfalfa.

"You Never Did Love Me, Frederick," he said. "Should be near the top of the queue. MaryAnne … and you certainly can, my dear … this'll be a breeze. Here're the lyrics and I've highlighted your parts. Just the intro here and then harmonies on the chorus and then the last out here … really, really big, 'Never, never, never, never …' And I'll just fade it out. It's in D sharp, perfect for your voice. How's Michael? Is he still perfect? Rich, handsome, industrious, great in the kitchen and in bed? I'm surprised you're still able to walk, I bet you never …"

"Jeremy, how 'bout shutting up and let's do this? Uh, Frederick, can you play it for me please a coupla times?"

"You didn't even tell me how you were," Jeremy said as she shut the door of the vocal tomb, cutting off his voice.

"How are you, baby? It's been too long," he said, this time through the talk back.

MaryAnne stood behind the mic.

"I'm fine, Jeremy, great. Let's do this, sweetheart. I want to get home."

It took an hour but Jeremy was happy and instead of paying her he picked up her studio tab, a few hundred. MaryAnne thought it was overly generous but Jeremy's demos usually ended up on someone's video and he never worried about making the rent or spending the winter in Cuba, enjoying, as he said, "heat and meat."

She left the studio on Christophe Colomb and grabbed a cab for the Café Cherrier where she had an hour for a drink with Glenda before Michael was serving smoked Cornish hen, God bless him.

Several lives ago, starting out, Glenda sang with her in a band. The girl singers. Tambourine bruises on their thighs, short skirts, one part eye-candy, one-part two-part harmonies. Glenda hung it up when the band broke up, the guys always fighting, drinking, drugging, screwing. Amazing they ever made it on stage.

MaryAnne refused to die and was eventually discovered by Sid playing the El Mocambo in Toronto and was signed without having to lie down for him. Glenda got married to a finance guy who liked haunting rock 'n' roll dives, buying fine dinners and better hotel rooms for young girls used to road food and stained motels. Two years later she divorced him, married another broker and had hung in since, bringing a few kids into the world while her husband flew around the world.

She had said more than a few times life was best when her husband was on a plane.

The years had not been kind. She had always loved frozen vodka and still did. She had jowls and sagging cheeks and was easily two hundred pounds, a good section of it swaddling her waist like a life preserver.

She talked about her children, their problems, their successes, her grandchildren and their problems and triumphs and the TV shows she watched.

MaryAnne listened, asked questions, trying to find out if there was any of the old "good-time Glenda" left, the woman who liked to rent a bike when they were out of town and explore, take hikes, long walks after gigs down unfamiliar streets in strange towns. She used to be fun.

But the conversation always came back to the kids. She knocked back shots effortlessly, but it changed neither her tone nor the subject of her monologue.

She said she found exercise boring, her knees and hips

hurt, nutrition nothing more than transitory fads, and she had given up on losing weight. She was a big woman and so be it.

She was enthralled by the wonders of a website where she could download TV shows, movies, books and music for free.

Right, MaryAnne wanted to say, why would you want to pay for artists' work? We'll spend our lives so you can sit on your fat ass and enjoy yourself while we eat Kraft Dinner. Where did Glenda go?

She followed the vodka with chocolate cheesecake and ice cream, then gathered her phone and keys and handbag, kissed MaryAnne on both cheeks, promised to call soon. "But with the grandchildren's soccer and theatre and baby-sitting them and the sale of my daughter's house and and … uh … the move and you know I've been totally addicted to that series *True Hero*, been binging on six seasons, like a hundred shows. It's amazing. You have to see it. I downloaded the whole thing. Didn't cost a cent … I'm so, sooo busy, can barely breathe."

"She used to be beautiful, had a great voice, better than mine, got hit on backstage way more than me," she told Michael from her seat at the table as he sculpted dinner. "Now, she's a walking time bomb, booze, tobacco, no exercise and 70 pounds overweight easy. What the hell happened?"

She had meant the question to be rhetorical.

Michael splashed some wine into his clam sauce—he

couldn't find fresh Cornish hen and the guy would lacerate himself before serving a frozen bird—and stirred affectionately. He was wearing the apron she had bought him for no reason other than she had fallen in love with him, its admonition—"Don't fuck with the chef"—more appropriate than most of their dinner guests realized.

"I'm no therapist," he said. "But it's a safe bet your friend doesn't like herself. And it's a chicken and egg question."

He speed-chopped some jalapeño peppers and scraped them into the sauce. He compensated for the lacklustre flavour of the canned clams he complained about by jacking up the heat. Michael did not let obstacles or shortcomings shape his dinners or his destiny. He always found a way to add flavour.

"Did she stop living because she didn't like herself or did she stop liking herself so stopped living, which, of course, makes her dislike herself even more?"

"If I hadn't met you," MaryAnne said, "I could've been her."

"No way, darling," he said, reducing the gas under his sauce to an almost invisible blue flame with his right hand as he turned the gas under the water up high with his left. The guy could've conducted an orchestra.

"You've always known what you want. You're like a great running back. The mediocre ones, when the O line doesn't open a hole for them, they bull their way in, gain a yard or two and blame the blocking. You, when the hole isn't there, you change directions, try going off tackle and if that doesn't work, you'll go wide, around the end, or maybe right to the sideline, run over a linebacker and get six, seven yards or break a tackle for 10 or more. One of the reasons I love you."

"'Cause I'm like a football player? Two hundred eighty pounds with a thick neck holding up a concussion-addled brain?"

"I guess you've never seen lingerie football," he said as he slid the Italian linguine into the boiling water.

When he was 25, he was making more money than he knew what to do with. He was travelling a lot and whatever impresario or band he was working with paid the freight. Hotel, per diem, salary. And there was always good food backstage. And while everyone around him was drinking their money, putting it up their noses and keeping women happy, Michael banked it. He wasn't much of a consumer.

When everyone was partying and tearing hotel rooms apart, he was usually alone in his room, reading, holed up in a multiplex or walking around town. Scaling towers like a monkey and hanging speaker boxes and lights 30–50 feet in the air was excitement enough. Hangovers wouldn't make things easier. The women he tended to meet backstage or in the hotels liked to use the crew to get to the band. Empty sex left him hollow and cold. He lost interest.

When he was home, he walked the streets and back alleys of Montreal. It was the early 80s, and there were For Sale signs everywhere in his favourite neighbourhood of

Italian cafés, Greek souvlaki joints, Hasidic grocers, fish-mongers, butchers and bagel shops. It was five minutes from Parc and Mount Royal, the mountain and the boule-vard; one bus from downtown and the homes were tri-plexes and duplexes and six-plexes made of brick and stone, built in the '20s. The money sat in his bank account, and one day, bored with the news and sports pages, he bravely ventured into new territory, the business section. He dis-covered banks were making a killing with his money. Why shouldn't he? He bought an old house. Then another, and then another, regularly emptying his bank account for down payments on places and buying mortgages from in-surance companies. The banks didn't like customers in jeans and rusty cars and their offered rates reflected that.

But, the more property he owned, the more the banks wanted to be his best friend, throwing low-interest loans at him or better mortgage rates or lines of credit and the mortgage brokers would outbid the banks and Michael was getting another education in the three-ring circus that was finance. Money lenders were fickle. The more prop-erty he bought, the more mortgages he owned, the more the banks groveled.

All these loan officers in their Moore's suits and ties treated him like Elon Musk. When he was starting out at 20, living from paycheque to paycheque, they wouldn't give him a credit card. Now, indifferent owner of six or seven rental properties, impressive cash flow from the rents, it was raining plastic. He took it all, prepping for Armageddon.

And, as people scrambled to sell, convinced Montreal

was dying, sure their futures were in Toronto, Calgary or on the Coast, Michael was happy to buy their homes and wish them well.

He was happy right where he was then and now.

He pulled his Mazda truck up to the curb in front of a six-plex he had bought on Waverly for $135,000 30 years ago. Realtors were harassing him to sell for more than a million, but he didn't see the point. What would he do with the money? And looking after the old buildings was what he did, the tenants were people he liked. There were no curtain times to worry about, no inflated egos to deal with, no stoned dramas to complicate life, no hearing loss.

People raised families in his buildings, people retired here. He tried to make life easier for a dozen or two, and him and MaryAnne.

Rigging days were over. He didn't need a lot of money back in the day and didn't need a lot now. MaryAnne was into playing and painting, not buying. All he had to do was keep the places in good shape and keep MaryAnne happy. And make sure he had time to grocery shop and cook dinner and read. The mortgages were paid, the rents paid the taxes and expenses and the cash left over was more than Michael and MaryAnne cared about spending.

Friends who didn't know him well suggested he raise the rents. Friends who knew him well admired him. The guy owned four worn shirts for warm weather, four for cold. His entire wardrobe could probably fit into a single suitcase. He had more pots and pans than socks, and his stove cost twice what his beat-up truck did.

He grabbed his tool box. Today he had a hot water

tank to fix. Then he'd shuffle down Saint Viateur, hit Parc, hunt for dinner and cook for the singer in his life. He didn't think life could be better.

Took him more than 50 years to get here but it had been a good trip. Sometimes he thought he should be doing something more, what or why he wasn't sure. But the feeling generally passed.

Mrs. Gross was another matter. She and her son had this two-bedroom since he bought the building. She was 92. Her son was 75, give or take. His mental competency was maybe 12, give or take. Born in Auschwitz. Michael never asked about the father, never asked about the camps. The blue numbers on her forearm were faded but easy to read when she was in her wardrobe of two or three short-sleeved synthetic housecoats, a few months short of being rags, all five feet of her, shrinking steadily. Every few years Michael painted a room for her. She would put up a fight.

"Why you paint for?" she'd say. "I don't need new paint. I'll be in my grave soon. You want some rugula? I make some coffee."

She had called because her hot water wasn't hot. She was always apologetic. She had been paying the same rent for the 25 years Michael owned the building. He could've doubled it. Tripled it. He didn't need the extra $500 or $1,000 a month. And how many more years could she live?

"Don't worry about Lebby," she had told him a dozen times. "When I die, he's going to go live at a home. You don't need to worry. He'll be fine."

Another time she had told him, "God thought I had it too good at Auschwitz, so he gave me a son without a proper brain. A real mitzvah." Michael had to ask a Jewish friend to find out she was being sarcastic.

Doing repairs for Mrs. Gross necessitated a half hour of civilized intercourse over strong coffee, a habit she had picked up during her meandering migration to Canada, and several pieces of rugula, to which he had become addicted and was one of the reasons he happily rushed to repair anything.

She also insisted he collect the rent personally, once a month, she was too old and tired to walk to the mailbox that "the goniffs in the government" had moved two blocks farther away, because "they were sure she hadn't suffered enough."

"Today I made jam and walnut," she said. "I know you like better cinnamon and chocolate but I don't want you should get spoiled." Then she laughed. Michael didn't know how anyone could laugh after the path life had led her on but somehow it put a little more steel in his spine.

If he came near noon, she would whip up German fried potatoes with bacon.

"They're not kosher but what can God do to me that he hasn't already done?" she said more than a few times.

Rent days he aimed for lunch. He had watched her make the potatoes a dozen times, there was nothing exotic or artistic about them, but he couldn't come close. Either the bacon was overdone or the potatoes were not cooked through or the onions burnt. It was like what Eric Clapton said about B.B. King, "I play the same notes, but it doesn't sound the same." Maybe making her potatoes was like playing the blues. You had to suffer.

He ate the golden brown potatoes, shiny with oil, on a circa 1950s table, topped with something akin to Formica, skirted with dulled stainless steel, sitting on four inverted tripods of tubular stainless steel.

Over his head was a framed cheque from Volkswagen for $6,472.00, dated 2002. Also framed was the letter, explaining the money was part of the settlement agreed to by one of the world's biggest carmakers to pay the surviving slave labourers they had used during the Second World War.

"What am I going to do with their six thousand dollars?" she said. "Better they should all drop dead."

In a crawl space above Mrs. Gross's bathroom, pulling out a fried heating element from a hot water tank, encrusted with white scales, he was a long way from setting up for the Stones. And stuffed with fried potatoes and rugula, it was tough to think about what to put together for dinner.

Cooking was a rediscovered joy. Celine had not liked him coming home looking like a plumber, driving a pick-up. She liked the best restaurants after 8 p.m. She was tall and slim and worked 70 hours a week as executive assistant to the town's top impresario, a rock 'n' millionaire whose signature was on most of Michael's cheques. If the act was a hot ticket, Celine was the one working the bank of phones, negotiating contracts with artists, venues, caterers, hotels, media. Every show Michael worked he would run into Celine, a great mind for the smallest detail, a perfect eye for the bottom line, a great body for tight clothes.

They had made it through 10 exhausting years. As Michael sealed the tank, he told himself forget Celine, think dinner. Souvlaki and a beer would've been good but they had turned the Greek joint into a martini bar. Dimitri had packed it in, packed it up, and taken his wife back to Greece. He had shouldered working seven days a week over a grill, adapted to winter, but avaricious rent increases and business tax hikes chased him and the family home, only to run into the ever-tightening vice of the IMF.

Greece was no longer the paradise of the youthful Irving Laytons and Leonard Cohens. Michael wondered how Dimitri was doing. A lot of other familiar faces had evacuated the neighbourhood, turned off by high rents, ambitious, childless couples and their duos of expensive European cars dueling for parking, rumbling delivery trucks feeding the stores and café conversations about real-estate prices and second-world vacation spots.

Michael's thoughts segued to Cantonese lobster and steamed oysters in Chinatown, a carrot to end the day.

This was the fourth time in 10 years he had changed the element. Mrs. Gross liked the water near boiling, but the hotter the water, the more minerals collected and the quicker the element cooked.

"I spent enough years being cold," she said. "I want hot. I deserve hot."

So Michael changed elements and changed tanks and raised the rents regularly on her neighbour, Charles, who had been renting out rooms on AirBnB, claiming they were cousins, uncles, friends and friends of friends. MaryAnne had found he was renting rooms online for $100 a night. Charles was making a fortune turning Michael's flat into a rooming house. He was paying $1,200 a month, but was making about $2,000–$3,000 a month. Michael wasn't sure why it pissed him off, but it did.

"It's because you're charging what you think is a fair

price," MaryAnne said, "and he's taking advantage of your decency to screw other people and make a killing."

"No laws against it," Michael said.

"No laws against greed, sweetie. It's a virtue these days."

One thing MaryAnne was not, was greedy. Give her something to smoke, a guitar to play, she was more than fine.

Celine, on the other hand, defined the word. There was no such thing as enough or too much. Food, wine, drugs, money, property, sex, rancor, squabbles, she always needed more.

Nights were marathons. She had a nose for coke, but he had given up on drugs. Reminded him, maybe he should abandon alcohol; it wasn't sitting too well lately.

Good ol' Celine loved to work 14 hours, shouting into landlines and two cell phones, pop in, do two lines and take him to bed. An hour later she'd do two more and jump him again. Seemed fun at first, but it hit him one morning at 4 a.m., as she was performing her hyperactive magic, that it wasn't really him that was the attraction. It was the drug. He was just in the right place at the tight time.

The exhaustion and fried nerves meant she could catch fire any time over anything. It was exhausting. But, he admired her efficiency, energy, commitment to whatever task she was doing. And, he had to admit later, he was but a man, and Celine's beauty and talents were cheese in the trap.

In Michael, she found stability and moderation, qualities she was pondering, the way an atheist might read the bible.

For a couple of years, she cut back on cocaine, at least when he was around, slept better, put on a few pounds in the right places, had more energy. They made a lively couple.

But, Celine wanted more. She wanted real estate and lessons from Michael on how to bag it.

"I don't do that anymore," he told her. "That was a long time ago. I was a kid with more money than brains. Now, I work shows nights and I janitor days. It's not a fun gig."

The rock 'n' roll shows were getting old. The quiet, solitary repairs were welcome. Dirty hands, no egos. The only keening in his ears outside of work was Celine's temper tantrums. His old brick properties provided refuge.

But, Celine dove in, buying mortgages and properties at inflated prices, renovating with contractors, charging killer rents, living on the edge, scrambling to meet payments. Then the drugs made a comeback.

"Mike, I have so much to do, not enough hours in the day," she said, wiping her nose with a crumpled tissue that seemed to have grown roots into her left hand. He hated being called Mike.

Then her tenant stopped paying his $2,000 a month rent, and another moved before his lease was up and she was short $4,000 a month and counting. In three months, her credit line was chewed through—mortgage payments, classified ads, Hydro bills, cocaine by the ounce and she asked Michael for money. It wasn't the first time her go-go lifestyle and powder habit had drained her bank accounts.

"Short-term, until I get the places rented and the hearing at the rental board. You know Mike, you should really raise your rents. Tell them you're going to move in and want to renovate. You could double your income in two years. Your flats are worth a fortune. Then we could sell it all and go live in Hawaii. It's time we lived together anyways."

He wrote her a cheque for $10,000. Then told her he wanted time alone. And not in Hawaii. She didn't understand. He never saw her or the money again. The concert company she worked for was sold and she was dispatched. Michael did less monkey work, more supervision and number crunching, more time at a desk or in his truck, computer on his lap, his mind drifting.

Last he heard Celine was selling real estate in the U.S. during the pre-bubble days in 2005-7. He didn't know whether she crashed with the crash.

Michael found life easier alone and mostly celibate. He relished the quiet and lack of drama. Work was always akin to climbing the high wire and that was enough excitement for him.

There was Marsha, a mother of two who rented a three-bedroom from him on Waverly. Her divorce had been messy and unexpected. Every few weeks, they spent some time together while her kids slept. He'd bring a bottle of wine, follow her into the bedroom where glasses and candles waited and a few hours later he'd quietly slip down the stairs and walk home down the empty streets under the orange streetlamps, feeling more than a little empty himself.

A year before he met MaryAnne, Marsha told him she was moving to Toronto, trying to find better work. She wasn't going to renew the lease. He wished her well and tore up her last rent cheque. He didn't hear from her again. What was she doing now? And where was she doing it?

Curious the pages of his past that he flipped to when

he was sardined into a crawl space, up to his elbows in a hot-water tank.

He said goodbye to Mrs. Gross and her son. She gave him an aluminum foil pouch of rugula.

"You leaving?" Lebby said. "Why you leaving? You going to work? You going to school? You going to bed? Mama, why he going?"

"He's going," Mrs. Gross said. "It's not your business where he's going. Michael, you come back. I'll make you cinnamon chocolate like you like."

He threw the tool box in the truck, thinking about dinner and the evening ahead. Maybe he'd pick up something, cook while MaryAnne got a buzz on, told him about her day as she played bits and pieces of songs she was working on. He was tired. The climb into the truck seemed higher.

"Whaddya think? A or D?" she'd ask. Or, "Ya think the chorus should come after the second and fourth verse or second and third and end on a verse? Or maybe just hit them with the chorus first?"

He'd serve, they'd talk, he'd clean up, she'd play at the kitchen table. She was better than any radio station. It was a habit they carved out during their courting months. He never asked guests to clean so she would play for him. And now, when vestiges of dinner were put away, she liked to climb to her studio, paint a bit or play a bit. He wasn't yet used to having his nights free, and he enjoyed it. He walked. Sometimes she walked with him. He read. Sometimes he shopped. The fine-food stores in the neighbourhood were endlessly fascinating. They'd meet again later in bed, read, exchange horrors from the news. Their libidos had greyed with their hair. But they were fine lying side by side, hips touching.

"What'd you hear from Joey?" Michael said. He was cutting into chicken Milanaise he had served with a large salad and black-eyed peas he had slowly cooked a few days ago.

"I'm a lousy mother, that's what I hear from my daughter," MaryAnne said. "And she's right. She screwed up again; was stuck in NDG and I was in the studio and didn't go riding to the rescue. I should've. I was being a bitch."

Michael knew when to listen and when to shut up. There was no right answer here.

"She's a smart kid but always screws up. And now she's pregnant and …"

"Next time, unless you'd rather I mind my own business, you can call me. I'll drive her."

"I hope I am a bit of your business, baby. But interrupt an afternoon with Mrs. Gross and her fried potatoes?"

He looked at her with the Michael look, the one where he cocked his head slightly and raised his eyelids, his "don't-be-stupid" look. She hadn't learned yet how to take it. Lots she hadn't learned to take yet. Long silences. Long walks. He could disappear for a couple of hours and tell her he had been walking on the mountain. Of course, she had been in her studio, lost in whatever she was doing, why shouldn't he get lost wandering around the city?

MaryAnne thought he didn't really need her, not in

any tangible way. He was self-contained, almost maddeningly so. But maybe that's why it worked. MaryAnne didn't want to be needed. She wanted love, liked companionship, enjoyed his warm body, but when need was inserted she recoiled, certain she couldn't deliver. She would fail. She would disappoint.

Couldn't her daughter give a Ted Talk on her shortcomings?

"That's kind of you, but if she's going to have a kid, and indications are, as of this hour, she won't, but she still has to get her shit together. Don't you think?"

"I don't know."

He chewed slowly, staring at her. "But I can and will happily help, regardless of what you need, at any time. I like Joey. She's messed up but she's a good kid."

"You're so bloody chivalrous," she said. How she'd find this guy?

"I don't know what the word means," he said. "I think it's about love and I don't think, in case you're wondering, that a quid pro quo is required."

"Michael, you make a better mother than I do."

Michael, the momma. Maybe there was a song there.

"It's much easier when you don't have 20-plus years invested."

"Or maybe you're just not a self-absorbed asshole."

"There's that."

She flipped her napkin at him. It fell on his plate. He ceremoniously folded it, placed it next to her dinner plate, and happily resumed eating.

He had coated the chicken with homemade bread crumbs punched up with salt and pepper, of course, and fresh garlic, Romano cheese, powdered thyme, sage, dried oregano and just a touch of ground jalapeño peppers. It was too good to permit a little family dissension to allow it to go cold.

"Steve's a grandfather," she said. "Did I tell you? It's a disease. He even likes it. Takes the kid for walks in his carriage every chance he gets. Steve! If he tries to tell me how wonderful it is I'm going to wrap a bass string around his neck. How come that sweater's so big on you? It get stretched?"

"I must've screwed it up on the spin cycle," Michael said. "Maybe I need to do heavier weights at the gym, pump up like Arnold."

"Please don't," she said. "Oversized clothes are in fashion."

They ate in comfortable silence.

How did this happen? MaryAnne had bounced around a three bedroom for the first years of Joey's life, her and Joey's father living in that grey stone on Saint André.

But she was used to hotel rooms and once Joey had found her wings and discovered men and substance abuse, she downsized to a studio on Saint Christophe, an embellished back alley east of Saint Denis. One large room with kitchenette and a corner for a bed, another for playing. The big space with its big windows on two sides was all she needed.

Michael had a two-bedroom in his own building a few steps from the Italian Social Club. One day they pulled the curtains wide, opened the doors and invited the neighbourhood to join the old men playing cards around oversized tables. Michael was the first through the door and turned coffee and whatever into a morning ritual. The thick espresso Louie served him and then them every morning was their wakeup call, until the place became trendy, line-ups at the bar grew and Michael popped into Saeco on St. Laurent near Little Italy and dropped $700 for an espresso machine. The ritual coffee remained, only the location changed. One in his bed and one with breakfast.

Not much larger than MaryAnne's studio, but he had gussied up the kitchen. Also used to hotels and being on the road, it was all he needed. He and MaryAnne spent two years enjoying nights in one place or another. Their routines remained the same. She played, he cooked, though not happily when he was at her place.

One summer night, they were eating on her cramped balcony. He had smoked a small pork roast on the little Weber he had bought her, though they both knew it was for him.

"You know, MaryAnne," he said. "Your kitchen … no counter space, you have to pray the stove heats and the temperature is anyone's guess. The fridge is the size of my grandmother's ice box, though I think the ice box was colder."

"I'm so used to being away, I never paid attention to the kitchen. And before I met you I was eating in restaurants. I guess I should think of moving to something more befitting a grownup. Maybe install a real kitchen. I'm not on the road that much anymore."

"I think I'm going to stop travelling, too," he said. "My vocation needs an upgrade. Rock 'n' roll shows, 36 years, maybe it's enough. I think my ears would appreciate the break. And I'm tired."

He sliced a few slivers of roast, slid them on her plate. Unlike many women he had known, MaryAnne liked to eat.

"I have my eyes on a duplex, small, beat up, most of it would have to be torn out. The price is fair. I was thinking of buying it, fixing it up. A great kitchen for me. Maybe a studio for you. The street's quiet. I could soundproof a room. About 1,800 sq ft total."

"Michael, are you inviting me to co-habitate?"

"Is that what they call it now?" he said. "I thought we'd be shacking up. The house would be mine. You wouldn't have to pay anything. You could rent out this place, keep paying the mortgage on it. Good investment. Maybe one day you sell it, fatten up your nest egg. We could even renovate it. But your input entirely welcome on the reno of the new place. I'm not fussy. We'll do whatever you like."

Took three months. They got their hands dirty as electricians, drywallers, plumbers, carpenters, roofers and cabinet makers; swarmed the old place, stripping it to its skeleton and then putting it back together. Michael supervised, painted, wired, shuttled from home to store several times a day while MaryAnne buzzed between her house, a studio or two, shows here and there and spent off days and evenings in the construction zone and later the paint store, contemplating colours.

It was as good a way as any to get to know each other. Neither was neurotic or demanding—their world didn't depend on if the countertops were butcher block or tile or on the colour of the paint in the diningroom. It was a good time with many more to come.

She watched Michael finish eating, looking at her with

that same ain't-life-grand look he always had when they ate alone. She wished she wasn't getting on a plane. But she was looking forward to tonight.

Esther had called, asking her to come out and play and MaryAnne needed no convincing. She stood in the door-way of l'Express, traffic behind her on St. Denis noisy and impatient, hunting for her old friend until she caught a glimpse of Essie at the bar, her right hand on a glass of wine, her left on the empty stool beside her, chatting to a slick guy in a suit.

MaryAnne had ironed a black silk blouse for the occasion and still felt underdressed. Essie always looked game; hair in glossy rows, eyes lined, cheeks subtly shaded, lips inviting, clothes tight, accenting a body that still liked to shake it, ready for the spotlight. She had always been gorgeous. Always been tough. The sister she never had.

Essie's face lit up when she spotted MaryAnne and she exploded out of the bar stool and they hugged and kissed each other on the lips and then on each cheek.

"Told you we were gay, honey," she said to the guy in the suit, who tried to look like there was nothing wrong with it but waved for his bill.

"Mary, Mary you look like pure honey, make me feel like a slug," Esther said. "Let me take your coat."

"You're full of shit," MaryAnne said. "I spent three hours trying to make sure I wouldn't look like your poor cousin from West Virginia."

"Look like my younger sister from Fifth Avenue," she said. She waved at the waiter, always alert for a beautiful woman. "Give my sister here a glass of ... no, hell with it,

give us a bottle of good red, something from California."
And she hustled off to hang up MaryAnne's jacket on a
rack of hooks on the wall next to the bar.

"What you doing here?" Mary Anne said. "You playing or visiting?"

"Both. We're doing three nights at PDA then four at
Roy Thomson in TO, another in Winnipeg, Regina, you
know. I think three in Vancouver and Victoria, something
like that. I'm too old for this and I miss everyone. But at
least I can see you. How are you?"

"I'm on the treadmill, Es, but I'm getting slower and
it's getting faster," she said. "But I ain't hanging it up yet.
Touring soon."

"I envy you, woman," Essie said, sliding a glass of fresh-
ly poured, shiny Cabernet toward MaryAnne and taking a
taste herself. "I never had the balls you had. I used to be 20
feet from stardom. Now I'm 30 or more but you went for
it. I listened to your last tunes. Shit, I still listen to all your
tunes. Ya keep getting better."

"You are a bullshitter and I love you for it."

"No, I'm not, least not to you. Bobby or Slate, as the
world calls him, is insane over your stuff. Loves your pipes,
girl, and I'm sure he'd love the whole package if he got a
good look at you."

"You like working for him?" MaryAnne asked.

"He's a piece of work," she said. "The star thing gets to
them all eventually, you know. First they want to fuck you
and then they want to fuck you over. But he's still paying
well and goes after younger game, leaves me alone. I do a
couple of tunes myself a night, give him time to do the

drug du jour, get a nice hotel room to myself, decent per diem, and if we have a few days off between towns, I get to fly home, spend some time with Henry, see the kids and … I didn't tell you, the grandkids."

"No shit," MaryAnne said. "You got grandkids? You!?

"My girls got their own girls," she said. "You'd think they never heard of contraception but they hit twenty and they both got knocked up. But they got good men. JenJen is 10 and Mauricio is eight."

"Been too long since I've seen you, Essie," MaryAnne said. "Congrats. I'm happy for you. You doing babysitting and that shit."

"A bit, when I can, but I'm not around much. When I'm not on the road and Slate loves the road, the whole super-star thing and he don't mind much that I'm not 25 any-more. And I have a little business I run on the side, out of Atlanta, but, you know, now I can work anywhere, bustier and laptop will travel. How's Michael the dream boat?"

"Keeps me sane," MaryAnne said. "He's a little under the weather but he'll be fine. Cooks like a bastard."

"In more ways than one, I hope," Essie said.

"My stew pot is full, sweetie. I'm lucky."

"And how's your daughter, Jackie? I forgot her name. Jackie?"

"Joey. Twenty-nine and preggers and in love with every vice," MaryAnne said. "She's a good woman but a work-in-progress."

'Oh my. She gonna have the kid? She have a man?"

"Don't know. Don't know. But I do know I'm not really ready to do the grandma thing."

"I envy you, MaryAnne. You're still on the stage, front and centre. You've always been the one with go. When we started as the Trash Sisters, 'member that, about nineteen oh two? I knew you wouldn't stay 20 feet from the spotlight too long. I'm still doing harmonies and showing skin but you're the headliner."

"'Cause there's something wrong with my head. Ship's going down, girl. Just a matter of time. Market's drying up for an old broad. What kind've business you running?"

The bottle was half full or half empty depending on how one viewed these things. The restaurant, as was its habit, full of clinking and clacking and laughing in three languages, ambitious service people rushing and smiling, a tasty bite of Montreal, but the two women were in their own bubble, oblivious of everything but each other and their past of shared secrets and big shows.

"Well, don't laugh but I book acts and performers. I have about 45 people under contract. Do mostly weddings and large corporate parties, birthdays for rich assholes, bar mitzvahs, but only for real green. It's my day job. I take these musician kiddies, mostly kids, some got the chops and mix and match 'em. Give 'em repertoires, get them costumes, rehearsal hall which is mine, kick ass and make decent money."

"You're kidding."

"Nope. It's my retirement, MaryAnne. You want crooners for your father's 75th, I got 'em. Dance music for a wedding, bar mitzvah, golden oldie band, music for down the aisle, I got 'em. They're paying ten, fifteen thousand for an eight-piece. Band gets half, I get half. Last year

I grossed close to a hundred thousand, so I'm doing fine. The kids are doing fine. The future is here, MA, no more hustling for gigs. They come to me. And if whoever comes to town or Miami, even, they need a bunch of black soul singers or even white, I book that, too. Did a few shows for Cocker and Seal and Paul Simon wanted some African soul, didn't want to tour with all them people, I hooked 'im up. They paid fine."

"Shit, I'm exhausted just listening to you. Pass the wine."

"MaryAnne, know what?" Essie said. "You can get off the treadmill. You're tired. I can book you gigs as a backup, studio sessions, you don't have to do anything but show up and sing, get green, per diem, travel, hotels, food, top shelf, woman, no worries. Almost as much as you want. Probably have to beat the dicks away with a stick. And, for you, you can keep it all. I don't need to make money off you."

MaryAnne watched the bustle, the moules and frites, the rognons aux dijonnaise go by, couples holding hands, wooing at the bar, business guys talking business or maybe trying to forget it. Where did the time go?

"Essie, that's generous, really, but I can't," MaryAnne said.

"You're a stubborn bitch," Essie said. "You always were. But woman, maybe you can take it easy a bit and stop hustling. You still painting? ... Great. So you'd have more time to paint, maybe get into the granny thing. It's not all diapers, woman. They keep you young."

"Esther, you always were the smartest one on stage, hands down. Everyone else, maybe they sold the records, made the money, played the celebrity, got the groupies but you had the brains and the beauty."

"Don't forget the soul, sister."

"And the soul," MaryAnne said. "In spades. Whoops! Was I politically incorrect?"

"Fuck off," Essie said and laughed. "You going to think about it?"

"I have a small tour coming up, not Roy Thomson Hall like a big shot but ... And I'm trying to finish a CD. Backup singing, shaking my ass, not me."

"What's not you is taking it easy," Essie said. "Nothing wrong with not having to hustle for every breath. And every lousy dollar. You're not under the big lights but at least you do what you do best, sing, and not worry. Think about it. I'm going to call you. Or text you. Whatever."

MaryAnne shrugged, drained her wine glass. She knew better than to argue with Esther.

"I love you, sister. Always have, since that first gig in ... where was it?"

"I haven't a clue," MaryAnne said. And she didn't. And it made her feel old. "It was a century ago. We were five years old."

They toasted and laughed, tears in their eyes.

"Take a load off, Fannie," Essie sang softly.

"Take a load for free," MaryAnne sang louder, climbing off the bar stool and putting some hips and shoulders into it.

"Take a load of Fannie," Essie sang louder, joining in the dance, the 20-foot-from-stardom, shake-your-bootie of their youth. Their voices melded, going with the Staple Singers vibe. The restaurant froze.

"And ... and ... and put the load ..."

"And put the load ..."

"Right on me ..." They sang together, in perfect harmony, shaking their hips, swinging their arms. People clapped at the bar and every table and the two women bowed, then put their arms around each other, ignoring the fluorescent glare and applause and the fact it was all so long ago.

"I was in a car accident and the police insisted I go to the hospital, rear-ended, they were worried about my neck and I don't know what happened to my phone," Joey said into her iPhone, working on sounding suffering, though it didn't take much work. ... "Yes, I'm all right, but it was a real bad day so is there anyway the doctor could see me today? I'm so sorry about yesterday, really."

It was classic Joey, improvising made it real. Maybe she should go into theatre.

She had to be at work collecting cash for swill in 12 minutes which meant a taxi for sure if she could get this bitch to give her another appointment after messing up her first day off, getting stuck with Manon's bill. Took a lot of skating and smiling to convince the café manager she'd be right back with the money. Which she didn't do and wasn't going to. Drag herself over to NDG to pay someone else's tab? Maybe in the next life.

They gave her an appointment to see an OBGYN in two days and as Joey scrambled to dress she wondered how she'd get off work and how she'd get through the day since she hadn't slept. Not drinking sucked enough without being able to escape by sleeping. She'd been awake most of the night. Got dressed at one to hit the pretentious Whiskey Café meat market. Just one drink. Walked two blocks but changed her mind, ran home, and climbed under the covers dressed. Lay in the dark. Thought of calling Josh, maybe sex would knock her out but he'd bring wine and dope. Maybe dope would be okay.

"What do ya think, kid? Wanna get high?" Shit. She had to eat for two and stay sober for two. She may have slept on and off, almost made a run for the bar at 2:30, just a quick glass, but dug deeper into the cocoon of warm sheets and chewed her lip.

She ran through the varieties of coffees and so-called coffees or coffee-flavoured milk and sugar drinks the café sold and fell asleep for about two hours, waking up sweat-drenched and shaky. Must be what MaryAnne's menopause felt like, short-circuited thermostat and all. Something else to look forward to. Why did her body seem to revolt so often and so regularly? And surprise her, often unpleasantly.

She had waited for her first period like a five-year-old waiting for Christmas. It was to be her key card into a new life as an adult, the circus, the show of earthly delights. Yes, there had been delights. True. But they came with a price. Blood and pain and embarrassment. She hated buying tampons from a geek at the pharmacy. Hated talking about it with men she barely knew. Somehow it was way more intimate than sex. She had met Québécoise women at parties that talked about their periods as if they were talking grocery shopping. Not her.

She rubbed her belly with her right hand, slowly, trying to divine if there was really an embryo there. She tried to see down that long, dark funhouse tunnel of life. To where MaryAnne was. Hot flashes and weird moods and dry and cranky and out of the game. Though good ol' mom seemed to have a good time and caught herself a good man.

He often called her, inviting her to dinner, buying her lunch, took her to a couple of those romcoms where everyone had great clothes, lots of money, perfect jobs and worried only about getting hitched.

The last time they left after 20 minutes and he took her to Burger de Ville on Saint Laurent, bought her a steak.

"Michael," she said, "that film was hideous."

"Truly," he said. Guy didn't talk much.

"Why did you want to go see it?"

"It's a chick flick," he said. "Seemed like a good idea at the time."

"I hate chick flicks," Joey said.

"Me too," he said, "but I figured you're a chick and ..."

"I have a brain, Michael. It's sometimes pickled but I have a brain."

He smiled.

"Sorry," he said.

"No, no ... I'm sorry. I'm being stupid. You took the afternoon off and took me out and now a great lunch or dinner or whatever, I'm being a bitch. I had fun. I never go to those movie places. I just stream shit. It was fun."

"You're lying," he said, laughing.

"No, I'm not," she said. Then she started to laugh. "Yes, I am."

She was suddenly jealous of her mother. She had a good man and she seemed to be right where she wanted to be. And here she was, alone, rubbing her belly. Do I want to keep you?

And she drifted off again until the alarm blasted her awake and she was force-feeding herself coffee in between punching the cash and giving change and trying her best to smile and care that every customer's order was "perfect" and all was "awesome."

From double espresso with milk to diarrhea latte with whipped cream and sprinkles it was, "Of course, no problem, perfect, awesome."

She was knocking back single shot espressos between smiling like an idiot. She had read an Elmore Leonard novel where recovering alcoholics drank a lot of coffee. Recovering? She was going to have to recover from this so-called recovery. It was killing her. The two million mgs. of caffeine only over-amped her and made her want to guzzle a gallon of bad red to pacify her fried nervous system.

Caffeine couldn't be good for the creature curled up in her black lagoon, either. No coffee, no booze, and now sex didn't seem like such a good deal. It was unimaginable. "Double espresso, please. Just a bit allongé."

There was Felix, hair longer, welcome tilt to his head, curious smile taking her in.

"Joey? Joey?" His long arms reached across the counter, squeezing her shoulders. She thought he was going to climb over the counter.

"Felix," she said, real joy in it, almost as good as a doctor saying, "There was a mistake. You're not pregnant. Your monthly visitor's taking a brief vacation."

But, it was only Felix, and she was surprisingly thrilled, even more so 'cause he seemed the same. There was a whole kind of Hollywood thing happening and she was helpless. Bring on the popcorn. And the Kleenex.

She flashed on waking up on the kitchen table, nude, of course. She had met him at some bar on St. Laurent and had brought him home. He was clean, funny, not overly anxious, polite and a stud. Didn't take long, he was naked on the floor next to her, out cold. Detritus of depravity was everywhere. Empty bottles, full ashtrays, empty cigarette packs, empty glassine envelopes, crumpled clothes and pieces of a broken ceramic something or other. And her brain, chopped in half, an ax sticking out her head. Torn, stretched and limp condom on the floor. Yeah, she remembered now. The condom tore but they hadn't skipped a beat. He had known all the right buttons to push and they were orbiting Pluto at the time and had no Earthly concerns. *But the comedown's been a bitch*, she thought.

"What're you doing here?" he said, ignoring the caffeine-crazed lining up behind him.

"I don't know," she said. "Keeping out of trouble."

"How are you?"

"Ahh, can you guys maybe flirt on your own time. I need to get back to work and I need a coffee, if you're not too busy," said a 60-year-old guy in a suit behind Felix.

"This is my own time," Felix said to the guy. "Nice suit. New York or Hong Kong?"

To Joey: "How long you been here? Make it a macchiato, just a cloud of mousse. How are you? You okay? And give me some really sweet, tooth-destroying chocolate stuff. I tried to call you but never found your number. I've been in New York. Brooklyn, you know, hipster city. Maybe I'll have a cherry flavoured … No, how about an

Iced Coconut Milk Mocha Macchiato? Does it have any coffee in it?"

"Jesus, can I just get a coffee?" the guy in the suit said.

"I don't know, man, I don't work here," Felix said to the guy. He turned back to Joey, un peu dans la lune. "When are you off?"

"Now," Joey said. "I can't stand this shit."

"Janis." She called to a woman in the requisite green apron, pouring milk into a metal can. "Take the cash, 'kay? I'm leaving."

"Leaving? You okay? You can't just leave."

Joey pulled her apron off and dropped it in the sink behind her and walked around the corner and popped her arm through Felix's and steered him out the door.

"Buy me lunch," she said.

"Sure," he said. "Where?"

"Doesn't matter, but you have to buy for two," she said. "I'm pregnant."

She smiled at him. It was time she told a man.

MaryAnne lay beside him in the dark, listened to him breathe. He was a good sleeper. A man without a guilty conscience. Or perhaps no conscience at all. Michael was happy in solitude. He easily slipped inside himself; could spend hours with her in the car or reading in the garden, not saying a word. When alone, as far as she knew, he lived like a monk. Sometimes, it drove her crazy.

His pursuits were equally solitary. Cooking and the well-oiled movements between fridge, stove, pantry and counter that she liked to watch as she picked at her scarred Gibson.

In his backyard garden, patches of French radishes, Lebanese cucumbers, tomatoes and green beans, he had planted empty upturned paint cans to sit on. His days of stoop labour were over. All year, he attacked the weight room; three times a week, he quick marched to the Y or rode his bike like a courier through traffic, home an hour later for a shower. Though he hadn't gone this week. Said he needed a break.

In winter, he walked or drove to the park or arena. Early mornings, if the ice was good and the kids were in school, he chased a puck by himself on the outdoor rink on Saint Dominique and Laurier. If not, he'd join the free skate at the arena at 4 p.m., weaving circles, dodging tumbling children and near-spastic beginners for 20–30 minutes, seemingly amused as hell, made it look easy, much like his kitchen time. His mind was she knew not where. She came once, had a coffee in the seats, and watched.

"What do you think about when you go round and round and round?" she said that day as he wiped his blades dry with a ratty Kleenex he pulled from his pocket.

"As little as possible," he said.

"Well, something must be going on up there as your legs are pumping down there."

"Mostly, how to avoid crashing head first into the boards and breaking my neck," he said, straight-faced. He often made her feel as if she was trying to pry open a locked drawer. "Sometimes I wonder what the hell I'm doing going round and round in circles trying to avoid crashing head first into the boards and breaking my neck. I was thinking steamed fish with ginger and shallots, red rice, and maybe Brussels sprouts and roasted cauliflower."

Maybe that's why he slept so well. There were places out of bounds, maybe even to him, locked compartments where compulsions, mistakes and remembrances best forgotten were sealed away, out of sight, out of mind.

He was a be-here-now kind of guy while the romantic in her was always looking for stories from the past, heartaches and heartbreaks or notches in the win column to twist into verses and choruses or shape with paint on canvas. Everything was fodder.

Some nights she'd climb out of bed and pad to her studio, cloister herself behind the insulated door, smoke a little, play and scribble. Maybe paint or sketch. She didn't worry about getting up in the morning, hadn't since school days. The middle of the night had always welcomed her, especially after shows, when the noise and adrenaline dissipated and she could be herself. On tour it was her favourite time.

Night after night, shows sometimes a grind, music only part of it. You had to be on, play the part, pacify the beast, then the bus or plane or van and, if you were lucky, you might find yourself alone behind a closed door by 3 or 4 a.m. Put your feet up, smoke a little, hold on to the moments you wanted to hold on to as long as you could, the songs you nailed, the look in their eyes, those times when you were no longer a solitary, alienated human but had, somehow, through some miracle, touched the souls of strangers.

"This is how I feel. What do you think?"

She'd hold on to those moments. This is what love is,

Ma. Besides, what else was there? The whole trip was nothing but a too-brief escape from emptiness.

Michael didn't need an explanation. He just let her be, show or no show. He was there if she needed an ear or shoulder or more. Many a night she'd come home, pour an once of brandy for each of them, climb into bed beside him and stare into space. He was good with that, too. Didn't mind waking up to hear about the show. Share the highs and lows. The damn guy didn't ask for much. And he never spouted homilies at her when she was down. He just put his arm around her and let her lie on his chest—a better place than most after a hard night. But what was going through his head? When did he need comfort? How come he never seemed pissed?

She was working with an envelope, pencil and calculator.

Michael came up behind her and rubbed her neck. It was his way of saying: "How you doing?" She loved him for it.

"If all goes almost as planned, I'll break even," she said. "With a little luck, good weather, no playoff in some sport, no terrorist attacks or new COVID terrors, I'll make a few thousand for the retirement fund."

"Hell of a lot more than I'll make sitting on my ass and you'll make money for having a good time. Pretty sweet."

"Darling, it's not more than you'll make sitting on your ass," she said. "The rents keep coming and you have stocks that seem to only go up and …"

"I'm another oracle, the oracle of Le Plateau. And they don't keep going up. They jerk me around pretty good and the rents pay for keeping the roofs from blowing to Kansas and the walls from getting blown down by the Big Bad Wolf."

"What do you love, Michael?"

"You. And French radishes."

"If you could do anything, what would you do?"

"What I'm doing. Watching you plan your tour, see your forehead get all furrowed as you think. Know we'll be reading in bed together soon, maybe make love, ponder breakfast."

"Dreams?" she asked.

"What do you think we're living?"

"You are such a sweet talker, you. I bet you were never celibate for more than 48 hours ... maybe we can go away when I get back. Sit on a beach. Maybe someplace exotic. Someplace far. Leave my guitar ... that might be a lyric." She scribbled it down on the envelope below the rows of expenses and revenues for the 10-city tour locked in for next month.

"If you want," he said.

"What do *you* want, Michael?"

"I have what I want. I told you. And I've travelled to most places a few times. Used to fly charters most of the groups I worked with. Didn't have all the paranoid security to deal with. But I'll go anywhere you want."

"There must be something you want, someplace you want to go."

"Yeah," he said. "Not to be psychoanalyzed and to go to bed with you. How does that sound?"

"You're shutting me down and shutting me out."

"No, I'm not. You have this fairy-tale notion, maybe a writer's notion, that we all have stars we're reaching for, some sublimated desires, frustrated ambitions. I don't. I look around and see people chasing a rabbit or doing nothing, all a waste of time to me. I'm not chasing and I'm not wasting. You have music and you like to paint. I don't have an art form or a dream. I just live. Like to cook. Shoot pool. Fix shit. I like how we're living. That's my art. It's enough. I'm sorry if my life bores you."

"No, Michael …"

He left her at the dining room table, frustrated, working on keeping a lid on her unexpected anger and she listened to him climb upstairs. MaryAnne wondered. *Were there places he didn't want to go or was she unable to accept he was happy right where he was?*

"A baby would sure change the colour of the light," Felix said. He had been green-lighted at noon, time to soothe the aches and pains of body and soul. They were in a pho joint drinking tea waiting for the soup. "You going to keep it?"

"Don't know," Joey said. She liked the Jasmine tea and how perfect its temperature was. Were her doubling HCG levels starting to make her crazy? Maybe she was reading too much.

"Do you know who the father is?" Felix said. No bullshit about Ol' Flix.

"I think it's you," she said as a gym rat in a tight black shirt, tomato can biceps covered in tats, placed their wide bowls of pho on the table, smiled and walked away on air. Ballet, for sure, she thought. Or maybe her progesterone was kicking up.

"Condoms kept coming off," he said, digging through the racks on the table for chopsticks and a spoon. He gave them to Joey then found a set for himself, wiping them with a paper napkin. "Could be me."

"It didn't seem your dick was too small," she said, trying to smile.

"You didn't seem to think so that night," he said, laughing. He dug into his soup, twirling the vermicelli around his chopsticks and filling the ceramic spoon with soup. He chewed and smiled.

"My Father Felix," he said. "If we had a kid he or she could write a book, call it *My Father Felix*, maybe a play, I could play myself."

He dug around in his bowl of soup.

"What do you want to do?"

"I don't know," she said. "Except I'd really like to eat."

She gave him the "you're not a priority look" and grabbed her spoon and went to work.

"Where you been?" she said, slurping.

Felix had gone to take acting lessons in New York, meaning Manhattan, ending up in Brooklyn on someone's sofa and someone else's floor or car. Til broke, hungry, sore, tired, he came home to the room in his parents' basement and joined the fulfillment world. And there he'd been for a couple of weeks.

"But last I saw you, though I can't really say we saw much of each other that night, that was only, what, two months ago?"

"It was kind of dark and we had a hell of a time and I took acting lessons for a month, every day, but how can you afford to live there? I'm no waiter. And I tried to call you but I had the wrong number," he said.

"I do that. The first time a guy asks for my number, I invert a couple of digits. I have your number, if I want to see you I call and if not, you can't bug me."

"You have a bloody system," he said.

"Experience," she said. "Flix, we had a great time. I was hoping to see you again. I know the condoms slipped off twice. And I haven't been turning tricks at the Motel Amazon. So you're probably the guy, unless you're infertile."

He contemplated the face in front of him. A lot to read there. Her eyes said, "I'm afraid. I think I'm fucked."

The lips said, "Don't fuck with me." Her body language, arms hard on the table, head up, said, "I'm not taking any shit. I don't need you."

"History has proven me anything but," he said.

He needed time to parse all this. He was living in a cave under his parents, an embarrassing cliché. Working in a new-age hell. That would never get better. A pregnant woman carrying who the hell knew whose baby though it was probably his. Wouldn't be the first time. Get stoned, lose control and common sense. End up holding a woman's hand at the clinic. And then the relationship dies.

He could/should pay the cheque. That would be a valiant symbol, and get the hell out. He had his own problems. Yeah, he told himself, call for the waiter. But his hands stayed caressing his bowl.

"Down there, there are like a million gorgeous chicks and beautiful men, buffed and sculpted, great eyes, great chins, all hustling, hustling, hustling," Felix said. He wasn't ready to call for the cheque. "I didn't have a green card, I couldn't even work as a dishwasher. I spent my money on classes. That's what everybody does. Take shitty day jobs in between acting classes or dance classes or movement and yoga classes, workout, run to auditions if you can get one. The place is awesome but ..."

Joey hit her forehead, grimacing. The word made her crazy.

"What?"

"Awesome, don't say awesome, please. No awesome."

He shrugged, foraged for another slice of beef.

"Can't get auditions without an agent, can't get an agent if you haven't worked, and everyone's trying to sell you something guaranteed to get some director's attention or teach you to act or audition or dress. It's a racket. They sell audition apps. Funny thing is, except for the multi-million-dollar tourist musicals and big-name plays, there ain't that much anymore. Little theatres full of empty seats, off-off-off-off Broadway.

"But it's cool. On stage pretending to be someone else. Everyone acts all the time, but in the theatre you have a script and a director to help you not make an ass of yourself. Sometimes you even get paid.

"But only so many nights I could sponge off people I barely knew. So I came home. Working in a fulfillment centre."

"Sponging off your parents," she said. "Shit, I'd love a glass or six of wine."

"They're not licensed, that's why you wanted to come

here," he said. "Maybe I'll spend the rest of my life as a picker and a sponge. Maybe I can get a Canada Council grant, write a play about working in hell."

"You ever write a play?" she said.

"No, but I read a lot. I took English and philosophy in school." He sounded guilty.

"You can philosophize about life in proper English?" she said. "That'll pay the rent."

"How do you pay the rent?"

"Daddy," she said. "He died and left me a trust fund. I'm what you call a trust-fund baby who might have to feed a baby on the trust fund. So maybe an abortion."

The hot soup felt good, salty and spicy and full of life.

"Joey, maybe the kid is mine but what the hell, I mean, I'm not making a whole lot, but if you need help, I'll be there."

Her own mother had not made the offer. Manon drove off into the sunset, left her with the cheque. Maybe Flix was more than a dick.

"Flix, if I have a kid, the party's over, no wine and meth and coke and ecstasy and dope and staying up all night screwing," she said. "These days are … Well, if I have the kid, over, maybe permanently. I don't want to be like my old lady, stoned all the time."

"Joey, I said I'd help. I didn't say you had to give me unfettered access to your great body and impressive network of drug dealers. We did have a hell of a night, didn't we? It worked."

"Worked in more ways than one. It was two nights tied together with a day," she said. "We didn't eat or sleep."

"Did a lot of other better stuff," he said. "Plus maybe changed the world, man. What if you have a prime minister in your belly? Or a scientist that discovers a cure for cancer?"

It was her turn to forage in the soup. She was looking to bag a sliver of onion.

"I don't really know you," she said. "A couple of nights ..."

"'Cause there's not much to know. I'm living in my parents' basement. I'm 31 with two hundred and thirty dollars in the bank and sixty-two bucks on my credit card? I work when the traffic light let's me."

"What?"

"I'll tell you one day. I have an audition at a little theatre day after tomorrow, if I can get away from work at Santa's Workshop. Not a hope in hell. I'm not Equity. So I'll have a little time and a few bucks I make being a slave to the robots. But, what you want me to do?"

"How the hell do I know what I want you to do when I don't even know what I want to do?"

She arranged the chopsticks neatly beside her large bowl, printed with red snake-like dragons. He was one of those guys, needed a mother to tell them what to do.

"Give me your number," she said. "If I think of something, I'll text you."

Michael hated these places. He had visited them too often when his father was diagnosed, about his age now. Took six months. He was gone. Now it was his turn in the barrel. He wasn't hopeful. Why was everything so white and bright, as if colours would slight the profession.

"Ya can't trust the guy, his office is blue."

And why did they call you in to sit in an empty office for ten minutes? Maybe to save the doctor the 30 seconds it would take the patient to make his way from the waiting room. There was a clock on the desk. MaryAnne would be landing now, probably already in the van, heading to the motel.

The doctor came in, still 10 years older than Michael and looking it. He had abandoned his white smocks a few years ago, was into golf casual, bright Polo shirts, brown slacks, file under his arm.

"How you doing, Robert?" Michael said.

"Not bad, Michael, not bad," he said. "How you feeling?"

"Good. Real good."

"Lost a few pounds?"

"I don't know, I don't check, don't have a scale."

"I do. Let's check."

The scale looked older than Michael. He weighed in at 167 lbs. Down four from last month.

"I've been neglectful at the gym, less weight, muscle mass I guess shrinking."

Robert nodded, went back behind his desk. Michael sat down to face him.

Robert didn't open the file.

"We've done the MRI, the endoscopic ultrasound, I can do an ERCP, go in for a biopsy," he said. "I'm sorry, Michael, the tests look identical to your father's. I'm not hopeful. There's stuff we can do. I can hit you up with radiation, maybe chemo, slow it down, but … you know. It's ticking in your genes."

"I don't want to go through that shit," Michael said. "How long?"

"No one knows. But Michael, you could get another two, three years with treatment. Maybe. And in two, three years, there might be new treatments. Don't be so quick to want to die. Think, talk it over with MaryAnne. The treatments are significantly less onerous than in your father's day. You're not a quitter, man. Get back to me when you can."

He scribbled a script; gave it to him.

"For pain and for sleep. The little green ones, Dilaudid, will dull the pain, let you function. When it's real bad, the Oxycodone will dull most of the pain but you best not drive or mess around on the stove. There's no nobility in suffering. Take the drugs, keep on top of the pain. Don't let it settle in. Late in the day to worry about getting addicted. Sleeping pills will knock you out, pain or no pain. Don't take more than two. With the rest of the drugs in you, you might not wake up. Watch the booze. Go easy. Come see me in a couple of weeks, we'll re-evaluate. Or call if you change your mind."

Robert just stared at him. Michael nodded, shook his hand and left.

Waited for the elevator in the hallway. How many people got death sentences here every day? Nothing to get worked up about. It was part of the deal.

MaryAnne would probably be unpacking now, which meant turning the suitcase upside down over an open drawer. How would he tell her? When would he tell her? Why would he tell her?

The elevator came but he ignored it, pulled out his

phone, looked up a number and pressed the buttons, asked for his lawyer.

Fucking Musak.

"Marty, Michael. Fine, fine. I need to change my will. You got time today?"

The hallway was still empty, the elevator had departed. He took the stairs. It was only twelve flights. Might as well stay in shape.

MaryAnne wasn't crazy about these little planes. Could barely stand in the can. If you sat in the window seat, easy to whack your head, twist your neck on the overhead.

But she was looking forward. Took her almost a year to book this little tour, 10 towns, 15 nights, fly, rent a van, not too much driving. She shared a room with Stephen —they were too old for modesty—saved her more than $1,000, might be the difference between profit and loss. Drums and guitar in another room, per diems for everyone. She needed to sell seats. But small cities, little towns, less competition, venues were cheap to rent, usually easy to get 150 people at $20–$25, usually easy to make more than her nut.

Place des Arts and Thomson Hall were a long time ago. She should check out the Cinquiéme Salle at Place des Arts. That might work. It would be nice to play at home again.

Things brightened up at the bigger venues, 250–300 seats and merch—she hated that word—CDs, T-shirts, posters, caps sold. She had no idea why they did, but they did. Good night, you could make $300–$400 on the stuff, paid the motels and rent a car. That and the butts in the seat made for a pretty good night. These days.

But the scene was changing by the hour. The surprises were usually unhappy ones that blew holes in her ego.

She was counting on ticket sales to pay the band and pump up the nest egg not to mention her confidence. Maybe buy some groceries for a change. Michael loved Quebec lamb. Maybe knock him over with half a beast butchered and ready to whatever.

Made her smile. Michael didn't like the way she shopped, preferred to do it himself, wouldn't even take money for food. She picked up a cheque when they went out, but really his food was better and a hell of a lot cheaper.

But sometimes she needed to go out, see faces and not feel guilty about being cooked for, served and cleaned up after.

He was spoiling her and she loved it and made sure not to abuse it. Maybe he was atoning for some long-ago sins, she thought staring at the floor of clouds beneath her. Maybe the sins weren't that long ago.

The plane banked and lined up with the runway at Sault Ste Marie. Van was waiting.

They were doing the Sault tomorrow night, had time to get the scent of the place. Then Sudbury, North Bay, Kirkland Lake, Timmins, Thunder Bay and then a long drive to Toronto, a 400-seat venue and then next night a little place in Hamilton, 250 seats. Guelph a couple of hundred. Some towns two nights. Advance sales had been good. Then they'd fly home.

Fall was show time. No hockey yet, baseball gearing down, but the Jays were out of it. Canadian football wasn't a factor except on the Prairies. Golf was not yet under the lights. Didn't have to worry about Jewish holidays too much in Northern Ontario and too early for Kirkland Lake to fret over missing NFL Monday nights.

She was going to have fun.

The landing gear opened with the familiar thunk that sounded like a wing had torn off.

She would have to call Joey, see what she was doing. Might be easier to have fun if all was well with the kid. Maybe buy her something. But the kid was so picky, easier to just give her money, let her spend it as she liked. If she wanted to blow it on booze and drugs, who was she to tell her different?

Stephen drove the van to the motel, the guys jumped out, MayAnne drove to the venue, Stephen riding shotgun.

It was a converted movie theatre, her name was on the marquee, still a charge. She existed.

"Hey, ma, if you could only see me now."

Did the old lady ever play Sault Ste Marie?

She went through the front door, over the cracked mosaic tiles, up the worn marble stairs, the walls coated with posters of shows come and gone, her face, guitar in hand, in a frame that read "Coming Soon."

So far so good. She opened the old theatre doors, walked around the back of the last row of seats on faded, threadbare carpet into an office where Byron was sitting at his desk, looking at his computer.

"Hey MaryAnne, you're looking sexier than ever, it's so good to see you," he said, his 300-plus pounds rising out of the chair and kissing her on the cheek. "Sit down, sit down. Hi Stephen. Going to be a great night."

"Tell me," she said.

"Got 132 sold, think we'll get a walk up another 40–50. I paid the radio station a few hundred, they've been playing your last CD and some oldies all week, plugging the show, gave them 10 sets of tickets to give away, we'll do okay."

"Show me," she said. "Show me the money."

"Okay. So far here's the gross, before tonight's walk up, twenty-one hundred and change, my percentage off the top, radio payola, print ads, publicist, posters, I have $1,660 for you now, and then the walk up at $25 a ticket, probably give us another $1,000, you get $750 and I have a table and girl to sell merch. Nothing to complain about."

"Not yet," she said. "Show me the money and I want the walk up e-mailed to me before I get on stage. I check my phone, when the money goes ding, we hit the stage, play two sets, 50 minutes each, everyone has a good time."

"Always a hard on," he said, smiling. "Always a hard on."

"From being surrounded by men day and night," she said. "Trust but verify. Show me the money, we all have a good time."

"Email the same?"

"Yep," she said. "I like to pay the guys just before we get on stage, a great motivator."

"I play much better after warming up my fingers counting cash," Stephen said.

Byron clicked some keys, stared at the screen, clicked a few more.

"It's gone, you'll get it by the time you get to your motel."

"Okay, By. You're looking good. Keeping away from the booze?"

"Yeah, right. For an old NFL lineman, maybe. Cut back, lost 10 pounds. Only a couple of drinks a night."

"Stay well, see you tonight, as long as my phone goes ding, Byron. No ding, no show."

"You and your fucking dings."

Her phone went ding. She checked it.

"Thanks, By. See you at sound check. Six p.m.?"

"Yep, same as always."

"Thanks for the ding," she said, and kissed his cheek. "Don't forget, another ding before we get on stage, the walk ups."

"Yeah, yeah, ding dong, Jesus. Ding dong."

Byron knew better than to mess with MaryAnne. He and she went back a ways. Started out at the same time. He backstage, she on stage.

She began at 20, doing backup with Glenda, didn't find herself until she was 35. Perry liked that about her. She kept working to figure out who she was. Always comfortable on stage, but one day she drove in and she was a new woman, bluesier, more soul, stopped wearing skirts. It wasn't about her legs. Took to wearing jackets. It wasn't about her breasts. It was about her heart and she put all of it into every night.

He asked her what she was scribbling so feverishly one evening before curtain in the shabby dressing room he kept meaning to paint, maybe drag out the beer cases and faded posters and she told him. She made notes before shows, jokes about the town, the room, the news, the guys behind her, get the audience laughing, relaxed. Learned to pace the show, a few songs, a few words, a few jokes, some local politics or news. Byron had seen a lot of girl singers come and go. Pretty voices, great bodies, nothing special. MaryAnne was special. She had ambition and a take-no-prisoners determination. And talent. She could turn a phrase, touch you. And audiences left smiling.

Nicky managed her for six years. Everyone called him Nick the Prick but only behind her back.

Gigs weren't great, but she was playing. Paydays were disappointing, but, it turned out, not for Nicky. He was showing her dummy contracts. If she was getting paid $3,000 for a show, he showed her fake contracts for $2,000, took his fifteen per cent off that. What did MaryAnne know?

Byron came into her dressing room after a gig, told her, "You were worth every one of those four thousand bucks, next time I'll make it five." Kissed her on both cheeks. He was a genuine fan.

Nick the Prick was outside, smiling, envelope in hand. "Great show, dear, here's the sushi." MaryAnne counted and found $1,700. Byron had heard gossip about Nicky, the music biz was a large fraternity where everyone shat on everyone, but now he was seeing it.

"Seventeen hundred? That's it?" she said.

"More when we tally the merch," he said, looking at her, wondering why she wasn't smiling.

And, Byron couldn't believe this shit, the broad reached back with her right arm and punched Nick the prick in the mouth. The little bastard wasn't more than two inches taller. He took a step back, holding his mouth, shocked, stunned and then the chick kicked him between the legs and slugged him again. She was all fury and flying limbs and Byron would've pulled her off but he was having too much fun watching her beat the crap out of Nicky. He was going to dine out on this story for a decade or two.

"How many years, you asshole? How many years?" Stephen had all his hair back then. He pulled her off him.

"Fucking guy's been stealing from me, probably for years, you motherfucker!"

"Don't hit him, MaryAnne, you'll bust a finger," Stephen said.

Nicky was bent over.

"I can pay you back, it was administrative fees, overhead," Nicky said, breathing fast, teeth clenched, lip split, eye cut, blood dripping from both.

"Don't bleed on my boots, Nicky," Stephen said and kicked him in the ribs. "Bastard. Rip off MaryAnne, you're ripping us all off."

Nicky was coughing and groaning as Stephen reached into Nicky's jacket pockets and found a couple of hundred in one and a wad of hundreds in the other. He handed the cash to MaryAnne.

Byron learned—don't mess with MaryAnne.

She drove back to the motel. So far, so good.

Stephen dropped his bass and bag in the room, went to hang with the guys. Grandpa and grandma, sharing a room. She'd have to ask him how the grandfather thing was working for him. She'd bathe and fluff later. She'd been in a thousand rooms like this in a thousand towns. Polyester bed spreads and curtains, cigarette burns on the carpets and fake wood furniture, five-and-dime art on the walls, pillows filled with foam, plastic glasses and soap that was more a sliver than a bar.

Maybe she could call Essie.

"Take me away from all this, Essie, and I'll stand in the shadows and shake my ass for whoever and sing whatever and not worry anymore."

She called her daughter.

"Where are you, Mother?"

"Northern Ontario. I think Kirkland Lake or Timmins or Sault Ste Marie. ... Somewhere like that. How are you, Daughter?"

"I don't know, MaryAnne, really. Shit's happening, feels like the Alien is growing in there, playing with my insides. It's weird."

"Mother nature can be a bitch," she said. "You know what you're doing?"

"I do. Then in five minutes I'll think I'm doing something else. But, I'm running out of time. It's been maybe 10 weeks I think. I have another few weeks to make up my mind. I think. How many weeks until they won't do it anymore?"

"I ... I ... I don't know. You'll have to check with ... I guess your obstetrician or gyno. I don't know, Jo. But you have time. This ain't the States. You drinking?"

"No, mother, I'm not drinking. You smoking?"

"Not yet, too early. I like to wait until after a show or my timing goes, pisses Stephen off. Don't want to piss Grandpa off."

"I don't know what to do, MaryAnne."

"Joey, I'm a lousy mother. I can't tell you what to do,

especially from a dive in Northern Ontario. It's your call. I want you to be happy. But ... if you go through with this, I'll help but don't depend on me to babysit and ... I work all hours. This'll be your baby. As long as they're buying tickets and songs, this is who I am. You need anything now? Need money?"

"A case of red. By the way, Felix has returned. He was in New York taking acting classes. He's back, working in hell, living at his parents, a basement rat."

"Felix?" MaryAnne said, trying to hide the skepticism.

"MaryAnne, I told you, it was not immaculate conception and Flix is the father. So yes, he's a real human, two arms, two legs, etcetera. He's the daddy. I think. I'm pretty sure. He says he'd help."

"Really?"

"Yes, really."

"You trust Felix?"

"Course, not. That was a weird week and I did some stupid stuff, okay? I fucked up. I was out of it most of the week and I ... It was just stupid. I'm not 16 for Christ's sake."

"Joey, listen to me, listen to me," MaryAnne said. "You're not the first woman who slept with more than one man in one week and shit happens and stop beating yourself up over it. You got pregnant, most women do and we don't always choose the time or even the man. Do you want to keep it? That's the question now. If you have the baby, that's a lifetime commitment."

"I know that, Jesus. Think I'm a fucking idiot? Why do you think I'm curled up in the fetal position every night, I think I have the DTs from not drinking, just in case I want the little ... Having me wasn't a lifetime for you. You're flying around playing rock star and I'm not holding you back."

The conversation was going south and MaryAnne was struggling to drag it back to civility.

"That's true, but I'm a shitty mother. Probably worse grandmother. Did you get to the clinic?"

"Tomorrow. Tomorrow. It's a one-stop shop. They give me a check up, give me info on how to proceed with the pregnancy or terminate it. Love that term. Terminate with extreme prejudice, like one of those blow 'em up movies with Matt Damon running around trashing people."

"I'm sorry I can't be there with you."

"I can always ask Flix. He'd come. He's probably not working. He has one of those gigs, maybe you work, maybe you don't. But what's he going to do? And you got a tour. Hip grandma the rock star."

"You should have someone with you, in case you don't feel well or just to buy you lunch."

"I think of food, I think of puking."

"Lovely being a woman, isn't it? What about Manon?"

"She's usually showing houses. MaryAnne, you're play-ing mom, and it's not a usual role," Joey said, exasperated. "I'll work it out, I always do. My friends work, or try to. Don't you have a sound check or something?"

MaryAnne was trying, her daughter was resisting. Neither enjoyed the moment. *Maybe that's why I don't try*, MaryAnne thought. *My daughter is a pain in the ass. Maybe her mother is a pain in the ass.*

"Yeah, sound check or something," MaryAnne said. "Call me when … whenever."

She ended the call. Clicked another button to speak to

Michael. He always cheered her up. His voice was enough. The guy was always calm. Talk about Zen.

He sounded asleep.

"Did I wake you?" she said.

"No, I don't think so," he said. "I was reveling in the quiet. Zoned out, I guess."

He was asleep. One minute he was reading, the next minute he was gone. Weird dreams, too.

"How you doing and where you doing it?" he asked.

"My motel room, heading for sound check, got a stash of cash from old Byron. Says he lost ten but it looks like he gained 30. Seems we'll get a good crowd, make a dollar."

"Why don't you sound happy?"

"Joey, she has an appointment at the women's clinic, no one to go with, but you know what, Michael? It's not my business. She's grownup, she'll do what she has to do, or not, and doesn't need me to hold her hand. And I have a set list to do. How are you, other than enjoying the fact I'm not around?"

"Great," he said. "I'm taking the day off. Though I think I'm supposed to paint someone's bathroom. I put in new medicine chests last week and I promised I'd repaint. So, I might mosey over there."

He felt like going back to sleep.

"Not quite as glamorous as thrilling thousands in …"

"Hundreds, if I'm lucky," she said. "You okay?"

"Fine. It gets so boring here without you I went into a traumatic stupor. I'll sniff paint, get me right back on course."

"Okay, darling, see you soon. Miss you."

"Have fun tonight. Muchos merde," he said, and the line went dead.

MaryAnne tossed the phone on the bedside table. Two calls, zero for two. Nothing clicking today. Better be better tonight.

Naps were good, a blessing, really. Time, aches, worries suspended. *Sleeping the sleep of the dead*, he told himself, laughing.

"Getting kinda morbid there, Michael," he said to the empty house.

His thumb did its thing, checked his email, his habitual response when finding consciousness again. Mixed in with the usual "world gone awry" news flashes and a couple of "let's eat or drink" requests was a note from his former tenant/lover, Marsha. Short and cryptic.

"I'm back in Montreal. Come share some red." She left an address on Mentana, not far from Mount Royal, and a phone number. His heart rate increased, a Pavlovian response. She had always been good company in the days before she left, before he met MaryAnne, now doing her thing in Northern Ontario.

Best take a shower, shoot some pool. It was not the time to do something stupid.

The long, worn marble staircase seemed higher than the last time he climbed it, maybe two weeks ago. The cigarette butts and roaches and dead bugs swept into the dusty corners of each step had been there since Moses carried the tablets down from the mountain. Didn't bother Michael a bit. Only added to its cachet. This was his second home, caught in time like a fly in a web.

He pushed open the swinging glass doors and smiled. Ten antique snooker tables, all but three of them dark, their pockets made of webbed leather, scents of marijuana and hashish framed by cigarette smoke clouded the room, the clack of balls at tables under white neon the sound track. And a bit of laughter from Desmond, tall, skinny Haitian who seemed to live here and was once again trying to strip Bonnie of a few bucks.

"You can bend over all you like, Miss Bonnie, and unbutton all the buttons of your beautiful shirt but you will not succeed in distracting me," he said. "Ha ha ha."

But Bonnie did succeed in not only distracting him but running through the coloured balls as Desmond laughed at his own futility. Bonnie was a pro. She chewed gum with the precision of a metronome, about 120 chews per minute. Wore tight jeans and shirts, kept her hair clipped short to keep it out of her eyes and was as good at pocketing other people's money as sinking snooker balls. Michael stood in the shadows, between empty black café tables and long snooker tables, watching Bonnie shoot, face blank, eyes analyzing the options, following the intended trails of the red balls she was hunting.

"Life is all about a big stick, balls, a snug pocket, and how you get there, wouldn't you say?" she asked him over a post-game beer a few years back. "All about working the angles." He couldn't argue with her and had to smile re-membering it. Bonnie reminded him of some of the artists he had talked with backstage during his thirty or so years.

Reminded him of MaryAnne, too. Their profession was who they were, most of the time. They wanted it more. He thought of his lover, getting ready to step on a stage 1,000 kilometres away. She had wanted it more, it just hadn't wanted her as much and time was no longer on her side. It pained him she kept running into the brick wall of time and change, made him weary that her heart and soul, lyrics and melodies could not get her what she deserved.

Maybe nobody deserved what they got, he thought.

Michael made his way down the row of tables. Henry, behind the bar, filled a glass with Boreale Rousse and slid it toward Michael and nodded. There was another couple playing that Michael didn't recognize. Léo and François stopped playing to give him hugs and ask what was up.

Michael came here to get away from whatever was up. Here or the motel room—four hours, $40—where he had started to cop his clandestine naps, not wanting MaryAnne to know he was exhausted much of the time.

There was purity in pool, sanctuary in the darkness, freedom from rancor. In this faded joint, there were no TVs, no music, no electric glossy beer ads, no video games and no one shouting at him. No "Buy this!" or "Think that!" It was a rare and comfortable no-tech zone. The last time a guy used a cell phone here, he came back from the can to find it twirling slowly on the bottom of a fresh mug of beer.

Under the long lights that made the perfect green felt shine, there was only one truth—sink more than the other guy.

Where else could anyone pay only a few bucks and enter a sanctum where geometry and physics and hand-eye coordination ruled. All you had to do was understand angles, that action bred reaction and know how to use a stick. Gender, age, race, weight or beauty mattered not. And there was no app to rescue you.

Michael knew most of the real players that came through, poker-faced all. Bonnie used her cleavage. François used feigned contempt. Sally used stone-faced confidence. Beverly liked to talk trash. And they all had stick. And they all worked at it day and night.

Michael had played and paid them all, supporting the arts, he called it. They played on the same table but they lived and played on an exalted plane.

He took his beer and climbed up a few steps to the dark tables overlooking the snooker tables, what passed for a spectators' gallery, a throwback to the pre-video game era, when people would leave their homes and shoot a game or two and watch the pros play.

Desmond handed Bonnie a few bills, laughed as if it was the happiest day of his life, then racked them up. Guy was a masochist. But, Michael thought, thinking of Haiti's history, losing at pool was a walk in the sunshine. And Bonnie, maybe 30, was not hard to look at.

Self-conscious, Michael went to the can, locked himself in a stall and read Marsha's note again. His hands texted her while he watched.

"What you doing?"

He sat on the toilet, feeling adolescent but alive, better than he had in a while. His phone chimed. He fiddled with it to kill the sounds. The ignominy of being caught texting in the can would be hard to live down.

"Want to eradicate my boredom?"

Michael flushed the toilet so he'd have something to do between the graffiti-scarred grey steel walls. Took a deep breath, thought of MaryAnne. He was just going to visit an old friend. Why was he making such a deal? Grow the fuck up.

"30 minutes?"

"I'll let the wine breathe."

He went back to his perch overlooking the tables. He had 15 minutes to kill. Watching Bonnie clear the table would be an excellent way to do it. He wondered why his palms were damp. His right foot tapped. His heart rate increased. His mind was invaded by thoughts of Marsha, naked, lovely, loving. His pants grew tight. He felt stupid. Eighteen again. He wanted nothing more than he wanted Marsha at this moment. He had had sex thousands of times and yet he was now obsessed with making love with a woman not his partner, a primordial need awakened, boiling.

His days were numbered, he told himself, grab everything you can. And, without regret, he buried thoughts of MaryAnne and kept checking his watch. What was wrong with him?

After Bonnie cleaned the table, he went through the narrow corridor that had washrooms and a storage room on each side, pushed open the emergency exit and was on a rusted steel balcony, littered with butts and roaches, anchoring a winding, rusted staircase that brought him down to the back alley.

Montreal seemed to have more back alleys than streets, crisscrossing each other anywhere families and shops had housed horses in their back yards, in tin stables and wood garages. Most of the remnants of the horse and buggy days had been torn down, a few had been converted to garages for the imported cars the tiny streets could not contain. There were no Chevies in this neighbourhood. The alleys were bordered by tall fences of wood or wire, some mangled and cracked and torn, others fresh and trying again. Graffiti was everywhere.

This part of Le Plateau was in the throes of another renaissance. The renovated flats were being renovated. Increasingly interiors of multiple dwelling buildings were being demolished to create spacious, impressive single-family dwellings. Prices kept climbing, demand kept growing, traffic was suffocating and dark, musty convenience stores had given way to hair salons and designer clothes boutiques and architects' and designers and engineers' offices feeding off the endless rehabs fueled by the invasion of deep pockets. The former occupants were pushed off island, to the 'burbs, where you could get three bedrooms, a backyard, a front yard, a garage and a short drive to malls, large and small, for half the price of half the space in the city. And spend a good chunk of time and money buying cars to commute. There didn't seem to be many good choices.

Michael loved the alleys, the startled cats and the quiet. He wandered down a few alleys, came out on Mentana, found her flat and rang the bell.

She came to the door, kissed his cheeks three times, gave him a gentle hug.

Did she sense he was hurting?

It had been five, six years but the memories rushed in and the anticipation grew, just as it always had when he made his way to her door. He was tongue tied, awkward —the guy who had been there and done most of that— didn't know what to do or why he was here. She hadn't changed. No emerging lines, no new sadness in the brown-green eyes, no visible physical or psychic scars.

She wore a clinging one-piece shirt-dress, a thick black belt hanging loosely from her hips. It fell a foot above her knees and Michael imagined her taking it off, which was the effect she was working at, provocative but subtle. And his obsession grew. He wanted that dress off, he wanted to touch her everywhere.

There was colour in her cheeks, no makeup on her eyes and she seemed anxiety-free, happy in her skin. But, he remembered, she always had.

They sat on a supple, black leather sofa, and she handed him a rocks glass filled with thick red wine. She had spent time in Greece years ago and had no use for glasses perched on stems.

"Are you well, Michael?"

"As well as can be expected." He wasn't and that was all the rationale he needed. *Time was short, live for today*, he whispered to himself.

"Still climbing the high wire? Or have you come down to Earth, a simple man of brick and mortar?"

"What brought you back to Montreal?"

"Montreal," she said. "Ever go to the dog races in Florida? I like Sarasota. Dogs chase the rabbit. They never catch it and they probably don't know why they chase it but they keep doing it. Toronto's like that. The bobbles are trendier and, of course, costlier, the food's to die for, but they've turned that to a bobble too. People there collect fine restaurant meals like charms on a bracelet, something to get you through a cocktail party."

She finished her wine and poured another half tumbler.

"My children hated it. They said it was too noisy and there were too many shadows. The office towers, the condos blocked the sun. If they want sunshine they grab a plane to Maui. Or take vitamin D."

She put her glass on the table at their feet.

"And no one made me laugh."

"What were you doing?"

"Risk assessment, big time. Big bank, big money. But the real risk was to my soul so I made a run for it. And to keep me from working for the competition they gave me a lovely severance package, soothed my soul and paid a big down payment on this place. I'm very soothed."

"How are the kids? They close to the tree?"

"Not till school starts in a few weeks," she said. "They're lovely and own my heart but they're with their father in Vancouver."

"You haven't laughed," Michael said. "I can tell. I prescribe suppers of spicy Korean soup, Saturday morning walks around the bird sanctuary and, if you're flush, brunch at the Ritz. You'll be giggling by autumn."

She laughed.

"You haven't changed, Michael, though there is something in your eyes," she said. "You always brought food and talked food. You were always a man of appetite. Are you still insatiable?"

"No," he said. "But I am hungry."

"Do you feel like making me laugh?" she said as she stood and took his hand. He put his drink down and followed her down the corridor to her bedroom. Her queen-size bed had only a sheet and a few pillows on it, lit by two soft lamps on either side. She pulled her dress over her head and there was nothing he wanted more at that moment than to be where he was. It was almost as if he could hear a clock ticking. She stood comfortable in her nudity, replaying a scene they had performed many times. She exuded confidence and a playful challenge. Are you up for a good time? He stepped out of his pants as she lifted his sweater over his head, ran her hands down his ribs.

"You can tell me later about the woman you're in love with," she said.

The grace was in finding someone and losing oneself. Michael couldn't quite pull it off. She found him detached, gentle and loving, but removed.

Michael did not think about dying for a minute or two and was especially glad to be alive for the rest of the time they shared her bed.

"You've changed," she said, staring at the ceiling, her cheek orange in the lamplight. "You're either in love and guilty or wishing you were somewhere else."

So he told her. He felt vulnerable in his nakedness, embarrassed that skin hung in places muscles used to swell, so he adopted an it-is-what-it-is pose. Life had been good, he was good with the prognosis, at peace and grateful for the sweet moments. Like now.

"What does MaryAnne think? How she doing?"

"How did you know about MaryAnne?"

"I read about her, online. I like her songs. The story mentioned she was living with you. They called you a real-estate developer. I laughed. Is she all right?"

"She doesn't know."

They thought about that.

"You told me 'cause I don't matter," she said. "You don't love me, it's easier. Nothing to risk." She turned toward him, threw a leg over his, ran her hand along his ribs.

"Relationships are sticky affairs," she said. "Exhausting. It's why I've always liked spending time with you. You don't expect, you don't demand ... Michael, don't be so quick to die."

Michael had nothing to say to that. He was tired and was thinking perhaps this had been a mistake and their conversation would orbit his impending demise.

"You're a good man and it will matter to a lot of people and not a lot of people can say that, you know?"

"I worked with a guy, a good guy, Jerry St-Onge, 57 years old," Michael said. "We'd do a lot of the same shows. He did sound. Was good at it. He called me one afternoon. He was at the Neuro. He'd been sending out email. Seemed perfectly sensible to him. Problem was, he was writing gibberish. A chimp would've made more sense banging away at a keyboard than Jerry, except Jerry didn't know till someone called and said, 'What's up, man, you stoned?' Had a brain tumour. One day he was fine, the next he wasn't. And I went to see him, brought his favourite chocolates, spent 20 minutes in his room. They had shaved his head, waiting to operate."

Marsha was staring at him, sitting up, the sheet had fallen, exposing her breasts.

"But, see, he knew the surgery was, like, maybe more for the surgeon to practice his chops than save Jerry 'cause they knew he wasn't going to make it. The tumour was too big. He told me then. He knew. And after, when he was home, he called me up. He was doing okay but the doctors, they gave him maybe six months, maybe a year. Jerry said he was watching hockey a lot, taking a few walks, invited me over. He said no one was coming to see him. 'Cancer ain't communicable,' he said. 'You ain't going to catch it watching the Habs lose.'

"No one wanted to see him die. No one wanted to be reminded it could happen to them. So maybe no one has to know I'm ... whatever. Don't need my friends to feel guilty."

She moved down the bed, smiled as she pulled the covers back.

"I think we should party."

"I never saw him again, never called," Michael said. "I didn't even go to the funeral. I was a prick."

"You're human, Michael," she said, as she bent over him. "I'll show you."

Felix was working on it like a surgeon, slowly pulling a taste of crème brulée from the bottom of the miniature bowl trying to avoid cracking the cover of hard, burnt sugar. He liked to save that for the end.

"How many calories you figure?" he said.

"Fifteen hundred easy," Joey said. "Equivalent to about a bottle of wine, depending, you know?"

"I could use it," he said. "I ran for 10 hours today behind that fucking robobeast. You don't want a taste?"

"No, thanks," she said. "Just lookin' at it, wanna gag."

He ignored her, worked on the dessert.

"Before the Big Apple, I was a financial analyst, advisor, broker, whatever," he said. "Pretended I knew what I was doing selling investments. My uncle's company. Took a few courses and would just sell shit the way my uncle told me. I had a script, answers to questions, just had to add hype, enthusiasm, like an actor, playin' a part.

"'Mr. Fuckface, this is a once-in-a-generation opportunity. Digital printing is the next hot technology, like a laptop or smartphone except with Express Printing or Salex 2020 you're getting in on the ground floor and ...'" He dug for more sweet, thick cream. "'This is a bargain price. And I only have a few hundred thousand shares left. We can sell them for $18.30, 35, so for only fifty thousand ...' Lasted a week, figured maybe Broadway wouldn't make me think of jumping off a building every night."

Joey watched. Felix was in there pitching. *Bay St., Broadway, then working for a robot, big ambitions, meagre returns*, she thought. The working person's future had arrived. She had watched with him videos on YouTube of fulfillment centres, a spin doctor's label for modern retailing warehouses.

"Where consumers' dreams are fulfilled," Flix said. "And we're all worked to death."

He had just showed up, Friday night, after 11. She had been thinking the dep is closed but the bars aren't. Just hang in for a few hours and go to bed. And then there was Felix, jonesing not for dope but for the best crème brulé in the city. She grabbed her thin black leather jacket, something MaryAnne had brought back for her from she couldn't remember where and walked with him to the bus stop on Van Horne.

She didn't want to wait for a bus after 11 on a Friday night on Van Horne but maybe it would take her mind off the delights of the convenience store on the other corner.

And it did. The glare of the lights and the ads in the bus made her wince but the vibrations and the chugging motor calmed her and Felix's chattering kept her brain semi-engaged. She couldn't remember the last time she had seen the city late on a Friday night through a bus window. Hipsters on the make had taken over. Good clothes, good hair, lots of laughter on the streets, phones shining. Its promises had grown increasingly irrelevant since she became pregnant. Everyone on overdrive, fun to watch. Not tempting to join. It looked exhausting, chasing someone you'd eagerly dispose of a couple of hours later and then wash the sheets if you weren't too messed up to find the machine. Listening to Flix seemed easier.

"So I was thinking, maybe do what you did, Starbucks," he said. "Or maybe borrow a car and drive for Uber a few times a week after the unfulfilling fulfillment centre, make a few extra bucks. I never know how much I'm going to make in Roboland and if I can make more money, I can at least pay some rent."

"You nuts?" she said.

"No, just for a while. I can help with the baby. If you have the baby. You're going to need stuff, right? Clothes and diapers and shit. So I'll work a bit more. If I'm going to be a father, I'm not going to be chasing women, right? That'll save a fortune right there."

"I didn't know cheap condoms cost that much."

"Why you gotta be a bitch?"

"Mother's milk," she said.

He finished the bowl, scraping the sides, as Joey sipped tea.

God, she thought. *From red wine to mint tea. Sucks.*

Felix wiped his mouth, grabbed the cheque and his overstuffed knapsack, slung it over his shoulder.

"C'mon Jo, going to take you on a real trip."

She wasn't tired but wasn't feeling overly trippy, a word her mother used, but she followed. Was she turning into the proverbial obedient wifey, two steps behind the man who's paying the bill, following blindly?

She grabbed the cheque from his hand, said, "My treat."

"Why?" he asked.

"You left me such a delightful gift that just keeps on growing, least I can do is buy you a dessert," she said, and paid the bill and followed him to the bus stop.

"Where we going?" she said.

"Someplace absolutely insane, you'll see," he said.

The bus made enough noise to camouflage their conversation. There were maybe eight people under the rumbling glare, heading east, lost in their lives, going or coming back from work. All people of colour, looking dazed. The streets had not only not been paved with precious metals, they were a maze of potholes, detours and dead ends.

"You're going to do Starbucks and the warehouse, live in your parents' basement, give me money for diapers?"

"I was thinking maybe we could live together."

"Live together, you, me and the baby? Like a bad movie?"

"Well, it's my baby and I wanna be there."

Joey really wanted a drink. Live with Flix? She didn't even know him. Her mind couldn't track that option.

"Where's this crazy place we're going?" Joey said.

She followed him off the bus and had no idea where she was. It was dark and industrial, a no-man's land of low-slung depressed offices, windows dark, small industry with loading ramps and parked silent semis, empty sidewalks, orange street lights glowing for she knew not who.

She followed blindly as Felix walked down a wide driveway that led to a loading dock and three graffiti-scarred garage doors. There were four or five silent 18-wheelers, giant shining grills, monstrous, abandoned and mute. He heaved his backpack higher on his shoulder, walked around the back of the building and stopped at an iron staircase hidden behind a cracked concrete wall. It was going down and was covered by a rusty gate and locked with a padlock.

"What the fuck, Flix?" She was weary, depressed, catching a glimpse of her future, here, bleak, dark and empty. She wanted to go home and climb into bed and try not to weep.

"You'll see," he said. He pulled a key from his pocket and opened the lock.

"I cut the original off and bought my own," he said. "No one knows. No one goes here."

"No kidding," she said. "It's such a garden spot."

"You sound like my father," he said. He pulled the gate back, revealing another rusty staircase that descended into the black.

"Giving me a taste of my future?" Joey said. "Welcome to hell."

He clicked on a little flashlight, revealed the gloomy stairs.

"Follow me," he said and clanged down. "And close the gate behind you, just in case anyone is checking."

"Can we go home?" she said.

"C'mon Jo, where's your sense of adventure?" he said. "Here's a flashlight."

They walked slowly down the stairs, hands pressed against the walls. She could see nothing but darkness ahead of the splash of white light from the LED she was holding.

The stairs ended and he stopped, pulled off his knapsack and yanked out two pairs of Billy boots.

"Put these on," he said. "I think they're probably close enough. Give me your shoes. I'll put them in the knapsack."

"Why do I ..." Then she saw why. There were several inches of water under her feet that had now saturated her shoes and socks. She pointed the flashlight right and left and saw a long tunnel, made of cracked and broken red brick, stretching as far as she could see in both directions. She heard water trickle. Other than that there was silence.

"This is hell," she said, pulling the boots on.

"This is urban caving, exploring," he said. "It's wild shit, man, you'll see."

They splashed through the six or seven inches of water, the current pushing her forward, following the beams of their flashlights, down the tunnel.

She was frightened and fascinated at the same time. How was this wet world under the city?

"This place was built late 1800s," he said. "Channels rain water. It's not sewage, don't worry. It takes water to an underground river, eventually out to the St. Lawrence."

"Why are we here?" she said, determined to be a pain in the ass despite the fact that she found it pretty, well, awesome.

"Exploring," he said. "No one comes down here ever, except a few guys I know. It's cool unless you come down and there's a really heavy rain, then you might get a little fucked up."

"Like get drowned," she said.

"More like get carried along with the current, maybe rammed into a wall or two, break a rib, bust your nose. But there's no rain coming. We're okay."

They walked silently, swung left and the tunnel widened at a fork. On the left was a larger tunnel pebbled with a rocky coating, making it look like a cave formed a million years ago.

"Holy shit," she said. "That's really awesome ... I hate that word."

"Yeah, cool, eh? The water from a hundred years or so leaves behind minerals and whatever it picks up along the way and hardens and coats the walls, like stalagmites, like a natural cave. The city is above us but no one knows what's down here. It goes for hundreds of kilometres in all directions. A secret world. This might've one day been a real river and they just shoved it underground, built shit on top of it."

She had to admit it beat watching the traffic going by her front door as she sucked on a wine bottle.

"So, like, I can help pay for the baby, I want to help," he said. "It's mine. Like, I wanna do the right thing."

"Give me a break, Flix. What's the 'right thing'? I don't even know if I'm keeping the kid. Doing the right thing would've been to buy decent fucking condoms that don't come off."

"Those were your condoms," he said. "You gave them to me. You even put them on."

"Well, it's not my fault your dick's so small," she said.

"Don't be an asshole," he said.

"Why didn't you bring your own condoms?"

"Why'd you insist we mix the coke and speed?" he said. "We kind of seriously lost it there for a few hours. Messed up, man. I was bouncing off the walls."

"Yeah, me too," and their laughter echoed off the walls, carried by the water and into the gloom. She caught an image of them, just hyped to the max, rolling around in the dark. She couldn't get enough. The guy was a rabbit that night. One part of her was mortified. All the crap she had shoved up her nose and smoked and drank. If there was a blue sky anywhere it was only that she was needle shy. She was suddenly horny and wet, a Pavlovian reaction to the memory and the substance abuse that seemed to end up with her on her back with some sweaty guy. Who was that woman?

The tired brick tunnel opened up to a large concrete cathedral with giant shelves under wide square tunnels.

"It's a catchway for major storms, kind of holds the water here, prevent floods," he said. He seemed to know what he was talking about. Indiana Flix. Maybe he had a bullwhip in his knapsack.

There was a ladder from the tunnel up to what appeared to be a wide concrete table. She started climbing.

"Where you …?" Felix said, and started climbing after her.

She stepped off the ladder, walked along the dry hard floor of a concrete cathedral with vaulted ceilings 20-feet high. She felt like she was in a horror film and Dracula would descend from an unseen trapdoor any second. Her blood was banging in her head and groin. Weird. Felix joined her.

"Cool, eh?" he said, looking down at the tunnel of ancient brick and mortar and its river of running water.

"Alone under the world," he said, taking her arm in his hand. "Joey, listen, I can do this. Me and you. And the baby. I got nothing else going. You neither. We're in the same canoe, flying down the rapids, bouncing off the rocks, going over the falls. Splash! Crash! But, together, you know, you're fucking brilliant. And a baby. We'd be a family. We can fix up your apartment, paint and get some furniture and I'll work, get away from my parents and my father's shit. It'll be awesome ... uh ... just excellent. Three of us ..."

"Shut up!" she said. Her head was spinning. "Take off your clothes and shut up." She started shedding layers, throwing them on the cold concrete floor. He was too slow for her so she pulled at his belt as he threw his backpack on the floor and then his shirt and T-shirt and kicked off his pants.

"Just be quiet," she said.

They fell onto their discarded clothes, the flashlights bouncing off the bare concrete, the running water in the tunnel below their soundtrack. They were beneath the ground, under the world, away from reality and the cha cha of the city. The only two people on this shadowy planet. Maybe three people, she thought, but she was all alone.

She kicked off her underwear and pulled him down on top of her, wrapped her bare legs around his back and squeezed.

She needed to stop feeling.

"Show me," she whispered.

They lay side by side, breathing hard, staring up at the concrete ceiling high over their heads, comfortable in their nakedness but Joey was fighting dark thoughts.

"What am I doing screwing this guy in a tomb? What's wrong with me?"

The reprieve from reality was sweet but short. Felix knew what he was doing. She wasn't sure about his other qualities, or lack of same, but he got her motor running and knew how to happily shut it down.

"They want me to help organize a union at the warehouse," he said, looking at nothing. "The place is a jungle, the Team Leaders make the rules, we follow like sheep, everybody's pissed, everybody's exhausted all the time. Not human."

"You're an actor," she said. "What do you know about unions? You have a script or something to tell you what to do and say? Scene one, Flix gets fired, goes back to living with Mummy and Daddy in the basement."

Why was she angry? The orgasm wasn't making her all warm and fuzzy. She stood and collected her clothes, started pulling and snapping them.

Felix hadn't known her long enough to be used to

the moods but he kept his temper and hurt to himself. Naked and pregnant in this vast space, Joey seemed lost and vulnerable.

"Joey, they treat us all like shit. Feel like a whipped dog. I should do something. It's just wrong. It's the 21st century and I feel like I'm working in a modern remake of a Dickens novel."

"You ever read Dickens?"

"Stop being an asshole," he said. "Every day, all day, we all live in fear of either the Team Leader jerkoff or the red light or taking too long to take a shit. It's fucked up and we gotta do something."

"You don't know anything about unions," she said, buttoning her shirt. "And since when did you become Joe Hill?"

"Who's Joe Hill?"

"Exactly." She was slipping back into her boots, listening to the echo of water trickling somewhere in the spooky tunnel down below. "He was a union organizer and they hung him. Remember, 'I dreamed I saw Joe Hill last night, alive as you and me?'"

"What're you talking about?"

"If you read a bit you'd know," she said. She looked around for an exit out of this tomb. She felt dirty and stupid. What was she doing here? "Union guys get shot, killed, fired, blackballed. It's not for basement rats who like to get drunk and stoned and hookup with any female with a pulse. You gotta have real balls."

"Why are you being such an asshole?"

"'Cause I'm buried below ground, I'm cold and tired and I'm listening to this bullshit about you organizing a union. I'm not sure you can even spell the word. You're working for a huge company that'll happily pick and pack you in a box and ship you to Greenland and no one will give a crap. You think you can beat these guys? Get real."

She started to climb down the ladder.

"Joey, you're going to get lost and you're being a jerk. We just made love. What's wrong with you?"

"We didn't make love. We had sex. We had sex. Sex! That's all it was. Now can you please get me out of here?"

He climbed into his clothes, fought with the boots and followed her down the ladder. They didn't speak as they trooped behind the glow of their flashlights down the long, dirty, fascinating tunnel.

Michael climbed into his truck. The bed was already loaded with paint, brushes, ladder, Varsol. Two trips into the basement and he was bagged. Of course last night had been exhausting. He was too old for these interludes, forbidden or not. Curiously, he checked his psyche for guilt the way he checked his body for malignant pain. The former was absent, unlike the latter.

He double parked, ran into the café, nodded to the familiar faces. He didn't feel like talking.

"Macchiato coming up," Louis said. "How you doing, Mike? You don't love us no more, you never come in?"

"I love you, I love you," Michael said. "I told you I bought a machine at home, so I can practice being a barista as good as you, something to do when I get tired of having to deal with tenants."

Louis liked to hide his impressive pasta and parmesan-plugged belly behind long, black dress shirts. He wore a permanent smile. And why not? He made about 800 coffees a day, was tipped 25 or 50 cents per, cash the government knew nothing about. He also owned the café with his three brothers. They all took shifts; they all had buckets of coins stashed here and there.

"Listen Mike, you know that big duplex just on the other side of Saint Viateur?" Louis leaned over the counter, lowered his voice. "I hear it's for sale. The guy wants $750,000. The realtor said he could get eight hundred for it. Eight hundred. Fucking crazy. I was thinking maybe I should buy it. What you think? It seems high to me."

"Depends whether you really want to live in it and then it's worth whatever you think it's worth to live in it," Michael said, sipping his espresso. They used a good black bean here, not double roasted like he used at home, but passable. "If you buy it to rent, as an investment, the mortgage payments are going to hurt and the interest rates are not staying this way forever. To break even, you'll have to charge a killing in rent and find someone willing to pay Outremont prices to live in Mile End and listen to the trucks unloading at the grocery stores and restaurants all day."

"Yeah, that's true, eh? Why do I need the fucking headache?"

"I don't know," Michael said. "Why do you need the headache? It's a shitty time to buy, prices are too high. Wait until the bubble bursts or whatever. It's a seller's market. I got to run."

"Hey, thanks Michael. No charge. Keep your money.

You just saved me almost a million bucks. Don't be a fucking stranger."

He beat a cop to his truck and drove off, turned left onto Waverly heading to Van Horne to take another couple of lefts and run south along Esplanade to a triplex that needed some paint. Just before the corner he saw Joey sitting on her stoop, a large green plastic glass in her hand. He swung the truck over and parked.

"I know you, girl," he said, slamming his door, walking in front of his ticking motor. "How you doing?"

"Fucking peachy," she said. "How are you?"

"Pretty peachy myself. Good day for a peach, warm sun, blue sky, slight breeze keeps the leaves fluttering. What you doing?"

"Drinking ice water, believe it or not. Contemplating my future, you know? Have a baby, kill the baby, kill myself. Regular stuff."

"Funny, I was contemplating the same thing, without the baby. A good day for suicide. I'm hung up on the means, though. If I lie down in front of the truck, will you run over me? Or maybe you got good drugs. Nah, I already got some."

"You have good drugs? Really?"

"If I did, your mother would've eaten them," he said. He got a shot in the gut and winced but caught himself. Son of a bitch.

"You okay?" Joey asked.

"Yep," he said. "Gas, too much coffee."

"Tell me about it," she said. "Me too. I could play tuba in a marching band. Gross."

"Wanna keep me company? I need to eat and do some

stuff and your mother's away so I'm a lonely man looking for some beautiful female companionship."

The lie brought up images of last night and he caught himself looking at Joey and seeing Marsha over him, smiling.

"I ... there's shit I ..."

"I hate being alone on a sunny day," Michael said. "I think sunshine is for sharing. We can have some sushi or souvlaki or how about Thai?"

"Have you tried the empanadas at that place on Parc? I love their seafood empanadas."

"Sounds good to me," Michael said. "I'm buying."

They each ordered three empanadas and a Coke with lemon slices, sat on a table in the sun watching the buses and the trucks throttle by. It was an unholy din but it was their din, the price you paid to eat empanadas under the bright sky in the big city.

"I don't mind taking you to the clinic," Michael said. "In fact, I'd be honoured. And you'd be doing me a favour. I wouldn't have to spend the afternoon painting."

"You'd rather sit with a bunch of pregnant women?"

"Worse things," he said. "It's the great bagel of life. Round and round, birth and death. In between, empanadas and cold Coke."

"You ever have a kid, Michael?"

He put the empanada down. His appetite disappeared. He had never told MaryAnne but there seemed little point to secrets anymore.

"I had a son," he said. "I wasn't married but I was with a woman, obviously, we lived together, not far from here."

"What is or was she like?"

"Smart. Smart enough not to hang too long with me," he said. Picked up the empanada, but put it back on his plate. Poured some hot sauce on it.

"She was a dancer, long legs, man. Like a Bob Fosse dancer. You're too young ..."

"I've seen *All That Jazz* and *Cabaret*. Pretty hot. You must've been a stud, man."

"I'm still a stud, girl ... She was pretty good. Gorgeous. We were young and horny and not too careful. Sound familiar? She got pregnant. I was 20. Crazy. But she figured, have it, get right back to dancing while she was still young enough. Benjamin, good kid. Beautiful. Didn't cry all the time. It was tough, but fun. We both worked nights, but now she was staying home, slowly trying to get back in shape. She liked being a mother. It was cool. She didn't run off to work out or audition or work the phones. She liked being with Benjamin. I was home a lot of days, worked nights, travelled a bit. It was the three of us. Kid was beautiful. Babies are babies. They just want to be held, loved. They don't need BMWs or designer food. It's hard to be unhappy when you're young and life is cheesecake with fresh cherries."

"Is it?" Joey said.

He was still and silent waiting for a dump truck to run north on Parc, thrashing through its gears, spewing black diesel fumes. Waiting for a pain that was getting shriller to blossom and then move on, he hoped.

"Down the block Cheskies, cherry cheescake, ten bucks. But not for Benjamin. He died. He was one. Three days after his birthday. Maybe crib death, they didn't really know. Cops asked me if Dominique had ever hurt the boy. Stupid. He just died."

Michael had no idea why he was relating this tale he had never shared with MaryAnne. Maybe that's what she meant when she said he was closed. Maybe it just hurt too much. It hit him then, staring at a half-eaten empanada, after that, nothing else seemed as important as it used to. Life lost a pantry full of flavour. Maybe he compensated by cooking, obsessing over making food just right. Now he was in the barrel, trying to keep a straight face as the pain vibrated between moderate and severe.

"Hey, Michael, sure you're okay?"

"Yeah, course, I was ... you're right, this is good," he said, feeling as dark as the exhaust that hung in the air. "I just can't eat anymore."

He picked up the damn empanada but dropped it.

"You wanna have a kid, have it. You want to not have it, don't have it. Keep on trucking. Just live, every day, fuck 'em all. You're young. There's almost always a tomorrow."

He had believed that of himself only a few months ago.

She was chewing enthusiastically, two and a half down, a half to go, bits of dough clinging to the corners of her mouth.

"What're you doing after?" he said.

"Going to the clinic. What happened to Dominique?"

"She lay around the house for a while, six, eight months, went to Vancouver, visit a friend, hang out at Kitsilano, get her groove back," he said. "Never came back. Wrote me a letter, thanks and goodbye."

"Cold, man," she said.

He shrugged. It was what it was.

"I'll drive you to the clinic."

"Michael, that'd be incredibly uncool. People'll think you're the father or I'm your poor, knocked-up daughter."

He put $20 on the table, drank the Coke. It felt good, the caffeine and carbonation gave him a bit of a boost. Stood up, offered his hand gallantly to Joey, who took it, smiling.

"Who gives a shit what they think?"

MaryAnne loved the sound check. Liked to watch good techies do their thing, liked it better when she arrived on stage and found everything wired and ready to go. Plug and play, though she had switched to an acoustic without a pickup and used a second mic for her guitar. No plugs at all; just play.

She embraced the warm up, tuning, giving the guy or girl behind the board the thumb up or down, getting all the levels and sound sweet, going through a few numbers to an empty room, no pressure. Just fun. She loved singing to a vacant theatre, band cracking it behind her and no one around to impress or to watch text, swipe or share pictures. More and more people in the seats took video of her performing and shared that with their fellow phone freaks in the seats next to them instead of watching or listening. The digital version was more important than the 3D reality. Time was moving too fast for her.

God bless Stephen who leaned his bass against the big amp and jumped off stage and walked to the back of the dark, ugly room and listened, talked to the techie. She trusted the guy in her motel room, she trusted him with her sound. He liked the band to play behind her, protected her voice, made sure nobody trampled on the lyrics. He was the de facto musical director and the guys listened, but MaryAnne always got what she wanted. Unless Stephen said, "Just try it this way, see what you think." He was often right and rarely minded when she thought he wasn't.

They ran through three songs, sound in the monitors getting sweeter each verse. The techie heightened the sound off the kick drum, reduced the cymbal crash a bit. Stephen knew she didn't like the sparkle of new strings and asked for more mids on her guitar.

A few of the staff, service people, security, were against the back wall, watching. MaryAnne knew it was going to be a good night.

"Let's do Climb the Walls."

It was a toe tapper, a story of an elevator operator going up and down all day in a little box then going home to his empty room. There was space for Stephen to do his finger ballet on the long neck of the electric bass and the drums to pound out the rapid heartbeat of an anxious, trapped man, going up and down and getting nowhere, as MaryAnne danced with her guitar, diving back to the mic to slip in the vocals while the guys wailed for the staff in the back of the room. They applauded and she waved and it was dinner time.

Stephen told the drummer, "Maybe just lay back a bit under MaryAnne when she's doing the Climb the Wall thing."

"Was I banging all over your lyric?" he said. "Sorry, MaryAnne. I'll go light on the sticks or I can use brushes."

"I think staying with sticks is okay," Stephen said.

"Sounded fine to me," MaryAnne said. "Where you guys eating?"

"There's a pizza joint across the street we're going to hit."

"Okay, enjoy. I'm going to walk a bit, see what I find."

Five years ago, she had stopped the ribs, burgers, pizza, wings, dried out chicken, ersatz Caesar salads and all the other crap of the standard menus of riding the road. She had a nose for Oriental, could find Thai, Vietnamese, decent Chinese or Korean in any town in the world. And off she went. A good sound check, where a song gels in an empty room, made her hungry. She'd hold off on smoking a joint till after the show.

This was all getting to be a little much. Like crazy. He had been following the robot—"Yes, I am a robot"—for a few weeks. His legs were stronger but his joints were increasingly inflamed as was his hunger for the pills, the happy pills, the smart pills, the little tabs that kickstarted his day and smoothed the wrinkles and the worries. When his knees, shoulders or back were screaming at him, he added a painkiller.

The last few days he'd been greenlighted early, working two hours, making not enough to keep his dreams alive. Back-to-school business was done and Gaetan told him the pre-Christmas lull was normal. Another month or so, it would be red lights every day and survival not a certainty. The little robots never flagged and the humans he crossed aisles with smiled and moved on and disappeared. There were new faces every day.

He had time to think, stalking the blinking machine from shelf to shelf. He wasn't sure about this daddy gig.

He was spending a few nights a week at Joey's. It got him away from his parents and out of the basement and she was kind of fun when she wasn't being a moron.

He had swiped right a few nights and hooked up with a few women but something didn't feel right. Jerking off would've been as much fun and less expensive. And he wouldn't feel he was auditioning during the pregame drink and meal. He wasn't opposed to having a kid but he had thought the process would be more romantic. He was pretty sure life wasn't about screens and social media and he was pretty sure Joey would not be his first choice for mother of the year. And this wouldn't be his first choice for a career. He wasn't leading a life. It was leading him.

Joey had problems. Moody as hell. Drank too much. Or did. And used her body as a test tube to test-drive any concoction of drugs. Or used to.

But, she made him laugh and she was an acrobat in bed when she was in the mood, which wasn't often lately. Did he want to pour his three-digit pay cheques into diapers and pajamas and baby cereal and sit home and play house? And he'd have to tell his parents sooner or later. And he wished Joey would just say move in so he could feel at home somewhere.

"Hey, how's your universe?"

It was Gaetan, all hyper and paranoid, vibrating and looking over his shoulder.

"You think about the You word?"

"Yeah, yeah, I'm down. Let's do it … What do we gotta do?"

"You speak to anyone? Anyone ask you about it?"

"No," Felix said. "I can talk to a few people."

"Maybe, just see if anyone's on board. But be careful, they got spies all over."

"Then how the hell can I talk to anyone?"

He saw Ronnie, Team Leader, heading their way, looking disgruntled. Ronnie always looked disgruntled.

"Gentlemen, this is not associates' break time," Ronnie said. He was looking at an iPad. It tracked everyone's production, how much they picked and how fast and where their mechanical companion was.

"We're analyzing the algorithm to use to follow best-practice to get between hemorrhoid creams and crotch rot spray," Gaetan said. "I'm not sure Gladys here has been updated on the new aisle arrangement ..."

"Gladys knows this shit before you guys do," Ronnie said. "Associates don't worry about algorithms. You worry about picking. Team Leaders worry about algorithms in cooperation with our IT and GFY teams. So, get back to work, please."

Ronnie walked away, poking at his iPad.

"What's a GFY team?" Felix said.

"Go Fuck Yourself," Gaetan said. "Who gives a shit? Listen, sniff around, see who's on our side. Be, you know, chill, just chat, don't be too serious. See who gives you the look. Let's go Gladys."

He walked a few paces and then turned and walked back to Felix, causing Gladys to spin.

"Maybe she'll blow a chip," Gaetan said. "Here, man, keep it cool and hang loose."

He shook his hand and in his palm was a white tablet. A nuvy. Nuvigil. Yum. Gaetan winked and he and Gladys slid away. Felix looked around, saw the camera overhead and pretended to cough, covering his mouth and sucking in the pill.

There were two men in the waiting room, five women, two about Joey's age, one Michael's age. The magazines on the coffee table between the eight or 10 chairs had been published when print was profitable. Michael closed his eyes. Took a deep breath, let it out slow, a pain-management technique.

He was 100 feet in the air, clamping lights onto a cross hatch he was straddling that hung between two grid towers bolted to the two front corners of the black stage. He had a safety belt clipped to a harness he was wearing. Below were more people than he could count and more gear than he could remember. But it would've been speaker boxes, monitors, drum kits yet unwrapped, packing tubes of mic stands and travel cases with microphones and probably a few film cameras and tripods. He liked it up there, above all the chaos and the noise and the stress, always the stress of getting all the pieces together by showtime.

It was going to be a big festival, starting tomorrow. A hundred thousand or so expected to be spread-eagled up in the stands and all over an old football field, yard lines and numbers faded. What city were they in? Detroit? Somewhere like that. They had only finished snapping together the stage at 4 a.m. Michael had been working since then, the sun slowly climbing behind him, pulling the towers up for the lights and sound.

He was wiring the big Kleigs that would wash the

stage with whatever light the designer fancied. Then he had to rig a whirly-gig that would spin the lights, add a little more spectacle to the smoke and bombs and fireworks and inflatable dolls and all the other shit some bands felt they needed to get the attention their music didn't merit.

He'd been doing this for a couple of decades or more, hanging high over a stage, the music already blasting from a temporary setup. The kids below couldn't work without being stoned and sonically assaulted, another reason Michael preferred to be in the sky.

He took his hand off the grid and swung over to the next light, it was easier than walking along the grid like one of the Flying Wallendas, when his safety line snapped. It seemed to happen in slo-mo. The realization that he was unleashed and about to fall 100 feet or so was like an afterthought. He saw his safety line fall from the grid, said, "Shit," flashed on himself broken and useless on the stage way down there, reached up with his right hand and grabbed the only bar he could. And hung there, swinging. He felt his shoulder pop and a startling pain shoot down his arm. Curious how he diagnosed a ripped rotator cuff as he dangled. He brought his left arm up to take some of his weight and swung there.

Then there was a lot of screaming down below. He was swinging there, the man on the flying trapeze, but he heard the "Holy fuck!" "Shit!" "Michael, you okay?! Mike?!" "Hang on, Mike," as everyone started running in circles.

Of course, he wasn't all right but he was going to hang on because he wasn't ready to die rigging lighting for an execrable rock band or two.

He was sitting in the doctor's office, waiting for Joey, asking himself, *Would I rather have died for a band I liked?*

There was a portable crane somewhere and someone was trying to drag a ladder that wasn't tall enough and Michael started to swing from one arm to another as the guys below cheered. Both shoulders were screaming at him but letting go wasn't an option. He had too much life to live. Arm over arm, he made it to a tower and easily climbed down to the waiting arms of the guys who hugged him and high-fived him and asked him if he was okay and did he need a line or two of blow.

He opened his eyes, saw Joey come out from the doctor, her face hard to read. He still had too much life to live.

"Where we going?" Joey said. The pickup was climbing Côte des Neiges and Michael made an illegal left onto Côte St. Catherine.

"Come help me paint," he said. "I promised Jennifer I'd paint her kid's room today, when they were away. She's a good person, lived there 15 years. I like painting. Instant gratification."

"Yeah, but doing it yourself doesn't mean I help."

"That's true, but I want to give you this once-in-a-lifetime opportunity to paint while pregnant. What'd the doctor say?"

"He asked if that old fart in the waiting room was my father or the baby's father," she said.

"You should be that lucky, have a kid with a guy as good looking as me," he said. "This Felix fellow, how ugly is he?"

"Depends on how much you've had to drink," she said. "I think he's hot, even sober. Passable, for sure. He wants to live with me, buy diapers and jammies from his salary at the house of robots, where he never knows how many hours he's going to work or how much he's going to make, and will never be enough to even pay half the rent, phone and Hydro so he'd be living off me, like a nanny with privileges. Least that's what he figures. And the doctor said I am definitely knocked up. No kidding. Mother and fetus healthy. Physically. Mental state uncertain."

They drove in silence, Joey staring out the window, Michael confident thinking was the most appropriate activity at this time.

It was rare he felt inadequate, but he did now. His experience with fatherhood had been short-lived but knew participating in conception bestowed no insights or special wisdom. It just kind of pushed you to a place where you had to make decisions without the skills to do it well. But he was living by a credo that had always served him—when in doubt, shut up and do something.

He handed Joey some poles for rollers and a few brushes and he grabbed a plastic tarp, a can of paint and a tray and ignored the pain corkscrewing into his belly, his mind singing Dylan's You're a Big Girl Now, "With a pain that stops and starts, like a corkscrew to my heart."

He spread the tarp, pried open the paint can and Joey grabbed a roller and screwed it onto a pole. Perhaps she needed something to do, too.

"Let's open the window," he said and did. "Don't want to poison the baby before he's born."

"If he's so fragile he won't make it in the city," Joey

said. "He'll have to be Bubble Boy or maybe we'll get him or her its own place in the country. I'll visit on weekends."

She started rolling pale green latex. She found it soothing.

"I guess whoever lives here's kind of laid back," Joey said. "Nothing too dramatic. A good colour to chill by."

She dipped the roller in the tray.

"Doctor says I'm 10 weeks, maybe 11," she said. "Gotta make up my mind."

"And what if you didn't have the kid?"

She pressed harder, the roller rebelled by dotting her face with paint. Michael smiled. In her vest and hat and now her painted face, Joey reminded him of Suzanne Hoschedé in Monet's *The Stroller*. And she reminded him of what MaryAnne must've looked like as a kid, probably less troubled, but they insulated their flesh with multiple layers—shirts and undershirts and vests and sweaters, jackets and hats. He found MaryAnne sexy as hell, found her daughter cute, the girl next door with substance-abuse problems. Mother and daughter.

Joey didn't bother to wipe her face, might as well wait and do it once. What would life be without a kid? *Like it is now, asshole,* she thought. *I'd sit on my stoop and watch the world go by and drink. Where would I put a crib in that dump? Am I supposed to sit home all day and listen to the baby cry? Chew Xanax?*

Again, she took her anxiety out on the roller, slathering more laid-back green on her than the wall.

"Don't babies make you happy?" Joey said. "'Goo goo, gaga, ain't she cute?' Except for the diaper part? Maybe you don't want to talk about … babies."

"Don't mind. My limited experience is not definitive. Some women hate being pregnant, hate being mothers, others live for all of it. I'm pretty sure babies aren't living, breathing anti-depressants. It's hard, alone with a baby all day. Some go nuts."

"I was just thinking about that," she said. "That's what daycare's for. Drop the kid off, let someone else worry about it for eight hours and then bring it home, feed it and say, 'night night.' That, or heavy downers."

She put the roller in the tray, dropped the pole.

"This is boring," she said. "Thanks for taking me to the clinic but I'm going to split."

She glanced out the window, saw the rain bounce off cars, rivers washing down the gutters.

"Shit. Can you give me a ride?"

"I gotta finish," Michael said. "It won't take long. You can just hang. It's latex, goes on easy."

"You own the place, who gives a shit if you finish?"

"She would. I would," he said. "I said I'd do it. Chinese revolution, they shot the landlords first. Look upon it as self-preservation."

"You're a strange dude," she said. "MaryAnne always had a thing for strange dudes."

She sat on the bare floor, back against the wall left to paint and watched Michael work the roller. There was nothing to talk about.

They were kicking ass. The joint was jumping. MaryAnne had put her guitar on its rack for the encore, grabbed the mic off the stand and was dancing back and forth across the stage, singing a new tune, *Take Me to the Party*, with the joy of a child at Christmas. The band was nailing it; Stephen rocking with that long-necked electric bass he loved, belting out harmonies and the audience was up on their feet, milking the last of their money's worth. Playing Sault Ste Marie was not a bad deal.

> *Take me to the party*
> *We'll let our hair down*
> *We'll drink to the hale and hearty*
> *Sing a toast to the clowns*
> *Take me to the party, baby*
> *Take me to the party*

She waved to everyone, said thank you, hung up the mic and skipped off the stage, the band still cooking. Byron met her with a cold beer and a clean white towel. She inhaled the beer, wiped her face watching the band finish up and listened to the hoots and hollers and whistles as she kissed each of the guys as they bounced backstage, wet and happy and eager for beer. And a hit on the joint she had fired up. Play sober, kick back post-game.

"Great show, guys, thank you," she said.

The curtain had come down, muffling the crowd and they could hear themselves.

"Pretty good for an old broad, MaryAnne," Stephen said. "Pretty damn good. Especially *Kill Me Before I Die.* You jumped an octave bang on. Lovely."

"Thank you, Stephen. Food? On me?"

There was a chorus of "yeahs" and they trooped off.

She liked men. They played, they ate, didn't worry about chipped nails, gaining weight, worn makeup, didn't talk too much about children and grandchildren—shit, she had to plan on seeing Joey—they liked to live. Maybe they didn't have that nurturing gene most women fed off— worry about everyone else before yourself. Michael had a pleasant set of nurturing genes, a bit of marshmallow interior.

Before him there had been Frederic. He had been a groupie. Had bucks. Once they got to know each other, he started to try and control her, picked her up after shows, wanted to travel with her, sat in on rehearsals, too many opinions, jealous of the guys in the band, always asked where she was going, when she was coming back, how much money she made and they weren't even living together. He asked her to move in, she told him to take his stuff from her closet and dresser and stop calling her. It wasn't pretty but she was finally able to breathe, spend time alone and meet Michael. And she was pretty sure Michael would be her last love. If only he'd open up a bit, let her in. Sometimes it was like living alone with a cook and a bed partner. She wasn't sure that was enough. He was like his favourite orange Creuset sauce pan: lid on tight, sometimes, maybe, a little steam would escape, a scent of dinner, but not too often. The guy was so self-contained, drove her nuts.

She led them to a Chinese joint and they ate steamed bass with vegetables and rice and swigged a lot of Tsingtao and talked about shows they had done and places they had played and rip offs they had endured and who was playing or not playing with who.

Around the overflowing table under the white fluorescent lights, with the sounds of the audience fresh in her ears and the mélange of garlic and salted black beans and ginger and beer wrapped around her tongue, life was good. Having Michael here would've been better, but it wasn't his scene. It was okay. He didn't mind her having a good time. She thought of calling him, but knew he enjoyed being alone. She wondered if he might even prefer it. The gentleman landlord and his toolbox and pool habit, her the aging doper and her guitar and the boys in the band. She was in the afterglow, a place he couldn't share.

What road did they share? She wasn't sure but hoped it was endless.

Her phone called to her and she fished it out of her jacket pocket expecting to be speaking to Joey. It was Essie. She gave the band her index finger, pulled away from the table and squeezed between tables to the front door.

"Essie, how you doing?" she said, pushing her way onto the sidewalk and an empty street.

"I didn't call too late, did I?" Esther said. "I don't figure you for an early-to-bed kind of sister."

"No. Having dinner with the guys after a show," she said. "I'm in Northern Ontario."

"You kill?"

"They are dead, woman. Just feeding our faces in celebration. What's up?"

"I was speaking to my main pain, Slate the superstar, who is paying for my grandchildren's education fund and he told me to call you up, see if you'd join us out in B.C. After that we're going down the West Coast, finishing in Oakland."

"Really?"

"Yeah, and he says he'd love you to do two or three tunes, and we'd do one together, you know? The Trash Girls be back, woman. Five hundred a night plus a hundred per diem and hotels and health insurance. For at least 10–12 nights, I think. And once you're working with us, there'd be more. He likes working all the time."

"Man, real money guaranteed and all I gotta do is sing a bit? You didn't sell him my body, did you?"

"You'll have to do that yourself but I don't think you'd be interested," Essie said. "He's a slimy snake. Besides, he likes 'em barely legal."

MaryAnne looked back into the restaurant, saw the band around the table laughing. It was after midnight and they were the only ones in the joint but the beer was flowing and the waiter was having a good time. MaryAnne had slipped him $40 before they sat down.

"Essie, I don't know. I'm kind've on the road and having a good time," MaryAnne said. "I don't think I'm your woman."

"MaryAnne, I hear you but don't be so quick to shut it down. This is a good, easy-on-the-back gig. Seventy-five to 90 minutes a night, good airplane, good hotels, easy money."

"I hear you, I do, but ..."

"Listen, you're in the middle of things, probably out with the guys at some Chinese joint. I know you, woman. Think about it. You have my number. Take a week or so. Get back to me. Have fun."

"Thank you, Essie. It's a good offer. I'll think about it."

She ended the call, knowing there was no way she'd think about it.

Michael took a deep breath and entered the forbidden sanctum—MaryAnne's dressing room, right off the bedroom. A room he added for her to store performance clothes and shoes and do makeup and test out looks between the mirrors he installed.

He had glimpses of it before but believed she had a right to privacy and her own space and had never walked in.

But, his was a humanitarian mission. Or maybe he was assuaging guilt he wasn't sure he felt. As expected, he had lifted the curtain on chaos. But the depth of it made him do a double take, then a full headshake with a "holy shit!"

Every dresser was topped with crumpled clothes, every drawer was open and drooling. Shirts, pants, bras, scarves hung out like coloured tongues. There were clothes on her makeup table and clothes on its chair. There were clothes on the ironing board and on the floor in a circle around it. The clothes tree was covered, and clothes were piled at its base, like rocks holding up a post.

He peeked into the water closet he had built for her and was relieved to find only a few wet towels bunched at the base of the tub.

He started gathering tops and jeans and underwear and found a broken cup and a soup spoon under it all, surrounded by cotton balls tinted with shades of eyeliner and blush, tissue with red lip prints and he knew not what. There was an ashtray among the wrinkled, castoff wardrobe—its treasure a dozen roaches. He found a small baggie of weed and five or six lighters from the dollar store.

They were more like acetylene torches than lighters, built for crack pipes and for igniting joints in any wind. He bought them for her by the dozen.

Pulling a pile from the makeup table revealed a few yellow legal pads scrawled with notes and verses and doodles and hearts. *Hearts were so her*, Michael thought. The romantic. It always surfaced in her songs. Love will win. Except when it didn't. That was her curious contradiction. She believed but with reservations, more an agnostic than an atheist.

He piled the clothes in a heap on the floor and shifted to recyclables—balls of paper, sheets of paper, envelopes, sheet music, tissues, gift wrap and started sorting. Yellow sheets from her legal pad were mostly crumpled in frustration. The smooth lined pages he started scooping and placing on her desk, then stopped. There was a letter in her hand, written in red pen, block letters:

"DON'T COME BACK. JOEY IS FINE.
WE'RE ALL FINE. I WON'T GIVE YOU HER
ADDRESS. SHE THINKS YOU'RE DEAD
AND AS FAR AS WE'RE CONCERNED YOU
ARE. IT'S BEEN 20 YEARS SO DON'T EVEN
BOTHER. STAY IN MALTA. DON'T WRITE
AGAIN. I'VE MOVED AND THEY WON'T
BE FORWARDING MY MAIL ANY LONGER.
HAVE A NICE LIFE."

Michael stared at the note, put it on top of the pile, gathered the laundry. The machines would do their thing while he slept. If he could sleep now. Her husband was alive? And,

Michael was supposed to be dead soon. How the hell was that going to work?

Stephen liked to sit on the side of the bed, his size 14 feet keeping time on the floor, the bass in his lap, no amp, and run his fingers up and down the neck, pluck at the strings with five fingers, talking and playing almost silently, as automatic as breathing.

MaryAnne was in Michael's white dress shirt and jockeys under the covers. Stephen was a better brother than her real brothers had ever been.

"I was thinking, uh, on *Lazy Old Bones*, instead of a four-bar intro, we go five. I can do this ..." He played a bass run ... "Stretch out the resolve on the one, then you sing. It'll be cool, man. Heighten the anticipation. They'll be wetting their drawers." He played the five bars over and over, tucking it away.

"I like it," she said. "Let's do that tomorrow night."

Her mind shifted gears.

"So, being a grandfather, one to ten? One being I'd rather be in Philadelphia."

"Twelve, man. Great." He was still playing silently, bent over the instrument. "They're so full of life. I got these creepy beatup joints, man. I'm sore, and every day I wonder uh, 'what if the car don't start? How much money's left in the bank or between the sofa cushions?' The kid, man, completely Third World 'change my diaper, give me a hug and I'm cool.' Righteous, basic stuff. That's really all life is, you know. 'Keep me warm, feed me, love me.' You write about that shit. Babies, they're pretty with it, except music-ally, of course, but they can sure hit the high notes."

Stephen looked up from his bass, nailed her with his great smile, and went back to playing.

"And," he said, walking up and down the neck, pluck-ing big, long, round notes, "you can love them completely unconditionally. 'Ah, kid, you're the best kid in the whole world, the smartest, most beautiful, have a Caramilk, don't tell your mother.' And then you hand them back, go do a gig, stay up till five, watch the sunrise, and there's no squealing rug rat to wake you an hour later. It's perfect. Makes me ask myself sometimes, 'Is there a God?'"

"You come up with an answer?"

"Yeah," he said, smiling. "Nah."

He went back to running his big fingers up and down the thick bass strings, his before-bed ritual, always happy as a boy with a new video game.

MaryAnne killed her bedside lamp.

"Joey in the family way?" Stephen asked.

"Yeah," MaryAnne said.

"That okay?"

"Sure," she said and turned over. "I don't know." And they left it at that, Stephen playing his bass quietly in the soft light of the lamp on his bedside table.

The numbers weren't as good as Sault Ste. Marie but she did her thing. The guys were pros and played like there were 10,000 in front of them. In the front row a young couple were hanging onto each other and smiling up at her.

"Try a little tenderness, makes it easier to bear," ran through her head as she sang her *Someone Turn on the Lights*. So, the place was half full but the young lovers were getting off and that was fine. Almost. Essie's offer began to nibble at the edges of her brain. Did she really need to do this?

They played the full show, did the requisite encore and the stage went dark. They gathered backstage, chatting with the few souls that braved approaching them at every show to say thanks or hello, ask for an autograph. She didn't get the autograph thing but it was part of the job and she did it happily.

MaryAnne wore her postgame smile. Ticket sales would not cover her nut but she was still in the black and was pretty sure by the time she got back to Montreal her bank account would be fatter. More importantly, the band sounded great. The arrangements were tight and fun and she was having a good time. Wasn't she?

She signed a few autographs, signed a few CDs, smiled into a few cell phone cameras, said a lot of thank yous and, when she was ready to head to the van, a guy about 35, good looking in a magazine model kind of way, in a short casual jacket and skinny jeans approached, smiling like a TV weatherman.

"MaryAnne, Miss MaryAnne, that was great, really awesome, the best show I've ever seen," he said.

MaryAnne's mind was going, "Wingnut Alert! Wingnut Alert!" and Stephen heard the guy and immediately stopped and stood by to protect and serve.

"Thank you, that's very kind," she said. "I'm glad you enjoyed the show."

She turned to leave and felt his hand on her shoulder.

"Don't touch," Stephen said, stepping between them. "Adulation welcome, touching verboten."

"Sure, sure, sorry, I was carried away. You know that last song, just great. It really got me."

"Thank you," MaryAnne said. "You'll have to excuse me, I'm going to change."

"I wanted to ask you for a drink or a late supper," he said. "I have all your records and, well, I love you and would love to talk to you."

"I'm sorry, I can't," MaryAnne said, trying to get to her dressing room. "Thank you."

"Just one martini and I'll take you right back, promise."

"No, really, I can't, thank you. I'll see you next show," she said.

"Well, fuck you, then," he said. "You look like an old woman anyway." He turned around and casually walked away, disappeared through the curtain.

"That was a quick love affair," Stephen said. "Not even a one-night stand."

The task was ridiculous but he had never been one to sit on his ass and leave his fate to others. Michael pushed thoughts of MaryAnne's husband and her lies about him to another one of the darker corners of his brain. He hadn't been so honest himself lately, so let the dogs sleep, he figured. For now.

He lay on the sofa, his favourite activity of late when

MaryAnne wasn't home, and flipped open his laptop and entered the maze that was the Internet. He was looking for the latest in cancer research. He had mastered lighting and sound when he was a kid, now he was going to excavate the latest on cancer cures. If he ignored miraculous cures by vitamin supplements, plant extracts, essential oils and pulverized fruit pits and went right to the science, there were only a few million entries. No sweat. He was under no illusions. He was undoubtedly wasting his time but at least he wasn't waving a white flag. If you have a problem, he had always reasoned, you find a way to solve it. Life went to the living. And the determined.

He started reading and opened a blank document and cut and pasted anything pertinent, though the medical lingo was only slightly more indecipherable than Urdu. Maybe, later, he'd go shoot pool and try not to think about Marsha.

He read what he could understand, made some notes. The pool hall intruded—the tables, the dim light, young, determined Bonnie. But behind that was Marsha, an hour of getting away from himself, what he was reading, his fate, MaryAnne and Joey. He figured he had every right. A dying man should get lots of wishes. And he was lonely. He had never felt lonely. Maybe it was the sound of the impatient grave.

He picked up his cell phone, took a deep breath, texted her and waited for her ding.

Michael was happy to see her, despite the eyelids at half-mast. He was so used to seeing her stoned, it wasn't until she was away for a week that he noticed when her brain was fogged in, her eyes half closed.

He needed her now and after locking the door, he unbuttoned her shirt, slipped off her jacket and took off her pants and with as little preliminaries as possible made love to her as she lay back on the sofa, her legs on his chest. The urgency surprised him, it had only been a few days since a quiet evening with Marsha but it seemed he needed to assert his love for this woman, reassert she was the only one that mattered, erase his infidelities, reassert life.

And she was hungry and willing and a little surprised by his need but accepted him happily. After, they lay together on the sofa, hearts banging, trying to catch their breath.

"We're going to drip all over the couch," she said, squeezing him tightly.

"Again," he said. "No better way to personalize your furniture."

"Did you miss me?" she said. "Jealous of the adoring multitudes that tossed rose petals and underwear and phone numbers at me?"

"They can toss what they want but I'm the one you're staining the sofa with."

"It wasn't all adoration," she said. "Had some tough nights."

She was almost embarrassed remembering Timmins. They drove all day, her phone turned off to avoid unpleasant surprises as she tried not to continue thinking about the previous night, the empty seats that outnumbered those supporting rear ends, the clean tabletops that outnumbered those with pitchers of beer and bottles of wine.

She was tired. It seemed sometimes she worked all that much harder when the place wasn't jumping, as if enthusiasm and energy would suck people away from their screens and into the club. It hadn't.

They drove north on the 101, along Lake Superior, through Batchawana Bay, Agama Bay and the irrepressible Wawa and finally pulled up to the club eight hours later. She had a raging case of white-line fever and an overdose of road-food grease.

All made worse when they pulled up to the Rockin' Road and saw her poster with a bright red strip of Cancelled through it.

"Aw shit," she said and climbed out of the van, Stephen with her. She found Richard behind the bar. He looked embarrassed. The place was big, dark, empty and ugly, the way most clubs looked when they weren't happening.

Richard kissed her but MaryAnne wasn't in the mood.

"What's going on, Richard? What the fuck?"

"MaryAnne, don't worry, I'll give you the guarantee. I'm not stiffing you. I said $1,500 and I have it upstairs, in cash, and …"

"I don't give a shit about the $1,500," she said, lying. "What's with the cancelled. What's going on?"

"We sold not even 20 tickets, MaryAnne. I can't staff the joint on that. Doesn't pay me to even turn on the lights. I'm paying you like I said but I had to cancel."

MaryAnne was struck dumb. Twenty tickets? Twenty?

"MaryAnne, I swear, lately, I don't think I can fill the place with a double bill of Elton John and Bruce Springsteen. I'm dying here. I fucked up. I should never have promised you. Since COVID, man … We go back and …"

"I don't want your sympathy, Richard. I want to play and I want some asses in the seats. I drove all fucking day."

"I can't, MaryAnne. It's a thousand to open the place. Tech, ticket taker, bar, servers, I can't do it. I'm already in the hole."

"I don't want your fifteen hundred. Give it to the staff. We're playing."

"MaryAnne, if …" Stephen said.

"Stephen, we're playing. No one's going to cancel my show but me. I don't care if the place is empty. We're playing. Richard, you call your people and give 'em my fifteen hundred or whatever it costs to get someone taking tickets and slinging drinks.

"Tech, we need sound, MaryAnne," Stephen said.

"Yeah, get your techie's ass in here," she said. "We'll do a sound check in two hours and play in three. I don't care who's here."

"MaryAnne, please."

"Richard, this show is going on, don't mess with me. I'm not in the mood. And make it free. Take off the cancelled sign and put up free. Big letters … Fucking Free."

The dressing room was gloomy. More like the green room at an execution.

The guys left her alone, went to flirt with the woman behind the bar. She called Essie, left a message.

"Give me a call."

"So you played a freebie?" Michael said. "Anyone show?"

"'Bout a dozen. We did about a dozen tunes, went out, drowned my misery in pizza and beer, more of the latter than the former. I stretched my waistline and paid the bills with a few hundred left over to keep you in MSG."

He rubbed her back with one hand, massaged her neck with the other.

"And I called Essie," she said, embarrassed she was contemplating the white flag. "I can meet them in Seattle or Portland in a couple of weeks. They'll book the tickets, send me cash for travel. Already sent me MP3s. I told her I'd think some more."

"What you going to do?"

"Think some more."

They lay silent, flipping through the files of secrets, lies and deflated ambitions.

"Joey called me," MaryAnne said finally. "Said you were pretty cool. Her words. I think you're hot … She was happy you took her to the clinic. She still hasn't made up her mind."

"I think she has," Michael said. "She just doesn't know it."

He braced himself on his forearms, looked in her eyes, red and not quite focused.

"How come you're stoned all the time?" he said softly, no attempt to injure. "And why is your daughter drunk or was drunk until she got pregnant?"

"I don't know," MaryAnne said, though she was sure the answer was there if she wanted to flip through the files. She pulled him back down to her, avoiding his eyes. "I think about it, 'specially when I smoke too late and I can't fall asleep. Started when I couldn't take the vibe at shows, crowded crazy bars, then bigger listening rooms, I was always afraid. Little girl in a little skirt. People screaming at me. Dope rounds off the edges, turns down the volume. Life seems easier when there's gauze over the lens. Sometimes, Michael, I'm just afraid. Of everything. Does it bother you?"

"Of all the drunks and dopers I've known, you probably have the least to fear and seem the least altered," he said. "I'm so used to you stoned, I guess it's just you. You're not all here but just a bit of you is more than all of most people. And, here can be a dark and ugly place."

"It can also be breathtaking," she said. "Like a few minutes ago."

"It can be breathtaking with our clothes on, too," he said.

She squeezed him and kissed his neck.

"We're doing okay, right?" she said. "It's not so dark and ugly here."

"It's paradise here," he said. He wanted to ask her about her husband, the dead guy that wasn't. He wanted to tell her darkness was coming, but he was tired. He wanted to sleep.

She didn't know if he was being sarcastic. Maybe she didn't want to know. He was in her arms but she felt he was somewhere else and wondered where and why and if this was the beginning of the end. Something was off kilter, ground beneath their feet less firm. Maybe it was her, partly still in the van or some dressing room. She remembered all that too well.

She chewed on her bottom lip then teased his ear with her tongue, trying to reel him back.

"Don't know why Joey drinks," she said. "She has a bit of money, she doesn't really want for much. Her own apartment, though it's a slum. She's good looking, men chase her."

"Maybe she has too much," Michael said, thinking of the letter he found. The dead man's trust fund was obviously not from a dead man. "No brass ring to reach for, why not stay drunk?"

"Maybe it's my fault," MaryAnne said. "Her old lady has reefer madness."

"My mother was a druggie, too," Michael said. "Loved dem bass notes. Darvon, Valium, Librium, Fiorinol, Seconal. Turned me off. I experimented a bit but really, I got high rigging. If you're going to get high might as well get high for real. Maybe I should get a pilot's license. Maybe there comes a time we're no longer our parents' responsibility, we are who we are because of us, not them."

He shifted position, took a deep breath.

"You okay?" she said.

He was exhausted. Too many half-truths to juggle.

"Yeah, just had your beautiful bones digging into my belly. Hey, we're having a dinner party Saturday, smallish."

"Really? I'm glad you told me. How small is smallish?"

"Eight, maybe 10. It's time. See some people, have a few laughs. Welcome the star home with proper pomp and ceremony."

"The star is a black hole so easy on the pomp and ceremony. Should I bake pies? I guess I should 'cause it's the only thing I can bake."

"I'd love you to bake pies," he said.

"How about a little more sugar, now Sweet Buns?"

"Please tell me that's from an old blues song."

"I worshipped at the altars of Ma Rainey, Alberta Hunter, Bessie, Fats Domino, too many to remember," she said. "Now 'nuf talking, time for sugar. She climbed on top of him, helped him get in the mood and took what she needed, lustrous smile brightening his night.

Be here now, he told himself.

He held her buttocks and let her do the work. His extracurricular activities had not only exhausted him but numbed him as well. He pushed Marsha out of his mind. The guilt was not there to ignore and that was curious. Be here now.

"You in me, I don't need the spotlight, baby," she said, reached behind to stroke him, smiling, breathing hard.

And she raised herself and teased him and then let herself slowly slide down on him as deep as she could and they grabbed for each other and held on tight.

Joey and MaryAnne were finishing the last tidbits of Michael's dinner in a bowl, grains and greens, a little Oriental-flavoured meat, some stir-fried veggies, in layers. MaryAnne trying not to overeat after a week on the road, her daughter stuffing herself.

Michael excused himself. He cleaned off the table, dropped the plates on the counter, headed upstairs.

"Michael, you don't have to hide," MaryAnne said.

"You ladies talk," he said from the foot of the stairs, his hand squeezing the newel post, fingers white. "I have some stuff to do."

He walked slowly, heavy tread. Had to lie down. The pill at 2 had worn off. He needed another and a few minutes to recharge. Do some deep breathing. Think through the pain. Listen to her songs. He knew them all, even the instrumental breaks, note by note. He lay back slowly on the bed, afraid to give anything an excuse to jolt him, his left arm digging into the night table drawer for the blister pack of painkillers. He popped two and swallowed them. And waited. It was going to be bad.

Took a breath. He had tried to keep busy. Avoid it. Probably a lot of self-help books he could grab. *How to Die Gracefully. Going Out in Style. The Zen of Dying. Your Time is Up, Get Over It.*

If he was religious, he could pacify his worries by thinking about heaven or paradise or wherever.

Nah, he told himself, waiting on the painkiller, this was it, he was going out not in style but in slow degeneration, with increasing pain and diminishing dignity. It was going to be a hell of a show. MaryAnne was going to have a hard time with this. She'd be okay coming out, after a time. He was going to leave her everything. She could tour, make a record or two in a great studio with the best session guys, she'll be set. But, what about the husband, whoever he was? Could he step in and get a chunk? He'd have to talk to her, find out what the hell was going on.

But, what difference would it make to him? None that he could think of. But did he want to leave it all to her if this lost-in-space fellow was going to rip half of it away. Dying was a complicated affair.

He couldn't think about that now.

He could feel the morphine light up his brain and the pain dial down. It was good shit. There was always a silver lining. Maybe he could do standup, the cancer comic.

It's the only time a man wants part of him to shrink, he thought. *Get great drugs and, you save a bundle on food and shampoo.*

"You're a riot, Michael," he said aloud. "You can do the late-night talk shows. 'Ladies and gentlemen, please welcome Michael tonight, 'cause he won't be here tomorrow.'"

"Flix talking about moving in, helping with the baby," Joey told her. "I don't even know if I'm keeping the baby."

"I have no answers for you," MaryAnne said. She wished she wasn't stoned. She couldn't concentrate. Maybe she should cut back on the shit. Why did Michael look so pale?

"I'm not expecting answers, MaryAnne," Joey said. "Just telling you, Felix wants to make an honest woman out of me. I won't be the poor little knocked-up lonely girl, the pathetic skank too dumb to use birth control."

"Screw that," MaryAnne said. "Anytime anyone does anything in life, assholes shit on them. Being shamed on Facebook, or getting stares from a few insignificant wretches, man, forget about it. Life's too short.

"You're almost 30, had an education, you made choices. You are who you want to be."

"Yeah? A pregnant drunk. Daughter of a superstar pot head," Joey said.

"Listen daughter, you gotta knock that shit off. You're not just one thing or even two or three. You're not just pregnant, you're not just a drinker or just out of work. You're an entire file cabinet of things and being pregnant is not necessarily a bad thing. Neither is being out of work. You have options, you can steer the boat. And I'm not a pothead. I'm a high-functioning connoisseur of herbal delights."

"Right, I'm a sober alcoholic," Joey said. "Isn't it getting boring driving all over, playing seedy joints? You're almost 60. If I had a great man in my life, I'd want to be home."

"You are home, even without the great man. Or is Felix great? And darlin', I've been playing seedy joints all my life and I love it. It's what I do. When the house lights go down and the spots go on, every club is Carnegie Hall. When you like what you do, every night is Christmas Eve. You find what you like, you'll see."

"Every night was Christmas Eve but for a different reason. And I miss it. Sometimes. Felix works, trying to show me he can be a ... provider. Pretty sure he wants a place to hang, get away from his parents, a place with fridge, TV and privileges, you know? You could just paint pretty pictures and every two years have an exhibit at one of those store fronts artists rent for a week 'cause no one will exhibit their stuff."

"Your hormones turning you all warm and fuzzy, daughter," MaryAnne said, now glad her mind was fogged enough to blunt her daughter's fangs. "I'm not the one sucking back wine at 10 a.m. Or is it six in the morning now? And those dumps and halls and festivals put a roof over your head, clothes on and food in that body of yours you're so happy to share with any asshole you meet in a bar with a can where you pack your nose with powder."

Well, maybe not so mellow after all, MaryAnne thought. The kid knew how to push her buttons.

"I never drank in the morning," Joey said. She was quiet, rancour erased. "Except a few times when I never went to bed so it wasn't like morning. And daddy pays for my roof."

"Sure," MaryAnne said.

"I remember when I was little, I knew you'd been up all night, probably doing coke, too messed up to pour me a bowl of cereal and get me out the door to school so you could crash. Or was it to get more blow?"

"Maybe it was because I came home from a gig at five and wanted the nanny to go home so I could make you breakfast and see you for a few minutes before you went to school? I wasn't really into coke. Except when I needed something after a gig to keep me awake until I made you breakfast, dressed you and shipped you off to school."

They sat silently glaring at each other. MaryAnne wished Michael would rescue her. Joey wished she had someone to rescue her.

"What if I get an abortion and never get pregnant again, never meet the right guy?" Joey said. "Or maybe my womb says, 'Abort, abort, this body is toxic?' And what's the upside to having this kid? It's all about no sleep, being a slave to a screaming, puking baby. And my place is a hole. I never clean. I think I need to take a flame-thrower to the dump. Flix could disappear any day, decide to move to Paris, become a painter. He talks a good game but I can't imagine growing old with him, you know? … Remember we used to go down to Vermont, camp on one of those little logging roads and run cross-country, eat at those diners?"

"You loved chicken-fried steak."

"Yeah, I did. Still don't know what it is 'cept it's greasy, tough and great when smothered in brown gravy," she said. "Be fun to do that again. Remember the High Peaks that rainy summer?"

"We had that little motel room, one bed, there was a women's hockey tournament in town."

"We went to a game, had no idea who was playing."

"Only slightly more exciting than changing strings," MaryAnne said. "Great feminist accomplishment. We, too, can take sticks and whack each other over the head."

"Yeah, we'll just stay home, have babies," Joey said. "Man, you're so last century."

"Think you're in any shape for cross-country running."

"I was running last week up Mount Royal, the mountain, not the latest hipster strip," Joey said. "And I think a coupla weeks before that. I'd like to run a half marathon one day. Then a real marathon, like Boston or New York."

"You might have to come off that liquid diet."

"I'm not drinking, I told you. How come you can't be even a little supportive? Is this your cynical artist's disdain on display?"

"All right, you're an Olympic athlete, you're not a problem drinker. I'm sorry. Listen, Joey, time has come for you to face facts. You figure out this pregnancy, you find a job or something, get your shit together. It's time. That trust fund might not last forever. I haven't checked how it was invested and what's going on with it. But if the markets crash and burn or whatever, that money might stop flowing."

"I thought it was forever," Joey said. "What would I do if I lost that? I'd be screwed."

"Guess what, Jo, nothing's forever. And some people get jobs."

"Doing what?"

They heard footsteps in the hallway.

"You ladies want some dessert or something?" Michael called out. "I was thinking of throwing together ... I haven't a clue. But I bet I can figure it out."

He was smiling, looking pale but had the characteristic bounce in his step. The guy thought he was on top of everything but MaryAnne figured, when she was away, he didn't really bother to look after himself all that well. Every man needed a mother sometimes. But then, like a light flashing in her socked-in brainpan, it hit her—a typical stoned paranoid thought? Or harsh reality? Her daughter thought she was a lousy mother. Was she a lousy partner, too? Was Michael pulling away? Would this too end in ashes and tears and sad songs? She shook her head, blew that cloud away.

"Joey and I just talking about heading down to Lake Placid, do some hiking, cross-country running, like we used to," MaryAnne said. "Maybe do some shopping. Have a girl weekend."

"What?" Joey said.

"A girls' weekend. Shopping, hiking, a little running, a movie at night, you know. Lake Placid has that old theatre, box of dark chocolate with those little candy beads on it for a buck? Sno-Caps?"

"Oh, mother, puleeze."

Michael gave good reunion. He was working on the dinner party, though MaryAnne was not feeling sunny side up.

"Be good to see people," he said. "It's been a while."

It had been only a month since the last feast with friends, but MaryAnne wasn't complaining. They were always good times and Michael loved to cook for a crowd. The guests had RSVPed, the menu was planned, ingredients bought and there he was at the counter, slicing and dicing. He had invited Joey but Joey passed. Then reality intruded. He was doing his thing in the kitchen. She rolled a joint and smoked just a few puffs, trying to cut down, contemplating the other reality of her life. Home. There were clubs, motels, bad restaurants, the van, the plane, and then there was home. Something was up with Michael, whatever it was and she didn't know how to deal with it. Her daughter and her daughter's womb. Thinking a lot about Essie's offer, being on a big stage but being in the background, harmonies and hip shakes and ohhs and ahhs. Thinking about the pay cheque, easy money. All she had to do was show up. No wonder she was stoned all the time.

MaryAnne was fearing her soul would leave her body.

She was the woman that had lyrics, melodies, demented colour combinations and twisted shapes she needed to get on canvas running through her head, sometimes even when she slept. She had an idea for a painting of a plane, taking off. Distorted, big windows, little wings, huge vapour trail. She was going to start sketching later.

She was the woman that choreographed stage moments, little movements, expressions, scripted spontaneous anecdotes to tell when she was tuning or when she needed a break between songs. Catch her breath, change tempos, make a connection. She was a singer/songwriter/performer/song and dance man, storyteller/painter/lover/mother. Where did granny fit in all that? Or even backup singer?

Through the haze she realized it irked her most that she wasn't in control of anything. Music was imploding, her partner seemed to be drifting away, her daughter was … her daughter and no one knew what she was going to do. Life was a runaway truck and she had to find the brakes. She'd take angry, resentful daughter away for a weekend, try for a bonding thing.

She wandered into her studio, stared at the half-finished canvas waiting for her on her easel. Michael had restocked her supplies while she was away—tubes of Stevenson— cerulean blue, zinc white, burnt sienna, yellow ochre, Indian yellow, ultramarine blue, Payne's Gray and alizarin red, a bunch of perfectly stretched canvases from Surface Support, a handful of sable brushes.

She picked up a brush and her palette, squeezed a few blobs of sienna and blue and mixed them. Here she was in control, here she could get lost—a one-woman band. Here was peace.

"Tell you what, Joey. I'll stop writing songs to look after your kid. Or stop painting. Or playing. Yeah, just put down the guitar. The brushes, easel? I'll put 'em all away, help look after the kid, the mistake, the gift that'll keep on giving until we die."

Or maybe shut down one part of my life. Stop painting, change diapers instead. Make baby food. Wash diapers. Did anyone wash diapers anymore? Grandkids were cool. Or so they said.

Or maybe Felix, the phantom, would hang in, do his part and MaryAnne would be a Sunday grandma, put a crib in the spare room, buy some crib toys, Michael would cook a Sunday brunch, the baby would sleep, they'd sit around a table like families on TV. It didn't seem so bad. Others did it.

They'd work it out in Lake Placid, she thought. Just ride out tonight, enjoy their friends, have a little wine, have a few laughs, enjoy being home.

Maybe she needed another puff or two. At this point, it seemed, getting wrecked was the suitable response. Or maybe she should take a stab at sobriety. Right!

"Maybe there's a happy medium," Michael said. He was sautéing something by sliding the pan back and forth across the fire, then giving it a little wrist flip, the bits and pieces doing pirouettes above the pan. He was always so damn reasonable.

"Yeah, I can join Essie, revive the Trash Sisters, make some decent money, be on the road a lot and stop worrying about my own songs, my own gigs, my own money. Just give up. And become grandma."

Her cell phone rattled somewhere in the house and she set about searching for it. It rang five times and went dead before she found it. She didn't recognize the number or the area code and when she was debating calling it back, it went off in her hand, the same number.

His name was Brian Campbell, he told her, and was owner, with his brother, of Campbell Soop Productions. "Two Os, no U," he said, and he was coming to Montreal and hoping to have lunch, dinner or coffee or drinks with her, whatever she preferred.

"What can I do for you, Mr. Campbell?"

"I produce, promote, manage acts, a few here, some down in Australia, in Europe, and South America. I have a proposal for you. You probably don't remember, you sent us your EPK."

"'Course I remember," she said. She didn't remember. She sent out dozens a month, planting the seeds for gigs around the world by email. Press send and forget about it. Few bothered to reply.

"This a pay-to-play deal, Mr. Campbell?"

"Call me Brian," he said. "No, well, maybe yes, 'cause I pay you to play. You don't pay me. It's not a hustle. We take on artists we think can make money for us and them. We like music and since we can't sing or play, we promote others. Kind of masochistic but we try. As you know, the biz ain't what it was, but I don't quit."

"Tell you what," MaryAnne said. "There's a quiet bar in the Ritz on Sherbrooke West. Do you know it? I can meet you Tuesday."

"Sure."

"By the way, Mr. Campbell, Brian, I've been in this

business a while so if you're trying to hustle me, screw me literally or figuratively, I'm not buying, I'm not interested. I've been fucked over and fucked around, lied to, cheated, ripped off, taken advantage of and just plain robbed. If you're selling something, don't waste my time. But, if you want to talk without picking my pocket or taking advantage of my fragile ego, meet me Tuesday for drinks. Okay? Say six?"

"I'm old enough to understand plain English, Mary-Anne. I appreciate your honesty and I'll be waiting for you at the bar," he said. "And by the way, I've been listening to you since I started breathing. My parents were big fans, last of the hippies, and here I am, still listening."

He wanted to lie down, take more pills, forget everything. But MaryAnne's stage was in a club or hall, while his was right here and nothing helped him keep it together like a good dinner party, lose himself in the food prep, the conversation, the smiles and laughs of people he liked and loved. His cast iron pan was his guitar. He smiled to himself.

"I know the tour wasn't the best," he said. "But I'm cooking, it's the best I can do over a stove and you made a few bucks and came home in one piece, so we're going to celebrate."

"No wonder I love you," she said, kissed him hard on the lips.

"If you get me in gear, dear, I'm going to screw up my jambalaya."

"Isn't screwing me worth screwing up the jambalaya?"

she said. "Stupid question. You'd cut off your dick before you'd ruin a meal."

"A man has to have priorities," he said, and went back to stirring. "Who called?"

"Some half-assed producer wants to buy me a drink next week," she said. "And promise to make me a star if I pay him a small fortune. These guys are the new aluminum siding salesmen."

"Here's to MaryAnne, and her safe return from a great tour, the terrific woman I love," Michael toasted. Glasses of red clinked, congratulations were chorused, the jambalaya was sampled and applauded.

MaryAnne was grilled about her tour and the best parts of Northern Ontario and then the affairs of the world were dissected.

Even with her brain marinating in dope and wine, MaryAnne had little patience for conversations of the helter skelter of politics in faraway places, including Washington. Without substances to soothe her, she would've left the table, lost herself in her guitar. She could sing about war and heartbreak. Didn't see any point in talking about it.

She noticed Michael was with her. He gave her a wink and listened as poker-faced as he could, nodding appropriately. She understood the fear the world was coming apart, but what the hell was she going to do about it? She had nothing to add about the shape of the Middle East or Korea or Africa or south of the border. Too far, too out of reach, too little she could do about any of it.

All she knew about these places were what the refugees served in the restaurants they opened once they crossed the ocean. Except, of course, for the States, where multiple daily calamities was part of the soundtrack of Canadian life. There weren't enough compartments in her brain to suffer for everyone suffering. Thinking about her little family and impotent career was enough for now. She remembered the empty seats and tried to refocus on the seats that weren't empty.

Michael smiled at her above the wine glass at his lips. He knew what she was thinking. They had unplugged. Their reserves were for keeping themselves, and the small coterie they cared for, sane. And MaryAnne wasn't sure they were doing a great job of that.

"Ah, but you know what?" Philippe said. "Hell with it. The whole world's on fire and pissing on it won't put it out, so you mind if I pour another glass of this divine Bordeaux, ma chère, and sleep in your spare room?"

"You can sleep in the spare room even if you don't pour another glass," MaryAnne said.

As always, with dessert, MaryAnne sang a few songs. She didn't like to; feared she was playing to a captive audience that thought listening to her was the price of admission. But their friends always insisted and eventually she gave up protesting and grabbed the downstairs Yamaha that always leaned against the sofa. She played a couple of new tunes she had baptized on tour.

As she sang, she watched. Michael was in his element, producing an evening of food, music, talk and wine and sitting back and relishing the show.

She also noticed discussions around careers had given

way to talk of hobbies and even, grandchildren. Nathan had spent his life as a rock 'n' roll electrician, wired a lot of the same shows as Michael. Now he was doing wood cuts, gardening, taking tennis lessons. Cecile liked to bake and loved to expound on the magic of sourdough. Robert was taking cello lessons and was always looking to MaryAnne for advice, even though her knowledge of cello was akin to her interest in the Middle East. But she admired his devotion. He was like a man with a new lover, brought chamber orchestra CDs with him, closed his eyes when the cello parts took centre stage.

When MaryAnne put down her guitar, Cecile and Nathan said they had to relieve their babysitter.

Their son and grandson lived with them and their son worked nights, so was rarely home. Their grandson had become their charge, his mother had fled to B.C. five years ago and Cecile and Nathan, edging toward their 70s, had her son and his son camped out in the spare room of their apartment condo.

Their life was MaryAnne's nightmare. Cecile was up with the roosters to make the little one breakfast, just like the old days, she laughed. The strain was showing in the new lines carved into her forehead and around her mouth. And her husband was not amused. It wasn't how he had pictured his retirement.

"Mitch gets up the same time as I do, so what's the big deal?" she said, on the defensive. "Can't leave the baby cook his own breakfast."

"And we wouldn't want our son getting out of bed before noon," Nathan said.

"He works late," she said. "He needs to sleep."

How easy had it been for her to go back to the grandeur of being a hovering mother, making sure everyone started off the day with a good meal. MaryAnne felt sweat roll down her rib cage. What gene was she missing?

Making breakfast for my kid and grandkid, MaryAnne thought. *I can see it now.*

"Hey, mom, you guys have a big house, can we come and live with you just for a bit until I find a better place? I like extra bacon and eggs over easy, please."

Of course, Michael, the bloody Zenmaster, collector of lost cats, dogs, women and children, would go along with it. Isn't that how she ended up here?

"How do you find it, the kids living with you?" MaryAnne said.

"Mitch is so cute," Cecile said, with a big smile. "He's growing so fast."

"Pain in the ass," Nathan said. "But what you going to do, your kid needs a roof? He has a kid that needs ..."

"Everything," Cecile said. "His mother took off, left her baby. What are we supposed to do, watch them starve, live in a shelter?"

"What's your son doing?" MaryAnne asked.

"He tends bar at a club," Cecile said.

"That's what he says," Nathan said. "I haven't seen the cash. Doesn't give us a dime. And, I went to the bar one night, asked for him. They knew him, all right, but he wasn't there. I'm not so sure he actually works there."

"So what's he doing?" Cecile said, an edge to her voice.

"Cecile, you weren't born in a turnip patch. Where there's a bar, there's drugs and where there's drugs, someone is selling them."

"C'mon," Cecile said. "Anyway, our grandson is gorgeous and smart. So cute watching him on a game on the phone, the little thumbs just clicking away, completely mesmerized. He's six but you'd swear he's 12."

"I wouldn't swear he's 12," Nathan said. "I'd swear he's six. And you know, our son, who knows who he's mixed up with. Who's going to break down the door one night with a big gun in their hand? A cop or a dealer he ripped off?"

"Don't be so bloody dramatic," his wife said. "He's tending bar in a nice club. He's not Pablo Escobar."

"Pablo Escobar didn't live with his parents," Nathan said. "C'mon, we should go. The babysitter's on the clock. Fifteen bucks an hour to watch TV and eat everything in the fridge. You believe that? Kid's like a swarm of locusts."

"Nathan, will you stop bitching and let's go. Mike and MaryAnne have heard enough. And you guys, don't listen to him. The grandchild is a wonder. I don't care how much it costs to have a babysitter to get out and have a beautiful night like tonight. Thanks so much. And thanks for the music."

Everyone else left except Philippe, whom MaryAnne escorted to the spare room, arm in arm, making sure he didn't topple over and have to be dragged off the floor. He fell into bed, tried to take off his shoes, but fell back on the bed, lifting his feet to give MaryAnne access to his laces.

"You're a very gracious host," he said. "And Michael is a hell of a cook. Sometimes I think being drunk is the only sensible response to just about everything these days. Don't you agree?"

MaryAnne had both his shoes off and steered his legs onto the bed and pulled the blankets off the empty half of the bed and covered him.

"I don't drink much," she said. "But I sympathize. You need anything?"

"Right, you're a doper. We all need something. How else can you cope? Is Michael all right? He looks ... I don't know, different."

"Of course he's all right," MaryAnne said, closing the light. "You let me know if you need anything. There's Tylenol and 222s in the bathroom."

"I love you, MaryAnne. You guys are the best."

"Thank you, Philippe. We love you too. Get some sleep. I'll bake cheese scones in the morning."

Michael was still at the dining room table, sipping water. Usually he was loading the dishwasher.

"Philippe asked me if you're okay," she said, grabbing the plates in one hand and a fist full of cutlery in another.

"Why wouldn't I be okay? Sometimes, I'm not in a rush to erase the evening. I like to keep hearing the conversation. Like revelling in the last notes of a good show. Remember? Perhaps the counters can stay sullied another few minutes, the table rumpled, stained and cluttered. Who gives a shit?"

"You've been smoking my hash?"

"No, but why don't we?" he said. "Smoke a little and go to bed?"

"Why don't we?" she said and took his hand and led him to the bedroom, smiling. Maybe he was all right, after all.

Felix had chewed some Ritalin, today's smart pill of choice, and was cruising. His legs and back ached but an Oxy would take care of that. He was working books. He liked working books and, though there was a lot of porn, with the pills pumping through his system he didn't get distracted by titles and back covers. He used to get lost in reading them all and twice incurred the wrath of Team Leader, the little fascist. But now, he just chased his machine, dropping covers, hard and soft, into their respective maws. Nothing distracted him, nothing pissed him off. He was laser focused.

Those smart drugs were killer shit. Days flew by. And if he had to work a few more hours, no problem. When they green-lighted him, though, he had no idea what to do with himself. Joey didn't seem to like him coming home in the middle of the day and he didn't want to be there anyway. He just walked and walked. The warehouse was out in Saint Michel and he stumbled upon Addison's, a discount electronics place, selling cheap Chinese knockoffs. He loved to rummage through the store for an hour looking at everything, playing the guitars and electric drums, picking up and analyzing connectors and adapters and chargers and tools and then he'd wander over to Kim Phat, just across the road. They had every Oriental food imaginable, and many he had never imagined and when that made him hungry enough, they had a restaurant with a pretty good menu where he could stuff himself on salt and pepper pork chops and Yang Chow rice and bring the leftovers home to Joey. Sometimes he'd bring them to his parents with a few extras like garlic and ginger, or, if feeling righteous, he'd buy some fresh fish, make his mother happy. The old man was never happy so he had given up on that score.

Sandra was a babe but knew it and flaunted it and was seriously unhappy with her lot in life. Felix had tried to turn her on to the magic tablets Gaetan was pushing but she looked at Felix like he was a roach. The woman wore tight jeans and tight T-shirts, her mysteries covered only barely, but seemed annoyed if any guy paid attention to her. Yet, here she was, sauntering toward him either on break or heading to the can and she was giving her walk a little extra, making sure Felix knew she had the goods. He did his best to ignore her, picking the books and following the robot. She surprised him by stopping.

"How you doing?" she said.

"Good," he said, trying not to look at her, pay her back for the scorn of the past. But she stayed there, a firing offence for sure. Chatting was right up there on the list of crimes with pissing on the products.

"You hear anything about a union?" she said.

"Not really," he said, but he stopped picking. He didn't know what to say.

"What does that mean, 'not really?' Either you did or you didn't."

"Hey, Sandra, chill, okay? What's with the hostility, man?"

"Flix, sorry, but it makes me nervous talking about this stuff but I've been hearing rumours, like, you know. I'm just wondering if you know if anything's going on."

"No, I haven't heard anything," he said.

"C'mon," she said. "This place is like a prison camp and we're the inmates. Gotta do something, you know. It's not right. Green light, red light. Crazy, man. I never know what I'm going to be making, which bill I can pay, when

I'm going to be working. Can't plan anything. It's seriously messed up."

Felix was getting paranoid. No one talked like this in the middle of hell. He didn't want to lose this job today, become one of those fulfillment centre pros, going from one hell to another, enduring one set of indignities after another, sleeping in your car in the parking lots. Course, he'd need to get a car first.

He had heard stories in the lunchroom. Strip searches, 20-minute meal breaks, 14-hour days, no OT. It was crazy out there. This was a hell he knew and Gaetan's chemical blandishments made it all possible.

"I know, I know," he said. "People are talking. If you're interested in, you know, seriously, let me know and I can talk to someone who can talk to someone. I gotta get back to work before our Team Leader for Life gets on my case."

"Well, I'm interested and I'm tired of blowing our Team Leader for Life just so he'll leave me alone. It's a fucking circus here. Talk to you."

She swung into motion and disappeared around a corner. He felt like a tornado had whipped through. But, brain soaked in Ritalin, he went back to picking.

MaryAnne loved the drive. Not the 87, not the border-crossing creeps, but once she left the Interstate and started climbing into and around the mountains and rivers, it was gold.

She was driving a new Miata Michael had floored her with, a present for persistence, he said. She came home and there it was sitting in front of the house. She almost wanted to drive it into the livingroom and spend the night looking at it. Instead they climbed on the autoroute and headed to a dairy in St. Jerome, ate a couple of scoops of a chocolate concoction and zoomed home, zipping between lanes, hair blowing in the wind.

She had always loved two-seaters and she loved the new wheels and how it glued itself to corners, climbed without a pause, had enough room for a few bags and her guitar in the back, even with the top down.

Joey was watching the scenery.

"Can't believe he just bought you a car," she said. "That's insane. I guess he really loves you."

"I guess he does," MaryAnne said, easing into a straightaway that bordered a river just before Whiteface. In the middle of the rushing water a man in waders was fly fishing, watching his line float as if he had not a worry in the world.

Lake Placid was built for the Olympics so it was not a place for a retreat but it had a few things going for it. A not-bad free beach, a not-quite dreadful Chinese restaurant when you needed vegetables other than French fries, an ancient movie theatre that sometimes had films that didn't involve carnage, and chain stores selling decent clothes at affordable prices, places to buy boots and sweaters and shirts and jeans and socks.

She was going to splurge on her daughter, buy her buckets of stuff. Then go home, conscience clear, and finish cutting the CD. Think of what to do with Essie.

"I've hired a producer, Eric West, big-league guy," MaryAnne said, above the wind, the car surging through the turns, accelerating down the straights. She loved it all, the mountains, the rivers, the car, her daughter, her future, the man at home, probably cooking or painting or plumbing or off on his bike, sailing through city streets, dodging cars. The guy was a maniac on wheels but he lived. Life was perfect. At least for this instant.

"So when I get back, I'll be in the studio for a bit more, just another tune or two and maybe join my friend Esther, do backups with this guy named Slate."

"He sucks," Joey said.

"Maybe but he has about 100 million plays on wherever, Spotify and YouTube and Apple and the pay is good. Bank account needs some fluffing."

"You're going to sing for someone else?" Joey said.

"I don't know. I have to think about it."

The town, courtesy of Olympic Games past, had more motel rooms than it knew what to do with, more restaurant seats than it could normally fill. Autumn and the changing leaves were a big time, summer vacation and winter skiing did not do too bad, but the restaurants were forever changing, looking for a formula that would survive four seasons.

The Chinese joint, white walls and Formica tables, stayed because it was cheap, run by a Vietnamese family that didn't appear to have BMW ambitions and were acquainted with long hours over hot woks pushing sweet, fried variations of Asian cuisine. MaryAnne liked it 'cause you could get broccoli and snow peas.

She found some real wool sweaters at Bass as they geared up for fall, bought a half dozen, three for each of them, some hiking boots, lots of socks for cold weather, real cotton and flannel shirts and they took turns in the changing room, pulling pants on and off and going out to model their rear ends to each other.

"You're doing pretty good for an old broad, Ma," Joey said, looking at her mother in tight, slim jeans.

"Thank you, Jo. But I gotta sweat to stay pretty good and I'm aiming for great. So let's hit the trail, do a little running, a little hiking and then eat ourselves silly."

"It's four o'clock," Joey said. She felt like a nap. "Can't we do it tomorrow?"

"Yep, we can. And today. We have lots of time. Sun doesn't go down until 8. We'll be eating Italian by then and deserving it."

They changed into new hiking boots and good socks at the motel, patted some bug spray all over and drove away in the little blue car.

Michael was sitting across from the doctor, today wearing a smock, file in front of him. The doc was straight-faced.

"I'm glad you've changed your mind, Michael. We've had success by using chemotherapies in combination so we're going to hit you with a triad of therapies. Three times a week for three weeks. If it don't kill you, it might cure you." The doctor smiled. "A little cancer humour. Listen, there's room for optimism, Mike. I can't give you odds, can't say this'll give you more months or years, I don't know. But you've got nothing to lose, depending on how well you tolerate the cocktail. And so far, this particular combo is as easy as vodka and tonic, except no buzz. I think you should try it."

"What percentage does this cocktail work on?"

"That's irrelevant," he said. The doctor, maybe 40, hadn't shaved in a day or two; there were bags under his eyes; his smock was wrinkled, not shimmering white. Maybe the guy wasn't sleeping. "It's kind of like stats in sports. A .300 hitter could easily strike out, the guy hitting .192 knocks it out of the park every once in a while. So we don't look at stats. We know it sometimes works and sometimes doesn't so we're going to think that this time it will work. That's what you focus on."

"I've been reading about iron oxide nanoworms used with doxorubicin," Michael said. "Experiments with mice."

"You've been scouring the Internet, looking for miracle cures," the doctor said.

"No, looking at the science," Michael said. "I don't believe in miracles."

The doctor looked at him. He hated when patients took a too-active role in their treatment. Complicated his life. Too many times they started talking about the magic of prune pits.

"I haven't worked a lot with doxorubicin," he said. "But I'll make some calls, check the research. But what I've prescribed often has a positive outcome. It can work. I won't tell you that positive thinking improves your odds, 'cause it doesn't matter what you think, but it can make the process easier to handle if you don't go down the dark road. Stay in the sun."

"You sound like a politician or a bad songwriter," Michael said.

"Politicians win elections and bad songs become hits," the doctor said. "Take comfort in the fact I'm neither. Just a doctor trying to keep you alive and I'm pretty good at it. C'mon in back and John'll hook you up. And I'll follow up on the doxorubicin."

"It's Saturday," Michael said.

"Disease isn't unionized," the doctor said. "Doesn't take weekends off. I don't take too many myself."

Michael sat in the La-Z-Boy, hooked up to the hat rack, the juice flowing, his mind racing. Funny thing was, he felt nothing. No sign his body was being poisoned, no burning, no glowing in the dark, no itch. Nothing.

It hadn't been so bad. MaryAnne rarely asked where he was going if she was home when he headed out. He took his toolbox as camouflage while she painted or played or scribbled. Michael hated lying but he checked into his little out-of-the-way motel with its four-hour siesta rates almost every day, slept a couple of hours and spent the rest of the time staring at the ceiling, trying to fathom what the future might hold and if and how he could keep it together.

His mind often drifted to MaryAnne. He knew almost every afternoon, if she wasn't in the studio, she was standing at a large slanted table with drawers, a wood piece circa 1920 that he had refinished for her. She wrote songs at the table on yellow pads, her guitar on a strap around her neck. She wasn't shy, didn't mind when he popped in and watched her work. She said she liked audiences, even when experimenting with a new tune. She'd play a verse, say, "Whayyda think?"

He always liked them. She had a poignancy about her writing. Or maybe there was a poignancy about her and he just liked everything she did.

"I'm hunting for a chorus," she said, more often than not.

"When in doubt go for the dominant minor," he'd say. He had no idea what it meant but he had heard Van Morrison say it one night when they were tearing down and a woman had just played him a tune as he was pouring drinks for the crew, though, as usual, Morrison was too drunk to do much more than spill drinks. But Michael had always remembered, "Go for the dominant minor."

"Already did, kid," she'd say, big smile. "Not working today."

One of the pleasant rituals that made them a couple, Michael thought. He didn't see any point in telling her this, not now, ruin all the good stuff. *They had their secrets*, he thought. *What's with the husband in Malta?*

He wore an elastic bandage over the little Band-Aid they placed on the puncture mark in his arm, told her he had strained it teaching a pipe wrench who was boss.

Maybe the new chemical would work, a magic potion, give him a few more years. He was lucky the cure wasn't killing him. Pretty easy, so far. A little nausea. He didn't feel like eating but ate anyways. Pain was controllable. Hardly any hair loss. And what came off with the comb he plucked out of the sink and washed down the toilet. Destroy the evidence.

Maybe it was all bullshit. Maybe he wasn't sick at all. He laughed. He was being sucked down Kübler-Ross's well-worn path.

"Hello denial," he said.

Shit, was he such a stereotype? It's not true. It can't be happening. Next supposedly would be anger. Maybe he should go and kick the shit out of someone. Be easy to find deserving candidates. Or, maybe skip right to acceptance and make it easier on everyone. The doctors were right. He might as well live with the fact he wasn't going to live too long. But, nothing said he had to tell anyone.

MaryAnne had accused him more than once of being closed, distant, hard to know. He wasn't closed. *What you see is what you get. I cook and clean and fix and sing your songs and admire you out there somewhere attacking a mountain. Or maybe a store. I just like living. And you know how to live, woman.* He admired her for her passions. No secrets. Until now.

When the worst happened there would be friends for her. Maybe he should talk to them? Philippe or Nathan or Robert. Maybe Stephen? Esther? And what would they do? There was nothing anyone could do except give him the sympathetic stare, then treat him like a leper. Screw that.

Lousy time to get sick, the kid was pregnant. Was there a good time? No point in anyone making a big deal about this.

Plath had written dying was an art. He thought life was an art. The original Dylan had advised fending off the inevitable with rage but that seemed a waste of energy. Death was pitching a perfect game.

Maybe it was a blessing. The world had turned dark and terrifying. What was the point in living long enough to lose himself in Alzheimer's, sitting in wet diapers and drool in a gilded seniors' home, fed by strangers from strange lands—ignored, pitied, and useless—death as much a gift as life had been?

"Hello acceptance," he said.

Wasn't that tough at all—five steps in a blink. Maybe

he'd shoot some pool tonight. Eternity was a long time to be alone.

Felix was in the can. Washing his hands, taking as long as he could. The cold water soothed his aching fingers. He figured he picked a few thousand items and the bloody light was still red. He could be stuck here all Friday night.

Thibeault came in. They had rarely talked but Thibeault, he knew, was a fulfillment lifer. Felix checked under the doors of the stalls making sure no one was sitting on a toilet.

"How's it going, Bobo?" Felix said.

"Like it always goes," he said. "I chase the machine, I pick and pack, I think about the beach my parents took me to when I was a kid. Old Orchard. I think about bikinis and hot sand and cold beer, man. Least tonight I'll get some cold beer."

"Thibeault, ever think of a union?" Felix was whispering. "A union here. Maybe better pay, better hours, you know." Felix kept looking over his shoulders, watching the door. His palms were sweaty.

"Unions? Fuck off," he said, his anxiety instantly climbing to near stroke level. "I don't want to hear about that shit, man. No fucking unions, okay. They hear you talk unions, they'll fire all of us. Unions just screw everything up, you know. They promise the moon, deliver shit."

He was washing his hands and face vigorously now as if he could scrub away the conversation.

"I worked at a place in New Brunswick, they went

there for the cheap labour and as soon as they started talking union, they shut the whole fucking place down. Went to work the doors were locked, done. I fucking lived on the street for three, four months. Got a lift here, slept in a hostel when I didn't sleep in a park under a bench. Ate crap, a lot of dumpster diving, standing on street corners with my hand out. They wouldn't give me welfare 'cause I didn't have an address, didn't live here long enough. I ain't doing that again."

"Union will get us more money, we'll have a real schedule, we'll ..."

"You stupid, man? If they don't close they'll just bring in more part timers, fire anyone they think was involved, if they'll ever sign a contract, which they won't. But, even if there's a miracle and they do, so what? These guys don't care if we live or die. Associates, my ass.

"They're into paying us as little as possible so they can keep their clients. And the bosses can live in fancy homes with swimming pools and cleaning ladies and drive Lexuses.

"Listen, man, I got myself a one-room in Pointe aux Trembles. It's a shithole but it's heated and furnished and no bed bugs. I got a TV and cable and Internet and an iPhone. All I need. Takes a half hour to get here by bus and when I get paid I can go to Harvey's and eat an Angus burger and all is good. Go home, watch a game, drink a six-pack. Don't need to spend money on girls. Got the Internet. Don't need no fucking union, either. Like life nice and simple. And if you're not careful, you'll be out on the street, dumpster diving, begging for change. Keep your mouth shut about a blood-sucking union."

"But Bobo ..."

"I don't want to hear it, man, get it? I don't want to hear it."

He stomped out of the can, kicking the door open with his foot.

"Where the hell is Pointe aux Trembles?" Felix said, and went to join his robot buddy blinking on the other side of the door.

By the time they found a trail and a place to stash the car, it was 5 p.m. They attacked the hill, brimming with optimism and good cheer. Mother and daughter on the mountain, MaryAnne carrying a water bottle, Joey a pocketful of apples and dried fruit. They were game. After a couple of hundred metres, MaryAnne started a slow jog, her daughter a few metres behind her, pointing her phone at her, shooting video.

"You can use this for your next video," Joey called at her.

"Joey, if you get too tired, tell me," MaryAnne said.

"Listen, old lady, you're going to be begging me to stop way before I even break a sweat."

And so they trotted, jumping over pools of mud, fallen trees, rocks, getting a good sweat going, smelling the fragrance of summer, ignoring the humidity moving in.

MaryAnne reasoned her daughter was pregnant and maybe tired but too proud to slow down, so she did.

"Okay, you win," she said. "I need some water and a breath."

They moved off the trail and sat on a tree, taking bites

of the same apple, eating figs and swigging from the water bottle.

"How you feeling?" MaryAnne said.

"Heavy and pregnant and tired and old and messed up," Joey said.

"That good, eh? First trimester tough."

"It gets easy after that?"

"Having you was no sweat. You were designed perfectly. Your father was a stud. Good genes, healthy body, if not mind, and I was in pretty good shape, too."

"Except for a little dope habit," Joey said.

"Except for a little dope habit," MaryAnne said. "You know, sweetie, not every conversation needs mention of my shortcomings, especially if I'm trying to tell you how great you were, emphasis on the 'were'."

"I'm sorry," Joey said.

"Anyways, I felt great when I was pregnant. You popped out easy and I was back on my feet and playing in no time. You were a great baby, a great kid. You probably don't remember but, when you were a little older, I had the sitter bring you backstage lot of shows. You'd inevitably fall asleep but I liked it when you were just where I could see you."

"Why didn't dad bring me to the shows?"

"He didn't like coming, didn't like me performing, didn't like me hanging out with the guys in the band, didn't dig the scene. Jealous. Always had plans the nights I had gigs, made me responsible for making sure you had a sitter, made me feel guilty, tried to anyway. Pissed him off I didn't feel guilty. I didn't see anything wrong with you being backstage when I was playing. Time you were 10, the band was way beyond the groupie thing, no one did anything stronger than a little dope or booze in the dressing room.

"Kids are shooting up in the can at McDonald's these days so you were safe enough. And the guys wanted to be your uncles. No one was going to hurt you. Nothing there to corrupt you."

"Why'd he kill himself?" Joey was looking at her feet as they made designs in the soil. She had rarely gone there. Dad was home one day and then he disappeared.

"I don't know," MaryAnne said, trying to avoid the quicksand a conversation about her husband could lead to. "He was into stuff I knew nothing about. He never told me what he was doing. 'A little of this, a little of that,' he'd say. So, it's been almost 20 years. I don't think about it. You wanna get going?"

"Why'd you marry him?"

"I have no idea," MaryAnne said. "He was good-looking, I was 27, thought I knew everything, kinda like you do. And he was, how should I say, gallant. At first. The kind of guy that would carry you over puddles or spread his coat on the street to spare your shoes, you know, at least in my fantasies. I think at first he thought being with a singer would be cool. Then he discovered the reality. I wasn't rich and I wasn't home many nights. I hung out with men. Pissed him off."

"I thought I had messed up somewhere," Joey said.

"Sweetie, no, that's ... that's just not true. He loved you. You were the only thing in his life that worked. He worshipped you. C'mon, let's keep moving before we get cold."

What if the asshole showed up? MaryAnne asked herself.

"Feeling your age, Ma?"

"Up yours," MaryAnne said, and started off in a slow jog, Joey behind her. After about a kilometre, they slowed to a march, ducking low-hanging branches, walking side by side, breathing hard.

"I think I've had it," Joey said. "Can we go back now?"

"Sure," MaryAnne said. "I'll buy you dinner."

They turned around. In 20 minutes they realized they were they knew not where. The path was not taking them down. It was bringing them higher.

"I think we zigged when we should've zagged," Mary-Anne said. "Let's have an apple and think."

"Great," Joey said. "Please don't tell me we're lost in the Adirondack Mountains."

"Okay, I won't tell you."

Michael was bent over the snooker table. Lately, it seemed, games were laborious, bending hurt, legs were tired, but that was okay. He didn't come to play. He came to hide. He tried not to watch the clock, he tried not to think of Marsha, he tried not to think of dying. Just concentrate on the geometry and put the ball in the hole. What could be simpler? Bonnie bopped by, handmade Brazilian Rosewood cue in hand. Only the best for the best.

"Looking for a game, old man?" she said, laughing.

Bonnie looked like Bonnie, three buttons undone on her form-hugging shirt, tailored black slacks, hair perfect, a hint of makeup around the eyes and lips. Michael had to admit he admired her. She was comfortable in her skin, comfortable in her clothes, good at what she did, happy to be alive. If he was younger …

"Not tonight, sweetheart," he said. "I'm not staying, and playing you is bad for my ego."

She bent over his table and made his shot, winked at him, pinched his butt and walked away.

He surveyed the remaining balls, trying to figure out a strategy but his mind kept going to his phone. He had texted Marsha more than 20 minutes ago and usually she responded within two or three. She was an iPhone junkie and was never far from it.

He told himself to go home, watch a film and go to sleep. But then his phone vibrated in his back pocket. He put the cue down and pulled out his phone.

"I was in the bath. I'll open a bottle."

He erased the text and left.

Felix was cruising. Had four fares tonight, made $61. His shoulders ached from working in hell all day but now at least he was sitting down and making a few bucks, driving for Uber with his father's car. Been a breeze. It was only weekends and nights, but not renting a car or paying for one, saved him a fortune—if his old man didn't start bitching about not having his car.

A few guys at work had started driving for Uber to stay alive during green-light weeks. Didn't seem bad. Listening to the radio, waiting for his phone to tell him a fare was waiting. Gaetan thought the union and a good raise were just a matter of time. Sandra and a few others were whispering about it, too. Maybe they could unionize the robots.

Saturday night on St. Laurent had to be good. Everyone was high with full pockets, all in a rush to get someplace, surge-pricing in effect. His phone lit up with a notice for a pickup on St. Laurent and Villeneuve, 10 seconds away, drive them only a few kilometres. No sweat, easy money.

He drove down the street and two guys and a chick, all about 30, hopped in the car.

"How's it going, man?" said a guy in a good tight black suit, the kind where the jacket barely covers your ass.

"Yeah, how's it going, handsome?" the woman said. She was a looker: tight top, small skirt. He checked her out in his mirror and she was smiling at him.

"Where you guys going?" Felix asked.

"You know Van Horne from Saint Urbain to Saint Denis, that overpass? Want to go under there. Meeting a guy, you know."

"I'm not sure how to get there," Felix said.

"No sweat, I'll show you," the guy said.

It took about six minutes and they were under the overpass, near the CN rail line that crossed the city, engine running.

"This is great," the guy in the suit said.

"Here?" Felix said. "There's nothing here."

"Exactly," the suit said.

The other guy reached over the back of Felix's seat and put him in a headlock. Felix starting to struggle, kicking the car floor, trying to get leverage. The more he struggled, the harder the guy squeezed.

"If I have to, I'll just strangle you, shithead," the guy said. "So, take it easy."

"Drop your wallet on the passenger seat," the guy in the suit said. "And open your door."

Felix struggled for a second but the guy's grip was too tight. He couldn't move; it was hard to breathe. Spots popped in front of his eyes. He pried his wallet out of his back pocket. He remembered he had his father's credit card for gas. The only cash he had was his own, maybe 40 bucks. No one paid cash, they paid Uber by credit card and Uber dropped money into your bank account. Everything was digital. He had nothing to rob.

He struggled to breathe and find the door latch, pushing the door open with his shoulder. His heart was banging in his chest.

He was gasping when he climbed out of the car and the guy just kicked his feet out from under him and down onto the glass and gravel he went. He heard the guy say, "I hate fucking union scumbags. Understand? Unions are for scum. And you're scum. Why don't you head out west and don't come back?"

Felix saw the guy's foot go back, felt an other-worldy pain in his ribs and passed out.

It was the most time they had spent together in a few years and they were having a good time. Until now.

"I don't have a compass or anything," MaryAnne said. "And no clue where we are."

"My phone has a compass," Joey said and pulled it out of the front pocket of her jeans. "There's no signal, not even half a bar. We're screwed."

"They teach you how to navigate by the stars?" Mary-Anne said.

"You're not funny, Mother."

"We have a couple of hours of daylight left, let's keep moving. We'll find a path down or maybe run into someone smarter than us who knows where to go."

"I'm beat," Joey said.

"I know and I'm sorry. I got turned around somehow. We'll go slow and we'll get out of here. Promise. Then you'll have a nice hot shower and I'll spring for dinner. Pasta, veal, a nice bottle of San Pellegrino."

"Really, Ma, sparkling water? Living large."

MaryAnne ignored her and picked up her pace. Getting her pregnant, hungry daughter lost in the High Peaks was Grammy-winning.

The path was not descending, not climbing. They were on a ridge, circling the mountain but MaryAnne had no idea where on the mountain they were. Or even which mountain. And she noticed the sun wasn't down yet but it was getting darker quickly in the shadow of the trees. They wouldn't even have until sundown to get out of there.

They trudged another 20 minutes and Joey stopped.

"I can't, Ma," Joey said. "I'm done."

"Just as well," MaryAnne said. "We are, I'm afraid, screwed. We better start gathering stuff to make a fire. Maybe someone will see it. If not, we'll at least have light and heat if it gets chilly and it'll keep the bears away."

"Are you fucking kidding me?" Joey said. "Bears? You want to stay here all night? I'm starving."

"I wish I was kidding but I'm not," MaryAnne said. "We have no choice, sweetie. We stumble around in the dark we'll fall off a cliff or break an ankle. If you're too beat to help, just find a spot and park it and I'll build us a fire."

"What you going to do, rub some sticks together? I can't believe this."

"Believe it," MaryAnne said. "It's summer, we'll be fine. We won't die of exposure."

"How you going to light …?"

"You're mother's a doper. I always have …" She reached into her breast pocket and pulled out a red Bic. "Fire."

"Great. We'll keep the bears away by smoking a joint or two. What about food?"

"We got some apples, we'll survive."

"I ate the apples. I was hungry. I'm eating for two."

"Well, I guess, we'll eat for none. We'll make it to morning."

MaryAnne started gathering twigs and dry leaves and a few bigger broken branches and piled them into a pyramid.

"Mama, the girl scout," Joey said. "You get a campfire badge?"

"Shut the fuck up already. You're not helping."

"This whole thing was stupid," Joey said. "Who the hell needs to be climbing mountains when they're pregnant? You got some dope at least?"

"I don't bring dope across the border," MaryAnne said. "Americans would give me life. You can't smoke when you're pregnant anyway."

"That's bullshit. Probably going to have an abortion anyway so it doesn't matter."

"Okay, have a toke after the abortion. I have no idea what dope does to a fetus."

"Maybe the little turkey would enjoy getting off," Joey said.

"If the 'little turkey' enjoys getting off, he or she will tell you when they're old enough to make their own decisions, as ill-informed as they may be. Until then, no dope, no booze, no pills, no powders, no ..."

"I get it, I get it. So thrilled to see you care."

"What does that mean?" MaryAnne said, putting her lighter to the dry leaves under the cross hatch of twigs she had built, watching them smolder and start to burn.

"Nothing," Joey said.

"We're here because I care," MaryAnne said. "I ..."

"Lost in the mountains. I can feel the love."

MaryAnne started to laugh and then Joey chimed in. Tired and frightened, they were soon cackling in harmony.

"You can show me some real love by taking me out in the rapids without a paddle ..."

"I can always take us skydiving ..."

"Without parachutes," Joey said and they giggled some more. The fire was engaged now and MaryAnne was still laughing as she hunted bigger branches and bits of wood. Joey joined in, bent over, grabbing clumps of leaves and sticks and dropping them on the fire.

"We can do a demolition derby next or sign you up for Roller Derby, even better."

"Watch Preggers Roller Derby tonight on Fox," Joey

said. "Don't abort your baby, that's a sin. Crush it for big ratings on Fox Sports."

"That's gross," MaryAnne said.

"Can't help it if you're the one in the family with all the talent."

"Why do you say that?"

"It's true. You sing and write and paint and I might not be into all the shit you do but at least you do it. I just sit around and drink and wonder 'what the hell should I do?'"

"I'm neurotic," MaryAnne said. "Why would you want to do what I do?"

"I wouldn't but you're in love with a good guy. I want to fall in love, real romance, sweet talk, lacy, frilly stuff, candles, soft music, like the movies, like you and Michael. Instead I hook up. Get knocked up."

"Women get pregnant," MaryAnne said.

"Ma, it's not the first time. I've had two abortions. I don't even know how I got pregnant the other times."

MaryAnne was silent.

"Really, I didn't do anything. I was using an IUD, I hate the pill and I don't know how the hell I got pregnant."

"You need a biology lesson? We have nothing better to do. Why didn't you tell me the other times?"

"You didn't have to know," Joey said. "You ever have an abortion?"

MaryAnne started gathering more wood.

"Ma, did you ever have an abortion?"

"No. ... Yes. One. When you were five or six."

"I could've had a brother or a sister?"

"No, you couldn't. I didn't want another kid with your

father. It was not what you'd call a planned pregnancy. I stopped the pill. I wasn't using anything but I wasn't sleeping with your father. I wasn't sleeping with anyone."

"So you were, what? Touched by God?"

MaryAnne went farther into the dark, hunting combustibles.

"How'd you get pregnant, Ma?"

MaryAnne came back into the orange light of the little campfire.

"Your father raped me. He was drunk and he availed himself of the *droit du seigneur* and when I tried to push him away he slapped me hard enough to knock me down and then he threw himself on me as I lay on the floor, kind of dazed. I was wearing a short skirt, back from a show. Your father was over 200 pounds, mostly suet, and I'm sorry but your father was a pig. And that's how I got pregnant and that's why I had an abortion and that's why you don't have a brother or a sister."

She played with the fire.

"And after that he was gone. … It wasn't the only time."

"Ma …" Joey pulled herself up and wrapped her arms around her mother. "I didn't know. I didn't know. I'm sorry."

"Don't worry Jo, it wasn't my idea of a good time but I wasn't gang raped by the Hell's. Your father's idea of sweet talk and foreplay was, 'You ready yet?' You know, I shoulda left him, but I was a coward. A singer with little money and a kid, the business crumbling, so I stayed. I was chicken. I didn't deserve to get raped but with him it was part of the package.

"I smoked a hell of a lot of dope and if someone had coke backstage, what the hell. I did a bit even though I didn't like it. Maybe that's why I did it. I was punishing myself. More self-loathing. It was hell but I pushed it aside and moved on. Saw a therapist for a year. It helped.

"Sweetie, you can't live in the past. Can't dwell on why you got pregnant, how you got pregnant. Right now it's all about what you want for the future. And that's a head full right there.

"Listen to me. You're only 28. You don't have the kid now. You can have it later. You have ten more years easy. If you don't want a baby, you don't have to have a baby. It was an accident. Maybe you're not ready. Maybe at this stage of your life, it's not the right thing to do. You have a choice. You can do whatever you want."

They were surrounded by night, secure in the glow of the fire, MaryAnne wrapped her arms around her daughter, Joey's head was in her lap.

"I don't have a clue what I want," Joey said. "I got 50 years to go, give or take, what the fuck am I supposed to do? Maybe the bible thumpers are right. What right do I have to end the life of a two-legged turkey?"

"Joey, get a grip," Mary Anne said.

"Probably easier back when women just kept pushing out babies, an assembly line of diaper destroyers, spent their lives looking after them and became drunks when the kids left the nest. I'm just getting an early start on the drinking part."

"You were always precocious," her mother said. "I don't have a clue what you want, either. But, isolating yourself and drinking doesn't help. To figure it out you got to get out there, see what's doing. Get a job, go back to school, meet people that don't just want you for sex."

"Yeah, right. I look around, Ma. Good men aren't growing on trees waiting for me. I see people work in banks, I see people work in stores or restaurants, smiling for tips, but all the fun stuff, like music or dance or movies or news or radio, or even working in a fun store or selling cool clothes, you know, everything that might be fun and interesting, is truly insane. Felix says even his whacked out job in that stupid warehouse is going to be taken over by a robot and the robots will soon be writing code for the other robots. He says he's going to try and help unionize the place. Hasn't a clue what he's doing."

"But he's trying. That's cool, Joey. Least he has backbone. When am I going to meet this man?"

"I'm not sure he has the stick with-it-ness, you know. He was going to be an actor and then he wanted to work in Starbucks, become a manager. He doesn't know what he wants."

"But he's working and trying," MaryAnne said. "It's tough out there. Organizing unions, man, not many people have the guts to do that anymore. He can't be all bad."

"Maybe. I guess. I don't know. He's crazy, that's for sure. Bounces around a lot. I've bounced enough. I'm nearly 30, feel nearly 60."

"I feel nearly 60, sweetheart, and you're not even close, believe me."

"What am I going to do, Mom? Even if I wanted to spend my days typing, a screen monkey in one of those great places that give you free donuts and cappuccino, I couldn't, and I don't want to. Maybe I can learn to drive one of those big trucks and spend my life on the highway, town to town …"

"Fourteen, 16 hours a day, hopped up on speed and coffee," MaryAnne said. "Never home."

"I could drive a snowplough. They'll always be snowploughs, at least until they make machines to melt the snow. Or it stops snowing forever. Or maybe a gardener. 'Cept, soon nothing's going to grow. Maybe I could work in a greenhouse."

"Why not?"

MaryAnne kissed Joey on top of her head, smelling the shampoo. Pantene, she had always used Pantene. MaryAnne still remembered what Jo had smelled like as an infant. She squeezed her close, mesmerized by the fire and the feel of her daughter's warm body. They were lost in the woods but MaryAnne thought they had found something.

When Felix came to, the first thing was sound, the thrump thrump of cars bouncing over the expansion joints of the overpass above his head. He didn't know what the hell had happened. He was lying on gravel and broken glass, an empty plastic bottle for window washer fluid and probably something a dog left behind. Right above him was a concrete road—thrump thrump, thrump thrump—and around him was mangled and torn wire fencing. His father's car was gone. The trio that had messed him up was gone.

He sat up, a little lightheaded, his neck sore, his ribs stabbing him every breath. He dug around in his pockets. No money, no phone, no wallet, no watch, no wheels.

Uber screwed, he thought. What'd the guy say? "I hate fucking union scumbags." What the hell. Where did that come from?

He did have a few coins and a single key in his pocket —Joey's. And she lived, if he was where he thought he was, only a few blocks away.

Call the cops, he thought. He'd need the car's registration and plate number and that meant he had to call his father. That'd be fun. He knew Joey was away with her mother, he didn't know when she was coming back. He climbed up, everything aching, but the ribs were a 10. Probably busted. He lifted his shirt and found two red lesions. The asshole had kicked him twice.

"Son of a bitch," he said to no one. He slowly started walking, brushing pebbles and dust and who the hell knew what off his pants and shirt. It was a short walk but it felt like miles. He was maimed. Hard to breathe. He hobbled, slightly bent. Man, where was Gaetan and his pockets of goodies when he needed them?

Joey's lock was old and turned easy. He went to her fridge and knocked back half a carton of orange juice, some of it dribbling down his shirt. Felt good though even swallowing hurt his ribs.

There was no booze in the house and no money in his pockets to buy any. And she had no dope in the house. He checked the medicine chest and found Advil. He took four. Not a whole lot of fun this pregnancy shit and he wasn't even the one pregnant.

He wanted to call but she didn't have a landline and her cell was with her. He didn't know what time it was 'cause he used his phone as a watch. The clock on her Blue Ray was flashing midnight. Clock on the stove was flashing the same. Girl didn't seem hung up on time.

They could keep his dad's car but taking his phone was really crazy. He felt like they had kidnapped his brother. He had met Joey's neighbours once—two with-it women. They would have phones and something to drink. He really needed something to rearrange some brain cells. And something to kill the pain in his side. Maybe he should go to the hospital, sit in the ER for a couple of weeks, eating machine sandwiches, watching people bleed, listening to them groan. Maybe not.

No, next door for a little TLC and then he'd crash here, hopefully properly drugged and drunk. Bonus. Maybe Joey would come home, he'd get laid. More bonus. It was cool the way her breasts were growing, made her sexy as hell.

He laughed. He couldn't breathe without pain but here he was, thinking with his dick.

The women next door were dressed in jean cutoffs and T-shirts. The TV was on. He smelled grass. Their initial skepticism gave way to empathy, a cell phone and a large vodka with cranberry juice. Visions of a threesome danced in his brain. He'd milk it for all he could.

He sat down on their futon, groaning and wincing and Sylvia, God bless her, remembered she had a dozen Percocet from her last visit to the dentist. He washed two down with the vodka and soon was feeling no pain. Magic shit.

He called his father from their porch, scribbled numbers—he had never really told his father what he was using the car for—and the old guy almost had a coronary, seemed more worried about his wheels than the fact his son had been throttled. The old man spent the weekends watching sports, killing six-packs in front of the wide, wide, widescreen. Didn't even need the damn car.

Felix waited for the police at Joey's. That took some explaining. Cops, in creaking leather belts and bullet-proof vests, big guns and cop swagger, were suspicious. What was he doing in someone else's flat when that someone else was not there and he didn't live there? They wanted to take him in, just to be sure, but the neighbours were waiting with him, said he was Joey's boyfriend.

Then the police called an ambulance, wanted him checked out, go to the hospital. Felix figured it might have been crazy to swallow two vodka, two Percocet and inhale a blunt. But the cops saw the bruise on his neck, his right side, now blue, spoke to his father and chilled.

Felix had thought it was just a stolen car beef and they'd leave in five minutes. But the cops were into the assault. This was a big deal. They wanted pictures of his neck and ribs, medics checked him out, flashing lights from the ambulance coming through Joey's window, descriptions of the three fares. He didn't say anything about the guy's opinion on unions. He knew unionized cops in work-to-rule jeans and camo pants and jeans weren't pro-labour, except for themselves.

He was too messed up to think straight and there were way too many people in Joey's place. He just wanted every-one to go home. Maybe he could go next door with the women, play the victim, bathe in sympathy, get really stoned and party. Percocets were magic. He was feeling no pain. A few more couldn't hurt.

MaryAnne was hungry but big deal. It was quite pleasant in front of a fire, cool summer night, her big, grown daughter with child in her lap. There was no moon, only hot, bright red and yellow light from the fire doing its dance.

"If you were younger, would you have a kid with Michael?" Joey said, looking into the flames.

"Yes, I would, I think. Maybe not. I'd have to not play for a year or two. I'd like to think I'd take more time with a kid now than I did when you were born but the business is changing so fast, taking off a couple of years could kill me. The brass ring might still be there, kid, but it might be too late. One song is all it takes. You can dine out on it for a career but ..."

She was embarrassed to tell Joey about Essie, waving the white flag and going back to backup. It was probably just temporary. She'd find a way back to front of stage without having to lose her shirt.

"Your first tooth I was in Saskatoon, feeling guilty. First word, I was in Duncan, on Vancouver Island. I remember even the first night you didn't devastate a diaper, slept right through without an accident—I got a full report—I was in Lake George. We did the Adirondacks, Catskills, Spring Valley, bunch of towns in upper New York, good listening rooms, hotel bars, good money, American dollars, too, serious coin, but I missed a lot."

"I saw you on TV, I remember, when I was little," Joey said. "Can't remember the show. Nanny Carmen let me stay up. I thought it was cool but I think I was pissed I wasn't there. I was probably seven or eight. I thought Mom's doing all this neat stuff and I'm left behind. She doesn't want me with her."

"I didn't, Jo Jo," MaryAnne said, stroking her daughter's hair. "We weren't Franciscans. On the road, last set in those days was maybe 2 a.m. and I was going to bed at five. It was no place for a little girl. Not sure it was a place for a big girl. But it didn't mean I didn't want you with me. It's just the work, the nature of the beast. Easier on the guys, their women sit home and suffer and look after the kids. Boys in the band didn't entertain guilt. They entertained freedom and maybe a woman or two. Wives and children were at home."

"Guys pigs?" Joey said.

"I made it my business not to make it my business," MaryAnne said. "I'm not their mother and I'm not their wife. I front the band, write the songs, have a drink and a smoke after the gig and go back to my room, try to find a movie. I lived for the gigs and lived for getting home to see you. Working mothers are two people. I called the nanny after every show. Guys probably called a dealer or ..." She laughed. "Guys needed to come down after a show and they had their own ways. They were good guys, good musicians but, when they were young, they were, uh ... hormonally challenged."

"You mean they were horny men," Joey said.

"That's what I mean," she said. "But they had boundaries, otherwise I ..."

"Michael seems ... you know, together," Joey said. MaryAnne couldn't stop stroking her daughter's hair.

"Michael's the only man I've known that is self-contained, doesn't need me, just loves me. He's a gift, no strings attached. Maybe he's a patron of the arts. He seems to like who I am. Doesn't try to change me, he's not jealous, he's happy for my minute successes. He told me I was the last two pieces of the puzzle of life, music and love. Made me cry. And I got a song out of it. Makes audiences cry, too."

"You're lucky," Joey said.

"And he cooks, cleans, and has never asked me for a dime. Gotta fight to pay for groceries. Took all my life to find him and if I lost him ..."

"I've seen the look he gives you. He's never going to let you go."

"Joey, you're all grown up, a real woman, but you have a lot to learn about men."

"No kidding," Joey said.

They lay beside each other, shoulders touching, Marsha sipping wine, Michael wanting to chew a painkiller but not wanting to get up and dig into his pants pockets on the floor beside him to harvest one. She didn't need to know the post-coital glow was now a hot knife in his gut.

The sheets were pulled up to his neck. He was self-conscious of the weight he had lost, the shrinking biceps, dwindling pecs. She always looked pretty. The candlelight became her, the rosy glow painting her face and exposed breasts.

He shifted his thoughts to MaryAnne and Joey, having

a bonding experience, or maybe tearing each other's hair out in some restaurant in Lake Placid. Part of him wished he was there. He pushed the thought away. Be here now.

"Do you know what we're doing?" he said.

"Having a lovely evening," she said, sipping wine, looking at him with what he believed was genuine affection. "We're having what's called, I believe, an affair. All the rage in France and Italy. Very cosmopolitan. And it's a lovely affair. Are you about to complicate it?"

"No," he said. "My life is sufficiently complicated. I'm just wondering why you don't have a regular man in your life, live-in or otherwise. Maybe a husband."

"Michael, give me a break," she said, laughing. "Relationships are like drug addictions. Starts out great, getting high, feeling no pain, wow, isn't this the end of the world? Then, you stop feeling high. All you feel is pain. Therapist I spent some time with after my marriage imploded said, 'Marsha, relationships are investments, you put in the work and then you reap the rewards.' But you know what, Michael? I want to invest, I'll call my broker at Nesbitt Burns. I might make four per cent or eight per cent or even 20. Or lose it all. But I won't lose me and I won't be changing pillowcases soaked in tears. Maybe give that line to MaryAnne, make a good lyric. I've had relationships. I've had marriages. Two. Now, all I want is a tender man now and then to make me feel human, dissolve the loneliness for a time. The real question is, what are you doing here? Is your investment not maturing at a sufficient rate?"

Michael stared at the ceiling, traced the web of cracks in the paint. He had never thought about it.

"No, MaryAnne and I, we're doing okay," he said. "Better than okay ... With her I'm me. I think. And sometimes I need to get away from being me. Here, with you, I'm away, comfortably away. On vacation. No expectations."

"Oh, I do have expectations, sir, and you fulfill them very well."

She turned on her side, wine glass in the air, and kissed him on the lips.

"Very well," she said. "Life is short and for one reason or another, we spend so much time and energy trying to escape it. You're not an escape for me. You're part of living. I'd be sorry if this ended, but I wouldn't be changing pillow cases."

"I can tell you I'm not well, it won't turn your life upside down, you won't be ... changing pillow cases. The truth won't hurt you. You're not invested. There's that word again." He laughed. "Maybe that's why I'm here. I don't have to worry about hurting you."

"Not loving someone," she said, "brings a lot of freedom."

The fire hung in, fed bits and pieces of dried wood found stumbling around in the blackness. MaryAnne insisted Joey sit still, she didn't want her falling in the woods, as she sifted through the forest floor by the dwindling light of her phone.

No mattress, no bed of hay, no blankets or pillows. Sleep was illusive. Joey tried to get comfortable with her head on her mother's lap, MaryAnne leaning against a tree, her eyes closed. Her fingers still entranced by her daughter's hair.

"What if we die here?" Joey said. "Starved to death, eaten by bugs and bears, all they'll find is our bones. No baby, no worries. They'd put one of those little white crosses here. 'This is where idiot mother and daughter perished in their narcissistic quest for beautiful bodies. MaryAnne was a great musician. Her daughter was on the verge of being one of the world's greatest ballet dancers.' Then the years of our births and deaths."

"Try to sleep, Jo. We'll get out of here in the morning."

"You know, this is kind of like a vacation, don't have to think about shit. Maybe we can stay lost for a few years."

MaryAnne twisted strands of her daughter's hair around her fingers.

"You know Ubisoft, Ma, they're at the end of Saint Viateur, on Saint Laurent?"

"Sure."

"Every morning, like 2,000 drones, mostly my age, go into that building, work on computer games and shit," Joey said. "They come out at lunch and swarm the street like mosquitoes, looking for cheap eats and daylight 'cause they're zoned-out mushrooms from living hard-wired to computer screens. I have a friend that worked there. Seriously contemplated suicide. They're all pale, dress like they buy their clothes at the Salvation Army 'cause they get paid shit and live off free muffins and Red Bull."

"You're safe, you don't know code and you never were into games," MaryAnne said, watching Jo take pictures of the fire and the shadows that jumped around it. "You're not even an iPhone freak, 'cept maybe for the pictures. I raised you well."

"I'm not safe 'cause I don't know anyone doing anything that I would want to do, other than you."

"Me? Really?"

"You have fun," Joey said. "You play, you travel, you paint, you write. It's cool. But there's nothing out there, MaryAnne. There's nothing I want to do. I'm kind of over the hill to go to med school or be a lawyer. I'd be 40 by the time I graduated. Besides I hate the sight of blood. I have no idea what to do. I'm no better off than Flix, talking about organizing a union. Give me a break. He can barely organize his hair.

"Sonya works for National Public Relations, a PR twinkie. She's cute and wears clothes well and says she has so many files she doesn't know any of them. Says she gets paid to lie about everything, so she's sure she's going to hell. She can get me a job, too, talking bullshit. Says it's mostly about avoiding getting groped. Before that she'd go around to food fairs getting people to sample hemp smoothies. Said the crap made her gag. She flew around the country, trying not to throw up.

"Everyone I know hates their job. Was it like that when you got out of school?"

"No ... I don't know. I didn't go to university I just kept singing after CEGEP. It's all I wanted to do and there was money to be made, even in town. There were clubs that paid; hotels in Old Montreal had music, they paid you decent; even with a band, you could live off it, play three weeks in a row, four, five nights a week. Then we'd go to Quebec City or Toronto, Ottawa, even Trois Rivières;

there were clubs everywhere. Streaming was in no one's vocabulary. Believe it or not, it was normal to go out and listen to music a few times a week, go to two or three clubs a night, maybe go see a film first. We called it living.

"I guess there were straight jobs, before Amazon and Walmart took over the world. I just didn't know anyone that had them."

"I'm scared, Ma. Baby or no baby, I don't know what to do."

"Jo, it'll come, believe me, one day, might be a few years, but one day, you'll find something. You have the financial freedom to sit back and think about your future. Nothing says you have to have a career or your future plotted by 30. Shit, I still don't know what the hell I'm doing and I'm almost 60. Best I can figure, life is all about figuring life out. No rush."

"Dad's fund's not that much money, Mother," Joey said. "I pay the bills, buy food and whatever. I live in a pit. I don't feel I have financial freedom."

"You have more than most, way more than you realize, so I wouldn't complain," MaryAnne said, thinking about the money her daughter blew through and decided it best to leave it lie. She closed her eyes, trying to find a comfortable spot on the tree trunk for her head, her fingers firmly entwined in her daughter's hair.

Michael wasn't feeling well. His legs were shaky. They had gone two rounds but it felt like he had done 10 with Ali. He headed to Mount Royal and flagged a cab. He felt old pulling his frame out of the taxi and climbing his five stairs. Guilt sat on his shoulder, whispered in his ear. He popped a couple of pain pills and something they gave him for nausea, and collapsed on the sofa, tried to relax, did breathing exercises, threw up once, then settled into the sofa again; tried to keep his mind off how he had spent the night or skidding down the gravel roads of fear that beckoned.

He pulled his laptop out from under the sofa. Went to History and resumed looking at treatment options. He finally figured out what alkylating agents were and it seemed they were basically carcinogenic that might or might not destroy cancer cells. Maybe kill you doing it. He read about Altretamine, Busulfan, Carboplatin, Carmustine, Chlorambucil, Cisplatin, Cyclophosphamide, Dacarbazine, but nothing was sinking in. It was a fool's errand. There were men and women in lab coats spending their lives trying to figure out this shit. What was he going to do that they hadn't thought of?

'Course, they weren't dying. They worked for, or were funded by, Big Pharma. Probably not too concerned about him and the other 15 million every year that were told, "I'm afraid the news is not good."

He was just one of maybe—what?—a hundred million living with the disease. Or dying with it. He was about as important as a leaf in the forest. All he had to look forward to was autumn when the leaves were turned into fertilizer.

"Knock it off," he said to the ceiling.

He took another painkiller and dragged himself to the wine cabinet where he had a bottle of Bushmills. Poured himself about four inches.

"Fuck it all," he said, and let about half of it slide down his throat. The impact was instant. He slowly stumbled to the sofa and fell into it, careful not to spill the whisky. He looked at the glass. He knew mixing meds and booze was not smart.

"Fuck it," he said, and knocked it back. The room tilted, his stomach lurched, he threw up on his shirt, the sofa, the carpet. His last thought was, "I'm going to die."

Felix finally went next door to pry some sympathy from the neighbours, show them his bruised side, slowly turning black. Royally messed up on a stew of dope and booze, he was transfixed by both women's legs until they said they were crashing and then he went back to Joey's and lay down on her bed. He liked it here. The room smelled of her perfume. Or maybe soap. It was neat, uncluttered, the sheets fresh. Maybe she spent too much time getting messed up in the livingroom to do much more in her bedroom than sleep and have sex, which was usually limited geographically to the bed, though memories of their first night together told him otherwise. The woman knew how to get loose.

It would sure beat living at his parents. They rarely spoke to him, but then again he spent most of his time in the basement or out. He climbed up for meals. He had to eat. What did they expect? His mother was not a bad cook and it was a hell of a lot cheaper eating her food than all the disappearing bargain spots on St. Laurent or Saint Viateur.

Uber was out of the question, now. His father's insurance would replace his car but somehow he was pretty sure he wouldn't be getting the keys. He could buy his own. They gave car loans to blind people now, but he had friends trapped by loans that kept demanding higher payments, interest rates higher than the department store credit cards, cars that kept needing tow trucks and repairs they couldn't afford. Buying a car had turned into a nightmare. Everywhere he turned, someone was out to screw him.

And now the warehouse. Or fulfillment centre. What the fuck was he going to do about that? All he wanted to do was try and help with the union and they almost killed him. Next time they might do it. Joey said they killed Joe Hill, whoever he was. Nothing made sense.

Here seemed safe. Joey was cool. He figured if she let him, he'd hang here, help her, help with the kid. Until something better came along.

And Joey had money. He wouldn't starve and wouldn't have to put up with his parents. Always on his case. It wasn't like it was fun being broke, living in their house, being fed, having no say in what you ate. Only jobs were in Santa's workshop or IT or selling derivatives and crap for his uncle. Making coffee at Starbucks or wherever. Least he could talk to people making coffees. It was somewhat human.

Nah, it wasn't going to happen. It made his skin crawl. Computers were insane but all day, every day, staring at a screen, probably some other computer counting your keystrokes or chasing a damn robot all day until the light turned green, it wasn't going to happen. Life with Joey and a kid, they'd eat beans and rice but maybe have fun, as long as her daddy kept the money coming. Maybe he could sell chill and pain pills, like Gaetan; maybe the guy would franchise.

He had sent out CVs, no one wrote back. Even bloody McDonald's had him fill an application, never called. Costco never called. Walmart made him want to gag so being ignored by them was cool. He was invisible.

He wanted more Percocet.

MaryAnne dozed off and on, mostly off, trying not to move while ants, mosquitoes and flies feasted on her and Joey slept with her head on her mother's leg until the birds woke them with the dawn. MaryAnne's leg was asleep. Every joint ached. She was itchy as hell. Joey said she was starved.

They dragged themselves up and started walking, serenaded by a forest full of screaming, chattering chickadees and who knew what. They came to a fork, marked by a signpost with trail names that were meaningless to them. So, they took the one that said two miles instead of six miles.

It wasn't fun anymore. Neither spoke. It was damp and chilly. They were hungry. Legs were rubbery. Guilt was gnawing at MaryAnne for nearly killing her daughter and potential grandchild. She still might. Jesus, when would she grow up? They weren't out of the woods yet. Literally. It was supposed to be a bonding experience. She was sure Joey would never talk to her again.

The path had started to ascend, straining their backs and legs, weak and exhausted. They had no idea what time it was but MaryAnne guessed it was around 5:30.

"I'd love bacon, now," Joey said.

"I'd even take a McMuffin whatever," MaryAnne said. "With one of their double espressos. With cheese."

"And bacon, extra bacon, even if it does taste like one of my little leather belts, smoked and salted."

They kept climbing and MaryAnne kept stopping, looking for any indication of how to get down the damn mountain. She was feeling all of her near-60 years, spiced with anger and frustration. The sun was not over the trees, the ground and branches wet with dew. They heard creatures scurry in the underbrush.

Her blood sugar had collapsed. As did her relationship with her daughter.

"Let's take a break, and figure this out," MaryAnne said and sat down on a log. Joey took her lead and parked it beside her.

"I'm sorry, daughter," MaryAnne said. "I screwed up."

"It's okay. At least we'll die together. I'm really hungry."

"I know," MaryAnne said. "It was stupid coming into the woods without real food, water, a compass. Your mother's an idiot."

"We agree on something," Joey said.

They sat, staring at the ground, birds shrieking at their intrusion.

"What's that?" Joey said.

"Birds," MaryAnne said.

"No," she said. "Listen."

There was something coming through the woods and whatever it was wasn't being quiet about it.

MaryAnne got up and started rummaging through the forest floor.

"It could be a bloody bear, need to find a stick, a big stick, club it in the nose," she said.

"Right, good Ma, we'll piss off a grizzly—perfect end to a delightful weekend."

The crashing grew louder and two women in green uniforms appeared, wearing caps and belts with radios and flashlights and leather pouches.

"You ladies lost? Leave this on the windshield of a little car down there?" said one of the women. She held up a piece of yellow legal paper, "Gone hiking," scrawled thick in lipstick.

"It is indeed us," said MaryAnne.

"Thank you, thank you, thank you," Joey said.

"Are you all right?" the woman said. "Do you need medical assistance? Is it only two of you?"

"No, just need bacon and eggs and a shower."

The woman nodded. Another couple of fools from the city. She unhooked her radio and held it to her mouth.

"We found two women," she said. "Everyone's all right. We're coming down."

"I'm buying breakfast," MaryAnne said.

They followed the Rangers down a path to two shiny ATVs, MaryAnne wondering if she was more embarrassed than hungry.

"You went hiking yesterday, no compass, no food or flares?" one of the women in uniform said.

"I was dumb," MaryAnne said.

"I would suggest that would be correct," the Ranger in blond hair said, a ponytail sticking through the back of her cap. "Good thing you left that note on your car. Saw it last night, saw it this morning. Otherwise ..."

"I'm not always stupid," MaryAnne said, visions of bacon, sausages, pancakes and eggs dancing in her head.

"Good thing," the Ranger said as she started the ATV and headed down the mountain.

The smell was vile. Hit her as she opened the door. Michael's head was hanging off the sofa, dried vomit on his face, clothes, the carpet. His eyes were closed. He was dead. She was sure.

"Michael? Michael!" She dropped her bag and guitar, a first, and knelt beside him, gently slapping his face, then trying to get a pulse from his arm but was too anxious to find it. And then he moved and moaned and she wanted to hug him. He was a mess. But he was alive.

"Michael!" she was almost screaming now. She took her phone from her pocket to call 9-1-1 but it was dead. Michael moved, groaned, blinked, tried to sit up. Mary-Anne pushed him back down.

"Michael, what happened? Are you all right? Are you sick? Let me get something to clean you up. Don't move."

"I'm fine. I think. I'm fine."

MaryAnne was running to the bathroom, grabbed a cloth, saturated it, grabbed a roll of paper towels from the kitchen counter, always running, heart pounding. Michael was sitting up, looking lost, embarrassed, pale.

She fell to her knees, started cleaning his face and then his shirt but he gently pushed her arms away.

"MaryAnne, I'm okay. I'm good. I can clean myself. I just got sick, I guess."

He stood, a little wobbly, started toward the bathroom.

"You guess? You guess? You were passed out, could've choked on your own vomit. What's going on?"

She had slept hardly at all and her nerves were frayed and now shocked. Michael had never seemed vulnerable. She had never seen him sick. He was a "keep-on-trucking" guy. She sat on the carpet, eyes wet with fear and exhaustion.

Michael came back, hair combed, in a fresh shirt, face clean, uncharacteristically self-conscious.

"I just got a little nauseous, no big deal," he said, falling back into the sofa.

"Don't bullshit me. What's going on? People keep asking me, 'What's wrong with Michael?' 'Michael's lost weight. Is he okay?'"

"I'm fine. Nothing to worry about."

"Michael, damn it. Talk to me!"

"No big deal, MaryAnne. Chill … Doctor thinks I have a form of Celiac you know, no gluten, but they're not sure. Seems there're all kinds of Celiac. He gave me some stuff to take and I guess I shouldn't have mixed it with booze but I had a drink and …"

"What kind of stuff?"

"Something for intestinal problems and something for pain. Relax."

"What do you mean something for pain?"

"What's with the 100 questions?" he said. He hated being probed, his private life exposed.

"Michael?"

"Painkillers," he said. "I don't know, but they obviously don't mix too well with booze. I was alone, you know, so I said what the hell, might as well have a drink or two and I had forgotten the pills I took ..."

"Pills, as in more than one?"

"Yeah, yeah, I took two, I was hurting ... I had a sandwich and I guess the bread didn't agree with me. I don't know. But I'm fine."

"You have Celiac's? All of a sudden?"

"They're not sure. I still gotta do some tests but that's what they think. It's a weird disease, all kinds of symptoms and it's not that easy to diagnose. I read up on it. Like three per cent of the population has it and lots don't even know. And I guess I'm one."

"What kind of painkillers you on?" MaryAnne said. "I've never heard of painkillers for Celiac's."

"I don't know," he said. "I didn't check the label."

"Bullshit," she said.

"Oxycodone," he said.

"Oh, shit," she said.

"Yeah," he said.

"You must be in a lot of pain," she said.

"Sometimes," he said.

"Why do I think you're not telling me the truth?"

"'Cause most men are lying, sleazy fucks?" he said. "I'm hungry. I seem to have lost my dinner and I slept through breakfast. What're you doing home so early? I thought you were going to spend another night, come home tomorrow."

"Let me make you something," she said.

"I'm fine. I'll take a shower and change clothes and I'll have some soup or something."

"We had an adventure. It was a little hairy but coming home to find you out cold was hairier. Want some eggs?"

"I can make 'em," he said.

"I know you can make 'em. But so can I. So please take it easy and let me make you breakfast, without a whole grain bagel, right? No bread?"

"Right," he said. "What happened? Tell me about your adventure?"

"Sure. Come in the kitchen while I make you a fabulous, gluten-free breakfast," she said. But she was thinking: *He has Celiac's like I have Celiac's. He was eating bread and multi-grain pasta two days ago. What isn't he telling me?*

She couldn't remember too many other people's medicine chests, let alone her own from previous living arrangements, but the cabinet she shared with Michael was always a bit of helter skelter, tubes lying on bottles, blister packs slipped between boxes of whatevers. Last night, after her shower, she opened it, looking for floss, her once-a-month ritual to avoid dental guilt and saw a row of four pill bottles with clean, bright labels. She picked them up. Two were painkillers, Dilaudid and Oxycodone, another was a minor tranquillizer and muscle relaxer. She had taken them a few years back. But she had had a script for 30 half-milligram tablets. Orange. Michael's script was for 100 two-milligram tabs. White. Serious downers. The other she had no idea what it was. But the doctor's name was easy enough to remember. Freedman, Ernest Freedman.

She climbed naked into bed beside Michael. He was reading a James Lee Burke novel, said Burke always brought him back to the good times he had had in New Orleans, before the hurricanes. But she knew he went there when he needed solace, when his insides were ragged or raging.

He made room for her and when she was settled with her iPad, he squeezed in beside her, gave her a smile and a pushed his bare hip against hers and went back to New Orleans.

It took her less than a minute. She googled Dr. Earnest Freedman, and his name popped up with the word oncologist beside it. She froze. Looked at Michael, killed the iPad and climbed out of bed. Michael was used to her late-hour meanderings. Often it was to try something on the guitar or to listen to something. He was probably reading about oyster po' boys.

MaryAnne's heart was a bass drum in her ears, her head was hot, eyes weepy, legs trembling. From the bedroom she made a sharp right and held on to the wall, fighting for some oxygen. Her eyes kept dripping. Leaning against the wall she made it to her room. Went to the dope box and found a joint—elixir for all her ills—and lit it, hands shaking.

Was he going to die? How much was he suffering? Why did he lie to her? What did he have? How much time did he have? What did the doctor tell him? What was going on? How could he just lie there and read? Why didn't he tell her?

She was shivering. She hadn't even put on the silk summer robe Michael had bought her just a few months before. She pulled a blanket around herself and hunched over on her little daybed, joint plugged in her mouth.

Maybe it wasn't so bad. If it wasn't so bad, why didn't he tell her? If it wasn't so bad, why all the pills?

Blanket over her naked shoulders, joint between her

lips, smoke curling up into her eyes, she reached for the Gibson, her oldest, bestest friend.

She went for her sweet spot, F# minor and then to the major 7th and started to sing, the words came without bidding. She sang the saddest lament she ever wrote and recorded not a word, just kept repeating two or three verses that came from she knew not where.

> *Where did all the good times go?*
> *I asked the doctor, he didn't know*
> *And the man upstairs said say a prayer*
> *I never told you life was fair*

He had slept little and was in her black robe when he came down for breakfast. MaryAnne had put out some berries and melon and cereal and toasted bagels.

He poured some cereal then stopped.

"Forgot," he said. "No gluten." His smile was half-hearted.

He spooned strawberry slices and blueberries into his bowl, started eating.

MaryAnne watched.

"Anything you want to tell me, Michael? Anything you keeping from me?"

"Like what? What're you talking about?"

"Just … You still love me, baby?"

"As of 9:20 this morning, you bet. Listen, I'm fine. Just got to deal with the Celiac thing, find the right diet and all shall be well. I'm probably going to lose a few pounds, the doctor said, so don't let your artist's imagination go wild. They'll find out the best treatment for it, seems not all Celiacs are created equal and I'll be fine. Maybe a little pain here and there, from time to time, but I'm a junkyard dog, Sweetie, I can handle it."

She wanted to believe him. She always had. She'd try to now. Even though she knew it was bullshit.

"Maybe we should go away for a bit. A week or two, go back to the mountains. Not get lost this time, just you and me. Someplace not about shopping like Lake Placid but someplace we could get lost, a cabin on a lake somewhere, just swim and screw and sleep and sit in the sun," Mary-Anne said.

"You're back in the studio this week," he said. "Maybe we'll take off on the weekend. Or how about some smoked meat tonight? Harry Barry's playing. We'll eat meat."

He was busy with his berries. The subject was closed.

MaryAnne placed her hand on his. He lay down his spoon, looked straight into her eyes.

"We going to be okay, right, baby?" she said.

"Till the end." But he wasn't looking into her eyes when he said it.

"You're not yelling me the truth, I know it. Goddamn it, I know it," she said, trying not to lose it but failing. "You're lying to me. You need to tell me what's happening with you. Enough of the cool detached, Michael. I need the truth. The real truth. I know Celiac's is bullshit. And your 'everything is going to be all right,' is bullshit. We're a couple, partners, remember? I deserve the truth. Tell me what the fucking doctors are saying."

Michael pushed his chair back from the table.

"Celiac's," he said. "It's Celiac's." He took his plate to the kitchen.

"Relationships are not based on bullshit," she said. "Michael, what you're doing's not fair; it's not right; it's cruel. I don't deserve this."

"You're getting a little dramatic, don't you think?" he said. "Why don't you take it easy?"

"Take it easy? Take it easy? Are you kidding me? You have a pharmacy full of junk upstairs and the doctor is a cancer doctor. Why aren't you telling me the truth?"

"What makes you think anyone knows the truth? I don't know what the truth is. Just let me be." He dropped his plate in the sink and walked out the front door.

She had a few hours until the studio.

She went to her room to commiserate with her best friend, her '56 Gibson, J-50. Lots of men had let her down, but never the Gibson. The varnish had worn off the spruce top, but that only made for a livelier, deeper sound. Pick guard and the mahogany on the back and sides were scratched, testament to its resilience and her determination. Rosewood fingerboard was scarred, notched and gouged. The keys had lost their gloss; pegs were gnarled and chewed. Yeah, the thing looked like she felt. It had a lot of miles in it, but the action was great, sound was warm and, best of all, the guitar never lied.

For Michael, it was one of life's little pleasures, and maybe because it was so simple, it was really so great. Music and spicy, greasy, fatty, food—delicious—and the woman he loved across the table from him, enjoying it too, little slivers of meat juice dripping from the corner of her mouth. He leaned forward and kissed her, inhaling the flavours. MaryAnne didn't need Paris and Le Toqué to be happy. Another reason he loved her.

They were at The Smoked Meat Seat. Took a 40-minute drive but every once in a while it was worth it. Maybe you had to be a true carnivore with a gene or two of Eastern European blood in you, but the grilled karnaztel and club rolls, two inches thick, the way they were designed, were worth the trip. As was the Harry Barry Band that played there Tuesday nights. They were paid shit but a gig was a gig, the audiences were tuned in, the food was good, if you didn't worry about your arteries.

And they always made a point of asking MaryAnne to sing a few songs. She stopped playing restaurants a hundred years ago, but she loved the guys in the band and it was part of the trip of going to the Meat Seat. A lot of meat, a lot of fries or latkes or both, a little MaryAnne. And Michael loved listening to her from only eight feet away.

Always a good night—if their nerves could accommodate the incessant construction jams. The drive was intimate, two of them alone, on their way to a shared experience or on their way back to a home they loved. Nothing wrong with any of it. Until tonight.

She was looking at him now, happily chewing, but not the wild-wolf way he usually attacked a club roll. And he had pushed the bread aside, eating the sandwich with a knife and fork. The band was working behind her but she wanted to watch her lover. The song ended and she applauded with everyone else without thinking. She wasn't sure she had even heard the song.

"Thank you everyone, don't forget to get your cholesterol checked tomorrow, make sure you can keep on coming here to consume smoked, spicy cow," Barry said, with a twinkle in his eye. He liked poking fun at the food when the owner was not around. MaryAnne turned to watch him. She would've been happy to work with him, but he didn't like touring. He gave up on motels and bad restaurants 20 years ago.

"We have a friend and great artist and singer with us tonight, MaryAnne, and I'm going to ask her to come up and sing a few songs. My throat's too old to do a whole gig myself so I'm hoping MaryAnne will take pity on me and let me take a break. MaryAnne?"

She wasn't in the mood, didn't want to play for people. She frowned at Barry but he wasn't buying.

"MaryAnne, I know you don't want to let your smoked meat go cold but we'd really love a tune or two," he said into the microphone. "C'mon. I'd ask her to marry me but she already has a good man who probably makes more than fifty bucks and a sandwich when he works. And she might not want to associate with us riff raff."

MaryAnne smiled and stood and the thirty or so people in the restaurant clapped and she climbed on the tiny stage, slipping between the neck of a bass and the neck of a guitar. Barry kissed her on both cheeks and she kissed Marty the guitar player and said "C'mon Over Baby," and Paul the drummer just kicked it, a simple 12-bar blues she had written for Michael.

When I'm hungry,
Not a drop to drink
There's a screaming in my head
I can't hear myself think
I call you up
and beg you please save me
You laugh and say,
C'mon over baby

"Can you imagine hell as a sweaty, fluorescent-lit warehouse where you never stop chasing stuff, getting down on your knees to pluck shit off a shelf along the floor or climbing a small ladder to grab something off a top shelf. You're a machine that never stops. The orders never end. You're looking at the scanner and looking at the row and bin numbers and trying to avoid getting run over by a cart or another asshole. It's insane. By noon, man, my knees, back, shoulders, everything hurts. It's insane. I barely make my quota now so no way I can make extra money. Everyone's chewing Oxies or smart pills to get through the day. They even have underwear. I had to find six bras, dozens of candy-coloured panties; must've been a hooker."

"Flix, think of it as a big stage and you're the star of the show, giving people what they want," Joey said.

"It's fucking depressing, Jo. Think about people sitting in front of their computer and dropping crap into their online cart, buying and buying and buying. Never leaving home."

"You're a shopping addiction enabler," she said.

"Exactly. I can see the future, half of us buy crap online, never moving, while the other half run up and down aisles loading what you dragged into your online crap cart into a real cart. There won't be any stores or malls or humans to talk to about what you're buying. You'll walk down Parc and the stores will be gone, turned into condos or restaurants we'll never afford."

"What are the other robopeople like?"

"It's kind've like what you said about the drones at Ubisoft," he said. "Almost everyone is our age, give or take a few years. Everyone wears crappy clothes, 'cause, like what's the point? But a few of them, this is their career, man, I'm serious. At lunch, we get 45 minutes, eat, piss and smoke a joint; this guy Gaetan told me it's the only work he's ever done."

"That's why you're riding to the rescue, being the union guy, shove a contract up the Team leader's ass," she said. "You'll be my hero. People'll love you."

"They almost fucking killed me," he said. The pain was fresh, the anger and frustration building. "Fuck the union. I'm not dying for a bunch of brainless assholes who want to spend their days picking and packing. French's 375 ml ketchup—Aisle 302G. I'm having nightmares."

"I thought you'd be my working-class hero," Joey said. "How about we buy a car and take turns driving for Uber?"

She thought it was pretty funny but apparently Felix was not amused.

"You nuts?" Felix screamed and started pacing.

"Chill, Flix, you're cool, you got your parents' place. Keep it smooth."

"It's fucking embarrassing living at my parents'," Felix said. "Billy went back to his parents, with his girlfriend.

Imagine, trying to screw, worrying your parents are listening. Johanna's living with her mother, too. She has a kid and a job but her rent was twelve hundred, paying for daycare, too, phone and cable and Internet, fancy clothes they told her she had to wear, working a shitty office gig. She said she has no money to eat."

"Flix, I got my own shit to worry about," she said. "I gotta make up my mind about the kid. I'm kind've fucked up about it, you know? So take a pill."

"Joey, maybe I'm the dad, maybe I'm not. It doesn't matter. We're happening, you know, and like a kid is permanent, you know? No one ever says when they're 60, I wish I had never had kids. ... I don't think ... Everybody has them, well, not everybody, but that's what life is about. I mean, I see it every day, man; it's not about buying shit. That's way out insane. I think, you know, it's really about having kids. I do. And you'll slow down on the drinking and doping and it'll be cool. I'll help. Really. I'll get an extra job, like Starbucks maybe or Second Cup or wherever, like I said, where you can talk to people. And if they make you manager, you make decent coin. I'll like it, I think, making coffee, chatting everybody up, like being a drug dealer; give 'em their caffeine fix, everybody loves you. I think you should have the kid and we'll live together and, like, I'll be his dad. It'll be great."

"We don't even know each other, how the hell we going to live together?" Joey said. "Maybe you gotta stop chewing those smart pills. They make you stupid."

"C'mon, we'll get to know each other," he said. He sat down beside her, took her hand. "We have a good time together and I think the baby would be great. And even if you start hating me and throw my ass out, you'll still have the kid."

"I need a drink," Joey said. "Listen, Flix, you're sweet. I'm really tired. Getting lost in the mountains was crazy. I want a bath and I want to go to bed so how 'bout I think about this shit and the baby and you, and you do your own thing tonight, sleep at your parents'? I need time."

He really didn't want to face his father, deal with the shit around the car.

"I don't want to go home. I can just hang on the sofa, leave you alone. There's a baseball game on, maybe a movie. I'll be real quiet. And if you need anything, you just gotta call."

"Sure," she said, too tired to argue. Maybe he hated being home, maybe he even really cared for her ... Nah.

"I'll see you tomorrow," she said and left him to fill the bathtub. She poured some lavender-scented oil into it, sat on the toilet contemplating the rushing water, thinking about Felix camped out in the livingroom, MaryAnne, the baby, the mouldy ceramic, a metaphor for her life, she thought. Life was eating her brain.

She fell into the bath and chewed on the future. The next 10 minutes and the next 10 years. Have a baby, have Felix in her kitchen, in her bed, on her sofa, watching baseball. Maybe it would work. Right. Maybe she'd kill herself. Just like good ol' Dad.

The sound of a beer commercial came through the door. Party, party. Gorgeous guys and girls in bathing suits, no doubt, drinking and having a good time and not worrying about fucking abortions and babies. Screw it. She was going to terminate it. Good, cold word that. No Felix in the living room, no baby in the belly.

She threw a faded Mick Jagger T-shirt on, came down to just over her butt, and instead of going left to her bedroom made a right for the kitchen. In the cupboard, under the sink, behind some laundry soap, a bottle of bleach and a lot of dusty crap, was a stash of three bottles of cheap red, screw off tops. Emergency supply.

She took one, slipped it under her shirt, the neck between her breasts, and walked to her bedroom. Felix saw her pass the entrance to the livingroom and waved, smiling. She waved back.

"See ya tomorrow, okay?"

He nodded and she slipped into the room and closed her door, lay down, held the bottle tight on her belly and stared at it. First the bottle, then the belly. Was there anybody home in there?

She saw herself in a bunch of months, lying here, infant in her arms, Felix watching a game in the livingroom, her trying to get the little drooling, burping mess to sleep. She could see Felix saying, "I'm going out for a drink, I'll be home not too late." And maybe he'd come home and maybe he wouldn't. And maybe he'd work and maybe he wouldn't. Either way, how was this little family unit going to survive? Her father's stipend, before taxes, barely covered her. And that's 'cause she never went anywhere, never did anything. What happened if they condoized her place? She could see herself living in a dump in Laval, staring out the window at the tribe of single mothers, people of colour struggling to learn English and French and find decent work, unemployed losers, methheads and junkies and the rest of the army of people who took refuge in the suburbs, driving egg beaters across the bridges to shitty jobs in the city. Or you spent your life on buses and subways. Friends laughed about end-of-month candle-lit dinners of Catelli pasta doused in ketchup.

It was hell out there. She kept hearing on TV about the middle class but where were they? Everybody she knew lived from paycheque to paycheque with ever-growing credit card bills. They were the 'working-their-ass-off class.' And if they kept paying their bills, the banks gave them more and more credit. Andrea had three cards, $18,000 in debt. Jennifer $24,000 on six cards. And she was always game to spring for a good dinner on Mount Royal and pick up the tab.

"Screw 'em," she'd say.

Five years ago, she ran up $30,000 in debt, quit her job, declared bankruptcy, collected employment insurance, moved in with her parents, and when that was all done, she started fresh. New job, new credit cards, new debt. No guilt.

"Banks write off hundreds of millions of loans to big companies all the time," she said over a bottle of fine wine one night, paid for by Mastercard. "Screw 'em. Bastards always upping their fucking fees, have no scruples. Why should I?"

But Joey couldn't do it. Some months just paying for her iPhone was a challenge. So, she'd be here or somewhere, broke, sober, with a crying baby, alone, binging on Netflix and Hulu. She'd even get used to it. Start drinking again 'cause who wouldn't?

No way. She twisted the top of the wine bottle and

took a long swig. She coughed and waited to be wrapped in alcohol's warm, soft blanket. She'd make an appointment tomorrow. Tonight she'd get drunk.

"Sorry kid."

Really drunk.

Felix watched a few innings and had to admit the beer commercials worked. He wanted a beer and one of those women shaking their booty in the endless ads they pried between each half inning. Beer would mean going to the store and asking Joey for money. Not a good idea. But sex, that was always a possibility. Even if Joey was asleep, when loving came to call she could go from zero to 60 in the time it took to pull back the covers.

He gently opened the bedroom door and there she was, sitting up, wide awake, bottle in her hand, smiling.

"I've said, 'fuck it,' Flix. Fuck the baby and fuck me and fuck you," she said. "And I'm having a lovely time getting drunk. I've only had about ..." She held the bottle up. "Half, but I'm going for this and another I have hidden far, far away."

"Joey, what're you doing?"

"I'm definitely drinking," she said. "Definitely. That's what I'm doing. How else am I s'posed to be dealing with this shit? Fuck you."

She guzzled a good bit from the bottle and smiled at him. The smile said, "What're you going to do about it?"

Felix marched toward the bed and made a grab for the bottle. She pulled it away and splashed wine over her far wall.

"Aw, shit, look what you made me do," she said. "Fuck off, Flix, and leave me alone."

"No," he said and jumped on her and grabbed the bottle. She kneed him in the stomach and then kicked him in the thigh, knocking him off the bed. He and the bottle toppled, the bottle bouncing off the wall, Felix off the floor, whacking his head. Wine was dripping down the wall.

"You crazy?" He was screaming at her. "You coulda killed me. And you're killing the baby."

"I don't give a shit and it's not a baby, it's a fetus, and I don't want either of you, so fuck you."

Felix was lying on the floor, holding his head.

"You're acting like an asshole," he said. "You should stick to drugs. Least they don't turn you into a bitch."

"Leave me alone," she said, and tried stomping him from her perch on the side of the bed. He scuttled away on all fours and climbed back on his feet.

"If you don't want to have the baby, that's your business," he said, breathing hard, his head and heart banging. "But it's not something you decide drunk."

"What the fuck do you know? You're just another man, you don't know anything."

"Have the abortion, go ahead, but don't poison the thing."

Even in her drunken haze, she had to admit the asshole made sense. And that made her cry. Large, gasping sobs. Felix climbed on the bed and took her in his arms and she succumbed, let herself be held. Her shirt had climbed up exposing her belly.

Felix looked down, saw her bare flesh and surprised himself. He pulled her shirt down to cover her and held her tight. But then a batch of other wine-drenched neurons sparked and she pushed him away.

"Leave me the fuck alone," she said and pushed him off the bed and onto the floor. "You won't leave so I will."

She pulled on jeans she had left on the floor, grabbed her wallet off the night table, didn't bother with underwear, took her old leather jacket off the Ikea arm chair.

"Get the fuck out of my house," she said and stomped out, heading for Le Meat Bar on St. Laurent. Good music, cold beer, resident coke dealer and lots of horny men. Fuck Felix and fuck the baby or fetus or whatever the hell it was.

MaryAnne showered, got dressed and paused. If the guy was legit, if there was real business on the table, she had to adjust. She did her eyes, some lip liner, discreet, changed her bra to something with a little more structural enhancement, give him a little cleavage. It was still sex, drugs and rock 'n' roll, even if her drug intake was limited to a toke or two. She couldn't look like a grandmother.

She lit a joint, took two puffs, killed it inside the toilet bowl, flushed the black cinders, gargled with mouthwash and slipped out leaving the fan roaring. Checked herself again in the hall mirror.

"What's the matter with you?" she said, "You going GaGa?" and took off her jacket and shirt, covered herself with a well-worn turtle neck sweater, climbed into the jacket again and went to find out Brian's scam.

They sat in two armchairs in front of a small, ornate table in the far corner of the Ritz bar where a waiter, dressed in crisp white shirt and a black vest, materialized almost immediately, tea towel draped over one arm. She felt like she was in a Bogart movie when drinking was still romantic and you could imbibe for hours and never get delusional.

They ordered soft drinks. MaryAnne preferred doing business sober and she considered a paltry two hits on a joint pretty sober.

"I know you're between contracts now," Brian said. "And I think that's a major screwup for someone. I talked it over with my brother quite a bit. We'd like to sign you, if you're willing, of course, for what we can pay. We'd like to finance a record, against future royalties but not concert receipts. We don't do that. We won't do a Stones' budget CD but we'll do it right, studio of your choice, musicians of your choice, if we can afford them, some videos. We're new millennium guys, lots of social media; we put a lot of stuff on YouTube, Instagram, Facebook, SnapChat, Twitter, Tik Tok. Got a woman does only that. We want you to sell, too. And we'd like you to tour Australia, then the U.K and France, Belgium, Germany, Austria. Pent-up demand. COVID. We've already been in touch with promoters, floating the idea. Most are cool. Again, with a band of your choice. And, I'm guessing, within the budget. The contract would be for five years, recording and publishing. But we can negotiate the details."

"What kind of budget for the record? I have some tunes I've already started working on in a cheap studio."

"That's great," he said. "Gives us a head start. If we hire a producer, there's less money for studio and mixing and sidemen. 'Course, that depends on the producer. Most aren't asking the moon and the stars anymore. But if you produce yourself like you like to do, I've been told, we can use the money for the music. We can put up $35,000, maybe $40,000, but, CDs aren't selling, even in Europe that well, so I'd like to record, say, four tracks, release them online, tour a bit, build buzz, record another four tracks, continue touring, put the new tracks online and then replicate the whole package and sell it online and at concerts and wherever. But, recording is not only about recording, as you know. It's great rehearsal and arrangement time, so it's an investment in the tours, too. You get an affordable producer/musical director, it's a good investment."

"What's the catch?" MaryAnne said.

"There's no catch," Brian said. "I think we can both make money. You're great. Your songs are great. We believe in you, MaryAnne. I think in Australia we can fill concert halls, get you into some large outdoor festivals. And my brother's plugged into the show bookers. You'll get a lot of exposure."

"You sound a little too confident."

"I am confident. What I didn't tell you is my brother and I also own 27 radio stations Down Under. And we're already playing you every day on every station. If you sign on the dotted line, you'll be a household name by the time you fly in."

"When do you want to do this?"

"You tell me," he said. "I work on trust."

He reached into his jacket pocket, pulled out an envelope and gave it to her.

Inside was a certified cheque in her name for $10,000 U.S.

"It's yours," he said. "If you come on board, I'll send you the paperwork by email. You can have it in 30 seconds. It's all on my phone."

She gave it back to him.

"I need time to think. It's a little much to compute all of a sudden. Send me the contract and let me talk it over with my partner and I'll call you. That work?" She pulled a business card from the back pocket of her jeans and put it on the table in front of him.

"No worries, MaryAnne. Want you to be comfortable, happy. We'll do right by you. I promise. And," he said, sliding the cheque back to her, "hold on to that. You can always tear it up if you decide now's not the time."

"This guy's talking ... Shit, this is a big deal. It's not all talk. The cheque is real. I think. I'd be thrilled to finish the CD with some real money, tour Australia, the U.K., Europe. You can come. I'd want to do it for months. Grow my name in Europe, Australia, play some bigger venues, maybe add a keyboard, or just piano. It's like now or never, Michael. The big six oh not that far away.

"It'd be cool. Except ... How do I leave my daughter for a year if she's a new mother? She's allergic to work. She'll end up sitting home drinking while the kid's in front of the TV or the tablet. And that's exactly what'll happen if I leave for a year."

"MaryAnne, I can't just takeoff for a few months," Michael said. He needed a deep breath. "I can't go away for ... Mrs. Gross probably won't make it another year." His brain was racing. He could easily get away, everything could wait except his death. Travelling with her, ending up in some hospital in Brisbane or Buenos Aires would really screw up her tour. Staying home, he could keep up a façade of good health by text and email. Best to stay the course, keep lying. "Melanie says she may move in with her guy, has his own place near Jean Talon market. Going to have to find a tenant. Can't leave."

"You could get one of those agencies to look after the property. You could afford it. I gotta grab it now before my parts start heading south. Well, my parts have already begun a glacial descent but with some creative use of miracle undergarments it's not readily apparent, at least not to the audience, but I'm not naive enough to think I sell tickets 'cause I'm a hot broad."

"You are hot, baby."

"Yeah, yeah. I gotta at least be easy on the eyes. It's part of the game. Guys are supposed to want to fuck you and women supposed to want to be you, phallic guitar neck in hand and all that. Just like what actors go through. I don't have many years left. This is the last chance. I've been waiting for this. I've been dreaming of this. Guaranteed money, a label behind me again. It'll be like a fountain of youth. And, I'll have to stop smoking; too many planes and borders and I'm too old to send a roadie out to score for me. So, if the deal is real, I'm there. I have to be. You going to be okay with that? I'd really like you to come, be together. Down Under, Europe."

"Sorry, MaryAnne. Want you to be happy. The world should hear your songs. You're like the bird of Paradise. But, I need to look after things here. And, Joey, too. Good if one of us is here."

The new studio was Cadillac. The board was huge with more tracks and tech magic than she'd ever need and there were stacks of electronics she'd never understand. There was a drum room or tomb and a vocal chamber, as they called it, and a big open space with mics suspended from the ceiling and carpets on a large space for horns and guitars and bass, a small orchestra if you could pay for it. And a couple of sofas, a few armchairs, racks of head-phones, banks of speakers, large and small. MaryAnne was in Shangri-La.

Chester, the engineer, scraggly beard, long dirty hair and the clawed face of a long-time cigarette junkie, could make the room sound like the inside of a car—the preferred listening spot for CD consumers. He'd change the mix for online streaming, where much of the sound was sacrificed to the glory of technology—1,000 songs on your phone.

Eric was fanatical about it all. Wanted every last byte of sound audible in every environment. He talked of highs and lows and mids and booms and tweaks as he puffed on little Cuban cigars, stretched out on one of the sofas. She had worked with Eric before, his reputation was platinum and now she was pissed.

"MaryAnne trust me, woman, it's going to sound great," he said, smiling like he did when he was trying to charm you into something.

"I want the bass," she said. "I don't want to do it just me and the guitar. And I want the drums."

Stephen and her drummer, Jackson, were sitting on

the other sofa, debating whether Dr. Pepper gave you a preferable buzz to Pepsi when you had to play all day and were sick of coffee. Cocaine didn't enter the debate.

"You don't need them," Eric said. "You'll see, just go in and sing it. It'll be great. It's a perfect tune for your voice alone, crystal clear."

"Remember Muscle Shoals, man, bass and drums, bass and drums," MaryAnne said.

They'd cut one tune in the three days she'd been working here, trying to keep her mind on the music and not Michael. He was going to the doctor today. "Just a follow up," he said. She felt the scaffolding supporting her life was threatening to collapse and this was all she had to hang on to.

"This isn't Muscle Shoals and we're not in the '70s, girl," Eric said. "Time to move on. Just keep it simple. Your voice is the instrument. That's where the magic is."

"Goddammit, Eric. It's my fucking record and I want the guys on the tune." She was losing it, raising her voice. "Can I just please get my way? I know you're the world's best producer but can I do my song, this one song, my way, please?"

Eric sat up, adjusted the driving cap he liked to wear to hide his bare pate, crushed out his cigar.

"Guys," he said to Stephen and Jackson. "Can we have a few minutes alone?"

"Eric," Stephen said. "Why not just do it with drums and bass? Let MaryAnne sing it and then just strip us out, see what it sounds like both ways. It's not like her voice is going to bleed into the drum mics. He's in a tomb."

"Okay," he said, taking off his cap, rubbing his hand

over his bare scalp, his habit when he was doing something he'd rather not. "It'll take more time but let's give it a shot. If that's what you want, MaryAnne, it's cool. But Jackson, let's use sticks, no brushes, maybe we add brushes later, yeah?"

"Okay, man."

"Maybe every 4th beat, a rim shot on the down … Bap!" he said, swinging his right arm and snapping it back as if he was slapping a snare. "And don't worry about the volume. I want it to resonate. I'll fix it in here."

MaryAnne locked herself in the vocal booth, Jackson the drum tomb. He had 10 mics around him. Eric wanted every vibration of every skin, cymbal and rim. Jackson had asked him if it was okay to breathe and Eric told him only if he was silent about it.

Eric didn't want a click track and didn't want to lay down a rhythm bed for MaryAnne to sing on top of.

"If we're going to go with bass and drums let's record them together, live, get the emotion," he said. "And do as many takes as we have to. Whatever it takes, so stay cool and relaxed. Get with it. We got time."

MaryAnne had the lyrics on a stand in front of the mic. She heard Stephen's one long note intro, his finger sliding the length of the neck and she started to sing:

> *There'll come a time*
> *It's the grand design*
> *There'll come a time*
> *I won't find the rhyme*
> *There'll come a time*
> *You won't hear me cryin'*

There'll come a time
You won't be mine ...

As the bass went to the resolve, she asked for a little more sweetener in her headphones. Eric gave her a thumbs up and she sang the rest of the song to Michael, one tear sliding down her right cheek. She finished and brushed it away.

Eric clapped.

"You nailed it, MaryAnne. You got it. Fucking perfect."

"Let me hear it, please," she said.

Eric nodded to Chester and he pushed a few faders, pressed a few buttons.

MaryAnne heard the tune, bass and drums in the background, Chester bringing them up a touch when the vocals stopped.

She liked it. Not bad at all. She'd been right.

"Sounds good, guys, thanks. Should we do another take for the fun of it?"

"Listen to it without drums and bass, okay?" Eric said.

"Sure," MaryAnne said.

She heard it again, the bass and drums erased, just her voice and simple guitar, sad and longing and plaintive. Her eyes got moist again.

Stephen had put down his bass and Jackson had left the drum tomb to stare at MaryAnne on the other side of the glass, listening.

"You don't need us, MaryAnne," Stephen said. "It sounds better without us."

"Yeah," Jackson said. "We just get in the way."

"Fucking guys," MaryAnne said to herself. Men. They were right. The song sounded great without them.

MaryAnne nodded to them. Eric smiled, blew her a kiss through the glass.

"I'm going to mix the guitar level and the voice a little different, maybe add a few violins, just a little, then master it, you're going to love it," he said into his talk back. "There's money there, girl. Let's do another take with the guys. You feed off them."

MaryAnne left the studio, headed into the washroom, sat on a toilet and wept.

Michael's nurse plugging him into the Jesus juice was Sondra, wearing one of those smiles and cloying voices reserved for the aged, the demented and the doomed.

"Doctor has a new regimen for you, Mike," she said. He hated being called Mike but he had more important things to irritate him. "Going to plug this magic potion into you for only an hour today. Then I'm going to take some blood. Then I'm going to give you a dozen tablets. You're going to take them four a day for three days, okay? And then you'll see the doctor on Monday. Is that okay? They may make you ill, so you probably should stay home those days. Then I think he's going to take more blood. How's that sound?"

He didn't answer, just sat back, closed his eyes and let her plug him in.

He could live with the treatments and he could live with the dying. When he got right down to it, living was better than dying but since he had no choice, life was, after all, just memories—hadn't Jesse sung it so well?—and he had collected a full, good-sized basket of them. He wasn't going to put up with one of those shrinking, gasping, morphine deaths. You're dead but your body hasn't figured it out yet and your family gathers around you as you gasp for air, your mouth hanging open, your eyes closed. He wasn't going there.

The doctor's message had been clear. Here are the pills you'll need if you've had enough. If it was a done deal, he'd wash the bottle of tabs down with a bottle of Irish when MaryAnne was in the studio or maybe Down Under and he'd make sure he'd said what he had to say and that the paperwork was in order. She'd have it all. Her and Joey, give the kid a break. He'd have to see a lawyer, find out if this undead husband could snack on some of it. Where was the guy? And why? A Nazi hanging out in Paraguay? An importer on the run from the cartel? A snitch hiding from the Mob, leaving a stack of money in the bank for Joey? He'd find out but now he was going to ride it out. He had popped a trank before the treatment, thinking it would be like the other, a few hours of nothing. He was almost floating, flipping through the scrapbook of his former life: parties in crowded flats. A woman in jeans and a leather vest over a denim shirt with whom he shared a bottle of wine as they leaned against a kitchen counter, talking politics and blues guitarists. Maybe 40 years ago? He was with another woman, couldn't remember who, and so he never asked for the woman in the vest's number. Tried to track her down and couldn't. Forgot her name but not her. More than 40 years and he still thought of her.

There were intimate dinners in places that still had checkered tablecloths and Chianti bottles holding candles.

He could remember most of the women he had made love with. Most were pretty good, some were unbelievable, a few not worth remembering. There was Rachel and her Gregorian chant obsession. A hot bath in candlelight, the chants on those massive MacIntosh speakers, the house shaking, the little bit of hash they smoked in a small hand-carved pipe, the hot oil she had by the bed and how she blindfolded him and made him feel things he had never felt before. Or since, when he got down to it. Where was Rachel now? Was she still doing oily candle-lit Gregorian sensory delight? She would be 60 now. If she was alive.

There was Stella, eager to learn about oral sex. They were what? Twenty-five? She succeeded in pleasing him but immediately threw up all over him. Anna liked skiing downhill. He was 20 and didn't mind falling back then. They got stuck on a chairlift for an hour or more at Tremblant. She recited Yeats and then Poe. She had a thing for *The Raven*. Swinging in the wind on this tiny chairlift, under a thick blanket in the cold sunshine, surrounded by the white mountain, green pines and blue, blue sky. Beautiful woman, smart as hell, perfect memory and really, really nuts. First time she climbed on top of him and started reciting Robert Frost as she made love to him, was kind of funny. When she started with Sylvia Plath at 5 a.m. or e.e. cummings, when sexual circumstances dictated a less distracting form of verbal communication, Michael realized this wouldn't work. Last he heard, she had three kids and was living alone.

Hiking through Athens by himself, that was a trip. Snorkeling in the Bahamas. He just jumped on a plane one weekend and flew away and spent much of it under water.

With two days left, someone in a jazz club in Nassau, owned by a couple from Montreal, had offered him cocaine and he said what the hell and spent 48 hours staring out the window of his room, looking at the cruise ships and feeling better than he had a right to, deciding he better not do this again. Maybe he should reconsider that now, all things considered.

Iguazu, in Brazil, the falls by moonlight, the night-clubs, neighbourhood bars, the dancers, the grilled meats, the real tango in Buenos Aires, the French student he danced with—Camille. Shared a room with her for a couple of weeks before she went back to Paris. She came to Montreal two years later with her husband, married a few years before she had met Michael. He was Jean-Pierre, a good guy who knew his way around a keyboard and then an editing machine. Now, a spreadsheet and a balance book. He ran a music video business and, he had told Michael over cognac last year, juggling the flaming swords of shrinking budgets and staff who preferred video games and texting as they sipped their lattés.

Michael had arranged a few gigs for him, introduced him to some people then later helped find work for his video start-up.

Every year or so they would have dinner and drink too much. Camille had disappeared a couple of decades ago. One night, J-P told Michael he had known all along he had spent two weeks with his wife. But, he laughed, he knew a few dozen others had been naked with her behind closed doors during their marriage. Couldn't blame them, he said, laughing. She was a good time.

J-P had a kid in his 20s with Suzanne, now 250 lbs,

thighs the diameter of snare drums. J-P said he never worried about her screwing around on him. His adherence to monogamy was not discussed.

There had been Alison, midnight post-coital summer bike rides to Chinatown for live fried crab almost as good as the lovemaking, a slow pedal back home along empty streets. Montreal was a city that slept, but Chinatown rarely did. She left him for a TV twit and had no idea where she was.

The shows he had rigged and then skipped out on, spending the evening instead at Rockhead's little bar with the hookers waiting by the pay phone and Billy Symonds playing jazz guitar. Sometimes the Mustache, l'Air du Temps, the dive on Ontario St., G Sharp on St. Laurent or The Rainbow downtown, holes in the wall with great blues inside for a few bucks or simply the price of a beer. Those days, those clubs, the whole scene, was gone.

But, filtered through time and the portent of an IV, it had all been good. It had all been great.

The times he had been hollow-eyed and heartbroken didn't seem important anymore. He rationalized that death wasn't hard on the dead. It was the living that suffered. The dead knew nothing.

Joey had a headache that was drilling down to her toes. She saw her reflection in the glass pane embedded in her front door as she dug through every pocket, looking for her key. She looked like hell, amazing the cab had picked her up. Amazing she had money for the cab. Amazing she remembered where she lived. It was 7 a.m. and all she remembered was having a few drinks at Le Meat Bar and some guy buying her shooters and then waking up beside him in a bed in some part of town she didn't recognize. The cloudy memories were embarrassing. It was bad. She was pregnant and she was out like a kid, hooking up with strangers in a bar. She did remember the guy had given her a twenty for a cab and she took it. She couldn't believe it. She took the money though she had a pocketful. She disgusted herself.

Felix was asleep on the couch. Just what she needed. This was no way to live. She tiptoed into her bathroom, locked the door and ran a tub. The light was overwhelming and she opened the medicine chest door to avoid looking at herself in the mirror. She swallowed four Advil. She took off her clothes and stuffed them in the hamper.

Felix pounded on the door.

"You good?"

"Great, great," she said.

"I'm going to grab breakfast at Beauty's and go to work," he said through the door, yelling to be heard over the rush of water.

"Have a good day," she said.

"See you later?" he said.

She didn't answer. Felix was used to her moods. Pregnant women and their hormones, he said to himself, and slipped out, thinking that Beauty's fresh orange juice would be pretty good with some blueberry pancakes. Today was payday.

Joey climbed into the tub and lay back, wondering how difficult it would be to drown herself.

Friday evening, 7 p.m., Stephen and Jackson had a gig that night, and Eric wanted to spend the weekend with his wife and two kids. Everyone was happy with the week's work. Eric had not let her wait to take a shot on final vocals until after all the bed tracks were done. He pushed her to do each song along with the band and then after a number of takes, her voice warm and strong, would ask her to do a few more tracks, the band humming along in her headset. They now had a good start on about five tunes and were celebrating by sipping a bit of Irish, before they went their separate ways.

Brian had flown in from Europe and was listening on headphones, tapping his toes, eyes closed, smiling.

Finally MaryAnne was locked into the music, thoughts of Michael barricaded back in the dark recesses of a brain delightfully marinating in whisky and marijuana. She was having fun, felt secure, looked after, in the right place at a good time. Here, neither daughter nor partner could intrude. Music made her free. Isn't that what the scene was about?

When everyone cleared out, MaryAnne asked Brian if he was staying the weekend, did he want to come home for dinner, spend the night.

'No, I'm good. Going to see some old friends in Pointe Claire and grab a late flight," he said. "Tracks sound great,

MaryAnne. Band is tight, Eric knows what he's doing. I'm looking forward to the final mixes."

"I think another three, four weeks," MaryAnne said.

"I'll talk to him, be good to get it done in a little less time, have more money to tour on."

MaryAnne didn't like talking money, especially not with promoters and managers that held a chunk of her future in their bank account.

Brian was enjoying his whisky. The studio was perfectly silent—a rarity—and MaryAnne's ears were ringing.

"I wanted to talk to you about the tour in the fall," Brian said.

MaryAnne tightened up, the good vibe vaporizing. She finished her glass, poured another inch. She wanted another joint.

"We're having trouble getting a few venues we wanted in France and Belgium," he said. "We don't own radio stations there, can't control the press or publicity like we can in Australia. I think Down Under, reaction and presales, pretty good. Can't say the same for parts of Europe. We can scale down the size of the venues but that doesn't help our bottom line. We're hooked up with a producer down there and he rents the venues and he's not confident he can make money in the more, you know, prestigious rooms."

"What does that mean?" MaryAnne said.

"Not sure," Brian said. "Smaller rooms mean smaller gates, more risk. Travel costs the same regardless of the size of the room, you know, and if you're only playing one night in Paris rather than two or three, well, that means they go up. I don't have to tell you how it works. So, my brother and I, with you, have to look again at Europe and how to best work it. Maybe wait a few months, try and build market there before we invest in a tour, or go right after Australia and just play smaller rooms, come back a year later, and hit the bigger rooms, look on Europe as a long-term investment, you know. Maybe it's worth losing a few dollars now and make it up next year, when you're an international star."

"What're you really thinking?" MaryAnne said. "Be straight."

"We obviously underestimated Europe's infatuation with streaming and YouTube, Instagram, Apple and all that," he said. "We thought the market was still there for middle acts like yours. But it's not as large as we hoped. Could be wrong but it's an expensive mistake if you're losing five, ten thousand a night because you rent a 2,000-seat hall, pay for ads and posters and sell 200 tickets. So, we're thinking instead of 45 shows over two and a half months, 25 shows over six weeks, smaller rooms. You're not Bonnie Raitt, I know you hate that comparison, but we'll turn you into a big ... bigger star. Only concert halls, you'll see. You got the goods. It'll just take a couple of years."

"I don't have a couple of years, Brian. This is the last kick of the can. I'm getting too old. My husband's not real well. I'm not sure what I'll be able to do next year."

"I didn't know that, MaryAnne," he said. "I'm sorry. I hope he gets better. Listen. We're doing our best. We believe in you and if we felt we could make a buck, not even a lot of bucks, just not lose more than we can afford to lose, we'd do it. And we still have a couple of months before we get on the plane. We're doing our best."

"Yeah," she said, wishing she hadn't, wishing she hadn't started drinking. She had a problem with anger and alcohol.

"Trust me," he said. "We make money, you make money and we're all rowing together."

MartyAnne climbed out of the overstuffed armchair, took her keys off the console.

"I gotta get home, see what's what. You sure you're okay for the night, don't need a place to stay or anything?"

"I mean it, MaryAnne, we're doing our best," he said. "I'm good, I'll be in touch. The tracks sound great. We'll get you there, I promise."

"'I won't make promises that I can't keep, I won't make promises that I don't mean,'" MaryAnne said. "Def Leppard tune. Not a great song, but suddenly, don't know why, the lyric popped up. Have a good trip back. To lock the place, just close the door, locks automatically."

"Uh, MaryAnne, one more thing," he said. She held onto the door handle. This was not going to be good.

"We have some good musicians down in Australia, and can easily line up trios in Europe, send them the material, they'd be ready to go with just a few rehearsals."

"What?"

"Well, you know, flying around with a band, and they're great guys, all of them, the airfare alone, that's thousands. If we use local guys, we save a bundle. And they'd be top guys, believe me. And that's more than ten thousand saved on tickets and hotels … meals. Lot of money we can use elsewhere."

"You want me to leave my guys at home? You serious?"

"Well, I want you to think about it, you know?"

"No way. I play with these guys. They're my band. I

love them all and they know the tunes and they know me and to even ask me that is insulting. They're part of the package. I can't believe you're asking that."

"MaryAnne, they're great players, I know, but there are other good musicians. And ..."

"They go or I stay, Brian, this is not negotiable," she said, asking herself, *What am I saying?*

"They're part of the deal. Yeah, there are lots of great players but these are my great players and they've booked off that time to travel with me, lost gigs. They're going, Brian. They're going or we're all sitting home."

She stared at him. He just looked sad and turned his gaze toward the floor and nodded.

"Okay, I understand," he said.

"Bullshit," MaryAnne said and left, wondering which man in her life, Michael or Brian, she was angrier with.

Michael wasn't feeling as good as he'd like but not as bad as he feared. He was driving east on Côte des Neiges when his phone lit up. Mrs. Gross. He pulled over in front of the Rockland apartments, across from the Mont Royal cemetery.

"Mrs. Gross, you have some rugula for me?" Michael said, though his stomach was not calling for sustenance. "Jam or chocolate or cinnamon, all good."

"Is not Mama, is Lebby. You come visit? You come over please? Now for Mama."

"What's wrong, Lebby? Everything all right? Your mother all right?"

"You come over. Mama need to see you. You come now. You come now."

He stopped thinking rugula and threaded his way through traffic. There was construction on Sherbrooke and des Pins for the 37th year; Penfield was backed up as it was every summer and every rush hour year-long. Man, he was starting to think abandoning the city might be a good idea. If he lived long enough.

He could've taken Van Horne east but as you neared Parc, the neighbourhood had been relentlessly condoized and a new campus for the Université du Montréal was where the rail yards had been, creating a gold rush for real estate and a migraine for anyone living there or driving through. Lots of cafés though.

Prices people were paying for a roof and a diet of carbon monoxide and horns, alarms, sirens and parking tickets was insane. But, he thought, what did make sense? The bakery was charging $7 for a loaf of decent bread. Was that what Cohen mean when he sang, "The good guys lost?"

Lebby was waiting for him outside, in his black trousers and jacket and broad-rimmed hat, his shirt white, stained and wrinkled.

"Come, come, Michael, come come."

Lebby led him into the house. It smelled bad. He found himself at the foot of Mrs. Gross's bed. She was dead. And her demise wasn't recent.

"Mama, Michael's here, you should get up and talk to him. Mama," Lebby said. And he shook her arm. "Mama."

"How long she been de ... like that?"

"Two days, I think. Yah, two days."

Michael noticed her head wasn't on a pillow, the

pillow was beside her face, stained with a bit of blood and he knew not what else.

"Lebby, that pillow, with the stain on it, you do anything with that pillow? Put it on your mother's face?"

"Yeah. Mama was coughing bad, very bad. I tried to get her to stop and it worked. She stopped coughing. See?"

"Maybe you should take it and put it in the wash, wash the pillow cover, you know. Can you use the washing machine?"

"Yeah, yeah, Mama show me. I know how."

"Okay. I'll call a doctor. Why'd you call me, Lebby?"

Lebby took the pillow, put it under his arm like a book. He was a big guy, overfed and stooped shouldered. He had trouble looking Michael in the eye. He looked at the floor as he spoke.

"Mama always say, something wrong mit da house, call Michael. I remember that so I call you. Uh ... Thank you for coming. Can I make you coffee? I can make you coffee. Would you like coffee?"

"You have a brother or a sister in the city, Lebby, or aunt or uncle? Family?"

"My aunt Misha, is my mother's sister," he said. "She tells Mama I'm an idiot."

"You have her number somewhere?"

"I have it in my head," he said. "Mama made me remember it."

He gave Michael the number like a drone, area code included.

Michael called the number on his cell phone.

"Lebby, maybe better, give me the pillow case. It's too

dirty to clean, I'll get rid of it. You have another pillow case you can put on?"

Lebby handed him the stained cloth, neatly folded and left.

He introduced himself to the woman who answered the phone, explained as much as he could to a stranger who kept saying, "Oh my God, oh my God ... Oh my poor sister, oh my God." She lived on the other side of Outremont.

"I think I should send Lebby over by taxi, he's agitated and confused," Michael said. "You understand?"

"Why she die?" the woman asked. "I spoke to her a couple of days ago. She had a cough and a cold that's all, a cough and cold."

"I'm going to call 9-1-1 and they'll contact you, I guess. I don't know how she died but I think it's best if Lebby is gone before they get here. I'm sorry for your loss."

"What loss?" the woman said. "I get to figure out what to do with my idiot nephew. My sister is better off. Her life was nothing but hell. Here's my address. Send him. I pay taxi."

"Uh, madame, maybe Lebby's been living with you this week? He came for a visit, gave your sister a break, she was sick, you figured you'd help her and have her son stay with you?"

"What? Why would ...?

"She needed a rest. Was sick, you helped her out, you understand? I'm going to pack a bag for him and put him in a cab. He came to you last week, whatever, Tuesday or Wednesday, you don't remember. He stayed in your spare room."

"My spare room is full of ..."

"Clean it and put Lebby in there. He's been there since Tuesday. Remember? Tuesday."

"But he wasn't ... Oh, I ... Just send me some more clothes. He didn't know he'd be spending more than a week here. Send clothes and shoes. He's been here since Tuesday. God help me for a change."

"So when 9-1-1 came, I told them I always visit once a week to eat some rugula and to check on her," he told MaryAnne. "I told them her son was staying with his aunt, her sister, I think. She was over 90, I don't think anyone's going to send homicide detectives."

She was stoned, pale. Michael looked like he needed to lie down, the tour news was still gnawing at her. The great week in the studio had turned to shit. She was worried her relationship was going into the dumper or maybe Michael was headed to the grave. Life was getting in the way. She just wanted to lock herself in the studio and then hit the road and know everyone was all right and that wasn't going to happen. Of course, Brian had just shortened the road, eroding her patience and stamina in the process. Was she a shallow, selfish bitch? Good bet.

"Michael, I'm sorry, you liked the lady," she said. She didn't know if he looked like hell from seeing the doctor or seeing the corpse or both. "How did it go at the doctor's?"

"He gave me these new antibiotics, see if it's an infection rather than a form of Celiac's. Just a five-day protocol. Then I see him next week. Nothing to worry about."

He wasn't looking at her when he told her. She knew he was lying. He had never lied which made her all the more sad and frustrated and angry.

"Why won't you tell me the truth?" she said.

"I am," he said, looking her in the eye. "There's nothing to worry about. It's going to be fine."

MaryAnne popped her cheek out with her tongue, a nervous tick she resorted to when she was scrambling for something to say while her mind went tearing off to places she didn't want it to go.

"You think her son smothered her? *Of Mice and Men*?"

"Well, he wasn't trying to make love to her or touch her hair. Maybe it wasn't about stopping her coughing, like I thought, maybe he just had enough. I'm pretty sure he killed her but what was going through his mind, murder, mercy killing or just stopping her cough ..." He shrugged. "What am I supposed to do? The medics didn't seem to give a shit. How many old people you think they cart out a day? How much energy is a doctor going to expend on a dead woman that age? And if he decided she was smothered, what then? If cops find out he was not staying at his aunt's until I sent him there, they'll put him through the ringer. He wouldn't have any idea what was going on and he'd end up in some institution for the criminally insane instead of an institution for the demented. A better warehouse ... Shit, I don't know."

"How many do the same thing to their parents when they can't change their diapers or stand their weirdness anymore?" MaryAnne said. "I can see Joey dropping me off an overpass then emptying our wine rack."

"Dear old dad can't be left alone," Michael said. "You

can't afford the assisted living home, can't afford a nurse …
I imagine quite a few. When I get there, help me out, you
can smother me or just shoot me."

"Tough old lady in a tougher world. She beat everything but her own son," MaryAnne said. "Not fair."

"What the hell's fair?" Michael said. "There's nothing
fair anywhere."

"Fair is you telling me what's going on and don't give
me Celiac Tale No. 5. You're seeing an oncologist. They
don't give a shit about how much gluten you eat. I deserve
the truth. Now!"

"There is no 'truth' MaryAnne. Remember alternative
facts? Nobody knows anything. I feel not great now. Later
I'll feel better. Takes time. Don't know how long. Need a
little Zen. I'll be better. Don't worry about it."

"You're full of shit," she said, the volume rising. "I am
your partner and I deserve the truth. Maybe not about
everything … maybe I don't need to know about the nights
you play pool. Men like pool halls. But I need to know if
you're sick."

"MaryAnne, I don't even know anyone that's healthy.
We all got our things. My stomach's acting up, I'm taking
crap for it and …"

"Give me a break, Michael." She wanted to roll a joint
but she wanted to be thinking straight.

"I can't do this," she said. "I love you. I am not going to
get on a plane knowing you're sick and not knowing how
sick. I'm not getting on a plane leaving my daughter pregnant and confused and I'm not getting on a plane to do a
shitty tour of some dumps and fleabags in Europe. I'm staying home. I'm growing up. I'm going to look after you and

after Joey and maybe, even, myself. You won't tell me how sick you are, well, fuck you, but I'm not leaving you. Not leaving my daughter. I'm going to call Essie and do that gig. Just do a little backup, never more than a few hours from here by plane. Quit anytime, no rehearsals, real money. I give up."

"Don't do that," Michael said. "You want Europe."

"Not anymore and don't tell me what to do," she said, turning her back to him and setting out to find sanctuary, where and from what she wasn't sure. "You don't have the right."

"MaryAnne," Michael said but she didn't hear him. She was gone. He minded but he didn't. He needed to lie down.

MaryAnne found refuge in a basement bar on Parc, a hole with a couple of billiard tables and some VLTs, lots of traffic to the bathroom. Someone was selling something but she didn't care. No one would find her here and when she had enough of the mirror she was staring into and the Bushmill's she was sipping she'd flag a cab and go home.

How did she fall in love with him? It was that winter night. They'd been seeing each other six or seven weeks. He said he was taking her on a trip, dress warm, his eyes and face sparkling with playfulness. She asked no questions, happy to be along for the ride wherever. She liked being with him.

Knowing him, she thought live fried crabs at the Sun Sun, which tasted far better than they sounded, but he drove straight up the 15, lit by an endless line of amber lamplights, to the Laurentians.

It was cold and the full moon was interrupted by clouds pushed across it by a brisk wind. In less than an hour he rolled his pickup, the cab warm and cozy, down a fresh plowed road off a rolling two lane, 20 kilometres from the autoroute.

"Button up and let's go," he said, excited as a kid. "This only happens maybe once a year. If you're lucky."

He grabbed a flashlight and took her hand and led her down a path. They crashed through a thin crust, the snow to their knees, behind the light of Michael's little LED. All at once the Earth went from deep dark to glowing white as day, and there was empty bright white as far as she could see. The clouds had moved on, exposing a full moon, an exorbitant Kleig light tacked to the sky, shining onto end-less open space. He walked her across a frozen lake and said nothing. Another cloud buried the moon and he took her hand and they walked in darkness across the ice blown free of snow by the winds. The moon reappeared and dis-appeared and the lake glowed white off and on and off and on in rhythm to the moving clouds, an enormous white light flashing in time to the beating of her heart and she fell in love right then forever, she was sure, when everything was glossy white in the moonlight. The man turned night to day. And when the lake turned black and the night dark again, he put his arms around her and MaryAnne knew she could stay there.

She took her phone out of her jacket pocket and scrolled through numbers until she found what she needed and pressed "call."

It range three times, went to message. She listened, waited for the prompt as she watched a couple coming from the washroom, laughing. She was adjusting her skirt with one hand, trying to button her blouse with the other. At the beep, she said, "Hey Essie, how's it going? I'm in, girl. Send me text, where and when; send plane tickets. Love you. See you soon. It'll be fun."

Felix was showing Joey iMovie on his laptop. They didn't mention her night on the town. They were having fun. He had downloaded some of the videos she had shot of people zooming past her door and were splicing them together.

Joey was mesmerized. She had meant to go to the clinic today but the hangover from yesterday demanded a little hair of the dog so she had a half glass of wine that cut through the haze, lifted her spirits and made her nauseous. But piecing together bits and bytes of video on Felix's computer transfixed her.

He had fetched the machine and a pile of clothes from his parents' house and seemed to have moved in. Joey wasn't quite sure what was going on. Life was moving too fast for her and losing herself in the computer was a perfect way to spend the day and forget about life. Better than going to the abortion clinic. Or anywhere.

"I'm going to hit the cafés today, see if I can find a part-time job," he said. "I can say I am not truly fulfilled at the fucking fulfillment centre, 'specially since they beat the shit out of me." He left her in front of the machine, losing herself in a video she had shot of the guy at the Lebanese restaurant up the street carving crispy shish taouk off the red-hot rotisserie. He was smiling as he sliced, liked his work. The only people she had seen smiling on the job, she thought, were obsequious waiters sucking up for tips and some retailers, desperate for sales. She had a closeup of him sharpening his knife as nonchalantly as she combed her hair. And a woman, maybe 20, eating a shawarma, garlic sauce sliding down her chin, laughing, wiping it off with her finger and putting it in her boyfriend's mouth. Their good times made her jealous. She wasn't much for hanging with people but shooting them and rearranging their lives fascinated her. Joey, a virtual God.

MaryAnne slipped into the house, understanding for the first time in a while why people drowned their sorrows. Booze was a serious drug.

She had stopped at four watered down whiskies and didn't have to hold onto the wall but she was mellow. Almost happy to see Michael sitting on the sofa, staring at nothing.

"You all right?" he said.

"I'm fucking fine," she said, opting for belligerence.

"Maybe sit down, I want to talk to you," he said.

So she did.

"I have cancer and it'll probably kill me but no one knows when. Three to five years, maybe. Maybe more, maybe less." He shrugged. There. He told her.

MaryAnne had no words. She could only stare at him. In shock, But not really. She knew. She knew.

"What kind?" It was all she could muster.

"I can't even pronounce it. I'm on a new treatment.

The doctor's positive. 'Course, it's not his life but he's pretty sure I'll get to five, maybe more, new treatments and stuff."

"Michael ..." She got up and fell on him, pressing his head to her chest, stroking his hair. "Don't leave me. Don't leave me, Michael."

"I won't ... I want you to leave me," he said. "I want you to go. Tour Europe. Be happy. I'm not dead yet and I don't need you here staring at me waiting to see if I'll keel over or checking my face for every pain. I'm fine and I want you to go and enjoy yourself."

"Don't be stupid," she said. "I'm going to be here, like I said, for you and for my daughter."

"No. I don't want you here and Joey is fine. I'll be here when you leave and I'll be here when you get back. And you will play Paris and Belgium and Marseilles and Buenos Aires and Montevideo and who knows where but you need to go."

"I'm not going."

"Yeah, you are," he said, stroking her back. "I'm going to die. This is my dying wish. I want you to tour and play and kick ass and then come back to me. I don't want you here until you've done that tour. I want you to do it for me if you won't do it for you."

"Stop it."

"No. The cool thing about this dying wish is I can enjoy it. I'll still be alive when you come back. I'm not going to be pushing daisies for a while so I can share your success."

"I don't give a shit about my success. Who cares? I can't believe this."

"We both care. You can't stop living just because I

might. Death is part of the trip. And your trip is to perform and write and tour. You have no choice."

"Don't tell me what I'm going to do or how to handle this. You can't guilt me out with this dying wish bullshit!"

"You think you're going to roll up in a ball and cry and smoke a kilo of weed and feel sorry for yourself. Fuck that. Go out and play. We all die and there's nothing you can do about it. I'll keep an eye on Joey."

"You're a bastard. Not only are you going to die on me but you're trying to tell me how to mourn."

"Mourn between shows," Michael said. "Besides, I'm not dead yet. Don't be in such a rush to shuffle me off this mortal coil. Just pack your bags and get the hell out of here."

"Do you mind if I stay until the tour starts at least? Or do I have to leave now? Goddamn it. What 're the doctors saying?"

She was telling herself she was not going to cry. She could feel the tears threatening but she took a deep breath and refused to wipe the corners of her eyes. She was going to be tougher than him.

"Doctor, singular," he said. "I told you. Three to five. Maybe more. Maybe not. Listen, MaryAnne. This is a cross-country train ride and like VIA rail you never know when you'll get to the end of the line or even if. I can get my ticket punched tomorrow or I can live until I'm 80. So fuck it and keep on keeping on. That enough clichés and stock phrases for you? I never could be a songwriter."

"The tour's a bust. Joey needs me even if you don't. I can fly down and play with Essie and Slate for a week or two and come back and not have to worry about asses in the seats, doing radio and TV and whatever print they have, counting nickels and dimes so Brian doesn't lose his shirt. I'm too old for that shit. I'm done."

Michael squeezed her tight.

"You're not too old, you're not done and you're going and you're going to have a great time and do what you do best. I don't need you hovering around when we're awake, listening to me breathe when I'm asleep, waiting for me to stop breathing. Besides, it's my dying wish. You owe me that."

He slid his hand under her shirt. But MaryAnne pulled back and stood up.

"No, I'm not making love. I can't."

"You wanna eat?"

"Shit, you ever think of anything else?"

"Sex," he said. "Remember Jesse Winchester's first record, 'If we're skating on thin ice, might as well dance?'"

He lifted himself from the chair, slowly, and he put his arms around her as she wrapped her arms around his neck, and pressed him tight to her breasts, burying her face in his chest, and they waltzed without music around the dining room table. MaryAnne bit her lip to stop the tears and kept on dancing. She wanted this moment to last forever and knew, of course, it wouldn't.

Michael took an emergency baguette from the freezer, popped it in a hot oven, sliced it open when it was warm and filled it with smoked turkey, sliced sweet onion, sliced hard-boiled egg, pickles, dry salami, Swiss cheese, Dijon and mayonnaise. They each had half at their table for two on the clay-brick patio under an elm.

"You think Brian, who just killed half my tour, jailer or prisoner?" MaryAnne asked. "Great sandwich. Thanks."

"Don't know," Michael said. "Maybe both. Maybe he's a slave to the banks, living on borrowed money or investors that just want a litre of your blood ... Or maybe he just wants a new BMW and likes flying first class and drinking Champagne for breakfast. Don't know the man."

"What you going to do with the old lady's flat?"

"I guess I have some work to do. It's a big one. Three bedrooms. I can rent it for four times what they were paying. Just have to paint it and do some renos, new sink, shower."

"That's a ton of work."

"Give me something to do while you're being a superstar. Maybe use the extra rent to fly us somewhere when you get back, have a vacation from life. Find a hut on a beach in Thailand or somewhere, first-class airfare, splurge."

If he had the strength, he thought. Maybe he'd hire Tony to help with the painting and reno work. No way he felt like tackling an entire apartment himself.

"Why don't you hire that guy Tony to help you?" MaryAnne said.

"Maybe," Michael said. "But I can do it myself. Always have."

He wanted to lie down.

"What's with your husband?"

"Huh?"

"Your husband, the guy you married, the guy who died but didn't? Where's he at?"

"What are you talking about?"

"I found a draft of a letter you wrote to him, when I

was skulking around your dressing room, trying to clean it up and I ..."

"I didn't thank you for the custodial care but why do you clean my room? I'm not a teenager."

Michael looked at her, his head lowered, his eyes saying, "Get real."

"Okay, I am a teenager. My former husband is dead. Mercifully."

"You wrote him believing the force of your displeasure would raise him from the dead?"

"I was just venting," she said. "It was a bad day, that letter must've been buried in a time capsule."

"That's a unique way to describe the pile of dirty clothes, old roaches and stained and broken junk you were curating. It was beginning to compost. I don't believe you."

"Michael, you've never said that to me before. You're fucking full of surprises today."

"And you're deflecting. What about your husband?"

"He's not really my husband. We never got married. Somehow boyfriend didn't quite cut it."

"And ..."

"Jesus. I shipped him off. Okay? Joey was five or six and was fast asleep and he came home incredibly influenced. Drunk and stoned and a mess and he tried to, you know, rape me or whatever you want to call it."

"Rape works."

"Yeah, well, not that time. I hit him with a vase I had on my makeup table. Flowers from a gig. Knocked him cold. Knocked out two teeth. I packed his travel bag, called an airport limo. Woke him up, gave him a new credit card with a $5,000 limit, his suitcase and pushed him into the car, told the driver to take him to Dorval. Never had to send the letter you saw. He called and I told him if he came within a hundred yards of Joey or me, I would charge him with assault."

"If you had to give him a credit card ..."

"He was always sponging off me. In those days I was making money. A lot of studio work. Paid well."

"So, how does he afford to pay Joey?"

MaryAnne started shuffling the salt and pepper mills, moving napkins around, avoiding his eyes. She cupped a hand and wiped crumbs off the table into her other hand and walked over to the garbage next to the counter.

"It's my money. I deposit it."

Michael was silent.

"And it's running low," she said. "I made some good money a few years, invested it, but I'm giving her more than the investment generates. I never thought the music would dry up. Who saw the future? And I thought Joey would get a job, a career, make her own bed. I never thought the money would actually stop her from doing that. I thought it would make her self-sufficient. It did the opposite. She's addicted to, among other things, my money. I thought it was the least I could do, throwing out her father, the useless asshole, that money would compensate. I was stupid."

"What did you tell Joey?"

"The truth. That he went away and ... well, almost the truth. A couple of weeks later I told her he had died in a car accident in Italy while he was working. She was used to him not being around and she didn't take it too hard. It was what it was. Kids are Zen."

"You ever speak to him, hear from him?" Michael said.

"He's dead. He did get killed in a car accident. I have magical powers, so don't mess with me ... About eight or nine years ago. Left around a hundred twenty thousand to me. I put it in her trust fund."

"Maybe he wasn't a complete asshole," Michael said.

"No, he was," she said. "Leaving me a bit of money to assuage his guilt didn't make him less of an asshole. What I read, the bigger the asshole, the larger the charitable foundation they start."

Michael went to sleep. He was looking pale and stooped, as if his muscles were exhausted. MaryAnne was left with her grief and memories. She knew Michael had attacked every challenge not only with determination but with gusto. He was a "bring it on" kind of guy, the fight burning in his eyes. She didn't see that tonight. She knew being bested by an invisible demon, a problem he couldn't solve, would hurt him more than the physical pain.

MaryAnne smoked, scratched on her sketch pad. Not too long ago, he'd wake up, suggest, "Let's go get a bite in Chinatown."

She checked on him and saw he was curled up and sleeping contentedly. There'd be no late-night sorties.

She withdrew to her office, painted, paced, worried and was a wreck. She couldn't concentrate. Picked up the guitar and put it down a half-dozen times between tokes, sad, alone and helpless.

She picked up the guitar again, slid the capo to the fourth fret and started playing in E. Then the words came.

She turned on her iPad and recorded it and the verses and melody were a lock in seven or eight minutes. There were tears in the corners of her eyes when she called Eric.

"MaryAnne, it's three in the morning, man ..."

"Eric, now. Please. It has to be now or I'll lose it. I'll call Stephen. Can you get Chester?"

"Chester never leaves the studio," Eric said, voice still gravelly. "MaryAnne, you sure we have to do this now, why can't ..."

"Eric, I'm in the groove now; there's stuff in my brain I can't record. We got to do it now. I'm getting in my car and I'll meet you there in 10 minutes."

She killed that and called Stephen. He was always awake until four or five.

"I'm going to pick you up in 10, bring the standup."

"In the toy car?" he said, as if she always called a couple of hours before dawn.

"In the Miata, outside in ten."

She dropped the Gibson acoustic into its case, pulled a jacket over her pajamas, said the hell with a bra—she'd keep her jacket on—and danced down the stairs and out the door.

There was plenty of space to park in front of the studio and they pulled up as Eric was climbing out of his Caravan, cigar plugged between his lips, cap askew, keys in his hand.

MaryAnne kissed him on both cheeks.

"Sorry to wake you, Eric, but I gotta ..."

"Okay, Miss MaryAnne, it'll be great." He reached into his car and pulled out a cardboard tray with five large Starbucks cups. "Dark roast. With sugar. We're going to dance, Sister."

They paraded into the studio, turned on the lights and there was Chester, naked, on the floor of the control room, between the legs of a girl who looked barely 16.

"Whoa, shit, man!" Chester said as the couple scrambled for cover.

"Chester, we're going to record a tune, just bass, acoustic guitar and vox, as quick as we can," Eric said, as if the guy was behind the board instead of climbing into his pants. The young woman grabbed her clothes and disappeared into a washroom in the hallway.

"You coulda fucking called first," Chester said.

"Didn't want to interrupt the good times too early, man. Had your best interests at heart. How old is that girl?"

"I didn't ask," Chester said as he disappeared into the vocal chamber, pushing his broom-stick arms through the sleeves of a striped and faded shirt, then assembling mics and wires. His chest was white and concave. MaryAnne thought lifting wires seemed to be all the exercise the guy got. That and intercourse with teenage girls. MaryAnne thought, *Call the cops or do the tune?* She walked toward the mics.

He set up the mic and spit shield to her level as Eric hunkered down behind the console and waited for the bass to be miked.

MaryAnn adjusted the mic as Chester hung another over her head and then fiddled with two mics for her guitar, one for the fret board, another for the sound hole. The technology was making her impatient. She was hungry to sing.

"Sing it through one time, MA," Eric said, swallowing coffee. She checked her tuning, strummed a chord. Eric nodded as Chester sullenly adjusted the controls.

"Okay, here goes. It's in D sharp, Stephen, or D to you. Then we'll try it in E."

She leaned in to the mic, adjusted her own headphones and closed her eyes. The words were still fresh.

> Yes, the moon slipped away
> But we stayed and stayed
> And I didn't need a moon
> The night I fell in love with you
> The clouds they sailed
> On winds that failed
> To blow away the truth
> The night I couldn't help
> But fall in love with you
> No matter how battered
> No matter how bruised
> There was everything to win
> And nothing to lose, nothing to chose
> The night I fell, the bright night,
> I fell in love with you

She sang it through, letting Stephen see her hands move along the guitar neck. As always he picked it up in a flash and his big feet started to tap, and body started to swing. She sang it again and again and again, changing keys, hitting different words here and there, experimenting with the tempo, knowing if there wasn't one perfect performance the magic of digital would piece one together. Took an hour and a half. By the last take, MaryAnne sang "night" for six beats, added another guitar track and a harmony;

Stephen had found the bass groove he had been searching for; Eric went in and played a piano part, the bass keys, with a touch of sustain, substituting for drums and it was a lock.

When the last note faded away to frozen silence, she said, "What do you think, Eric?"

"Money, Miss MaryAnne, money. I'm going to stay and mix and master and send you an MP3. Email it to that cat promoting your tour. Worth missing a few hours sleep. Killer tune."

Stephen kissed her on the cheek and gave her a big-love hug. She dropped him as the sun was climbing over the streets of duplexes and triplexes, reminding her of the good old days when they played till 3 a.m., ate and drank until five and found their way home at dawn. She steered the Miata through empty streets, parked it in the place she had left a few hours before and climbed into bed beside Michael, lying there a long time listening to him breathe and finally fell asleep as he was stirring.

He was expecting a day like any other. He woke, MaryAnne asleep on her side, breathing lightly, comfortably naked, her rear pushed against his hips. But it wasn't a day like any other. His legs didn't ache, his head was not fogged in, he wanted to get out of bed. Anxious to get out of bed. So, he did, letting MaryAnne sleep. He walked downstairs in his underwear and bare feet, and rummaged through the fridge. He was hungry. There was strawberries and cereals, cold pork roast, fresh eggs from a farmer he had met rigging a country music festival out in Lachute. Every time the guy came to the big, bad city, he dropped off a few dozen.

He cut the strawberries, added blackberries sprinkled with sugar, threw in some blueberries, sprinkled some ancient grain flakes on them.

Sliced four thin slices of pork, set them on his hot cast-iron pan and when they sizzled and crisped, he flipped them, topped them with a raw egg, covered the pan and lowered the heat. Lifted the lid, poured in half a glass of water to steam the eggs and keep the pork juicy.

Popped the thick grain toast, spread some Dijon mayonnaise and slid the pork with egg on top of each half of the toast.

Dropped a touch of Mexican salsa over each, lay the plates on a tray with two double espressos and brought them upstairs. The stairs. They didn't weigh him down. He felt decent. The first time in a long time. Maybe they should go away for the weekend. Someplace where they could listen to the basso profundo of the bullfrogs, the soprano of the loons, listen to a lake or river ripple and splash. Get the hell out of here.

The last time they had rented a place on a lake in the Laurentians, a little cabin on the water, the frogs sounding like mules, MaryAnne had climbed into bed, delightfully naked and said, "Enough listening to the bullfrogs, baby. We're going to make our own music." And they did.

She was out cold. He didn't know when she had come to bed but she was a trooper. He woke her, rubbing her bare shoulder until her eyes popped open and she said, "Coffee."

She sat up, knocked back the espresso and devoured the plate.

"We cut a great track last night while you slept, darlin'. Me and the boys, and I only got home a couple of hours ago but it's a great song and this is a great breakfast or early dinner, I'm not sure, and you're a sweetheart. If you die on me I'll kill you. Thanks for this but I really need to sleep."

She nestled under the covers. Before closing her eyes, she said, "Thanks for the tune, sweetheart."

She was gone pretty fast. He left her to her dreams and the song that kept playing in her head.

Michael bought a few gallons of white paint, dragged out brushes, rollers, poles and drop cloths and headed to what had been Mrs. Gross's last address. But, he detoured and knocked on Joey's door.

Joey was still lost in her video enterprise. She seemed glad to see him. She had a little colour in her face and was wearing pajamas with small tigers on them. She kissed him on both cheeks.

"Wanna see something cool?" she said. Michael followed her to her coffee table where a computer sat bracketed by dirty glasses, an ashtray with a few roaches in it and an empty wine bottle. She saw him looking at it.

"Mostly Flix," she said. "Wanna look at this?"

She showed him a collage of bits of video she had taken at the restaurant. It lasted 29 seconds.

"I was wondering," she said. "You think I should put this piece here, with the guy sharpening his knife at the beginning, like the start of the process or at the end, like this?"

She began manipulating the mouse too fast for him to track what she was doing but the snippet of the happy chef and his carving knife ended up at the end and she ran the clip again.

"I think at the end," Michael said. "Makes it feel like he's keeping on, like there's a future there."

"Yeah, yeah, you're right. Kind of optimistic. The happy chef sharpens for another day. Great machine, this. A Mac something or other. It's Felix's."

She played with the mouse, manoeuvring images.

"He's moving in, piece by piece. He went looking for a job. He doesn't find the fulfillment centre fulfilling. You want some coffee or something?"

"No, I'm good," Michael said. "You look good, too. Feeling all right?"

"Yeah, I guess. I'm not sure how I'm supposed to feel but I'm not tired all the time anymore. I'm feeling alive. What's up? Is Mom okay?"

"She's in the studio and I have to work on an empty flat. Someone … someone moved out unexpectedly and I'm going to start painting it and cleaning it up. I thought maybe you'd like to inhale paint fumes with me, help me paint. It's easy, just going to roll on some latex, freshen the place up. Then I'll take you to Chinatown, have some dim sum or whatever. Maybe drop in on your mother, see how she's doing. You up for it?"

Joey was dug in with the video toy. She didn't want to go out but she didn't want to disappoint Michael who was probably sent by MaryAnne to get her off her ass. And she was hungry and dim sum was an express train of food.

"If you have enough space on that camera for more video, why not shoot the apartment transformation? I'll paint, you shoot, then after, you can put it on YouTube, before and after, maybe help me rent it."

"Can I help choose colours?" Joey said.

"You can choose all the colours," he said. "I have no taste. Except when it comes to your mother."

It took them two hours at a paint shop on Fairmount that had been there for three generations. Michael bought all his paint and supplies there, doing his bit to keep Walmartization at bay. The founders were dead but the kids ran it with their kids and seemed to do okay. Michael described the rooms, Joey pounced on the colour chips.

This for one wall in the living room where the window is and this for three other walls; this for the kitchen cabinets but this for the trim; this for two walls of the big bedroom, this for the other two walls. Michael watched, agreed to everything. He normally would've painted everything flat white and let the tenant do what they wanted. It was Joey's show and her smile and the way she screwed up her eyes when she concentrated reminded him of MaryAnne. And he fed off her fun. Day was turning out pretty good.

By the time they were done, they had 16 cans of paint, Joey had a game plan for each room punched into her phone, Michael had a bill for $870 and they were ready to go. They agreed eating lunch before they started work was undoubtedly smart so they headed to the clang and crackle of Chinatown where carts of steamed dumplings, spices and garlic and shrimp and pork and shouting waitresses and frazzled waiters beckoned. Here he travelled without travelling.

They sat like father and daughter, an unfamiliar feeling for Michael, but not unpleasant. Joey watched everything, took some video of steam baskets being pulled from the carts by tongs. She watched Chinese customers eat one dish at a time, read papers, cool among the chaos, elders sitting stolidly, staring at the wall-sized windows, far from home. White diners filled their tables immediately, as if they were on the clock and the kitchen was going to shut down any moment.

She was a lot like her mother, Michael thought. She soaked life up, not only alcohol, given the chance. He'd have to spend more time with her.

He ordered har kow and sticky rice, Joey shooting it on her phone, sending it off to who he did not know, and left it at that. Eating without nausea was a pleasant change and he wanted to hold onto it.

They ate silently, Joey torn between soaking in the beehive that is a dim sum barn and eating everything that rolled by. Michael ordered cuttle fish and sui mai, watched the woman eat. Was she a step-daughter, he wondered, or simply his partner's kid?

"Not my business, of course," he said, "but I think your mother's going to need you a bit more than she seems to down the road."

She had an array of sauces in front of her, hoisin, soya, mustard, hot sauce, vinegar and she was dipping and mixing and tasting and smiling.

"MaryAnne never needed me, Michael," she said. "She loves me and all that but need is not in our relationship. She needs you. Shit, she loves you but I'm kinda the black sheep on the periphery of the superstar dream. Maybe the black hole."

Michael had nothing to say. He had found silence was often the optimal reply.

"I don't want to spend my life watching, Michael. I want to do, I just don't know what. I don't have my mother's need to be a star."

He chewed on a piece of ginger-flavoured cuttle fish.

"She doesn't want to be a superstar," Michael said. "She just wants to sing to people and make them happy. She's really just lonely and that's what she does. Connecting with the people in the seats and the guys in the band is oxygen. She doesn't need to be on the *Late Show* or play Yankee Stadium. But, the business is changing. I don't know how much longer she'll be able to do it and, if that balloon pops, she's going to need her girl."

"She has you," Joey said, plucking a sui mai and rolling it in a pastiche of mustard and hot sauce and soya sauce and popping it whole into her mouth.

Michael looked around. Within the pungent chaos was privacy.

"She has you, right?" Joey said.

Michael didn't know what to say so he looked over her shoulder, mesmerized by the rushing waiters in their black vests, so far from home, working for tips, many living in tiny rooms, sending money home, gambling every night, the cards and the men around the table filling in the holes wrought by loneliness and time. China wasn't the China they left as children, and many North Americans used COVID to jack up their racism. Canada was more foreign, its people often as inhospitable as the weather. When the Chinese weren't running with soup and General Tao, rice and ribs, they were mostly invisible, the future promising only that they'd be taking more shit from overfed Caucasians.

"Michael?"

"I'm not feeling all that great these days."

Joey reached for another dumpling.

"You see a doctor?"

He nodded.

"I'm not dying. I'll be fine, but your mother will need you."

Joey took a deep swallow of a Coke and put down her chopsticks.

"What does that mean? How sick are you? Cancer?"

Michael shrugged.

"You can't get sick and MaryAnne loves you and you guys are the couple everyone wishes they were in. Have you seen other doctors, like maybe go to the States?"

"Americans aren't winning awards for health care," he said. "Everybody dies and few of us know when. So, just be there for your mother if you can. You'll find that she's a great woman if you give her a chance. She's courageous and doesn't take shit and goes after what she wants. Not a Netflix kind of gal, you know."

A waitress bumped a cart into Michael's chair.

"Fried squid, fried squid, fried squid, fried won ton, fried won ton, fried won ton."

Michael shook his head and the woman moved on, repeating her mantra at the next table. A waiter reached over and grabbed two empty steam baskets off their table. They waited.

"It would be good if she could depend on you, lean on you a bit, even if she resists. Be good if you can be there for her."

"Lean on me? MaryAnne's worried I'm going to have this baby and screw up her life by leaning on her," Joey said. "My friends with kids have to fight their parents to keep them away. I'd have to fight with Mom just to get her to see the kid, if I have the kid, which is unlikely. Michael, you can't die." She wiped her eyes with the heel of her hands.

"Your mother is in the middle of a recording session and planning a big tour. It's the focus of her life right now but, like everything else, this will pass and your kid, if you have the kid, will still be there and so will MaryAnne and, I think, if you cut through all the bluster and bitching, she probably would make a great grandmother and a great great grandmother who will teach your kids to sing and play guitar and round them up for a tour."

"You tell her? You're not leaving her for another woman, are you?"

He pushed away the memory of Marsha lying under him, eyes closed, as guilt choked off his appetite. He didn't answer, just tried for the look that said, "You're not really that dumb."

"They giving you good drugs?" she said.

"You listen to her lyrics?" he said. "She sings about the world falling apart, she sings about lonely and lost people and fucked over people and malevolent people and her cure for everything is to find someone to love, to have your lost love come back one day, to remember when you fell in love. That's the gospel according to your mother and that's what she believes. I've seen her write a song in 10 minutes, straight from her brain to her guitar and her subconscious is dictating love. It's her fortress, castle and moat. It's not really my business, I'm just a guy your mother loves, but I'm buying lunch so you owe me. I need you to remember that and to know you'll give your mother a chance."

"Can we get more sticky rice?"

MaryAnne regained consciousness to take a call from Eric. He was sending her the tune as an MP3 and larger WAV file in Drop Box, better for radio play. The computer was in the drawer of the night table. She lifted herself onto one elbow, blinked a few times, reached in and took out her laptop, opened it and was pleasantly surprised its battery was juiced.

She opened Mail and waited and there was a note from Drop Box. She forwarded it to Brian in Australia, punching out "New tune no title, give it some spins on those stations you own. Do you spin a WAV file?" in the message line and pressed send. When she was sure it had left her machine and was heading wherever email went, she returned the computer to the drawer, her head to the pillow and forgot about it. Just another of hundreds and hundreds of email containing tunes she wondered if anyone listened to.

They showed up at Mrs. Gross's former flat and were met by a woman in a black suit, white blouse and a Glock on her hip. She had been sitting in a big green Ford, waiting.

She flashed her badge and a fake smile and asked to talk. Her name was Piedmont and she followed them into the flat where they sat around Mrs. Gross's kitchen table.

"I didn't think you guys investigated deaths of the elderly," Michael said.

"Why would you think that?" Piedmont said.

Michael figured it was best to shut up. He shrugged.

"What can I do for you?" he said. "I own the property and I came here to paint, get it ready for the next tenant. This is my step daughter."

"How long you know Mrs. Gross?"

"Several years. She's been here or was here for, I don't know, maybe ten, 12 years. I'm not sure."

"She live alone?"

"Mostly with her son," Michael said, mind racing. "But he hasn't been around. He's been living with his aunt somewhere. I called her when I found Mrs. Gross's body. She said the son was with her. Had been staying there for a bit. The old lady was sick."

Piedmont listened but took no notes, just nodded.

"What's the story?" Michael said. "I thought she had pneumonia or something."

"She might have had," Piedmont said. "She also had a broken hyoid bone."

Piedmont put her fingers on her throat.

"Was crushed. Someone suffocated her. You going to make the place all shiny and new? How much you going to charge for it?

"Not sure," he said. He found the process curious, being questioned by a homicide detective, it dawning on him he might be a suspect.

"I guess she was not paying that much, an old Jewish lady, she probably got a good price from you and now you can rent it for … what? Two thousand, twenty-five hundred. Make yourself some real money. Good flats here hard to find."

"Detective Piedmont, you should be a rental agent. Great idea. I should go around and kill all my tenants—I have a few buildings—and then raise the rents everywhere. You found me out."

Joey started giggling. The cop was not amused.

"You know how to contact the woman the son is staying with?"

"The number was on the fridge," Michael said. "The old Jewish lady, as you call her, told me to call her sister if anything happened to her. I don't know her name."

Piedmont walked to the fridge.

"No number here," she said, without looking at him.

Michael shrugged.

"I don't know what I did with it," he said. "I was a little stressed finding her like that."

"Can I have your phone number and date of birth?"

Michael told her.

"Mind if I look around?" she said.

Michael shrugged. Piedmont started walking through the house.

"I knew you were a killer," Joey whispered, laughing. "The ruthless landlord, murdering tenants. Agatha Christie or maybe Lawrence Block."

Michael wasn't amused. He had grown up in a time when police were pigs. As far as he was concerned, they had never lost their oink. He had not seen too much protection and service.

"A lot of men's clothes," said Piedmont, in the doorway between kitchen and hallway. Michael noticed her face was frozen in a permanent frown.

Michael said nothing. Joey watched him, curious.

Piedmont walked over, dropped a card on the table between them.

"If you remember anything, think of anything, call me. The woman was sick and old but she didn't have to die."

Once Joey stopped laughing and Michael cooled, they started work. The flat took two weeks, Joey and Michael taking their relationship to a new place, between rolling, brushing and making video of the transformation. Michael admitted the girl had taste. The colours looked good, the combinations she had chosen for each room worked.

Michael told stories of the rock 'n' roll life and Joey had no trouble relating the travails of the 20-something drinker, laughing about the men she had found herself with, the woman she had found herself with, the hang-overs she had found herself with. Michael was easy to talk to, no baggage, no judgment, no lectures.

Michael found himself reliving the tired chapters of

his past, too. Maybe he was lonely, maybe looming mortality was unlocking corridors he had sealed off. He told her of his short-term flirtation with drugs, an inebriated superstar he had entertained one early morning, playing pool with Elton John and Leon Russell at his hangout on Mount Royal and how no one paid them any attention. Learning tai chi from a gay guy on a beach in Ecuador and then making the rounds of all the underground gay bars.

When they finished the last coat on the kitchen and Michael suggested a celebratory Korean lunch, August was slipping away and there was that annual sense of foreboding about the approach of autumn. More so for Michael who had to see the doctor in a few days and would prefer to keep painting with this young woman who had adventures ahead of her and took his mind off his misadventures of the past and what the future might hold.

"How about you come help me paint my place?" she said. "It's a dump."

"Sure," he said. "As long as you're buying lunch."

"Michael," she said, washing the roller in the deep, porcelain sink that had been there since the house was built, about 100 years ago, the soft green latex running off like liquid moss. "I think I'm going to keep the baby. I kept putting off doing something and I guess that's 'cause I didn't know what to do and then, then ... Probably too late anyway." Her voice just faded away.

"And then what?" Michael said.

"Then I went to a bar, Felix was at my place and wouldn't go home and I got drunk and I went to some guy's place and he did ... he did ... he did whatever he wanted to me and made me do ..." Michael put his arms around her and she pushed him away. She didn't want comfort. She wanted to feel the humiliation.

"Things I don't like to do and I didn't care 'cause I was drunk and pregnant and stupid. I felt stupid and useless. He had a roommate and I didn't care about anything."

She kept washing the roller though it was as clean as it would get, working it as if she was washing the memories down the drain.

Michael watched, wanted to comfort but didn't know how.

"And I know that's not a way to live and I know a baby is not the way to get my shit together but I don't think having an abortion is the way either so I think that I got pregnant for a reason so I'd stop wasting my life and my time being an awesome idiot and everything."

Joey stood in the middle of the room, the roller in her hand, bleeding tinted water down her arm and onto the floor, face passive, locked.

"And it doesn't matter what MaryAnne wants or doesn't want and maybe if you're sick it's just going to be one more hassle for her and maybe I'll go somewhere like B.C. or California and start a new life 'cause the old one is really getting old. I can't stand just being a drunk and a slut and I can't be a drunk with a baby so I'm going to have this baby and I'll get my shit together. I'm going to be a mom. It hasn't sunk in yet but maybe if I tell people. But don't tell MaryAnne, okay? I wanna tell her ... And I fucked up your floor. I'll clean it."

Michael put his arms on her shoulders and she didn't shrink away. He kissed her on the forehead.

"You're not just a drunk and you're not an idiot or a

slut," he said. "I'd be proud as hell if you were my daughter. I would. You're a great woman. Can you and the kid handle some spicy beef soup?"

"I can't believe you, man," she said, a big smile crumbling the heartache. "Do you ever think of anything other than food?"

"What else is there to think about?" he said.

"Spicy beef soup? I guess we'll see," she said, tossing the roller into the sink, rubbing her slight baby bump. "He or she better get used to it."

"I'd say we're in pretty good shape," the doctor said, his hands around an inch-thick file, smiling.

We're? Michael thought. *You're not wondering how much pain you can handle and or saying "at least I don't have to think about replacing the truck." Fuck off with the "we."*

Instead he returned the smile, nodded encouragingly.

"The new cocktail seems to have been somewhat successful. We were able to target the tumour cells with more accuracy than we had anticipated. But, Michael, there's no cure. It's taking a break. We knocked it down, but not sure we knocked it out. You're doing better than I expected."

"What am I looking at?" Michael said.

"You're looking at maybe living longer. I can't promise, but I'd say, 50–50 for five years, 20–35 per cent chance for another five after that. They'll be newer better treatments in another five, so who knows. For a guy your age, all in all, that's not bad odds. Another ten years gets you into your '70s. How's the pain?"

"Manageable. Not really noticeable the last couple of weeks. I feel not bad, more energy. Don't feel like there are 50 kilos of lead wrapped around my legs."

"Good. You might not have to think about it for a few more years. That's a better prognosis than I would've given you last month."

"Anything I should do to improve my odds?" Michael said.

"Sure. Eat blueberries and carrots, have a glass a wine a day, least you'll be buzzed, make love as often as you feel like, stay in bed when you feel like staying in bed, eat smoked meat and fries at The Main. I never really liked Schwartz's. Travel if you have the money, don't read the news, enjoy the sunshine and be happy."

"Blueberries and carrots?"

"Sure. And strawberries and raspberries and black-berries. I prefer Nantes carrots."

"Antioxidants?"

"Nah. They just taste good and they're in season. Why not eat 'em? Summer's so damn short, get 'em while you can and no one ever got hurt eating berries. Just live."

Michael was happy and thought Cantonese lobster with MaryAnne would be a great way to mark the occasion.

He shook the doctor's hand and went to his truck to see if MaryAnne could get away from the studio. He had not seen her anywhere near as much as he'd seen Joey, but he wasn't complaining. She was in her element, he was in his and might well be there for a few more years.

The sun seemed brighter, people seemed happier, the frenzy of midday in the city seemed tolerable and Michael found himself smiling. He climbed into his truck, the cab and his phone vibrated. It was MaryAnne.

"Darlin'," she said, "Brian called. That new tune I re-corded a few weeks ago in the middle of the night, he says it's taking off in Aussieland. Heavy rotation, he says, and not only on the stations he owns, all across the country and New Zealand, too. It's a hit. I'm a star, down there in a former prison colony."

"That's great, baby. Great."

"And, it's in the top 10 in Norway. Norway. I'm a star and he's booked me there for five shows after Australia. And added eight more shows in Australia. I might have to move there, people obviously have good taste."

"Wanna celebrate tonight?" he said. "Lobster and steamed pork with Chinese sausage, steamed oysters, the whole nine yards ... actually let's go the whole ten yards, Yang Chow rice, too."

She was giddy and he couldn't remember feeling so good.

"The bad news," she said.

"Bad news?"

"It's a hit on the Internet and on radio but like, every-one's streaming. No one's buying. He says maybe with stronger YouTube presence. Might sell seats for the shows but, more likely, I'm a star but as poor as always. Though, I might expect a cheque from Apple and Spotify and I don't know who else for a couple of hundred bucks. And, the asshole cancelled France and Belgium, all of Western Europe, advance sales suck, radio stations not playing me. I'm not touring Europe. Maybe next year."

"Shit," he said. "You okay with that?"

"No, I'm not okay. I wanted to play Paris and Marseilles

and Nice and Rome and Florence. But … Most people aren't playing anywhere anymore, the scene is fucked but I'm doing my Energizer Bunny thing. I don't give a shit and I'm going to keep on keeping on. I'm playing and I'm touring and I'm not going to cry over what used to be. I'll do the two months in Australia, then fly up north and meet some Norwegians, God bless 'em, and come home and go back into the studio. Almost seems like old times.

"I have three new songs, going to try and think up some video and Eric is great. I think Brian is pretty happy so he's already talking about recording a few new songs. He wants product. I'll give him product. How are you?"

"Looking forward to seeing you," he said. "I'll pick you up. What time?"

"How's seven? How's Joey?"

"We finished yesterday, so she's free from indentured slavery. Looks good, seems happy."

"The baby?"

"We didn't talk too much about it," he said, which wasn't a lie. "But that girl can sure paint. I'm trying to figure out how to pay her for her time."

"I'll think on it," she said. "Talk about it over Chinese. You still love me?"

"More than Cantonese lobster," he said and meant it.

"Shit, you make me weak in the knees with all that love talk," she said. "I think before I head overseas I'm going to meet Essie and do the Slate gigs, pump up the bank account. Would you mind?"

"Never," he said.

He put the truck into gear and aimed it toward home.

He wondered why he wasn't feeling elated. He was given a few more years. Maybe. Or given false hope, being mind-fucked. 'Course, tomorrow's a maybe for everyone. The great sinkhole of life can yawn anytime.

He should've been happier. But, he had to admit, he had never believed the doctors; had never believed he was going to buy it so quick. He had been mired in denial—a desperate cliché.

MaryAnne never gave up. Almost 60, she was still in the ring, punching. So why would he throw in the towel? Woman was better than blueberries. Time for anger.

Felix caught Gaetan in the cafeteria, his face tinged with the yellow vestiges of where it had met someone's shoe. His ribs still ached, as did his ego. On TV, guys got the shit beaten out of them and were good as new after the next commercial.

"Hey man, you put your face in one of those Braun food machines, aisle 2113B?" Gaetan said.

Felix sat down beside him at the long table where he was eating alone and pushed his tray away, spilling his glass of milk. The boiled canned peas on his plate jumped and rolled onto the floor.

"No, asshole," Felix said, whispering. "Someone beat the shit out of me 'cause they said I was talking about the union and who the hell would've told anyone in management about me talking about union? Pricks almost killed me."

Gaetan screwed up his face and squinted and began rubbing his head with his fists.

"You think I did that? You think I'm a motherfucking traitor?"

"Who the fuck else knew we were talking? Who else?"

"Me, a company stooge? Fuck you. Fuck your mother. Those smart pills I give you make you fucking stupid."

They were now talking in a loud whisper, Gaetan still rubbing his head in some kind of psychotic, bloodless mutilation.

"You hot today, Felix, feeling sweaty, thirsty all the time?"

"So what? It's like 30 degrees outside."

"Come with me," Gaetan said, grabbing him by the arm and leading him around the 100 or so tables and out the back door where there was a parking lot for Team Leaders and bosses. Associates took smoke breaks there at a few benches against the wall.

Gaetan was still holding onto his arm and pulled him across the lot to the gate. Six yellow ambulances were parked there.

"See those, man? See those?"

"Big deal. What about them?"

"They're waiting for you. They're waiting for you to keel over. Every time the temperature goes above 26, they hire ambulances so when the heat floors their fucking so-called associates they can rush them to hospitals. Usually about a dozen a day when it gets this hot. You think I'm part of that? You think I work for the company? I'm a company man, all for hiring ambulances rather than pay for air conditioning. You're crazy insane."

"I don't know," Felix said. "You and maybe three or four others were the only ones I talked to but you're the only one I was serious with."

"You have 33 seconds to pick and pack your order, you know that, eh?" Gaetan said. "They time everything. You know you walk at least 10 miles every day, depending how many hours you're chained here and you're not really walking you're chasing the robot, all day, man, all day and you think I'm happy with that, that I would have you beat up?"

He started scraping his head again with his fists, dandruff flying, his face scrunched in pain.

"You know how much I hate this place? You have any idea how much I hate coming in here and chasing a fucking, cock-sucking robot?

"We're just machines, man, we're the robots and soon, we'll be picked and packed. They'll sell us for parts. You'll see, someone needs a new kidney and they'll take one from us while they're shipping us to the hospital after we pass out from the heat. Then it'll be a heart or a lung or a new knee or whatever. We're not even machines, just parts of this great, big, piece-of-shit machine, as replaceable as one of those rolling robots except we're cheaper and soon they'll replace us with robot pickers and we'll be nothing at all. Just beggars on Mount Royal, fighting for a corner with other beggars. You understand? And you think I'd sell you out? Man, you're fucked up."

"Chill man, chill. I'm sorry."

Gaetan had his hands on the windows of a new green Camry and began banging his head on the roof, denting the tin.

"I hate this place, I hate this place and I try to make it better, and I need those damn pills to not go crazy and live like this," he said. "Smart pills one shift, painkillers another. Some days I can't walk, some nights I can't sleep."

He kept banging his forehead into the cars roof, glaring in the sunshine.

"Can't believe you'd think that," Gaetan said. "The union is the only way to save us. The only way."

He stopped hitting his head.

"I gotta get back to work," he said and headed toward the door. "You know, this is all Henry Ford's doing, man. Make workers just teeth of the gears but at least he made sure his slaves made enough to buy the cars they built. All I can afford in this place is porn and maybe a toothbrush."

"Gaetan," Felix said. "How many of these places have a union?"

Gaetan walked faster, his hair standing straight up with the heat and humidity and his frantic rubbing, his forehead red and swollen from where he had used it to punish the car.

"None," he said.

Joey stared at the screen, trying to figure how to get the girl walking by her house to walk backwards, reverse the sequence. She craved wine but shook it off and kept fiddling with the keyboard.

She had started just after dawn, sipping coffee and spooning scrambled eggs into her mouth and it was now noon. Hunger was nibbling at her insides again but she didn't want to stop.

She knew she was escaping the real world by creating her own worlds but didn't care. Isn't that what her mother did? Maybe everyone found escape somewhere. She could control this world, finesse it, manipulate it, improve it, colour it, speed it up or slow it down. She was God. Now if only she could make it go in reverse.

She knew some people made a lot of money on YouTube, usually making little films of themselves acting stupid or just being themselves, pretending to be stupid. But she had the luxury of not monetizing herself. She had a bit of money. Every month, it was always there, what she imagined a pension check would be like, enough to live on. Barely. Her mind slowly waking from years of an alcohol-induced fog, she had started to appreciate the gift her father had given her: freedom. All around her, except for the few wealthy people with real family money behind them that she knew, people were wrestling. Life was uphill, always would be, slipping and sliding from one gig to another, apartments getting condoized, moving farther and farther away, out east or into places in the burbs, always farther and further from any chance at an authentic life.

"It's quiet and there's a great store just a couple of kilometres away. I can bike everywhere and there's no traffic. It only takes me an hour to get to town by metro and bus. Gives me time to read. Love it."

Except soon, they stopped coming to town. Soon they had kids. Didn't want to come to town. Then mortgages. Couldn't afford to come to town. She had it better than most. It had taken her a decade to see it. But, what was she going to do now? And for the rest of her life. With a kid? How long could she play on the Mac?

Felix gave half his salary religiously to her for rent and groceries. By the time he got home after a day in hell, filling people's online baskets, looking over his shoulder, praying for the traffic light to be green, he had no energy left to shop for food. He usually got off the bus on St. Laurent and wandered down St. Viateur and grabbed something to eat. There was cheap Polish, Greek, Middle Eastern, Italian, Portuguese and it gave him time to steel himself for whatever mood Joey might be in. Lately it had been a bit better but she spent most of her time on the computer. It had replaced drinking.

If Joey made anything to eat, which was rare, he left her to eat it herself while he turned on the TV and channel surfed for an hour, sucking on a joint, dreading tomorrow, dreaming about the little helpers he hungered for. Just one tab made life so much easier.

Sometimes Joey suggested a movie, a walk, a dinner together, going out to hear a band, but he was too tired. The pills cranked him up, but once they wore off, he was dead.

"You know Flix, you're becoming a bloody bore," she told him a few weeks into their domestic arrangement.

"I work all fucking day," he said. "You get to sit home and contemplate your screen and your belly. I got to worry about where the hell someone's month's supply of KD is, then run with it and try to grab a couple of bottles of Cheez Whiz at the same time, save a trip, rack up those bonus dollars, keep us in fine style."

"Guess what Flix, the $200 you give me pays for the cable and the Internet and the cell phone you got as part of the package. Sometimes I have enough left over to buy you the 10 bags of Miss Vickie's you go through every week."

"Comfort food, Jo. Man, I need comfort."

"I'm going for a walk."

Once the computer had nearly blinded her she became restless, energy to burn, the apartment increasingly claustrophobic with Felix hard-wired to the TV.

She walked to the Italian café on Saint Viateur and ordered a short espresso, found herself watching the world go by again. She took a bit of video on her phone but told herself, enough. She called her mother.

MaryAnne was in the studio, packing up her things, feeling pretty good about what she heard. It hadn't been mixed but she had five tunes she liked. In the studio, reality was on the other side of the insulated door.

When the phone vibrated and her daughter's name popped up on the display, the sanctuary felt invaded.

"Hey Mother, am I bothering you?"

"No, just finishing at the studio. What's up?"

"Nothing, just wanted to see … how's the session going?"

"All good," MaryAnne said. "Where are you? What're you doing?"

"I'm on Saint Viateur, nowhere, doing nothing. Having a coffee. What're you doing?"

She wanted to see Michael, she wanted to see her daughter. She wanted to just kick back, get stoned, see no one. Least she had choices.

"How about I come pick you up? We'll, I don't know, have a drink or something to eat or just drive?"

"You sure?"

"Well, Elton called and asked me to do a duet with him in Vegas, but I said, 'I think I need to see my daughter.' So, I'm cool. See ya in fifteen."

It took her almost 30. The city had turned anti-car,

bike friendly. Roads that had been two-lane had been squeezed down to one with a bike lane tacked on. Lots of one-way streets, lots of cars backed up at every light and every light seemed red. She'd have to think about getting a bike, maybe a soft-shell case to carry her guitar on her back as she pedaled through the city. She could see the headline: "Norway's favourite pop star brain dead after motorist opens car door."

Her daughter looked lost and forlorn, sitting on a bench outside the café filled with the neighbourhood's army of freelancers killing the hours between work and dinner, after which they'd go back to the computers to work, browse, maybe hookup for the night. Of course, some still were on their computers at the café. In the screen was life.

Joey climbed over the closed door of the Miata and settled into the passenger seat and MaryAnne kissed her, smelled the Pantene and they squealed away. The city was their oyster. But what if you didn't feel like oysters?

They had a platter of spit-roasted lamb in front of them, beside a platter of French fries, Greek salad and grilled chicken on Jean Talon. The Panama was always jammed, overpriced and delicious. MaryAnne sipped a half bottle of retsina, her daughter stealing a sip here and there. How could a little wine hurt?

Michael was walking through what was once Mrs. Gross's home, thinking of German potatoes. He could've joined MaryAnne and Joey but he begged off; wanted mother and daughter to do their thing. Maybe he'd try and make the old lady's potatoes for himself.

The flat looked pretty good. The floors needed sanding and he had hired a guy to do that—he wasn't into inhaling Varathane and sawdust. He'd have to find a tenant but all he had to do was go to the café and tell Louis and he'd have half a dozen people lining up with a cheque for the first month's rent. He'd be happier if the old lady with the blue numbers on her arm was still around making rugula. Unless of course, the cop came back with handcuffs for him.

Joey had done a good job. The place was fresh with colour and promise. People could move in, begin lives here, have babies, hang pictures, throw down carpets, throw parties, make love, have fights, live a life in a place he rescued, decorated, cleaned, made welcoming. There were worse epitaphs.

He pulled out his phone and called Mrs. Gross's sister.

"How's Lebby?" he asked.

"Lebby will always by Lebby. He's making me crazy."

"Maybe he can go away somewhere," Michael said. "You have relatives, maybe, somewhere out of town?"

"No, no. I don't … My sister-in-law, she lives in Buenos Aires. Why?"

"Maybe Lebby can go visit there, stay there for a while," Michael said.

"What would she want with him? He's a big … He eats for two. The airplane ticket alone probably costs a fortune."

"The police have asked about him. I think it would be

better if he went away for a bit. Maybe a year or so, learn Spanish."

"He can barely speak English. Why should ...? Oh, the police?"

"I have a little extra money," Michael said. "Get him a passport. Today. Get the pictures at the pharmacy. I'll send you some money."

"Why you do this? My sister-in-law, she has no money. She ..."

"I'll send you enough for her. Give me your address. I have a few extra dollars. I like Lebby and he should go have a nice trip, get over his mother's death. She would've liked that. Can you get him a passport?"

"Of course. Lebby's the idiot, not me. Maybe I take him, yeah? I haven't seen my sister-in-law in a long time."

"I'll send money for your ticket, too," Michael said.

"You don't need to send money for me," she said. "I can look after myself."

He keyed her address into his phone.

They had been hungrier than they thought. They stared at the wreckage of dinner—lamb and chicken bones, bits of feta cheese and tomato floating in olive oil flecked with oregano, the retsina bottle empty.

"When you going to have the abortion?" MaryAnne said. "You're cutting it close."

"What makes you so sure I'm going to terminate?"

"I don't know anything. I'm asking."

"You said, 'When am I going to have the abortion?' You didn't ask me what I was going to do."

"Joey, please chill. You don't have a job, you tell me you don't know what to do with your life. So, I figured, you'd wait to have the baby. You got time."

"The time is now, MaryAnne. I'm going to have the baby. I don't know if it's right or wrong or how I'm going to swing it, but I don't want an abortion. I know my life is a mess. Flix is as useful as a nail without a hammer but even if I had a great guy, the thing is it's my body so I gotta do what's right for me and I don't know what's right but I don't want to have an abortion. Maybe I got pregnant for a reason, maybe this was supposed to happen just to wake me up and start living. A reason to get up in the morning. Something to look after and think about other than myself. I'll be doing something. Maybe that's all life's really about?"

"Joey, a kid is not a self-improvement project. Maybe it was just a mistake. Or an accident."

"How many kids are planned and how many accidents?"

"Probably 50–50," MaryAnne said. "But, it doesn't matter what happens to other people. This is your life."

"Maybe a baby is a self-improvement project," Joey said. "And waiting, well ... I could be waiting 10, 15 years to find the so-called right guy and I'll be an old lady by the time the kid leaves home. I got to do it now."

MaryAnne tried to wring a last drop from the wine bottle. She saw Joey when she was born and when she was learning to walk and when they went shopping for her first bra. The first time she didn't come home at night, the first time she got really drunk. The day she moved out.

"Joey, if that's what you want, if that's what you think will work for you then I think you're going to be a good mother and I'm proud of you."

"Really? I thought you'd be pissed."

"I'll be pissed if you show up at my door saying 'Ma, I can't deal with this screaming kid. Take it for a couple of years. I want to go out and party.' But I don't think that's going to happen."

"Could," Joey said.

"No, it couldn't," MaryAnne said.

"I don't know what I'm going to do for money," Joey said. "It's so weird, my father's dead and every month his hand reaches into my bank account and drops money into it. And I guess because the market's doing well, the last payment went up a couple of hundred dollars."

"Joey, you won't be going hungry. I won't be a model grandmother. But, I won't let you starve. And, if and when you need something, I'll help you, you know that. I was such a good mother, I can give you courses."

"In what not to do," Joey said.

"I love you, too, dear."

"I think I need heroin," MaryAnne said, watching Michael make his way through a plate of German friend potatoes. "Something to wrap my brain in foam rubber and get it to stop working for a bit. My kid's going to have a kid. She's still a kid. The baby will start to cry and she'll go running to the dep to buy a bottle of wine. Or a case."

"She's 28 years old, perfectly capable, smart. She'll be fine," Michael said. "Maybe next time more bacon, or smaller bits of bacon."

"Can you put aside the cooking lesson for another day, please? This is serious shit."

"It is," Michael said, putting down his fork. "But it's not your serious shit. It's Joey's. It's her life. You have a life of your own. And it's going quite well. Lots to be happy about. And if her baby is healthy, there'll be more to be happy about. I'm not sure heroin changes that equation. Besides, I have no idea where to find heroin. Want a taste?"

He speared a potato and offered it to her and she shook her head.

"I always admired your Zen but can you stick it for just this once?" she said. "I'm having a completely illogical, emotional reaction to this situation and I'm allowed. And I'd like a little empathy, maybe sympathy. I'm going to be a fucking grandmother. Jesus. I'm going on tour, Michael. I don't want to have to worry about how my daughter's doing. I'll be someplace like Melbourne when she goes into labour and there won't be anyone there for her. That Felix guy, the invisible Felix, he's working in a fulfillment centre, for Christ's sake."

"You'd prefer if he was a vice president of a bank? Or a marketing executive? Maybe drive around for Google, filming streets for Streetview? He's a kid. He'll find something."

"What about her? What'll she find?"

"Joey's a great kid," he said. "It was fun working with her. She did the whole flat, worked hard, didn't bitch.

Did a good job. Place looks great. She even took before and after video."

"I feel old," MaryAnne said. "I feel like I'm too old. Here I am heading out on a great adventure and my daughter has just reminded me that a new generation is coming which means we're going. I'm not ready to be old."

Michael took her hand.

"This is all stuff you're imposing on yourself. You're not any different or older than yesterday."

"That's not true," she said. "I have to confront this. It's her decision and her life but I can't pretend that it's not mine, too. There's going to be a new member of the family. She's single, hell with Felix, and she's going to need us and the baby is going to need us and our life is going to change forever and, baby, you're not even well."

She reached for the dope box and then pushed it farther away. Later.

"And I want life to be perfect and I want you to be healthy and my daughter to be happy and have a proper man to help her like I have and I want to be a success and make a decent living playing music like I used to do and nothing is the way I want it. Everything is wrong. Except for you and you're ... you have ..."

"Cancer. You can say it. Happens to the best of us. Listen, MaryAnne, you're doing better than most. You got a new contract and shit happening and good players and a producer and your daughter is healthy and yeah, she has or had a drinking problem but she's doing better than a lot of kids who live in the basement and are chewing opiates and snorting meth and shooting smack and turning tricks. So, life is not perfect but no one's life is perfect. There is no such thing as perfect. You have the mind of the hard-core alcoholic or druggie. Life's not perfect, I better get stoned. You want to know what hell is? Read the papers. Well, there are no more real papers but read the news online and count your blessings. You're making music, you're travelling, I love you, your daughter loves you, the guys in the band love you, the grandkid will love you and we all get old and die and that's life. So, enjoy what you got and stop bitching."

MaryAnne stood up and looked down at him.

"I'm going to work on that new painting I started," she said.

She walked out of the kitchen.

"You better not fucking die on me," she said as she disappeared through the door.

Felix had a buzz on, amped somewhat by two double espressos from McDonald's, and stood under the glare of the fluorescents and was trying to digest the news that Joey was really going to have the baby. Maybe even his baby. He had been sure she'd have an abortion. This was seriously fucked up. Robot waiting impatiently, lights flashing, Gaetan coming at him. Gaetan going crazy. He had a shitload of order slips to fulfill but he wandered with only half a mind to the great, heaping shelves of baby stuff.

Cribs and strollers and bassinets and car seats and high chairs and low chairs and toys, toys and more toys, all wrapped up in shiny images of beautiful, happy white babies. And clothes, miniature clothes. He'd have to buy all this stuff. Or maybe his parents would. He hadn't told them yet.

"Yeah, I'm going to be a father. With this girl I met a few months ago. I been kind of busy. I guess you'll meet her. In the fall, October or November, I'm not sure. I don't know why I'm not sure."

When was the kid due? Did that mean he'd have to spend his life here between rows of shit he'll probably never afford? Fulfilling orders for people he'd never meet? Somewhere, anywhere, someone clicked on a key and he started to run, a puppet on an invisible string. "Everything for everyone everywhere," was the corporate creed of greed. Seemed he was doing the everything for everyone himself, some days. He spent all day silently running, talking only during his 45-minute lunch, his two 15-minute breaks, the rest of the time, locked inside his own brain, his legs moving, his mind at a dead end, thanks to magic pharmaceuticals. He'd been here maybe four weeks and it seemed every time he got to know someone well enough to say, "How you doing?" they were gone and replaced by another robohuman looking lost and afraid. Where did they go? Were they fired or did they quit? Where was he going? And when? He committed one of the ultimate associate crimes. He pulled out his phone, called Dominique in Toronto.

Didn't need a calendar to know September had arrived. The nights were cooler, the traffic was multiplying, real life was cranking up. Jean-Pierre had suggested a terrasse on

Mount Royal for a drink and Michael, poised to ask for a favour, added a sweater and a layer of patience. Sitting on a sidewalk as cars, trucks and busses pumped exhaust at him was not his idea of a good time.

YouTube had made Jean-Pierre happy and wealthy. The medium was insatiable, everyone with ambition and an instrument was aiming to go viral with a video and Jean-Pierre was churning out a few hundred a year. He figured on riding this train 18 hours a day as long as he could and then spend his money.

"Trick is," he said, holding up his glass of Perrier, "you gotta stay sober, gotta stay in shape and stay away from the crazy women. Suck the life out of you. Now I live with a good woman, easy on my head, have a few friends, easy to meet people in this business, and then I go home. Everything's quiet; all is calm; I can think, work, sleep, whatever. I've given up on true love, man. Retired. Just want sanity. Don't need the headaches. What about you?"

"Life's good," he told him. "Don't miss work, don't miss the music. I'm enjoying quiet. I love the woman I'm with."

"You always were a romantic. Your heart must have calluses on the calluses."

"I need a favour."

"Sure," Jean-Pierre said. "What do you need?"

"A job," he said.

Jean-Pierre laughed.

"How about vice president of marketing or head of production or anything you want. I do it all. I could always use some help. As long as you'll work for minimum wage. No, wait, for you, I can pay 15 an hour."

"It's for my step-daughter," Michael said. "She's into

video shooting and editing and needs to learn more and I figure you're the man."

"What she using?"

"Something on her Mac but it doesn't matter, she can learn anything," Michael said. "She's smart and seems to love it."

"I can take her on as an unpaid apprentice, you know," Jean-Pierre said. "She can learn and when she's up to speed I maybe can pay her a bit."

"Jean-Pierre, unpaid apprentice is a euphemism for slave labour and it's not even legal in Québec," Michael said. "Joey will earn her keep. She learns fast."

"Michael, hiring someone, even for minimum wage, say $20,000, that costs me close to $30,000 and if you cost training her, which means the person teaching is not making money, that's a huge investment. I'm sure your daughter …"

"Step-daughter."

"Step-daughter is great but these kids, man, you never know when they're going to quit or even when they'll show up. I have 12 people under 40 working for me and I think the reason I'm avoiding women is these kids make me crazy enough. Most of them got no fucking backbone. You know some of them, their mothers call me. 'Can my son have a day off, can my daughter have a raise, she works so hard?' I fired a kid, 32. He would take a day or two off every week, deadlines meant nothing. See these grey hairs, one for every day the fucking kid didn't show. His father called me, threatened to sue me. I told him, 'Your son's a useless asshole. I'll give you my lawyer's address. You can send the papers right to him. See you in court.'

"I'm sure your step-daughter's different, she's probably perfect, but, thing about videos today, the margins are small, man. People aren't paying me $50,000 for a video, not here. Maybe down in L.A., but here it's nickel-and-dime stuff. I work on volume and I need people to churn it out. I can't afford to train and pay for the privilege."

Michael watched the traffic, a kid on a black bike in black clothes, no lights, zipping in between cars and then running into an SUV changing lanes. He had to drop his bike. The driver stopped and the kid started swearing at him and kicking in his door. The driver pushed his door open and grabbed the kid. Another guy got out of his car and then a pedestrian ran over. Everyone was screaming. Drinkers on the terrasse were smiling. Another night on the town.

"Jean-Pierre, the kid needs a break. I know most kids need a break but she's kind of mine and I can only worry about her and her mother."

"The woman you love."

"The woman I love."

"There are government programs. If she can do the paperwork, get a grant to pay her salary, I can maybe do something."

"No, buddy, you're going to give her a job, you're going to pay her, give her three months probation with pay. Fifteen an hour and you're going to teach her properly. I've read shit. A lot of companies take the free labour, don't do the training part, use the kids to chase sandwiches, wash floors, dust furniture and then kiss 'em off."

"Are you nuts, Michael? I'm going to pay 15 bucks an hour and then have her clean? What drugs you taking?"

"Not the good ones, believe me," Michael said. "And I'm going to do two things for you. MaryAnne needs about six videos, a few thousand each. I'll make sure you do them. And the little company I have for tax purposes, so I don't get all my rental income taxed to the max, is going to hire your company as a video consultant firm and pay you a thousand a month while Joey's in training. So you'll be happy, Joey'll be happy, I'll be happy, MaryAnne'll be happy."

"Jesus, you're a manipulative bastard," he said, laughing. "I'll still be losing money."

"No, you'll get a great employee and you'll be doing something good for someone else. Jews call it a mitzvah."

"I don't care what Jews call it. I call it getting screwed without Vaseline ... I owe ya and maybe this young woman is a genius and it'll be the best thing that ever happened to me. When can she start?"

"Give her a call," Michael said, and sent Jean-Pierre her coordinates from his cell phone. "Don't mention me. This is between you and me. Just tell her you always need people and her name came up."

Jean-Pierre nodded.

"I hope you're at least picking up the tab for my Perrier."

"One more thing," Michael said. "She's pregnant. Due in November. She'll need mat leave. I guess she'll decide how much time she wants."

Jean-Pierre opened his mouth but no sound came out. He picked up the cheque.

"You know, Michael, you've always had big balls. Quiet guy, reliable, did the job, never any problems, always in a pretty good mood, and when there was trouble people knew you were the guy to straighten shit out. You were the guy who walked on stage during a concert of—I don't know—AC DC or someone, told the lead singer if he didn't wrap the tune and say good night you were pulling the plug. They were over time, union regs, city sound ordinance, can't remember, but you hated their music, made no bones about it and you walked on stage and just yelled into the singer's ear ... what'd you say exactly?"

"Get off stage or you're going to be tearing down yourself. Time's up and the crew's going home."

"Yeah, yeah, and the guy with all the hair and the bare chest just killed the song and came looking for you."

"He was all of 140 pounds, with his pants on."

"Yeah, but he was in some kind of drunken rage, he was stalking backstage, screaming at everyone, 'Where is that fucking asshole?' He find you?"

"It's amazing the calming effects of a 12-inch pipe wrench. He was very gentlemanly when I explained the laws of the land."

"You always had big balls, man. You've done such a good job fucking up my head tonight, least I can do is pay for our Perrier. Been good to see you again. I'll call the kid."

"Her name's Joey."

Michael took the first side street, Hôtel-de-Ville, getting away from the late summer madness of the city's hippest street and walked north toward home. Like all the city's miniature side streets, built for working poor, it was renovated upon renovated, populated by cars on both sides but no people on the sidewalks and there were few stars not obscured by haze and light pollution. A couple were talking softly, perched on folding chairs on a third-floor balcony, their 24 square feet of the great outdoors.

He called Marsha.

"I wanted to tell you, the doctors say I'm doing well. Probably have a few years or more," Michael said as he walked. Her place was not far. "I thought you'd like to know."

"That's great, Michael. I'm glad you told me. I'm happy you'll be walking the Earth for a long time."

"Yeah, I'm feeling pretty good these days," he said. He crossed the street, headed toward her place a few blocks away, visions of her body dancing in the shadows of the lamp posts.

"Happy to hear it, Michael. I have to go, I have a friend here. You take care. I'm happy for you."

"Sure," he said. "Night."

He ended the call, killing the fantasy with it. Maybe she thought cancer was contagious. Maybe she thought healthy guys were more fun. He had no idea why he had called her or why he felt depressed.

It wasn't like she wasn't expecting it but it still had her sitting on the floor of her livingroom, tears in her eyes. In her hand was Felix's note.

"Got fired. Caught using my phone. Fuck them. Got a ride to Toronto for an acting gig in small theatre. Call you. F."

"Ef you!" she said, rereading the note. He wasn't man

enough to tell her. He just fucked off in the middle of the night, ride to Toronto was bullshit, she was sure. As soon as he heard she was going to keep the baby, he was making plans.

"What did you expect?" she said to the floor. "Are you insane?"

She crumpled up the note and threw it over her shoulder. It bounced off the wall and fell behind the sofa.

She wanted a drink but she always wanted a drink and now that she decided to have the kid, it was a bit easier to control the cravings. She had started to picture the little person inside her. Beginning to look forward to meeting him, her or it. Began to wonder what it would be like. The last time she had a bit of wine with MaryAnne, it made her nauseous. Little unborn shit was already controlling her life.

Her cellphone buzzed and vibrated and then rang. She looked at it. Jean-Pierre Daoust. Jean-Pierre Daoust? A real-estate agent? Marketing moron? Friend of Flix?

The guy asked for her.

"I'm Joey."

"Hello, Joey," he said, introducing himself. "I have a video production company and we need someone to edit and maybe shoot video for music and corporate videos for YouTube and corporate websites. Someone told me you were looking for work and were doing a lot of video at home. Would you be interested in coming in to meet us and look around?"

"Really?" she said. "Are you serious?"

"Well, yes, I am."

"I'd love to but ... I ... I'm pregnant. I could work for a while. I'd love to really but I'm going to have a baby in a few months and I'll have to, I guess, take mat leave. But, I'll work at home and I can maybe find someone to watch the kid or a day care as soon as it's old enough."

"Our firm is woman and family friendly," Jean-Pierre said making it up as he went along. He only had three women working for him and they were all past baby-making age.

"People even bring their dogs. We train you and, if we're a good match, you come back to work after the baby. Why not come in and talk?"

"Sure, yeah, of course, anytime, absolutely," she said.

"I'll send you the contact info with an appointment," he said. "If you can't make it, let me know. Otherwise, I'll be expecting you."

"Great, I'll be there. Thank you. Uh, how'd you get my name?"

"Someone told someone who told someone who told me," Jean-Pierre said. "Talk soon."

The phone went dead and a text message popped up with his company's address and a time to meet. How did he get her number?

MaryAnne was leaving in a week and she was spending her time rehearsing, shopping for a stage wardrobe, and worrying. If it was getting colder here, it was getting warmer there. And Slate was doing California and Texas and Florida. Be a lot of people watching her. His music sucked but no one seemed to care. He was getting one twenty five a ticket. She was lucky to get forty. How many tickets were being sold? How many shows would they really do? Would they dig her? How was Michael doing? How was Joey doing? What could she do to help them?

Joey had a new job and loved it. And she was getting bigger and was going to stop working about the same time she left town. Once again, she wasn't going to be there for a big moment. Guilt was not gnawing at her, it was chomping through an SUV-sized chunk of her conscience.

With most of the details in place, unless she took a few days off to fly home and see the baby and then get back on a plane, about 60 hours in the air, give or take, she'd see her grandchild about two months after it was born. The tour was three months. Two Down Under then one in Europe, mostly in the north. The song was no longer a hit in Norway or anywhere else. Music was pretty disposable these days but the shows were selling. Brian was happy. He had booked her into some small rooms in France, Belgium and Italy, jump on a plane for 14 hours and play a half-dozen nights in Buenos Aires and across the river in Monte-video. She might be able to get out of France for two days but that wouldn't be until December. The jet lag would fry her, she'd be in no shape to perform every night.

For the first time, staring at herself in a changing room at Simon's downtown, trying on pants, she wondered again: *Where was this road leading?* Michael would say: "Nowhere, so just enjoy the ride."

Who would judge her? Joey, now carrying the responsibility of a child and work, told her to go and be happy. Michael said enjoy the trip. Maybe he had ulterior motives for bidding her a bon voyage. He was maybe thrilled to put her on a plane and go back to whatever he was doing. There was something telling her it was another woman, something telling her when she came back he'd be gone. She was making herself crazy. The only person not happy for her was her.

Michael wasn't big on airport goodbyes. The guys in the band would meet her in Cairns in a couple of weeks, once she was through harmonizing and shaking her ass for Slate and padding her bank account. Brian had his office book them decent seats on Qantas so the flight wouldn't be complete hell. Only about 32 hours of claustrophobic anxiety, fear, boredom and a need to scream.

Michael accompanied her to Dorval in her Miata and gave her a big hug in front of the wide doors leading to the departure area.

"Facetime?" she said.

"Skype?" he said.

"Old fashioned phone calls?" she said.

"Is that legal?" he said.

"I think it still is in the States," she said. "I don't know about Australia."

"You're going to kill," he said. "Have a good time with Essie and try not to drive all the men wild."

"If it doesn't kill me," she said, stroking his face. "You going to be okay?"

"Of course," he said. "Why wouldn't I be?"

"I don't know," she said. "Why wouldn't you be?"

They stared at each, no smiles. Then he broke into a huge Michael grin, made her want to drag him into a washroom for a real goodbye.

She hugged him until a cop came over and told them to get the car out of there. Michael watched her as she rolled a huge suitcase and her guitar case through the sliding doors and disappeared. She didn't look back. He climbed into her little car and drove away.

Michael liked the little Miata and whipped it around the Dorval circle and headed toward the water. At the end of the boulevard, past the strip malls and old homes and big groomed lawns was a small ferry terminal. A few hundred yards across the river, was Dorval Island. He parked, watching the little ferry chug away and pulled out his phone and texted: "Doing anything for lunch?"

Joey was moving slow. The day was done, work was getting harder each shift. But it was fascinating to lose herself in the screen and get paid for it and not think about drinking all day. After work was another story.

Her body was getting heavier. Another two months. Her mother's flight left in three hours, she should maybe go to the airport to say goodbye but she'd be in security probably or through it and they had said their goodbyes a few days ago. In Chinatown, of course.

She was out on the sidewalk and heading to the bus when the blue Miata pulled up, Michael at the wheel.

He came around and opened the door for her, holding

her hand as she lowered herself into the little bucket seat. This was not the first time he had showed up at the end of day. Sometimes he drove her home, sometimes he took her to dinner with and without MaryAnne.

This time he drove her to their house, double parked, killed the engine.

"I was thinking, while your mother was away, I'm going to be pretty lonely. Maybe you could come live at our place while you have the baby and while MaryAnne's away."

"What about my place? Pay rent on it and not use it for three months?"

"Sublet it, easy. It's in decent shape. And, I owe you for all the work you did on Mrs. Gross's place. I guess I should stop calling it that. Take it. Three bedrooms. It's empty. One for you, one for the kid, one for an office or whatever."

"Michael, that place is gorgeous now. It's worth a fortune. I can't pay for it."

"You can pay what Mrs. Gross was paying," he said. "Rent control doesn't allow me to jack up the price. Besides, you're the one who put all the work into it to make it worth a fortune. The place was a dump."

"Michael, I can't."

"Yeah, you can. I got all these flats, you can take one. Your mother would be happy."

"I don't know, Michael. I guess I could stay with you while Mom is gone. That would be nice. I was afraid actually to be alone, waiting for the baby to tap dance right out. That would be cool. I wish MaryAnne was around."

"You'll probably get to see her sooner than you think."

MaryAnne was finally settled. She had wound her way through security with about 1,000 others, taking off her belt, shoes, sweater, starting her computer, and giving them her shoulder bag to paw through. She was then felt up, squeezed, scanned, patted and prodded by a 300-lb woman could've played an SS guard in one of those S&M movies the guys used to watch in the studio 100 years ago. Pulling her gear together, she walked the 18 kilometres to the gate, stopping to get ripped off on a bottle of water and a bag of stale sandwiches on ersatz whole wheat. Would she eat the inedible airline dinner, if one was served, or the inedible sandwich? Good to have choices.

She stood in the jetway where progress was slower than horse and buggy, waiting to board, mask already annoying her, already exhausted. She had done this often enough to know that there were probably two hundred people in front of her stuffing as much luggage as they could carry into small overhead containers, avoiding extra baggage charges. The stuff wouldn't fit but they wouldn't sit down until they found a way, ignoring the long line of sweating, exasperated people waiting to board, waiting for them.

This must be what cows felt on their way to be shot in the head and slaughtered. A lot of her fellow travellers were patient, texting or scrolling through their electronic teats, some were talking. No inconvenience was too great if you had a smart phone tethered to the world beyond the gate, because, she thought, that's where they really are anyway.

She had dropped an extra $100 for a seat next to an exit door. She could spread out, do some isometrics and avoid an embolism on this 32-hour elevator ride.

She had to admit, the Slate gigs had been a gas. She and Essie had shaken their things and oohed and aahed and spent a lot of evenings drinking wine and a lot of mornings wishing they hadn't. Slate had asked her to stay with them but accepted a maybe for when she came back from her little overseas and Down Under adventure. Her bank account was fatter. She was fatter. But happily exhausted.

Somehow, sometime, she had become old. She pulled out her compact, looked at her face. She used to be a little girl, then a young woman. Didn't know what she was now. Except, curiously, she was happy. It was not that familiar a feeling.

It hadn't gone by that fast. It had been a good, long time. Maybe that's what grandchildren were about. You left a gene or two and the world kept spinning.

She wasn't going to be there but she'd be thinking of Joey, rolling around in pain, and later, full of the magic at what she had created. She would call her again when she landed. The check in calls from the road had been ok this time, hadn't they? Joey and Michael both sounded decent, right?

The compact looked back at her. She was old. What was she doing on this damn plane, guitar in oversized baggage? Who was she kidding? Her heart started to pound. Hands and armpits pumped out sweat. Maybe she should just get off the plane. Playing with Essie and Slate was one thing. Her own tour? She was too old for this shit. Centre stage, all these phones pointed at her. Hiding in the background had been comfortable. And Michael and Joey needed her. Or maybe they didn't.

She closed her eyes, snapped the compact closed and heard the attendant seal the door of the plane. She was trapped behind a few inches of aluminum on the tarmac in Miami while her whole life was in Montréal.

She had her iPad and headphones to listen to the latest mixes, some crime fiction to read but she kept looking onto the tarmac, seeing her daughter's face, seeing Michael, worried she'd never see him again.

Why had she let him get away with the game, blowing off her worries, lying that he wasn't really that sick? She could see it in his eyes, his slowed movements, his zest for life leeching away. All she had done was pretend it wasn't happening rather than facing it and dealing with it and not climbing into another can with wings and risking coming back to a funeral.

The Airbus started rolling backwards and she was fighting dread and terror and regret. She dug into her purse. Stephen had given her a bottle of white tabs.

"Minor tranks," he said. "Pop two. When you wake up, we'll be landing. Only way to fly."

She took four. What the hell?

She was groggy when they landed in Cairns, two stops and a million days later. The sun was dazzling, the heat surprising. She was stiff and feeling a decade older than when she left.

When much of the plane had emptied, she dragged

her stuff from the overhead and wrestled with grim thoughts and fear of a grimmer future. She followed people mindlessly and found herself at a baggage carousel.

There were more people than she wanted to count and beyond that was a row of sullen customs guards with guns and vests, masks and cold eyes and then a glass wall where friends and families and chauffeurs waited, holding up signs.

The little white tabs had worked—she had taken quite a few—and the bad airline coffee had injected a bit of caffeine into her blood. She was waking up and no longer ready for a coffin. Just a little groggy, a little lost. There were people waving and jumping up and down in the arrivals lobby, the other side of the glass. Someone was holding up a large white card that said, "We Love you, Grandma." Made her smile.

But something caught her eye. Something, someone familiar. She started walking toward the exit, to the arrivals lobby, looking at the sign and the two people holding it and she started to run. She ran right through the customs checkpoint and didn't notice a guard start chasing her, didn't hear the alarm go off, didn't register the guard had pulled out his handgun. She ran through the door, chaos behind her, and grabbed Michael and Joey and someone was grabbing at her. She was holding on for dear life, tears flowing.

"Madam, you need to come with me, madam," said a guard with menace in his voice.

"She's my mom, she's going to be a grandmother," Joey said. "Really, she's not a terrorist, she's a musician."

The guard tugged but MaryAnne held on to Michael'

hand as another guard and a cop surrounded them, his hand on his revolver.

"What, how …?"

"Amazing thing these planes. Takes only 24 hours. We've been here a while," Michael said.

"Madam," said a guard, doing her best to be forceful. "You have to come with us."

"But," MaryAnne said, letting him go, letting herself be led away by a contingent in uniforms.

"Joey wanted to have her baby here, Mate, or maybe Europe," Michael called. "I wanted to ask you to marry me, maybe in Paris?"

They led MaryAnne away as her family and the guys in the band watched. She didn't even care where they were taking her.

Acknowledgements

This book would've been impossible without the keen eyes and encouragement of Earl Fowler, who read every page of every draft, listened to every song and asked for more. Also indispensable were the generous comments from readers, including Liz Braun, Peter Howell, Jim Withers, adopted sis, Susan Kastner, Marilyn Mill, and my loving partner, Reisa Manus, who read several drafts, took copious notes and indulged my myriad insecurities, moods and the sound of my head pounding walls. And, of course, many thanks to Guernica Editions for its support and editor, Gary Clairman, whose light touch immeasurably improved the book.

Finally, I owe a ton to bass player Stephen Barry, one of Canada's great bluesmen, who I had the good fortune to share a stage with on occasion. Stephen always insisted music should be fun, the spirit of which I hope permeates these pages.

About the Author

David Sherman came of age when a man was defined by the size of his stereo speakers. Only woofers big enough to rearrange your heartbeat would do. As a journalist, he often wrote about music. Free time was often for bars and clubs with music on stage. David worked as an editor, writer, filmmaker and playwright, but ended most nights plunking on a guitar, writing songs. At the age of 59, as the music biz began to crumble under the tsunami of streaming, he was signed to a recording contract and played listening rooms and bars from Nova Scotia to Victoria.

If one sees life with three legs—love, work and music —one knows music can see you through days of empty pockets and nights in an empty bed.

After decades of writing and playing, *Momma's Got the Blues* is the author's way of writing about playing, fashioning a tale set in Montreal's Le Plateau, Canada's bagel capital.

Printed in February 2022
by Gauvin Press,
Gatineau, Québec